BALDWIN GREENER

To all the individuals and corporations
who give their time and expertise to save planet Earth

PREFACE

According to Professor Stephen Hawking, climate change is one of five possible threats to the survival of humanity.

> *"I am convinced that the human species is under threat of annihilation. It could be an asteroid hitting the Earth, a new virus, **climate change**, nuclear war or artificial intelligence going rogue. We must endeavour to leave Earth and look for another planet."*
> — Extract from a Stephen Hawking lecture

This novel considers whether the irreversible warming of the Earth and the collapse of its biosphere could bring about the end of humanity on Earth.

INTRODUCTION

The modern theory of **Climate Change** refers to the analysis of the long-term shifts in temperatures and weather patterns worldwide. It states that the cause of the current climate change is the intensive use of fossil fuels by humans. These changes started at the beginning of the 18th century with the discovery of the steam engine in Britain. The first locomotives burned coal as a source of energy. Further discoveries of fossil fuel-based sources of energy such as petrol (oil) and gas in Western Europe and America grew quickly, resulting in changes in the climate for the whole planet.

From the 19th century onwards, the various economies of the world transitioned from agricultural (use of the land for production of food) to industrial (production of goods).

That period is known as the "industrial revolution".

It is used as a <u>base line</u> for measuring the changes in several climate indexes, mainly the rise in temperature and the presence of greenhouse gas in the atmosphere -chiefly carbon dioxide (CO2) and methane-.

Changes in global surface temperatures have been measured with reliable instruments from the1850's. These days, modern measurements of land, sea and atmospheric temperatures are constantly transmitted by electronic sensors. Measurements prior to 1850 can be derived from tree rings, marine sediments and analysis of air bubbles in ice cores. Scientists can therefore calculate the sea and land temperatures for the past few million years with a reliable level of accuracy.

Long-term variations in the climate are attributed to geological or planetary reasons such as the wobbling of the Earth on its axis and its moving distances from the Sun. These external causes can be isolated in the compilation of the various modern indexes to concentrate on purely man-made activities.

From pre-industrial to the present (around 300 years) the global average land temperature has increased by 2.7 degrees Fahrenheit (1.5 degree Celsius).

The most important greenhouse gas is **carbon dioxide** (CO2).

Fossil fuels like coal and oil are mainly made up of carbon. The carbon that they contain has been produced by plants over millions of years through photosynthesis (the process by which they transform light into energy). When fossil fuels are burned- for instance in the internal combustion of motor vehicles- they release heat but also several gases. The carbon base fuels react with oxygen and release heat (energy) and gases, mainly CO2.

Another greenhouse gas**, Methane** (CH4) is released but the main sources of this gas are to be found in agriculture and the thawing of the permafrost.

Methane or natural gas is 80 times more powerful than CO2 in trapping heat in the upper atmosphere. The expected permafrost melt in the Arctic regions will contribute to a massive release of methane.

These two gases -carbon dioxide (CO2) and methane (CH4)- are invisible.

In view of their density, they rise in the air and find their way into the upper atmosphere where they aggregate. Due to their molecular structure, they trap some of the reflected terrestrial heat generated by the sun which would normally bounce back into space. These green gases act as a blanket and contribute to global warming.

CO2 remains in the upper atmosphere for hundreds of years.

The measurement of carbon dioxide (CO2) is calculated in parts per million or **ppm**. Samples of air are collected at high altitude like at the Mona Laua Observatory in Hawaii where their composition is analyzed.

The presence of Carbon dioxide is now 50 percent higher than it was before the industrial revolution (280 ppm).

The current reading is 420 ppm and rising.

Global warming is a result of climate change and refers to the overall increase in temperatures (land, sea and atmosphere) worldwide. Every degree Celsius increase causes a rise of about seven per cent in cloud evaporation in the atmosphere. This upsurge in greenhouse gas emissions is causing a strong deviation from the expected weather patterns. It has been calculated that since the industrial revolution the overall level of water vapor in the air has risen by around ten percent. This upsurge has caused major intensification of the weather systems, especially in the strength of storms and cyclones.

Conversely, in areas prone to desertification, warmer temperatures have dried out soils further due to rainfall deficiency.

CHAPTER 1
YEAR 2035—SIBERIAN TUNDRA, RUSSIA

The ice-cold wind hit their faces as they exited the plane. The three members of the UN Sustainability Development Group were wrapped in thick brown coats with large hoods to protect them from the cold. There was no evidence of the reported warmth of a few weeks ago which had caused the temperature in Siberia to exceed 100 degrees Fahrenheit for fourteen straight days. With the quickly diminishing amount of sunlight, fall had now well and truly arrived in the region.

They entered the small terminal at the Tiksi military helicopter base and were greeted by the Russian UN sustainability representative, Vladimir Kozorov, a stocky man with gray hair, a round face and dressed in a furry jacket.

Alexander "Sandy" Fraser, The Permanent Head of the UN group, shook his hand.

"Hello Vladimir. *Rad vstreche s vami.*" (I am pleased to see you.)

"*Privyet*. Same here, my friend," Vladimir replied.

Sandy presented his two colleagues. "May I introduce Professor Daniel Robson, our director and chief scientist, and Dr. Zara Naidu, our principal researcher."

Zara smiled at Vladimir.

Dan greeted him, "Good to see you, Mr. Kozorov."

"Please, please call me Vladimir," he replied in a heavy accent as he shook hands vigorously with them. "Thank you for coming. Long flight from Korea. Distances in Russia enormous. Please excuse me. I need to complete paperwork with authorities to get permission to travel to our destination. I need your passports." He raised his eyebrows comically. "I hope this is not too long.' He gestured across the terminal, "While you wait, have breakfast on me. Try kasha and tvorog, very nourishing."

As they walked the narrow hallway, Dan looked out the large windows, the endless Russian tundra expanded on kilometers upon kilometers of flat frozen land surrounding the airport. The sun had just risen, and the desolate treeless view was beautiful in its immensity.

The cafeteria was a relatively utilitarian setting as expected from a military base with long wooden benches. Several soldiers were lined up waiting for food. Dan, Sandy and Zara found a vacant table and sat down. Vladmir must have pulled a few strings as a petite old woman hurried over with plates full of food and steaming cups of coffee.

Although he had just turned forty, Dan had been the Director of the UN Office for Sustainable Development (UNOSD) in Incheon, Korea for the past five years. His quick promotion had been in recognition of his strong work ethic and his outstanding qualifications in climate and environmental biology from Princeton. His role involved supporting the UN member states to plan and implement sustainable development strategies.

Two days prior, Vladimir Kozorov, the Russian representative had called him. He had been insistent that he and Sandy, the Permanent Secretary of the Organization, needed to come to Siberia immediately and here they were in the middle of nowhere eating who knows what. Dan prodded the white substance on his plate, uncertain.

'Uh perfect', Sandy sighed in relief as he sat down stretching out. Dan had known Sandy for a few years. Who didn't? He was a legend in the international community. The larger-than-life Australian diplomat who charmed everyone was also the ultimate pragmatist especially when it came to food.

Sandy removed his hooded jacket, his carefully styled crop of wavy blond hair remaining in place, he looked at his watch- 'just long enough for us to refuel before the next leg'. He picked up his fork and began rapidly eating.

Zara, meekly sat to Dan's left, laughed awkwardly obviously intimidated. Dan had been insistent that he brought the principal U.N. Sustainability researcher Doctor Zara Naidu. Even though she was junior, she was a genius with numbers and the primary project lead.

Sensing her unease, Sandy smiled gently at her.

'Zara, I heard you completed a Ph.D. on the release of methane in the Arctic Circle. Perfect for our expedition. Dan sent me a copy of your thesis which I read with interest.'

Zara's eyebrows rose in surprise. Sandy continued 'Fascinating deductions and I mean that. I don't give praise lightly. Your work is professionally researched and the way you present the data is clear and persuasive. Not a straightforward thing to do.' I'm impressed!

————

After thirty minutes, Vladimir had cleared the lengthy paperwork required by the airport authorities and rejoined them. They walked on the nearby tarmac, and he waved the permit in the air to the Russian pilots, who signaled him "thumbs-up" to board the helicopter.

As he ducked under the whipping blades, Dan could feel a childlike enthusiasm rise in him. The aircraft was an MRK—a high-speed compound Arctic-coast surveillance rotorcraft. He had loved helicopters since he was a young boy and had been in a few, but he'd never been in this model. He slowly climbed aboard, taking the forward-facing seat next to Zara and across from Sandy Fraser. Vladimir offered them each a set of headphones. While the pilots warmed the engines up, a map of the East Siberian Sea coastline appeared on the screens in front of them.

Vladimir, who was sitting next to Sandy, began to explain the most recent developments through the audio system. "First you can see picture of Stolbovoy Island, here in North Siberia, taken by Kamov reconnaissance helicopter three years ago in June 2032. This is where we go today. Now I show you more recent images taken by this rotorcraft a few weeks ago, August 2035, after the heat wave. For best contrast, I use blue color to compare areas affected by rise of the sea."

A diagram of the same island appeared, looking noticeably smaller in view of the loss of the landmass caused by retrogressive thaw slumps and landslides. Dan gasped, surprised by how significant the difference was.

Vladimir noticed Dan's reaction. "You can see loss of land. Ten percent of island disappears very short period due to melting of permafrost. This going to get worse. In few years, maybe no island left. Russian research ship also detected that high levels of methane offshore on continental slope have escaped. Temperatures in this region rise three times more than global average. Warm Atlantic currents now come in Laptev Sea. Arctic becomes warmer in summer months. Ice melts faster and releases more gases. Tundra absorbs more energy from sun and so on."

Dan nodded his understanding and commented, "The dreaded runaway feedback cycle."

———

After receiving the green light from the tower, the two pilots took the craft to an altitude of 500 meters. Dan's mouth dropped as the pilots folded the rotor blades to a wing shape, thanks to the hybrid design features of their vehicle, and they began to fly it like a quasi-airplane with the power of the thruster. However, his enthusiasm was short-lived. As he looked out on the horizon, to his alarm, he spotted dozens of large wildfires in the distance.

Vladimir explained, "These fires, out of control for months. Dried-up peat burns. Sets entire areas on fire."

Dan shook his head in disbelief. *Wildfires in the Arctic.* He remembered his tutors at Princeton saying the Arctic was one of the few places on Earth where it was almost impossible for fires to occur.

As they arrived closer to the island, the pilots reverted to the main helicopter configuration, which Dan noticed allowed them to better maneuver at a lower altitude and at a reduced speed.

At the southern end of the island, they passed over a large crater in the ground adjacent to the seashore. The ocean was foaming at the water level, bubbling due to burning methane escaping from loaded sinkholes. Large gas columns were being released in the form of jet streams directly into the atmosphere. It looked like something out of a horror movie. Dan glanced at Sandy and Zara, whose faces revealed equal measures of shock and alarm.

Vladimir's voice came in over the intercom. "This island catches fire two months ago. Some fishermen go too close and BOOM! Methane explodes, island has not stopped burning since. Now, Russian government makes all Laptev Sea islands forbidden to any traffic. Too dangerous."

Sandy activated his push-to-talk button. "Vlad, can they take us down for a closer look at this?"

Vladimir instructed the pilots to take them lower.

Dan peered out as they descended. The island appeared totally singed, and flames could be seen coming from the barren land. The air inside the cabin suddenly felt quite warm.

Vladimir's voice came over the intercom again. "Sorry, pilots can't get closer. Too dangerous. They say we must go back."

———

The journey back to the airport passed quickly, but Dan's head was filled with a thousand thoughts. He'd never seen anything like it. The release of greenhouse gases had been like a warm water flow generated by a volcano. The warming of the frozen methane on the seafloor—known as clathrates—expelled a mix of hot air gas and water. Columns of burning methane vented directly into the atmosphere. He thought back to the classes he had taught. They had theorized about this happening, but it was supposed to be impossible. It was almost comparable to a wild gas field releasing uncontrollable amounts of methane, and it was unstoppable.

After they had landed back at the airport, Vladimir summarized the prospects of the phenomenon. "Our forecast, hundreds of gigatons of methane, carbon dioxide, and carbon monoxide discharge in Siberian region in the next few years. Some burn, some don't. Gas and heat drift toward Arctic Circle, increases melting of ice and so on. Then, all falls back on Arctic pole, melting it more."

He gestured toward the control tower. "Please come join me for a drink at the cafeteria. We can talk further. We need some vodka to warm up."

The shutters were now closed in the kitchen area, but there was alcohol available, and Vladimir proved generous with his servings as he poured some vodka.

Zara declined. "Not for me, thank you. I don't drink alcohol."

"This will warm you up," Vladimir insisted, filling her glass anyway. "That's how we Russians survive in winter."

Reluctantly, Zara agreed to have one drink only. Sandy happily accepted the vodka. Dan eyed his own shot with a touch of apprehension. He normally enjoyed a honey ale but this looked significantly more potent.

Vladimir proposed a toast, calling out, "*Nostrovia!*"

Dan took a sip. The fire burned down his throat. *Whoa*, he thought. *I'm going to take this slowly.*

Sitting down around the third large wooden table, Dan explained, "As a consequence of the summer heat dome and the direct release of methane into the atmosphere, it will be impossible to meet next year's Paris Agreement target and the ones after that. Anything we'd hoped for in containing the rise of greenhouse gas emissions will miss the forecast. From now on, the effects of climate change will become unpredictable. The more permafrost melts, the more greenhouse gases are released, increasing the temperatures, and again melting more permafrost. The feedback loops will trigger a runaway warming not only in this region but for the entire globe. This is an undeniable indicator of climate breakdown. This process is taking place right in front of our eyes."

Sandy asked anxiously, "Is it irreversible?"

Dan and Zara answered almost at the same time. "Yes."

Dan clarified the process further. "If we were able to stop putting greenhouse gases in the atmosphere today, the climate would continue to warm up for a few hundred years. Eventually it would reach equilibrium after maybe a thousand years *unless* we can find a way of pulling the CO_2 back out of the sea and sky in massive quantities and very quickly, but so far, we don't have any clear solutions to that. There's some hope, but it's very remote."

Zara looking worried, chimed in. "Dan's right, excessive temperatures in the Arctic region will become an ongoing issue. As sea ice melts, this results in a reduced area of bright surfaces. This means there will be fewer surfaces to reflect sunlight back into space, and more solar energy will be absorbed by the land and sea. This will begin a permanent cycle. I estimate the increased temperatures together with the releases of methane will accelerate the content of greenhouse gases in the atmosphere by a factor of 10 percent in the short to medium term." She added, "Permafrost covers two-thirds of the exposed Russian land, so more than 11 million square kilometers."

Sandy's eyes widened and he exclaimed loudly, "Bloody hell. That's huge! Nearly twice the size of Australia."

"And that's just Siberia, Sandy," Dan explained. "Significant discharges of methane and CO_2 in Greenland, Scandinavia, Alaska, Canada, and Antarctica have also been recorded." He zoomed in on the screen of his laptop, which revealed drawings of what lay beneath the surface of the map.

Dan turned to Zara pointedly. *Time for her to show Sandy her skills*, he thought.

"Zara, can you tell Sandy the exact amounts of carbon and methane we expect to be released?"

"Sure. Locked into the permafrost is an estimated 1.7 trillion metric tons of carbon and 60 billion metric tons of methane in the form of frozen organic matter. The vast tracts of permanently frozen regions in the world hold billions of metric tons of greenhouse gases. Global warming of 2 degrees will release 25 percent of these gases. An increase of 4 degrees will double the amount of the gases currently present in the atmosphere. At the current rate of increase, according to my calculations, we'll reach these levels well before the next century. However, there is a far bigger danger: the release of fossil methane."

The Permanent Secretary frowned. "What does that imply?"

"Putting it simply, further down, under the permafrost soil itself, there's an ice cork, meters thick, which has been there for perhaps millions of years. Below this cork are vast reservoirs of fossil greenhouse gases. If they are released, they will trigger a tsunami of methane and carbon dioxide. Nobody has any idea about the quantity that will be discharged, but it will be huge. I believe that this destabilization is the most dangerous threat to an abrupt climate change."

Vladimir poured Sandy another shot. Sandy drank it quickly. Vladimir offered one to Dan, who accepted.

Why not, Dan thought.

Zara pulled at her clothing. "It's getting warm in here." She shed her big jacket and was now kitted out in a bright blue thermal wear jumpsuit. She appeared flushed in the face. She stood up, swaying slightly. "I think we've reached the dreaded climate tipping point."

Dan poured her some water and passed it to her. "Here. Drink this."

Zara sipped the water and claimed again, "This is the beginning of the end!" Then she sat down heavily.

Dan looked at her, concerned.

Vladimir leaned over and whispered, "Not used to vodka. She'll be okay."

————

Vladimir offered more shots. After Dan counted what must have been his eight shot, he started to sing the first bars of "*Kalinka,*" a beloved Russian folk song. He was soon joined by the helicopter pilots and some of the staff from the control tower who had assembled in the function room. Dan watched as one of them brought out his balalaika, an instrument like a banjo, and started strumming it.

Encouraged, Dan and the others began to clap their hands to the ever-increasing tempo of the melody.

Vladimir explained, "*Kalinka* means my little snowberry. Gardener tries to get attention of pretty maid and calls her 'my little snowberry.' *Malinka* means 'my little raspberry.'"

Zara grinned and giggled. "That's so cute."

Dan had heard the song before but didn't know the lyrics. "Vladimir, can you tell me the words of the song?"

"Sure. Goes like this: '*Kalinka, kalinka, kalinka maya.*'" He spoke more slowly, "*f sadu yagoda malinka, malinka maya.*"

Then he said, "Easy. Should I repeat?"

"I think I've got it," said Dan.

"Do you want to sing it with me?" he suggested.

"Sure."

Dan's warm baritone voice rang out and, as he suspected, the Russians were surprised. Vladimir gestured to him to sing solo.

They all applauded when he finished.

"Wow, where did you learn to sing like that, Comrade?" Vladimir asked.

"Well," Dan admitted, "I was part of the Greater Central

Baptist Church choir, where my father was one of the deacons."

"Famous Harlem Gospel Choir?"

Dan smiled. "Yes, Vladimir, that one."

"Can you sing one of their songs for us, Dan?"

"Sure, what about 'Oh, when the saints go marching in'? All you need to do is to clap your hands and keep saying, 'Go marching in,' like this and rock to the music." He stood up and directed them.

The Russians didn't have to be asked twice. They got the gist of the simple refrain in no time and joined in as the chorus. When they finished, they applauded loudly.

They sang and danced until their return flight was ready to take off. Despite their differences, Dan smiled at the genuine friendship that seemed to have been created between them all.

The wonders of alcohol and music, he thought.

―――――

After they had boarded the plane, Dan turned to Sandy. "I never thought Russians could be so friendly."

"Oh, yes, they're a happy lot. They like singing, dancing, and drinking together, and I mean drinking, as you've noticed." Sandy wiggled his eyebrows.

Dan laughed as he settled into his seat across the aisle from Sandy. Zara didn't answer. She was already fast asleep.

―――――

After they had reached cruising altitude and the lights were back on, Sandy quizzed Dan in a stern tone. "From what we've seen today on the islands, what are your honest impressions?"

Dan frowned at him over his glasses. "Sandy, there's no

doubt in my mind that we've reached a dangerous juncture. According to my calculations, the methane release will now be on a scale so huge that no mitigation strategy has any chance of saving the planet. The Arctic will experience ice-free summers every year and cause Arctic amplification."

"Meaning all the oceans worldwide will get warmer?"

"Correct. They will now be influenced by a deep ocean process fueled by seas in the poles. The warmer waters of the Arctic and Antarctic will affect oceanic currents that determine global weather patterns. We're officially in the front seat to witness the collapse of Earth's weather pattern as we know it. We will literally be in unchartered waters."

Sandy whistled in shock. "Dan, we need to keep this in-house. You will need to watch the wording in your report."

"But Sandy, this is the science!"

Sandy eyed him carefully and spoke firmly, "Dan, I'm seriously concerned. I've been thinking about this since our trip in the chopper. If you are right and the world's climate has reached several tipping points. Well, if this gets out, there could be mass panic."

Dan thought back to his studies. Although humans were resourceful, in times of crisis, they weren't the most logical species. They tended to be highly irrational about issues such as existential threat. He nodded slowly. "I understand what you mean, Sandy."

Sandy continued, "As for us, we need to think seriously about the direction our organization should take from here. We will have to move fast. I'll organize a meeting as soon as I can."

A few days later, Dan was concerned that he would be late for his morning staff meeting. A powerful typhoon had struck South Korea overnight, dumping huge amounts of rain and causing major flooding on the roads. Although the damage had mainly been on the east coast, he expected to encounter slower traffic on his way to the office.

The local authorities had decided to close the schools for the day, and his ten-year-old daughter had been holed up in the bathroom for almost twenty minutes. He checked his watch for what felt like the twentieth time before knocking on the bathroom door and calling, "Ava, please hurry up. I need to get going."

Ava sauntered out of the bathroom. Her hair was curly and tipped with purple highlights. She twirled, fluffed her hair, and smiled at him, oblivious to his timeline. "Morning, Dad. Do you like my new look?"

"Yes, yes, nice," he mumbled, more than a little distracted. He rushed to the bathroom, brushed his teeth, and peered at his reflection in the mirror. Lines had formed around his eyes over the past few months. He touched them and ran his hands through his normally jet-black, frizzy hair, which now showed multiple gray streaks.

He sighed. *I need a break.* Shaking his head, he forced himself back to reality. *Not going to happen. After our visit to the Arctic, our research is coming to a critical stage.*

Resigned, he grabbed his black bag from the counter next to the door and pocketed his electronic keys. As he headed toward the front door, Melanie, his wife of fifteen years, smiled at him across the island bench as she put the cutlery away.

"Don't forget that the Kims are coming over for dinner

tonight. Could you pick up dessert from the Soboro Bakery? Maybe that matcha cheesecake?" She grinned in delight.

He kissed her on the cheek and then looked at his watch again. "Sure darling, but I think I'm going to be late tonight." He checked his holoscreen, looking at his schedule. "Maybe around seven?" he guessed. "The 2035 figures have just come in."

Melanie folded her arms, her lips pursed. "Okay hon, but no later than that, please. You've been working till the small hours every night this week. We've rescheduled with the Kims twice already."

He went around the bench and hugged her from the side. "I know, I know. I'm sorry. I'll call this afternoon to check in."

"Hmm." She half smiled at him as she dried her hands. "You'd better. I've got to run myself. I have a call with the Emirates, but I'll hear from you this afternoon, mister. Be careful on the road." She kissed him lovingly and headed off to her study, where she worked when she was in town. He headed in the opposite direction downstairs to the car park.

As he buckled in, the control center of his electric car greeted him, "*Welcome, Professor Robson.*"

He settled into his seat and the vehicle took off.

———

He loved his second hometown of Seoul almost as much as his first, Manhattan. His office was in the Songdo International Business District, which had originally been envisioned as a sustainable, low carbon, high-tech futuristic city. It was just twenty miles away from Seoul but light years away in terms of sustainable planning. Rubbish was automatically recycled. There were large green areas and good access to public transport. It was the way cities were meant to be designed although as he looked out the window, he noticed that most cars had only one person in them just like him.

After an hour of slow driving, he reached his office, which forms part of the campus of Yonsei University. As he unpacked papers from his bag and plugged in his holoscreen at his desk, Zara walked in. She was dressed in a bright blue blouse and green pants which matched her green sneakers. Today her hair was even more intricate than his daughter's, woven in tiny braids with colorful ribbons through it.

He gestured to her to sit. "Morning, Zara. Come in, come in."

"Morning, Dan. I've just finished the spreadsheet with this year's final numbers." She slumped into his visitors' chair, pushing the graphs over to his desk. Zara was normally upbeat.

Dan looked at her, concerned. "Are the results that bad?"

She drummed her fingers. "With the projections on the Arctic meltdown, they look terrible. We'll miss the forecast targets by a serious margin. The numbers indicate that green-house gas readings will rise dramatically. Global temperatures will now continue to surge at an alarming rate. According to our modeling, we're on track to hit a full 2-degree Celsius increase from what's set in the Paris Agreement in the next twenty years."

Dan shook his head in disbelief. A few months ago, they'd all expected the numbers to remain steady. He took out his glasses to study the executive summary. After a few minutes of reading, he dropped the report on the conference table, frustrated. When he turned back to Zara, his heart was pounding. "This is so disappointing. The numbers are amplifying rapidly."

"I don't know what to say. The numbers are correct, Dan."

He trusted her. She was the best analyst they had.

Dan couldn't contain his frustration. "We keep telling them to slow down on burning coal, gas, and petrol. They just don't listen. Cars, trucks, power plants, and farms are still pumping out huge amounts of CO_2. They are literally cooking the planet."

Zara shook her head furiously. "Blind fools, as my grandpa would have said."

"Can we confirm the carbon dioxide projections for next year?"

"Sure. Five hundred parts per million."

"More than 50 percent of pre-industrial levels already. And the global temperature?"

"It will probably rise by 1.8 degrees Celsius or more."

He felt dizzy now, almost sick. He slammed his hand on the table, trying to wrestle back control. "Damn it! That's the red danger zone for several tipping points!" He saw the shock on her face. He breathed in hard, trying to calm down. "I'm sorry about the outburst, it's just so—"

"Disappointing?" Zara filled in. She was aware of how critical these levels were.

Trying to regain his composure, he walked to the window and gazed outside at the view overlooking the campus. His office was surrounded by trees just beginning to turn beautiful shades of orange and red in between expertly manicured lawns and structured flower beds. He breathed in and out again, slowly steadying himself. *Think practical Dan... practical*, he repeated in his head.

Calming down, he came back to his desk and looked at Zara apologetically. "Sorry. Let's run the numbers one final time and then we'll set up some calls to discuss the implications. No point ringing alarm bells until we're 100 percent sure. Thanks, Zara."

As she left the room, the frustration he had experienced earlier was replaced with immense sadness. They had been working for so long to implement measures to curb the use of fossil fuels but had been unable to reduce their consumption. There was no doubt in his mind that humanity was heading toward a defining moment. His thoughts went to his family. Melanie and the children would be fine and their future grandkids and their children too. After them, he wasn't sure.

He moved to his table and began to eat his breakfast of Banchan, which his assistant had put out for him. He chewed his food slowly and examined the report once more. He reassured himself. *Sandy will know the next steps. He always does.*

Dan looked at his watch. It was 9:30 a.m. in Korea... that would only be 8:30 p.m. in New York. Sandy would still be in the office. *Wait a minute, no...* He thought further. *He's probably traveling back from the UK, after meeting with the English environment minister. What—*

The sharp sound of his telecon line interrupted his thoughts. He saw on his screen that Zara had picked up the call. He walked to his door and peered out. She was at her workstation just five meters away. He had placed her there so she could hear him when he called from his desk. She pressed a button and turned to face him.

"It's Mr. Fraser."

"Thank you, Zara. I'll take it at my desk."

He walked back to his office, set his half-eaten food aside, and dusted off his pants before he sat back down. He picked up the call.

"Hi, Sandy. Wonderful to hear from you."

Sandy's tone was quick and urgent as he relayed his message to Dan.

After the call, Dan looked at the clock as he called out to Zara to come back into his office. Sandy had spoken in a virtual monologue for over half an hour. He perused the notes he'd written on his tablet.

Zara sat down opposite him. "What's the story?"

Dan grimaced. "Sandy's concerned, and rightly so." "He is going to talk to the Secretary General and wanted to go over all the facts again, the record temperatures, the impact of the permafrost, basically rehearsing the bad news for the big boss." He shook his head, "he also repeated again how we have to keep the meaning of the news to ourselves until he can navigate a plan."

———

When Dan arrived back home, his daughter, Ava, was sitting in the living room watching her favorite show. She'd tried to explain it to him several times. All he could work out was that there were six teenagers who hated each other but somehow continuously fell in love with one another.

He gave her a kiss on the head. "How was your day, darling?"

She looked up. "Oh good. Hey Dad, look, this is Lacey. Remember... I told you she likes Davis... well, she's just found out—"

Dan could sense where this was heading and decided to change the topic.

"I had an interesting day too. We analyzed the results of our trip to Siberia."

She raised an eyebrow, puzzled. "Where is that?"

"I'll show you."

He sat down next to her in the lounge room and pulled out

his handheld computer. He brought up a 3D image of the world and zoomed to Korea. "This is where we are."

He twisted it up and pointed, saying, "Asia, Russia, Siberia."

"Whoa, that's the middle of nowhere, Dad. Why did you go there?"

"We had to monitor an unusual rise in methane gas in the permafrost region, darling."

Ava was an inquisitive child. "Permafrost? What's that?"

"Let me explain. Thousands of years ago, the weather in the Arctic region was warmer than it is now. Trees were growing there and leaves from the forests fell on the ground every season at the end of autumn. This went on for thousands of years, right?"

"Right," Ava agreed.

"As the weather gradually cooled down into a cyclical ice age, all this material was progressively trapped and covered by ice, which didn't melt for millennia. The trees and leaves were PERMAnently FROZen, hence the name... Ava?"

"Perma... frost." She eyed him, checking that she was saying it correctly.

He could tell she was getting interested now. "Clever girl. These days, the layers vary in depth from a few meters to more than a hundred meters. Now, with the unusual warmer summer months, like Siberia has experienced this year, the added sunlight has increased the temperatures of the ground."

"Huh? They don't teach us this stuff at school, Dad."

Dan explained with his hands, layering them on top of each other. "See, Ava, most of the carbon stocks from these old, decomposed layers of leaves and wood reside close to the surface, which is covered by the permafrost. In summer, the sun warms up the surface of the ice, slowly melting it. The leaves containing the carbon then begin to break up. They become available to microorganisms, which start feeding on them. Munch, munch!" he exclaimed theatrically, trying to rile her up.

Ava's upper lip curled. "Yuck! The bugs are munching through that gross stuff?"

"Exactly. That stuff, as you say, is called organic matter and the bugs are called bacteria. They make a meal of it and in the process release the carbon that it holds. This is converted into carbon dioxide and methane. These are heat-trapping gases."

"The gases that have a greenhouse warming effect on the planet, right?"

"Right. Our concern is this: with the temperatures getting warmer, the upper layers, which have been frozen solid over huge areas, will release massive quantities of these greenhouse gases. You know how that works, don't you?"

"Well, sort of. Greenhouse is like the solar blanket on our swimming pool in summer, isn't it?"

"Spot on. The greenhouse gases rise in the atmosphere and act exactly like our swimming pool blanket does. It's like an invisible cover in the upper atmosphere that traps some of the heat generated by the sun. It can also be compared to the glasshouse where we grow our tomatoes in summer. The heat from the sun comes in, but some is only partially reflected. The burning of fossil fuels, like coal and petrol, also produces carbon dioxide—the main trapping gas. Hence, the term *global warming*."

"Global warming, like the ice caps melting." She looked quite interested now.

He smiled. "Yes. It has serious consequences for the overall climate. First, the rise in temperatures makes the ice caps melt, as you say. This melting produces fresh water, which makes the level of the oceans rise, flooding the low-lying areas of the planet like islands and city foreshores. It also increases the interaction of weather systems above their usual pattern. More cloud vapor is produced, the storms become more severe, the floods get heavier, and the regions prone to drought have harsher and longer spells. Many places on Earth will become uninhabitable in the future."

Melanie called from the kitchen. "Dan, the Kims have arrived."

He signaled to his daughter. "Come, Ava. We don't want to be late to the table."

She stood with him and gave him a hug. "Dad, when I grow up, I want to be a scientist like you."

———

Dan stayed up late after the Kim's left, going through the numbers again. At around 1am, he sighed, put his glasses down, shut his study door and headed into his bedroom. He looked at his wife sleeping peacefully, her skin the color of warm bronze under the glow of his bedside light. Her breathing was slow and steady, the type of sleep he now envied and felt he'd never experience again. She was so beautiful and serene.

He recalled how he had met Melanie at a class in Princeton. They had both arrived early to a mandatory undergraduate statistics course, not an easy subject. She was sitting right at the front, her pens all lined up, her computer switched on. He boldly walked right up to her and asked if he could sit next to her. She nodded, gesturing to the seat on her right. He pulled out an identical laptop with a "Save the World" sticker on the lid. They started chatting, and it developed into a beautiful romance.

Melanie had been a wonderful wife and mother. She still was, of course, but back then, they'd been so young and carefree. That wasn't the case now. He barely saw his family, and he felt stressed about his responsibility for the future of humanity. His dream of saving the planet weighed on him.

He looked at the photo on the wall with Melanie, Ava, and their two boys, taken for their fifteenth wedding anniversary. His eyes began to swell. He quickly wiped his face. He thought back to the permafrost, the warm air rising over the Arctic, the ice melting, and the runaway release of greenhouse gases. Everything he had been working on for all these years was literally melting away. *Have I just been fighting against the inevitable?*

He sighed too loudly. Melanie stirred and turned, looking at him through half-closed eyes. "Dan, go to sleep."

He didn't move and sighed again.

"Dan?" She was more awake now. "Are you alright? Are you still jet-lagged? I know you've traveled huge distances, but you were only gone for four days."

He wiped his eyes again. He could sense his wife's intuition was kicking into overdrive now. She turned her light on and sat up.

"What's going on? You haven't been the same since you came back from your trip. You barely talk to me about it. You come in late and you aren't sleeping. What happened there in Siberia, Dan?"

"Nothing, nothing. Sorry I woke you."

Her eyes flashed. "Daniel Robson! I've been married to you long enough to know when you're suppressing something. Out with it. Whatever it is, we will work through it, but if you keep hiding whatever it is from me, it will keep eating you up inside!"

He looked into her eyes—they were like cocoa—warm, accepting, and inviting. But he couldn't explain what was bothering him so much. It wasn't about trust. He trusted her more than himself and that was the problem. He'd gone into the office this week, managing the Office of Sustainable Development, when he knew that eventually there might not be anyone to look after the planet. If he told her, if he opened that door...

"I, I can't!"

"You can't?" She raised an eyebrow at him.

"Sorry, I can't, it's, I mean... Sandy made me..." He could barely find the words to explain himself.

Any emerging anger in her suddenly made way for concern and empathy. "What you saw was terrifying, wasn't it?" she said softly, reaching for his hand. "You know something so frightening that you can't talk about it and it's eating you up inside."

He shook his head, not wanting to say.

"What's going on, Dan?"

He hesitated. "I can't say much, but basically there are too many greenhouse gases in the Arctic. The recent heatwave has fast-tracked emissions, ahh, irreversibly."

She was more awake now, and he saw her joining the dots in her mind. Suddenly, she raised herself and sat up in bed. "You mean, we're destroying the planet?"

"Yes. It's heating too fast. I doubt our society will survive the upheaval it will cause. It will be a totally different planet, nothing like its current form. When the heavily populated parts of the globe start to suffer massive food shortages due to droughts, fires and floods, there's going to be hell on earth. I fear the resulting global conflicts will overwhelm us."

"Oh, my god! How long do we have?"

"A few hundred years, maybe more, but eventually it's going to happen."

She paused before grabbing the glass of water on her nightstand and taking a slow, deliberate drink. When she finished, she placed the glass back, obviously processing her thoughts. She turned back to him. "All right." She nodded. "Yes, I mean if that's the situation we are in. As your mother would say, 'What God hath given, he can taketh away.'"

"He hasn't taken away, Lanie, *we* have. We've been dreadful caretakers. We have totally mismanaged our custodianship."

"Daniel, Dan." She took his face in her hands and kissed him deeply. "You listen to me. You are the most dedicated man. You've been caring for this planet for as long as I have known you. You've given it your all." She paused. "Will the kids be all right?"

"Oh yes, we're talking about hundreds of years, maybe thousands, but eventually..."

His eyes began to swell again.

She reacted quickly. "Don't you dare do that, that's not you," she said firmly. "You don't give up easily. It's not like you!"

"The devastation is happening on my watch, hon. We are the generation who will be held responsible for the Earth's demise. I feel I haven't done enough to stop its downfall. I should have been more forceful. All the trends are pointing to a collapse of our environment."

"There's only so much you can do, honey. You're a scientist. You collect evidence, analyze the data, and issue guidelines. You are *not* the policeman of the health of the planet. You haven't got the authority to jail offenders who are not complying."

"True. I wish I did. There would be a lot of people in jail." He laughed. A calming thought began to blossom at the far reaches of his brain.

"Ah, now you've got that look which says you're working

on a solution. Go back to sleep, rest that brain. You know the science."

He kissed her deep, brown lips. "Thank you, Lanie."

"Anytime, my husband, and I get the feeling you may be taking me up on that."

He turned off the light, his brain still mulling over her words. *I'm not the policeman of the health of the planet.*

INCHEON INTERNATIONAL AIRPORT, SEOUL

Six weeks later, Dan and Zara were heading to Bonn. They were heading to a high-level working group meeting at the UN campus in Bonn, the seat of several organizations, including the Institute for the Environment. As the lead author of the "Human Sustainability Report 2035," Dan was expected to present the executive summary in front of hundreds of key delegates, including the Secretary General of the UN herself.

Dan unloading his small carry-on bag and his black satchel from the car. He could feel Melanie eyeing his clothing suspiciously. He wore his standard travel outfit of gray chinos, a white polo shirt, and a black windbreaker.

"Have you got everything?"

He nodded, triple checking his pockets. "Yes, holoscreen with online tickets, passport, paperwork, warm jacket."

She leaned over, kissed him, and rested her forehead on his. "Keep safe, my love."

"Always."

Dan spotted Zara as she came into the terminal with two rainbow-patterned suitcases trailing behind her. She had her hair in a dozen mini fluorescent buns. She wore a banana yellow skirt with a bright green jumper. He smiled. "Morning, Zara. That's a lot of luggage for a week."

"I need options, Dan... unlike some people." She surveyed his carry-on bag. "Did you bring any clothes at all?"

He laughed. He was proud of his packing skills. "Of course, but just enough."

BONN, GERMANY

They were halfway to Bonn and he had only managed a few hours of sleep. He started typing on his laptop again.

Zara poked him and peered over. "Are you still switching some of the words of your presentation around? What's going on? Normally you're not worried about public speaking."

He looked up, removed his glasses, and rubbed his eyes. "It's different this time, Zara. There's too much at stake and I must phrase the facts exactly right. Sandy was very clear about it." He raised his eyebrows at Zara to emphasize his point. "This meeting is critical in shaping the upcoming Sydney conference, which will be attended by delegates from around the world. If I don't get it right, we won't get support from the key countries."

Several hours later, as their Lufthansa flight started its descent to Cologne Bonn Airport, Dan finally closed his laptop. He looked out the window and was surprised to see how parched the region of Westphalia appeared for the season.

"Unbelievable! Look at the countryside! The last time I came here, Bonn was a veritable oasis in the middle of the flooded Rhine River. Now the ground is as dry as a bone. More and more, Europe keeps experiencing extreme weather events."

Zara leaned over him to look as well. "From what I've heard, they have been waiting for good rains for months in this region. Whereas last year they had way too much. Apparently, navigation along the Rhine has been disrupted due to the low level of the river."

"I'll make mention of it in my introduction. What do you think?"

"Excellent idea. Make it more personal to the audience."

Dan nodded. "That's the way I intend to present the report. However, we'll meet the Secretary General afterward to discuss our real concerns. Sandy has booked a room for the four of us after the presentation."

———

After collecting their luggage, they headed for the Lufthansa first-class lounge where they'd agreed to meet Sandy. His flight from New York had just landed. The Under-Secretary-General for Economic and Social Affairs was easy to spot. He had a booming voice and was the tallest in the room. Several French and German businessmen surrounded him, enthralled as he spoke to them, switching languages with ease.

Typical Sandy! Always the most popular guy in the room. He finally caught Sandy's eye and waved at him. Sandy nodded in his direction, bid farewell to the group, and headed over to him and Zara. Immaculately dressed, he wore a deep navy-blue Italian suit with a crisp white shirt and a bright red tie. Dan guessed his whole outfit probably cost as much as his own monthly salary.

Sandy greeted him with a smile and a slap on the back. "Good to see you again, Dan. How's the family?"

"All well thanks, Sandy. Melanie's working on a major project for the Emirates. Ava, well, you know, she's barely at home these days. She has about a dozen friends she constantly talks to on social media but somehow, she still manages to get straight As."

Sandy threw back his head and let out a booming laugh. "Sounds like she takes after her brilliant mother. Have the boys started playing soccer?"

Dan knew that Sandy loved soccer. Whenever they traveled together, they always tried to attend a game. "Harry's shaping up to be a good striker, but Jack is showing talent as a goalkeeper."

Sandy nodded. "A skilled goalkeeper is critical to a good game. While I was in Oxford doing my masters, I did a bit of goalkeeping and managed to keep the Uni's streak in check for a season or two."

He turned to Zara and smiled, sticking out his massive hand. She bowed, obviously still intimidated by him. Dan was taken aback. Zara was normally so confident, but Sandy did have a presence and after all, he was the big boss.

"Lovely to see you again, Zara. Talking about Oxford, Dan told me you're also an alumna. I'd like to know more about you. We didn't get much of a chance to chat in Tiksi."

She took a deep breath and then began to speak rapidly, "I did my undergraduate study in my hometown Chennai in India at the University of Madras. Then, I sat on the Board of the Environmentalist Foundation in India. That's when I received a scholarship to Oxford to do my PhD. I worked for a couple years for an NGO in London. You might know it, 'Greening our cities'?"

Sandy nodded. "Yes, I know it well."

Zara continued, "Well it was through the Board I heard about Dan's work and approached him. I'm deeply passionate about the environment, and like Dan, I want to do everything I can to save the planet."

Sandy nodded approvingly. "Very commendable. That's the spirit. Exactly what our organization is trying to achieve."

A black Mercedes EQS limousine was waiting for them at the terminal's entrance. As Dan headed to the car, he spotted two German Police Motorcycle Unit officers already saddled on their motorbikes waiting in front of the car.

Sandy was eyeing them too. "We don't normally need a police escort, Dan. Let's go and ask them why they're here."

They left their bags with Zara and the driver. As they walked over, Sandy elbowed Dan and gave him a complicit wink. "I also want to have a sticky beak at their motorbikes. They look like the latest BMW Electra model. I wonder what these new fully electric models have got in their bellies."

They both approached the police officers, waving to them. Sandy addressed them in German, pointing at himself and Dan. From the action of his hands clasping fictitious handlebars, Dan understood he was telling them that they were riders as well. The senior officer answered them in English.

"I'm Constable Hans Meyer from the Bundespolizei. My colleague is Support Officer Helmut Valken. We will be escorting you to town. I see that you are interested in our motorbikes. Do you ride as well?"

"I used to ride a BMW F650 in Australia when I was in my twenties," Sandy answered. "What a beast."

"So much power, sir. I have one at home. I ride it when I'm off duty. And you are a rider too, sir?"

Dan nodded. "I usually ride my Harley-Davidson Road King Classic with my wife across the country roads in the States when we go back to visit our parents. It's always the highlight of the trip. But ahh, don't tell my mother."

They all laughed.

"That's an American legend as well," the younger

policeman said. "I can tell you, compared to the old petrol engines, our bikes are very silent."

He started the engine with the press of a button.

Dan listened carefully. "I see what you mean. No roar of the exhaust system like the old motorbikes. Part of the fun was revving the engine up."

Sandy and Dan spent nearly a quarter of an hour looking at the bikes, talking about the pros and cons of American bikes versus German ones.

After a while, Zara wound the window down and shouted, "Dan, Sandy, the driver wants to get going."

Dan called back to her, "No problem." He signaled to Sandy that they needed to head off. Reluctantly, they left the two police officers.

"So, what did you find out, Dan?" Zara asked.

"Nice guys. They told us they've both previously ridden in California and Queensland. You know, there's always great camaraderie between motorbike riders."

She shot him a look of mock indignation. "Hey, same thing with push-bike riders for your information, and we don't pollute the environment! But seriously, did you find out why we need an escort?"

"Oh yes, that. The police have been informed that activists from the movement 'Youth for a Better Climate' have requested permission to organize a march ahead of the UN meeting this afternoon. Supposedly, the participants will assemble in some of the streets around the University Campus. The police have laid barricades around the venue, which can now only be accessed from the south. These motorized police have a permit to get us in."

"But we want to save the world too, Dan. We're on the

same side. I don't see why they need to demonstrate!" Zara complained.

"Couldn't agree more, but apparently these young people aren't happy with the way things are moving. In their eyes, there isn't enough progress being made by official organizations like ours. They think we're too conservative."

"I'll check the Deutsche News feed on my holo, Dan. Just a minute... Here we go. They report the crowd has already swelled to a few hundred."

As they drove closer toward the campus, the gathering of protestors seemed to get nearer to the car.

Thank goodness for the police escort, Dan thought.

He could see the protesters were carrying banners bearing the logo *Unsere Welt*. "What does it mean, Sandy?"

"It means 'Our World.'"

"They're also chanting something in German. Shh. What are they saying?"

"They're saying, 'It's our future, it's our world.'"

Shortly before their Mercedes reached the gates, a tall, blond protestor leapt over the barricades and tried to stop the car. Dan jumped in his seat and yelled, "Watch it!"

The driver hit the brakes, but replied calmly, "Relax, sir. No problem. The police will move him out. Then I can drive through. Our police know what to do. No problem."

As they dragged the protestor away, he turned toward them and raised a fist in anger.

Zara sucked in a breath. "This is getting scary."

Dan tried to reassure her, "Don't worry, the police are standing inside the high fences. They look well prepared."

"Hmm... even so, I hope they can withstand the pressure of hundreds of youths pushing against the barricades."

———

Despite the protests, the audience gathered in the university circular conference room, the former German Parliament which had been based in Bonn before the reunification of Germany.

Sandy tapped Dan on the shoulder. "Before we take our seats for the session, let me introduce you and Zara to the UN Secretary General, Dame Ngaire MacKenzie-Tarawane."

"Wasn't she the Prime Minister of New Zealand a few years ago?" Dan asked.

"Yes, and an excellent one. She's had a lot of experience in diplomacy. She's also a keen environmentalist and was instrumental in having large pristine areas of New Zealand decreed national parks."

"I'm an admirer," Zara remarked, running her fingers over her carved fern-shaped green-stone necklace. She'd worn it specially for the occasion.

Sandy greeted Dame Ngaire—Māori style—with the traditional *"hongi"* by pressing his nose and forehead on hers and saying, *"Kia Ora."*

With a dual Māori and Scottish ancestry, Dame Ngaire cut a powerful figure. At six feet tall with straight dark hair, she was easily recognizable by the traditional *"moko kauae"* (sacred chin tattoo) under her lower lip. She had been noticed as a skillful negotiator with an extraordinary intellect and had become the first indigenous woman to reach the top position as the United Nations Secretary.

"Dame Ngaire, may I introduce Professor Daniel Robson, our Director of Research, who will present the Executive Summary of the 2035 Sustainability Report," said Sandy.

She greeted Dan with a broad smile and a firm handshake, complimenting him in a commanding voice that still held slight traces of a Kiwi accent. "We're most impressed by the work you have undertaken to preserve the planet, Professor

Robson. I'm familiar with your contribution to the agenda for sustainable development. It's an excellent set of proposals. Good luck with the talk."

Sandy continued his introductions. "And this is Dr. Zara Naidu, our principal researcher."

Zara inclined her head respectfully. "I am very honored to meet you, ma'am."

Dame Ngaire admired Zara's necklace. "I like your *pounamu*. Yours is called a *koru*. The unfurling of the fern leaf symbolizes hope. It will bring you new beginnings in your life."

"Does that mean I'll find a husband?"

"I sincerely hope so if that is your wish."

Dame Ngaire showed Zara her own carved piece of jade, which looked like a contorted little devilish creature with seashell inserts for eyes. "Mine was gifted to me by the current Māori king. This symbol of power has been passed to the war leader for generations in New Zealand. This means that, officially, I have authority over the land and people of my country. Come and sit, Zara. You can brief me about your visit to the Arctic Circle."

Sandy sat next to the UN Secretary General as well. Dan proceeded to the podium to join the panel.

———

A tall, fair man with a large mustache walked onto the stage.

"Ladies and gentlemen, welcome. My name is Ludwig von Richter.

I am the Campus Director here in Bonn. Welcome to this working group meeting, which intends to review the agenda for the upcoming plenary World Conference that will take place in Sydney. We are certainly looking forward to that event."

Pointing outside the building, he tried to reassure the audience, "As you can hear, the demonstrators are causing a lot of noise, but don't worry. The German police have deployed sufficient personnel to keep the situation under control."

He turned toward the panel. "Now, please welcome our special guest speaker, Professor Daniel Robson, the Director of the UN Office for Sustainable Development in Incheon, Korea, who will present the Executive Summary of the 2035 Environmental Sustainability Report." The audience applauded Dan, and the Campus Director resumed his introductions.

"In homage to our favorite son, Beethoven, let us start this presentation by singing 'Ode to Joy.' We will all sing the first verse in German together, led by our special guest, Professor Dan Robson, who I've been told has a good voice. It will be my privilege to accompany him on the piano. Could you please be upstanding? Let's celebrate the brotherhood of man."

The Campus Director played the introduction on the piano. Dan sang the first line of Schiller's poem, followed by the members of the assembly, who were able to read the lyrics projected on a large screen behind him. At the end of the rendition, the delegates were visibly uplifted. Dan received tremendous applause.

"Thank you, Campus Director." He looked nervously around the room. "Ladies and gentlemen, can you hear me?"

The audience replied affirmatively. Zara gave him a discreet thumb-up.

He bowed humbly. "Thank you. As mentioned by the Campus Director, I will give you a preview of some of the key points of the 2035 Environment Sustainability Report." He steadied himself. "Among all the threats facing the environment of our planet, our main concern right now is the release of methane from the permafrost arctic shelves in the Arctic

Circle. Using satellite images, we've measured the rate of change over the years. It gives us an indication of its impact on climate change. The acceleration of the thawing of the permafrost has increased dramatically this summer due to a strong and lasting heat dome. Don't get me wrong; we're dealing with many other issues."

He looked at the audience in sympathy. "For example, right here in Bonn, you have also experienced temperatures above 35 degrees Celsius this summer. I am reliably informed this year's harvest yield in Westphalia is half that of the previous one. We're sorry to hear that."

He went back to his notes. "Anyway, back to the other side of Europe and the permafrost. This phenomenon is of concern to our organization. We became aware of this problem in the waters surrounding the Siberian shelf—"

His speech was interrupted by a loud disturbance near the entrance doors. Dan stopped talking and directed his gaze toward the back of the auditorium. Despite the heavy police presence, some demonstrators had managed to break through and reach the area where the working group was taking place. The security guards pounced and held a few in a headlock. One demonstrator struggled furiously and screamed, "I'm Franz Jürgen!"

Zara looked at him and exclaimed, "Hey, that's the guy who tried to stop our car!"

The UN Campus Director stood up from his chair. "That's Franz Jürgen, the leader of Youth for a Better Climate. Just give me a second, please."

He walked toward the group of protesters, calling to the guards, "*Lass ihn loss*" (Release him).

Dan overheard him talking to the leader of the protestors.

"Franz, Franz, relax, we're on your side."

Franz shouted, "We want YOU to hear OUR point of view!"

"Fair enough, Franz, I'll tell you what. You can say a few words at the end of this meeting and put your point of view to the assembly, but first tell your friends to stop this unrest, please."

Franz composed himself, pushed the security guards away in a condescending manner, and agreed to the request by waving back at the Director. "Okay, okay!"

He gathered his comrades and went outside with them. After a few minutes, the uproar calmed down. Franz then came back and sat in one of the rows of the auditorium.

Dan was shaken but resumed his presentation of the report.

———

At the end of Dan's lecture, as promised by the Campus Director, Franz was invited to express his point of view to the audience.

Strongly built and blond, he walked confidently to the podium. Pausing for a moment, he glared at the audience. In a commanding Luxembourgish accent, he spoke in short, theatrical sentences, "It is our future, our planet. We are fighting for the right of a healthy existence. We want a clean environment for us and for our children. We don't want to inherit a toxic world!"

Pointing at the officials, he demanded forcefully, "We want YOU to protect the future of the Earth for US young people. YOU must put the planet before profits. Our governments are failing us. They still finance dirty energy projects. We want renewable energy. Stop the extraction of oil and coal. They are both cooking our planet!"

His pitch increased, and he thumped the lectern repeatedly with his fist. "Stop destroying life on Earth!!"

He paused for a moment, as if trying to regain composure before his next tirade. Some of his friends near the doors started chanting, "It's our world! It's our world!"

The Campus Director frowned. Gesturing to two of his colleagues to join him, he climbed back to the podium and took control of the microphone. "Thank you, Franz. These problems are exactly what our organization is trying to solve. Come down now, please."

Franz ignored him. He shouted defiantly, "I'm not finished!"

The Campus Director and his two colleagues held Franz's arms and moved him away from the lectern. Dan overheard the Campus Director trying to reason with him quietly again. "Franz, we can work together. I'll talk to you personally after the meeting, okay?"

After the commotion settled down, Dame Ngaire leaned over and remarked to Sandy and Dan, "I can't believe how this fellow tried to control our conservative audience of scientists and officials. His group proposes far more aggressive climate action. How about we all meet in one of the executive rooms in half an hour? I'd like to talk to the three of you more privately."

————

As suggested by the Secretary General, Sandy, Dan, and Zara convened with her in a small meeting room that overlooked a private courtyard.

"Congratulations, Professor Robson. Your presentation was an excellent summary of the state of the planet. I must say, the disturbance was frightening. Luckily, the Campus Director managed the situation rather well. How are you feeling?"

Dan thought how best to answer this question. "Shaken, I

suppose, but I hope I was able to get the main points of the report across."

"You certainly did. However, I noticed you were rather cautious regarding any long-term forecast about climate change. Sandy has informed me that based on what you witnessed in Siberia, he didn't wish you to disclose your projections too early."

"Well, he's right, of course. Our function is to compile data, analyze the situation and suggest remedial action; not to officially predict the future."

"I agree with that view but Professor Robson, you've been involved in the drafting of the Agenda for Sustainable Development Charter. Based on your professional experience, may I ask you, just for my own understanding, what are your predictions regarding the future of the planet? Please speak freely."

"Sure. Do you mind if I first give you a bit of background, Dame Ngaire?"

"Please, go ahead."

"After the 2020 to 2023 and 2030 to 2033 global pandemics, the budgets of most countries ended up heavily in the red, as you know. To revive their economies, they were obliged to curtail their efforts to use sustainable sources of energy. They went back to exploiting cheap fossil fuels. Coal and oil were again regarded as the most affordable sources of energy."

"I remember it very well, Professor Robson. I became Prime Minister of New Zealand shortly after 2025. Although my government had committed the country to a net zero emission target by the second half of the century, our budgets went in deficit for a few years. The burden of debt didn't allow us to phase out fossil fuel energy supplies and invest in renewable energy programs sooner than we had planned. Most countries were faced with the same predicament. The big emitters opted to spend their budgets on rescue packages in sectors linked with fossil fuel production."

"Here is your answer, Madame Secretary. Unfortunately for the planet, that renewed surge in fossil fuel consumption has contributed over the past few years to a massive release of greenhouse gases. Our updated modeling projections tell us we're now looking at a major increase of CO_2 in the atmosphere, warming of 5 degrees Celsius, and a rise in sea levels of one meter, over the next two centuries. Greenhouse gases, ice melting, and global warming will feed on each other until they eventually break down the global atmospheric system. My fear is that their mutual interaction will drive the Earth's general climatic system to break down and become unpredictable."

"It's frightening. Future generations will face a mountain of debt and a broken planet. So, in your opinion, Professor Robson, is there a threat to the existence of humanity as we know it in the future?"

Dan paused for a few moments, reflecting. With sadness in his voice, he answered categorically, "It's inevitable, I'm afraid, Dame Ngaire."

She rocked back and forth nervously in her chair. "That's what concerns me. Governments have failed to enact our recommendations due to their short-term attitudes. Despite all the warning signs around us, they haven't put in place any policy for human survival. Yes, here and there individual countries create land reserves, protect endangered animals and plants, but are we taking any measures to preserve ourselves as a species?"

Dan looked briefly at Sandy. "As far as I know, we aren't, Dame Ngaire. Not at an international level, anyway."

She shook her head and sighed. "We have this vital information and yet we aren't acting to prevent an incoming disaster for humanity. For decades, scientists have warned us that levels of carbon dioxide in the atmosphere will keep rising. As a global organization, I believe we should be more proactive to preserve the human species in the future. What are your thoughts on this, Sandy?"

"It concerns us as well, Dame Ngaire. We can see the long-term signs of a threat to human existence everywhere."

"So, what can we do as an organization?"

"One idea would be for our team to submit a proposal to look at the various issues involved and suggest some solutions. Then, we need to put in place an infrastructure of policies and submit them for approval."

She smiled warmly. "Very constructive idea, Sandy. Shall we call it a 'long-term governance strategy'?" She leaned forward in her seat and said firmly, "But I want your proposals to be positive and non-threatening. The last thing we want to do is to create panic."

Sandy, Dan, and Zara all nodded.

"We should highlight the achievements that modern discoveries have made to enhance the quality of human life, like in the fields of agriculture, power generation, transport, and communications. But at the same time, we should warn people these improvements have come at a cost to the overall quality of the planet's safety, like excessive pollution and destruction of natural habitats. Then, we should propose some options to tackle these side-effects on humanity."

Sandy looked thoughtful. "A feasibility study, Dame Ngaire?"

"Exactly my thoughts. Time frame wise and for our own purpose, I'd like you to investigate the risks of this century. People are generally worried about what type of world their grandchildren will be living in. This is understandable; that's their immediate horizon, you could say. However, that time frame is too short. My personal concern is the type of world Earth's inhabitants will face, say, in five hundred or a thousand years. What will the planet look like? Will it still be able to support human life? Look how quickly the world has changed in our own generation."

As she rose from the table, she concluded, "Maybe in time for the Sydney Convention? You know, a draft we can start working on? But let's keep it in-house."

UN KNOWLEDGE CENTER, BONN

The following day, Dan and Zara walked to an adjacent building: the UN Knowledge Center for Sustainable Development, a medieval castle located in an English-style garden. Sandy had several meetings to attend and had insisted they talk to the Campus Director.

They entered his private office. He extended his hand, greeting them cordially, "Professor Robson, Dr. Naidu, nice to see you both again."

Dan inclined his head. "Good morning, Herr Director, nice to see you too."

Zara smiled at him. "Sir."

As Dan went to take a seat, he spotted the vista out the window. "Wow, look at this amazing view of the Rhine."

"Enjoy the view. Best seat in the house." Then his demeanor became more business-like. "Please sit down. I wonder if you can help me. I've invited Franz Jürgen to come in for a chat."

Dan felt his stomach churn with this announcement and raised his eyebrows. "Really?"

"Our relationship with his group has unfortunately deteriorated under his leadership. I would like to try and keep him on side of course. Sandy is convinced your presence and input could make a positive difference." He leaned forward and said confidentially, "Just a forewarning, Franz will probably not shake hands with you. Just say hello to him."

Zara was puzzled. "Any reason?"

The Director cleared his throat. "That's just the way he is. Not a friendly character. He isn't German, mind you. Originally a citizen from Luxemburg."

Zara gave Dan a pointed look. He knew the signs as well. He had seen the way Franz had eyed his dark skin. Even after all the laws of race equality had been passed worldwide, it was still not uncommon to experience this unpleasant type of behavior.

Franz arrived and without being asked by the Director, sat at the side of the desk. As forewarned, he didn't shake hands with either of them.

The Director started the conversation off. "Thank you for coming, Franz. I have asked Professor Robson and Dr. Naidu to join us as experts in the field."

"Fine with me," he replied.

The Director continued, "As I've said previously, Franz, let me tell you that we sympathize with the ideas and agenda of your group. It's great to see young people involved. Our organization is just as committed to making the world a safer place by monitoring our environment." The Director smiled warmly. "Let's work together, Franz. On our side, we'll deal with the authorities and the industries. Your group can encourage young people to have smaller families, travel less by car and plane, and avoid goods which have a high plastic content. What do you think?"

Dan was surprised by Franz's harsh reply. "What you recommend is already part of our policies, Herr Director, and what your organization is trying to achieve has been proposed for years without much to show for.”

“We are trying hard, Franz. It’s not easy to turn the ship around.”

Franz became more agitated, reinforcing his point with a clenched fist. “You must be more forceful, Herr Director. We are controlled by multinationals that constantly push for increased consumption of oil-based products and pollute our environment. This isn’t the world we want for our children!”

Reluctantly, Dan tried to intervene. “Franz, The United Nations is calling for action by all countries. We want to build global economic growth, while protecting the environment at the same time.”

Franz looked at Dan in defiance, pointing a finger at him in an unfriendly manner. “Words! Words!”

Dan was taken aback. He knew there was only one way to regain the ground of the polemic. “How do you propose to fix the world’s long-term pollution problems then, Franz?”

Franz hissed, “Too many consumers. That’s one of the main reasons for the planet’s deterioration.”

“Well, this is precisely one of the issues our organization is trying to solve through our various family planning campaigns. There is a lot of reckless behavior toward the environment out there, but I agree the majority is due to increased consumption.”

“Then, you should control the size of the world’s population as a priority.”

“Apart from family planning campaigns, how do you propose to regulate that, Franz?”

He smirked. “Simple. Compulsory management of family sizes worldwide. That’s how. Especially in Africa, South America, and Asia. The fastest-growing populations are in these poorest countries. They don’t listen to your family planning campaigns, sir. They have twice our birth rate and lots of children they cannot feed. Then, in desperation, their kids become illegal immigrants. We must stop that. These countries should cut down their population by half."

Dan looked skeptical. "By half?"

"Yes. Two children maximum per family. The UN should compel them by law." He narrowed his eyes. "After that, compulsory sterilization. If they don't comply, implement more radical solutions."

The Director eyed Dan and Zara, who appeared shocked at these extreme statements. He stood up and said calmly, "Franz, we thank you for your contribution today." Pointing at a strongly built security guard near the door, he politely invited Franz to leave the room, "This gentleman will escort you outside the building."

To Dan's surprise, Franz's expression suddenly became much friendlier. In a now polite tone, he thanked the Director. "It was a great pleasure to exchange views, Herr Director. I am grateful for the opportunity you gave me to talk about my group's goals. I'm sure we can cooperate to improve global sustainability. Let's keep in touch, shall we?"

He shook hands with Dan.

"It was nice to meet you both as well. Good luck with your work. I'm sure we will be in touch in the future as well." He raised his hand in the air and ambled toward the security guard with a broad smile. "*Auf Wiedersehen.*" He winked suggestively at Zara as he left. Dan watched her visibly shudder in response.

———

By this time, Sandy had finished talking to the UN officials and joined them after Franz had left.

He asked Dan, "I saw Franz leave. How did your meeting go?"

Dan replied without hesitation, "You were right, Sandy, dangerous fellow. Very cunning in my opinion. He even suggested radical solutions for population control."

"That's worrying."

"Indeed. As you said, Sandy, he clearly intends to take advantage of the current conditions to push his own agenda."

Sandy reinforced Dan's view. "I'm sure he's using his eco-friendly movement to raise his own profile and maybe further his political ambitions. We're likely to see an increase in power grabs by some determined extremists. Franz Jürgen is one of them, ambitious and shrewd. I would bet his 'climate concerns' are just window dressing to get young people to follow his cause. I suspect his agenda is more disturbing. For him, the end justifies the means, pure and simple. I'll ask my contacts in the intelligence community to run a background check on him and his group, but guys like these tend to be slippery."

CHAPTER 2
YEAR 2036—SONGDO, KOREA

It had been six months since the Bonn meeting and events had significantly escalated around the world. Dan added another red flag to his digital world map and stepped back. Over eighty hot spots were now spread across the globe. His latest concern was a late-night decision from the Tuvalu Prime Minister to evacuate their entire population to New Zealand. Rising sea levels were now making it impossible for the islanders to live safely on the tiny Pacific atoll.

He sighed. *The Sydney meeting can't come soon enough. We need clear decisive action by all the member states, otherwise my whole map will be covered with danger flags.*

"Knock, knock," Zara called out, interrupting his thoughts.

"Hi, morning." Dan checked his watch. It was 8:00 a.m. and he'd already been in the office since 5:00 a.m.

She eyed him and his clothes. "Did you go home last night?"

He nodded, distracted. "Yes, for a few hours until Sandy called me about Tuvalu."

"Tuvalu?"

He turned back and pointed at his world map. "Here. A

series of small islands in the South Pacific between Australia and Hawaii."

She looked at the computer screen. "What's happened?"

"It was finally submerged overnight by sea water because of king tides. Its entire population had to be evacuated urgently. They are probably the first 'climate change refugees.' We'll have to send out a press release today praising the Tuvalu Prime Minister for his decisive action. We need to draw the link to climate change at the Sydney conference and why it's so important to turn the tide."

Zara grinned. "What?"

He scratched his chin, confused.

She repeated herself slowly, "Turn the tide!"

"Oh yes, thanks. Uh, right. We can't use that wording, of course. Not appropriate."

She nodded. "I'll go and draft the release now."

"Good, and this afternoon, let's go over the Sydney conference details once more. It's only three months away. We must get the right message across to the delegates."

"No problem."

His thoughts were interrupted by the beep of the holo-screen. His assistant called from outside in a thick Korean accent. "It's Mr. Fraser."

"Oh, thank you." He headed to his desk.

"Morning, Sandy. Zara's drafting the press release for Tuvalu as we speak."

"Great. She's good at that. She'll get the message across, I'm sure."

Dan put his glasses on. "All right. We're getting the evidence together for the conference, but as soon as we collate it, additional information comes in. Issues are really intensifying."

"I know the feeling. I'm working hard on this end as well.

I've been talking to some of the delegates of the member countries. I was hopeful we could get a strong resolution. You know what? They told me they had already done what is required of them." He rolled his eyes. "Ridiculous! The major powers still need a lot more convincing to seriously adjust their course, Dan."

"Sandy, we know the overall evidence is undeniable. Tuvalu is just the latest in a long list of threats to the planet. We're now looking at an increase of three to 4 degrees Celsius by 2100. Thwaites Glacier in West Antarctica is breaking apart. This could raise sea levels by half a meter worldwide in less than twenty years. Jakarta, a city of thirty million people, is being reclaimed by the Java Sea. Its entire population will have to be resettled to higher ground. Melanie is working with the Indonesian government to redesign some of the major infrastructure in Kalimantan. The cost will be in the trillions."

Sandy breathed in, suddenly looking hesitant. "Dan, I hope you don't mind me saying this, mate. I understand you have plenty on your plate, but I think you could do with a break. You've been looking tired recently. Overworked and overwhelmed by the task ahead, I'd say."

Dan groaned. "There's just so much to do before Sydney."

"I know. The Secretary General was in my office this morning saying how critical the conference will be, but you've got to look after yourself, mate. Otherwise, you'll run out of steam. I think you should get away for a few days with Melanie."

"I know, I know, maybe after Sydney?"

Sandy raised his voice. "Dan don't make the same mistake as I did with my ex. Too much time in the office, too little time with the family. It can break a marriage. Melanie is a wonderful wife."

"I understand what you're saying, Sandy. Thanks for your concern."

"I tell you what. I own a unit in Queensland. You could stop over on your way to the conference. Take a holiday with Melanie for a few days. What do you think?"

Dan replied, distracted, "Sounds nice, Sandy, thanks. Could you send me the details? I'll have a chat with Melanie."

"More than a chat. I want you to sell her the idea, all right?"

Dan perused his map. "We'll discuss it, Sandy. Thanks for the offer. Now, getting back to the rising seas. In Tokyo, three million people live below sea level behind huge concrete levies. Last month, typhoon Hara made landfall on the east coast of Japan. It brought record-breaking rainfall, which flooded ten prefectures of the low-lying areas and closed two of their major airports. They're running out of time and options. The Japanese should acknowledge that at the conference. With this information, we should get them onside, surely."

"I'll work on it, Dan. Right now, the latest concern here is that a Category 5 hurricane is heading for the East Coast of the US. The warnings are across all the TV channels. Combined with a low-pressure system that has moved from the Great Lakes, it's expected to generate winds in excess of 250 kilometers an hour. A weather pattern of this intensity has never been recorded before. However, the big players don't want to admit that these events are connected to climate change. All they're concerned about is their profits. 'Not our problem,' they say. 'Let the insurance companies pay for the damage.' That's their attitude. Totally irresponsible, don't you think?"

"Agree, and if they don't change their mindset, it's going to cost them even more. That's been our argument all along. They still don't get it. They're so short-sighted. There is definitively a connection between these weather events and climate change. We have explained that link many times, but they don't want to listen."

Dan paused and went back to his holoscreen. "Now, let me have a look at these hurricane warnings. Good Lord! I'd better call my mother. She might still be still in Harlem along with the congregation. They need to evacuate from the low-lying grounds immediately!"

"Sure. Call her now. I'll send the details about the place in Queensland through. Dan, I mean it. Take a break. Talk to Melanie."

Dan was already dialing his mother. "Yes, sure, sure. Thanks, Sandy. Bye."

———

Melanie had insisted that no matter what was happening at work, Dan had to be home by midday on Sundays. Together, they'd taken to their new way of life and encouraged their children to eat the local food as much as possible. Dan chopped the vegetables for their evening meal: Korean chicken hotpot. Melanie was cooking the chicken as Ava set the table. The boys were due back any moment from their away soccer match.

Ava came up and sat at the island next to him. She tried to sound casual.

"So, Dad, you know how I'm super responsible, yes?"

His eyebrows raised. He knew this tone spelled trouble. "Yesss."

She smiled sweetly, putting her hands below her chin. "Well, there's this party later in the evening."

Melanie turned away from the stove. "Don't get sucked in, Dan. I've already said NO."

"Ho, you trickster! You're trying to get me into trouble with your mum." He grabbed his daughter and hugged her.

"Daaad, don't mess my hair up," she protested, patting her hair. Today she'd combed it into tight braids at the top, which cascaded down in tight ringlets interwoven with rainbow ribbons.

Melanie put the lid on the chicken for it to cook further. She wiped her hands and sat at the island across from them. Dan offered her some wine. She agreed gratefully.

Leaning forward across the bench, Melanie sipped her wine.

"So, Ava, you know you mentioned how responsible you are?"

Dan laughed to himself. *Ava was no match for his wife.*

It was Ava's turn to be suspicious now. "Yes, I did say that" she confirmed. "Oh no, I get it. You want me to look after the boys? Are you having a flash date night or something?"

"More like a vacation," Dan said as he took some of the roasted seaweed from the table and crunched on it.

"A vacation without us?" Ava looked downtrodden. "Where are you going?"

Dan slowly sneaked some more seaweed. "Australia."

Melanie moved the bowl down to the table. "Your father needed some convincing to take time off from his work, but after multiple talks from Zara and I, we've finally pried him away from his desk. Mr. Fraser, your dad's boss, has been very generous and has lent us a place on an island in Queensland."

Ava folded her arms across her chest. "You're going to a tropical island without us? Really!"

"It's part of a business trip, darling. Afterward, I'll go to the conference in Sydney and Mum has some work to do in Indonesia, so it seemed like the perfect timing."

Ava shook her head. "Who's going to look after us?"

"Mrs. Roberts. But we're counting on you to help her out."

"Good. She's cool. She's looked after us before."

The boys bounced through the door. Their soccer uniforms were covered with dirt.

"Oh my God," Melanie exclaimed, looking at them.

Dan shook his head. "Must have been a rough match."

"In the shower straight away, boys! Dan, can you go help them while I finish up here? Don't let them touch anything."

Dan grabbed the back of each boy's shirt and headed down the hall. "Did you at least win, boys?"

Jack turned around, grinning. "Sure did. You should have seen us, Dad," he exclaimed, grabbing his brother and slamming him into the wall.

"Ahh." Dan sighed. "I think I might need a wash too."

———

Later that night, Dan was woken by a loud beeping. He put his glasses on and looked at his watch—it was 2:00 a.m. He reached for his holo. The caller was his mother.

"Hi Mum, are you alright?"

"Yes, thank God. But your father isn't. We've had a terrible storm here. Dad went to help Mrs. Banks onto the community bus. As he came out, a tree branch fell on him. He's broken several ribs and apparently has some internal bleeding."

Dan sat bolt upright. "Where are you calling from?"

"From Central Park. They're about to take your dad to an emergency outpost."

"I'll get a flight."

"All the airports are closed, Dan."

His mind raced. There had to be something he could do. He heard his mother's voice again. "I've got to go, Dan. I'm running out of battery. Thought you'd want to know about Dad. Pray for us, son, especially for Dad."

"I will. I love you, Mum. I love you both."

"We love you too." The holo cut out.

Melanie turned. "Dan, what's going on?"

"That was Mum calling from New York.

Dad got injured in the storm—"

"Oh, honey! That's terrible!" She hugged him. "Let's check the latest news."

She checked her holoscreen and read out loud. "The damage caused by Hurricane Lea has been devastating. Hundreds of people have been injured. Many homes have been destroyed. Large parts of New York have been ravaged by floods and fires. Many of the sub-stations blew up. The subway system is under water. It is anticipated there won't be any electricity for weeks in most of the counties. There are no ferries or flights out of the airports. The governor has declared a state of emergency."

"That's why they needed to leave the city, but Dad got injured in the process. I'll organize a flight to New York as soon as I can and check on him."

NEW YORK

Thanks to Sandy, who'd pulled a few strings with the Secretary General's office, Dan had managed to get a flight to New York two days later.

He arrived in Washington Dulles International Airport and then transferred to Joint Base Andrews. There he was greeted by Captain Fergusson, a well-built National Guard officer who'd been assigned as his bodyguard and could help him to get access to some of the off-limits buildings. Dan was issued with a battlefield army uniform, an emergency kit, and a semi-automatic pistol. From the base, a Navy helicopter flew them into downtown New York.

Dan peered out of the window and drew in a sharp breath.

"I can't believe the devastation, Captain Fergusson. All the trees have been flattened. I grew up in this neighborhood. The noisy streets, the little cafes, the colorful pedestrians have completely disappeared. Instead, all I can see now is widespread destruction: trees down, buildings damaged, rubble and large pools of waters everywhere."

"It's a sobering sight. The death toll so far exceeds three hundred, sir. Many more are unaccounted for. Power is still out in most areas. There's no running water or holo coverage, which makes it hard for our troops to communicate. One of our priorities is to restore the communication networks."

As they flew over Central Park to land at the northern end, Dan noticed a series of tents erected and dozens of white containers to their right.

"What are these?" he asked the pilot.

The pilot grimaced. "Refrigerated trucks. They ran out of space at the mortuary."

Dan shook his head and tears sprang into his eyes. This felt so personal, not just because of his father but because this was his home. He'd spent many happy years there in his youth, and now it was an unrecognizable disaster zone.

"This is as close as I can get you," the pilot said as he set the helicopter down.

After the landing, he reminded Dan, "You've got your gear? Keep close to Captain Fergusson, sir. It's total chaos down there, extremely dangerous."

Dan nodded. In exchange for flights to New York, he'd agreed to head to the UN building to retrieve an electronic storage unit containing confidential information about Project Legacy as soon as he had seen his father.

As they made their way to the Central Park Emergency Field Hospital, they passed several teams of rescue workers searching through the rubble for survivors.

"There's still hope of finding some people alive, but it's now a recovery effort," Captain Fergusson explained. Thanks to his presence, Dan received priority access to the triage section.

He addressed one of the nurses on duty, "Excuse me, I'm looking for a patient called Reverend Joshua Robson. He was injured three days ago in this vicinity."

The nurse searched through the listing.

"Robson... Robson... Joshua. Here we are. According to our records, this patient was transferred yesterday to Lenox Hill Hospital. His injuries weren't too serious—a few broken ribs and a dislocated shoulder."

"Thank God for that!" Dan exclaimed.

"Yes, we've seen far more serious cases."

"If I remember well, the hospital is further down south?"

"Correct, sir. Keep going down Fifth Avenue, past The Met, until you reach 77th Street. It will be the third block on your right. Can't miss it. The hospital covers the whole area."

"Thank you, nurse. You've been most helpful!"

"You're welcome. Good luck. It is terrible what's happened here. I was born and bred in New York, and I've never seen anything like it. The weather's gone crazy."

Lenox Hill Hospital could usually be reached on foot in less than half an hour, but it took them the best part of two hours to get to the front entrance. Some of the roads were blocked by partially collapsed buildings. Trees had been uprooted and cars stood abandoned. Dan noticed most of the shops had broken windows. Shopkeepers stood at the front of those that were still reasonably in one piece, trying to protect their goods. Other shops had their shutters down.

Under normal circumstances, Lenox Hill was a high-class hospital providing the full spectrum of healthcare services. A concierge in a custom-made, stylish, double-breasted uniform and matching top hat would typically welcome patients and their families at the main entrance. However, now it was manned by New York Police Department officers in full riot gear. Ambulances and emergency vehicles were double parked all around the building and people were shouting at each other. The tension in the air was palpable.

Dan and Captain Fergusson showed their credentials and were taken to the third floor. In an overcrowded room with a dozen patients all kitted out in blue gowns and lying in beds with various monitoring equipment obstructing his view, Dan couldn't see his father.

Panic began to rise in his throat. There were just so many people. He looked at one man after another, no match. Captain Fergusson was about to head to another floor when he heard a voice call

"Dan. Here, son."

Dan rushed over to his father who had been hidden behind several full gurneys. "Oh Dad, are you okay?"

His father was sitting upright in bed but had a sling over his left arm and he could see significant bandaging across his middle

He hugged him gently.

"Good to see you son." He patted Dan's hand with his good arm. I've improved a lot. I'll be out of here in no time."

"Don't rush it, Dad. This is one of the best places to be right now. It' is chaotic outside. Ask Captain Fergusson."

"Your son's right, Reverend. We've just walked from Central Park and the city is still in a mess, although our troops are trying hard to restore some order."

"How did it happen, Dad?"

"Well, I was trying to help Mrs. Banks get on the bus to Albany with the other parishioners when a branch fell on my shoulder and knocked me down. What about Mum?"

"Relax, Dad. I heard from her before I left Korea. She's safe in Albany. The congregation there welcomed her and the other parishioners. She's staying with Reverend David's family."

"Good, good". They'll look after her well."

"Reverend David said she can stay for as long as she needs to. This might be a while. What do you think, Captain?"

"From my experience with this level of destruction, a couple of months at least, sir."

"Dad, unfortunately, I won't be able to visit you again. I'll stay in New York for another day, but I have some official duties to attend. I'm sorry."

"I understand, son."

"I'll organize to have you transferred to Albany when you're recovered."

"Thank you. I just want to be with your mum again."

"Do you need anything?"

"Some clothes. I have a list here. Don't know what happened to the ones I was wearing. All I have is this gown."

"Not a problem, Dad. I'll fix that and leave some cash for you as well. Take care. Love you."

As Dan was about to leave, he felt called to lift the morale of the victims of this tragedy. He stopped at the door, turned toward the patients in the ward, and addressed them in his powerful voice. "Folks, may I have your attention? The captain and I wish you all a prompt recovery and the best for our beloved city. Keep your spirits up!"

Then, in his booming baritone voice, he started singing the first verse of the national anthem. "Oh, say can you see, by the dawn's early light, what so proudly we hailed at the twilight's last gleaming..."

Soon the other patients joined in and gradually the other wards on the floor.

At the end of the last sentence, "...that star-spangled banner yet wave, O'er the land of the free, and the home of the brave," Dan shouted, "God bless you all!"

———

After they left the hospital, Captain Fergusson suggested a change of route. "Sir, if I may? I think the best way to the United Nations' headquarters is to keep going on Seventy-Seventh Street toward the East River and cross over FDR Drive, thereby avoiding the built-up areas. Then, we'll use John Finley Walk south along the river."

"Excellent idea."

At the end of Seventy-Seventh Street, they walked in on a gang of looters who were dragging goods from a supermarket. The captain stopped and held Dan back by putting his hand across his chest. He cautioned him, "Better not confront them. We're outnumbered. Let's draw our weapons in case they turn on us."

The looters hesitated for a second or two, but eventually this firm stand was sufficient to deter them. Sandy and Captain Fergusson continued on their way.

Walking along the East River, it took them another three hours to reach the UN building. Dan remarked, "Look... all the flags which normally ornate the Plaza have been shredded to pieces and there's water everywhere. There must have been flooding in the basements. Too close to the river, you see. In another one hundred years, with the rise of sea levels, the water will submerge large parts of New York, unfortunately. Our calculations indicate that with a 4-degree warming, the sea levels will rise by two feet."

The captain's eyebrows shot northward. "So soon?"

———

Temporary fences were protecting the area with an entrance gate manned by National Guard soldiers. Other law enforcement agency personnel were also present.

Captain Fergusson explained the nature of their visit to an officer of the UN Department for Safety and Security. Ironically, the area of the Sustainable Development Environmental floor had been left relatively untouched.

They were escorted to the second floor of the main building. In the "Green Room," they were introduced to a member of the cybersecurity section. He asked Dan several questions and handed him a small case containing an external drive, which Dan put in his backpack.

Dan turned to Captain Fergusson. "Sandy was insistent. Mission accomplished. Thanks a lot for your help, Captain. Could you organize a meal and accommodation for tonight? Tomorrow morning, we'll do the reverse journey and then we will fly back. In the meantime, we may be of assistance. Could you ask how we can help around here?"

QUEENSLAND, AUSTRALIA

Six weeks later, Dan and Melanie caught a plane in Brisbane bound for Hamilton Island. As they began their descent, Dan could see the outline of the Great Barrier Reef from his window seat.

He leaned over to Melanie. "There it is honey. Look how clear the water is around the reef."

She smiled and kissed him. "Paradise, here we come."

After they exited the plane, the warm, humid weather hit them. "Thank goodness I changed into shorts when we were in Brisbane."

"Oooh, me too," Melanie exclaimed. She had changed into a blue and white sundress. She removed her large straw hat from her yellow handbag. Grabbing his hand, she gave him a loving look and squeezed it. "A tropical island. Isn't this fantastic." She gestured at the water, which was just meters away from the tarmac.

He could already feel the tension he'd been holding onto begin to melt away. He smiled. "We should have done this ages ago, Lanie."

She grinned. It had taken a lot of convincing to get him here.

They picked up their luggage and headed outside the terminal. Dan checked his holo. "Sandy explained that our transport is in parking bay seven." His eyes widened as he walked past the area lined up with white golf carts.

Melanie laughed. "Isn't this exciting?"

Dan shook his head. "We're going to run out of adjectives before we get to our accommodation."

A tan, young blond man welcomed them with a smile. "Mr. and Mrs. Robson?"

He helped them by putting their luggage in the back of the buggy and handed them the keys to their accommodation and some maps.

He pointed ahead of them. "From here, pass the white gate, go onto Airport Drive, and then take a left on Marina Drive and drive until you can see Mango Tree Corner on your left at the roundabout. Mr. Fraser's unit will be the first one on your right. It's called 'Coolangatta'. Have a pleasant stay."

Melanie grabbed the keys and hopped into the driver's seat.

"Come on, let's go, Mr. Robson."

After a few initial jerks, the drive was relatively smooth. Dan looked at the townhouses and apartments nestled among beautiful gardens. The drive was short—only ten minutes. As they pulled up to a quaint green bungalow, Dan noticed the lagoon pool to the right.

———

They spent time sleeping in, eating fresh seafood at the island's many restaurants, going for bush walks, and enjoying much needed quality time together.

By the fourth day, Dan felt totally refreshed and restored. "This is the life!" he exclaimed.

As they drank their morning pineapple juices on the balcony overlooking the ocean, he could hear flocks of white cockatoos screeching loudly and coming close by for free feed. In the distance were several islands. Melanie was reading the newspaper; an old-fashioned habit she enjoyed during breakfast.

She handed him the crosswords. "Here, hon, try the cryptic."

He grinned. Melanie knew his little pleasures. The comfort of being known swept over him. He reached out and kissed her hand. "I love you."

She smiled warmly, nodding. "Likewise. We make a good team."

After a long, leisurely breakfast, Dan checked his holo. He

had purposefully left it silent most of their stay, as he didn't want to disturb the blissful atmosphere. There was a message from Sandy.

"Hmm."

Melanie stepped into the room to pick up her hat for their walk.

"Everything okay, hon?" she queried.

"Yes, yes. Sandy has arranged for the resort manager to take us sailing around the islands in his catamaran this afternoon, and tomorrow we're going out to the Great Barrier Reef by helicopter."

"Why? There's nothing left there."

Bringing up a map on the holoscreen, he pointed to an area. "I believe there are still a few reefs of live coral here which have been re-seeded."

"Are we going to see that?"

"Yes. Sandy wants us to look at Heart Reef as background information for the conference. It's part of the Great Barrier Reef Marine Park. Environmentalists have put lots of effort into preserving hard and soft coral in that area. We'll also visit a patch further up on the reef where there's nothing much left. He wants me to take a few pictures to show the contrast for the presentation in Sydney."

"Dan?" Melanie said, protesting, "I don't like this idea. We're having such a nice trip. Why ruin it with work?"

"It's okay, Lanie. I can take it. It's part of my job as a scientist to face reality and explain it to the public. I can't deny what's happening even if it's upsetting. The degradation in the Great Barrier Reef is further evidence of the urgency of the situation; it also shows just how little we're doing to halt the destruction of the planet. I must convince the delegates to listen to me somehow. We're facing a potential existential threat here!"

"So, is the honeymoon over?"

He laughed. "Never. The honeymoon still goes on. Thanks to you, I feel like a different man now." He flexed his biceps.

She laughed too. "Maybe I should be with you more often, hon? You know what I'd like? To see the koalas. They look so cute. I believe they have some here at the island's zoo."

"Great idea. Here again Sandy has a contact. Let me see what he says." Dan flicked through the e-book Sandy had left them. "According to him, the head keeper of the small wildlife park is an expert on the koala population. His name is Michael Wanjuru. I'll give Michael a call to see if he's available. We could go there this morning for our walk."

A couple of hours later, they met up with a burly Aboriginal man dressed in a khaki uniform who was waiting for them at the gates of the wildlife sanctuary.

"G'day. My name's Mick. Nice to meet you, Mr. and Mrs. Robson."

Dan extended his hand. "Hi Mick. I'm Dan and this is my wife, Melanie."

"Good to see you, folks. You're the friends of Sandy Fraser, right? Nice bloke, hey. We always have a few beers together when he visits. Is he around as well?"

"No. He's in Sydney. We're staying at his bungalow."

"Oh yes, 'Coolangatta.' I keep an eye on the place when he's away. Anyway, you want to see the koalas don't you, folks? Follow me to their enclosure, please. We've got three females for the moment. One just had a new joey. She hasn't got a name yet. Tell you what, maybe Melanie after you, Mrs. Robson?"

"I would prefer Lanie."

"Even better. We'll call her Lanie."

Melanie grinned, obviously thrilled with the idea. "That'd be fantastic. Thank you, Mick." Mick opened the pouch of the female koala, and a little one stuck its head out.

"Isn't she cute!" Melanie exclaimed.

"Yes. We've got a good breeding program here. They're all in good health, free of diseases. It's not always the case on the mainland. Not many left in the wild, regrettably. Droughts and bushfires have killed a lot."

"That's terrible," Melanie said as she fed the mother koala some gum leaves.

"We're experiencing continuous drying out of the land, which reduces the growth of the gum trees. What you are feeding them is their only source of food. Picky eaters they are. That's the main threat they face. Also, loss of their natural habitat from intensive urbanization and farming."

"They're also prone to specific diseases, aren't they?" Dan asked.

"Chlamydia. Awful infection! Highly contagious with some populations seeing a 100 percent infection rate. The poor creatures haven't got much of a chance in the wild. The only healthy ones left are in sanctuaries like this one, zoos, and on some islands which have been designated for their survival. So, you want to have a look at the reef as well?"

"Yes please, Mick. I'm a biologist and I'm giving a talk about the effects of climate change on the reef at the upcoming Sydney conference."

"No worries. What about tomorrow, hey?"

"Yes, we're free."

"Good on ya. I'll pick you up from your bungalow after breakfast, say ten?"

———

The following day, Dan greeted Mick, "You're a man of many hats."

He grinned. "You have to when you live on an island."

"So, you work with Sandy?"

"Yes. But as a scientist, not as a diplomat, of course. Not much difference between the two professions according to Sandy."

"What do you mean?"

"Well, I asked him one day. As an international diplomat, what do you actually do? Do you know what he answered?"

"Tell us."

"I'm like a marine biologist, Mick," he said. "I watch the big fish eat the smaller ones."

They all laughed. "Very funny," Dan said. "Sandy has a great sense of humor."

While he was warming up the helicopter's engine, Mick gave them some details about their destination. "First, we'll go to Heart Reef, one of the most famous sights of the Great Barrier Reef. Unmistakable and naturally formed, you know? We'll have a look from the air first and then I'll land on the nearby pontoon. The public isn't allowed to dive there. Protected area, but I have the necessary clearances. As a marine biologist researching the cause of climate change, you're also entitled to snorkel around the reef. The coral and associated marine life are still in excellent condition. Have you guys used snorkeling equipment before?"

Melanie smiled. "We have, Mick. We dive regularly in Florida and Hawaii."

After Mick brought the helicopter down on the pontoon, he provided Dan and Melanie with masks, flippers, and snorkels.

"No need for bottles here; the water isn't very deep as you can see."

As Dan readied his snorkel, fond memories flooded back.

He and Melanie loved the ocean and the diversity of its marine life. They had been diving on many islands over the years, mainly in Hawaii and the Caribbean islands.

They went down the steps and lowered themselves into the warm water. Dan's senses went into overload. The water was crystal clear, and they could see several meters ahead. All around them was a rich variety of brightly colored fish, corals, and anemones. Dan watched a school of orange fish swim and circle with the current. A large blue angelfish with yellow streaks came close to Melanie. She reached her hand out and pointed it out to Dan as he went past. Dan gave her an "okay" signal, which she answered by smiling and waving.

After half an hour, they surfaced back to the pontoon. Mick greeted them with bright blue towels. "What do you think?" he asked.

Melanie couldn't contain her enthusiasm. "Absolutely stunning."

Dan was overwhelmed as well. "The abundance of marine life is amazing, Mick. Everything looks so healthy down there. I can't get over how clear the water is!"

"Well, it's the icon of the Great Barrier Reef. We take great care of this patch. We've introduced a bio-engineered variety of coral that is more tolerant to temperature increases. Unfortunately, as you know, most of the coral elsewhere isn't in such a good condition. I'll fly a few miles further up north after this to another pontoon near Kennedy Reef to show you the difference."

This time Dan was horrified when he saw the extent of the damage. The coral was totally colorless. Some varieties were smothered in sediment and overgrown with algae. It felt like the shadow of a reef. He saw almost no fish. He spent just ten minutes in the water and couldn't wait to get out.

Back in the boat, he turned to Mick. "It's like a ghost town down there."

Mick sighed, "Yep, virtually no marine life left."

"So just a small rise in temperature can kill the coral?" Melanie asked.

"Yep. What happens is the rise in temperature kills the tiny ocean creatures which the polyps feed on, therefore cutting their food supply."

Melanie gaped. "So, the corals literally starve to death?"

"Exactly. The frightening part is that it happened so quickly. During my lifetime in fact. When I started monitoring the reef as a young biologist, the majority were still very healthy. With the rise in temperature—only 1.5 degrees—but in less than two hundred years, the coral hasn't had time to adapt."

Dan furrowed his brow. "It's frightening how quickly irreparable damage can occur, Mick. Our concern is that a lot of ecosystems will suffer the same rapid decline as climate change progresses."

"Here in the ocean," Mick added, "we estimate that within fifty years, the additional CO_2 will cause such acidification that the reef's underlying structure will start to crumble."

SYDNEY, AUSTRALIA

After a blissful week in Queensland, Dan caught a flight from Hamilton Island to Sydney, while Melanie boarded one to Cairns and then headed to Indonesia.

Dan woke up from a short sleep as the captain of the Qantas flight announced, "Ladies and gentlemen, our arrival at Sydney Kingsford-Smith Airport will be delayed due to poor landing conditions. A thick fog caused by a combination of pollution and smoke from bushfires in the Blue Mountains has engulfed the city and reduced visibility to less than one hundred meters."

"Today of all days," Dan grumbled.

He was to be one of the key guest presenters at the United Nations Framework Convention on Climate Change in Sydney. The 200 country members came together every year to report on their efforts to stabilize greenhouse gas concentrations "at a level that would prevent dangerous human-induced interference with the climate system." The rationale was that "such a level had to be achieved within a time-frame sufficient to allow ecosystems to adapt naturally to climate change and to enable economic development to proceed in a sustainable manner" (United Nations Framework on Climate Change guidelines).

According to the new numbers, this target was unlikely to be met. Sandy had stressed to him the need to point this out during his presentation. With this evidence, he would hopefully persuade the audience to push for quicker action on containment measures.

Dan scanned the 3D map to work out how much time he required to get from the airport to the Convention Center at Darling Harbor. Then he texted the updated information about the flight delay to Zara, who had arrived in Sydney a day earlier.

She replied, "Major chaos at the airport and in the city. Don't try to catch a taxi. I've arranged for a helicopter to take you from the airport to the BriteStar hotel. An agent of SydHelico will be waiting for you at the luggage pickup area."

One of Dan's fellow guest speakers at the Sydney Convention was Isobel Löfgren, a well-respected Swedish astrophysicist. Since her teenage years, she had regularly been in the news for her strong views on climate change. Given the present delay, Dan tuned into the recording of her speech on his seat's screen wall.

A distinguished brunette in her late twenties with her hair in a neat bun appeared on the screen. Her message to the audience was blunt. "Delegates, like Professor Stephen Hawking, I am concerned about the future of humanity due to the deterioration of our ecosystem. We have treated our planet so badly that it will eventually reach a dramatic end. Governments have not focused on the long-term consequences of population expansion and climate change. The leaders of our nations have provided ineffective solutions so far."

She paused before raising her voice. "Global warming is happening right now! It is quantifiable. Our main measurement is the atmospheric concentration of carbon dioxide in parts per million. This reading is increasing at a phenomenal rate. By burning fossil fuels like coal and oil, which took millions of years to form, we are returning that carbon to the atmosphere in only a few hundred years. Figures compiled over the past two hundred years show a direct correlation between the indiscriminate use of fossil fuels, which produce CO_2, and a rise in worldwide temperatures. With increases in population levels and subsequent excessive demands for resources and energy, our planet is facing an environmental catastrophe. Greenhouse gases in the atmosphere have grown exponentially, and their levels cannot be reversed. As a result, life on Earth as we know it will disappear over time and mankind won't be able to survive in the future."

Dan watched as the camera panned to the audience. There was an obvious reaction of disbelief. However, Dr. Löfgren continued, unperturbed. "Due to public apathy, political expediency, vested interests, and a lack of planning at the international level, we humans have compromised our own habitat and our own destiny."

She looked intently into the camera. "Our generation is now living in the golden age of humanity. We are the lucky ones. But while enjoying a bountiful lifestyle, we have thought little about our responsibility to keep Earth livable for future generations! We have also not focused on the survival of mankind. We have already reached several dangerous tipping points. Ladies and gentlemen, it might already be too late for remedial action. Our own species could be heading for extinction in the future."

Pausing, she opened her arms and smiled at the audience as if inviting them to follow her suggestion. "In the history of mankind, the increasing pressures on living conditions drove some groups from their ancestral land. The same forces will drive some visionary inhabitants of Earth to discover new territories on distant planets. I believe we can meet these challenges. We need to build a new high-level space program to look for other worlds to save our species. We can develop suitable technologies for some of us to leave Earth permanently and start a new human civilization."

She concluded her speech. "Like Stephen Hawking, my concern is that we might run out of time."

Dan guffawed to himself. *A space program to save our species? She can't say such things openly. That's what Sandy warned me about. Don't scare the public! Don't start a general panic. Stick to the known facts.*

The plane's holoscreen showed many of the delegates reacting in the same incredulous way. *How unwise of the organizers to bring this woman to the conference,* Dan thought. He further scanned the media feeds, which were blowing up with words such as "extreme, alarmist, and over the top" filling the headlines. He put his earphone set away as the captain signaled, they were commencing their descent toward Kingsford-Smith Airport.

As the Qantas flight approached Sydney, Dan looked out the window. Sure enough, all he could see was brown smog.

After a bumpy landing, the captain gave the passengers permission to leave the aircraft. A senior flight attendant helped him with his cabin luggage and they both raced to customs, where Dan had been granted advance clearance in view of his diplomatic credentials. On the other side of the terminal, they met up with his SydHelico contact, who helped him collect his suitcase from the carousel.

A white limousine was waiting for them in a restricted parking zone right outside the arrival terminal. The driver greeted him, "G'day, my name is Jon. Welcome to Sydney. Please take a seat, and I'll take you to the chopper." He loaded his luggage into the oversized trunk.

The driver took the back road, skirting the airport to the SydHelico site. After five minutes of steady driving, he stopped at gate A, showed his badge to the security guard, and parked on the side of a blue hangar—the designated area of the heliport terminal. Carrying Dan's luggage, he walked with him toward the waiting helicopter. He tried to reassure him.

"No worries. You'll make it in time. She'll be right."

Zara was already inside. "Dan, in here!" she yelled, barely audible over the rotating blades. "I know you like helicopters."

She dialed Sandy. "He's in. We're on our way," she shouted, partly out of breath.

Zara put her holo back in her bag and relaxed in her seat, relief evident in her eyes. "Glad you could make it. Such an important day!"

As the helicopter lifted off and flew toward the city, Dan did his best to see through the thick smog. He could just make out the traffic around the airport as the helicopter increased its altitude to navigate the thick soup. Silver cabs and other vehicles with their headlights were at a standstill. Cyclists wearing face masks and motorbike riders were racing on footpaths off the road and between the other vehicles. Everyone was trying to get around, but this just seemed to create even more chaos.

"This is unlike anything I've ever seen before, even in Manhattan," Dan said to Zara.

It was hard to see any of the famous attractions which defined Sydney. They could only recognize one iconic landmark. The pilot pointed out the upper arch of the Harbor Bridge sticking out in a sea of clouds like the top of a humpback whale. It was an eerie sight.

Soon, they landed on the helipad of the BriteStar, a luxury hotel in the heart of Darling Harbor. Dan grabbed his bag and ran to the lift entrance with Zara.

Sandy was waiting for them. "Welcome, Dan. Welcome to sunny Sydney," he said in greeting, tapping his blue Rolex. "Dan, we've adjusted the agenda. You're now presenting in two hours. Zara has already set up the equipment and collated the sustainability reports. Does that give you sufficient time?"

"Not a problem. I'll have a quick shower and a change after I've checked in." Dan shook his head in bemusement. "Oh Sandy, that speech from Dr. Löfgren was something."

Sandy raised an eyebrow. "Straight to the point, wasn't it?"

Dan smirked as he made his way down to the lobby. *Has Sandy seen the headlines? The whole world is ridiculing her proposal.*

As he waited in the foyer, Dan's attention was drawn by the sound of a didgeridoo played by a young Aboriginal man dressed in a red loincloth. It was the last week of the International Year of Indigenous People. In Australia, major hotels were encouraging the traditional custodians of the land to perform a welcoming ceremony for their guests.

As if out of nowhere, a gray-haired, shriveled Aboriginal man wrapped in kangaroo skins approached Dan. His face and body were decorated with lines of ochre. The man greeted him in a slow, craggy voice, "Orana, welcome to the land of my ancestors. We are the Gadigal people of the Eora Nation. We have taken care of this region for many generations, making sure this land is kept the way it was given to us by the Creation Spirit. Look at it now!" he said with disbelief, gesturing to the tall buildings around the hotel.

He waved his hand in a semicircle, holding a eucalyptus branch over Dan's head as if he was blessing him. "Our region only covers a small part of Sydney. You have been given the task to look after the whole of the Earth."

The man exhorted him, "Do everything you can to protect this planet from destruction, brother." He then passed Dan a message stick. On one side, burnt into the acacia wood, he could read the words: **"Look after the land,"** and on the other side, **"the land will look after you."**

Dan took his time pondering the significance of the meaning. "Wise words, my friend. Your people know how to live in harmony with the land." He shook his head. "*We* don't. We exploit it. That's our mistake."

"Good luck, brother. Pankina. Be happy."

As the concierge called him, Dan reflected, *how does this old Aboriginal man know about my work?*

———

When Dan arrived in the auditorium, he was feeling more refreshed. He surveyed the room. It was packed. He felt somewhat hopeful. If they could just convince the different countries of the urgent need for action, maybe they could turn this whole conference around toward stronger action on climate change.

It was Sandy's turn to address the participants. He cleared his throat and began in his somewhat muted Australian twang. "Delegates, we've had an informative opening session so far. As an Australian, I just want to say welcome to Smokey... sorry... sorry... Sydney."

The reaction was immediate. The general laughter relaxed everyone in the Convention Center. Sandy continued with a grin on his face, "Let's start again. Welcome to Sydney."

He introduced his team. "On my right, please welcome our Chief Scientist, the Director of our Office in Korea, Professor Dan Robson, and on my left Dr. Zara Naidu, our principal researcher."

He readied himself. "I'll give you some of the statistics first."

A large screen descended beside him, and a holographic image was projected.

Sandy pointed at a curve on a population growth diagram. "At the last count, the number of people on Earth is above eight billion, and the carbon dioxide levels are 480 parts per million. Agree?"

The attendees nodded.

"According to the consensus forecast, by 2100, the world's population is expected to reach ten billion, carbon dioxide levels will climb to seven hundred parts per million, and the temperature will increase by 3 to 4 degrees Celsius compared to pre-industrial measurements. At these 2100 levels, our agency estimates the worldwide demands for resources and energy will result in heavy pollution of the land, water, and the air. It's a simple projection of the current trends."

He turned to Dan. "Isn't that what scientists call 'the critical mass?'"

"Yes, it's an appropriate term for an ecosystem about to reach a dangerous limit."

Dan continued with the presentation. "I will now cover the Southern Pacific region. In Australia, climate change will be a story of two halves. On the eastern side, the summers will become wetter with major flooding of the rivers from Queensland to Victoria, even Tasmania, due to the increase of the sea water temperature in the Coral Sea. In contrast, on the western coast, the summers will become increasingly hotter and drier with some regions reaching temperatures in the fifties in summer. On the mainland, large areas of land will be decimated by uncontrollable bushfires. We have all witnessed it this morning in Sydney. In the red center, deserts will expand. The Murray-Darling Basin will reach a tipping point of agribusiness viability. Production of food will be dramatically curtailed. Two icons of Australia: the richness of the Great Barrier Reef and the uniqueness of the koala population in the wild will soon be images of the past."

Dan showed some of the pictures he'd had taken on his recent visit to the Whitsundays, with their bleached coral reefs and videos of koalas fleeing from bush fires.

Pictures of searing heat waves and dust storms also appeared alongside images of cattle and sheep dead on the ground in dried-up riverbeds.

"I can also brief you about the overall region of the South Pacific. Australia's low-lying neighboring countries will continue to face the worst impact of climate change. Sea levels have already risen substantially."

Large parts of Fiji, the Cook Islands, the Marshall Islands, and Vanuatu came into view on the screen, submerged in ocean water.

"Only a few months ago, the entire population of Tuvalu was relocated to New Zealand. They are the first climate change refugees. Mind you, the rise of the oceans is happening worldwide. Significant land masses of fifteen countries are disappearing. Large parts of Bangladesh and the Netherlands have also been affected. Major cities like Amsterdam, Jakarta, Tokyo, Singapore, New Orleans, Mumbai, Shanghai, and even New York have started to be reclaimed by the sea."

Sandy raised his voice. "It's happening, delegates. It's happening right now! The signs of climate change are undeniable. We need to act fast!"

He turned toward Zara. "Dr. Naidu, would you please address our other concern?"

"Happy to. Excessive air contamination by greenhouse gases has led to noticeable increases in world temperatures. Our latest Environment Panel Report has conclusive evidence of the damage that has already been inflicted on the Earth's atmosphere. Our models indicate this trend will increase exponentially."

She flicked to another image.

Dismay started to drift across the faces of the audience at the sight of pictures showing hundreds of people in face masks commuting to work in a heavily polluted Asian capital city.

"As a result of a rise in global temperatures, several major ice sheets in both hemispheres have lost half of their volume. The thawing of the permafrost in the Arctic Circle is releasing huge amounts of methane gas. Greenland glaciers are melting irreversibly. In Alaska and South America, glaciers are disappearing as well. In Antarctica, the ice sheets are breaking up. In India and Bangladesh, the high-density populations living on the Bay of Bengal will be dramatically affected by monsoons and the rise in the sea level. Many islands have disappeared already. Thousands of people have been displaced. With the predicted 2-degree rise in the Earth's temperature over the next five decades, the situation will be catastrophic. I thank you for your attention."

Sandy took the podium again. "Well said, Dr. Naidu."

He looked out into the audience. "Delegates, we're not doing enough to combat climate change. We cannot delay action any further. We need to act now! We must increase our effort to curb the production of greenhouse gases immediately. The numbers shown here today indicate the impacts of climate change are real. They are happening at this moment and will worsen in the future. We must act now to try to reverse the trend. The longer we leave it, the worse it's going to get. I also encourage your governments to act to change the behavior of your citizens at an individual level. Most of them still cannot live without their powerful cars, four-wheel-drive vehicles, jet skis, trailer bikes, and motorized leisure crafts. They also love to watch the Formula One Grand Prix, supercar races, and rallies. The fact is all these activities burn large quantities of fossil fuels unnecessarily. More effort to educate the public is required. Regrettably, human-induced climate change interests will affect our life-sustaining systems more than ever the longer we don't take radical action to curb our use of fossil fuels."

Sandy paused and swept his gaze around the room, looking serious. "Delegates, you have copies of our most recent report. In the next few days, I will invite you to discuss the resolutions we need to bring forward. Our final public statement must commit to radical measures to turn this current destructive trend around. It is paramount that we commit to a 'carbon-neutral' policy by 2050 at the latest to make a worthwhile difference."

———

The next two days were filled with frustrating discussions. Dan and Sandy worked the room one country after another, trying to convince delegates and cut deals but with little success. Zara tried to convince India to "phase out" its use of coal, but they insisted on using the term "phase down" without setting a specific target.

Dan suggested a new strongly worded summary public statement. He tabled some of the resolutions, but they were watered down by several of the major players who were still unwilling to commit to effective measures to curb greenhouse gas emissions.

The representatives of the world's largest polluters proposed incremental changes to some targets and mentioned minimal remedial action. All of them made motherhood statements filled with platitudes and pure rhetoric. Nothing new was suggested. Dan was concerned that the wording of the final statement required the agreement of all the participants.

During one debate, Zara whispered to Dan, "This is infuriating. We were expecting a major change of direction, but they won't even acknowledge the dangers of the current situation. They seem to think they can keep delaying the current approach without any danger to the future of the planet. It's a typical 'kick the can down the road' attitude. So disappointing."

Dan shook his head. "Disappointing" was too tame a word. By the end of the last session, he could barely control his temper. He took hold of Sandy, who looked drained.

"We're not getting anywhere, Sandy. Despite the overall evidence of the effects of climate change, the big players don't want to make meaningful concessions. A tweak here and there but nothing of real significance, nothing which is going to change the dreadful course to the destructive path we're facing. The superpowers are trying to slow down our proposals. They're just tinkering at the margins, following the directives of their governments, who themselves are at the mercy of the fossil fuel industries. Same old story."

Sandy nodded. "You're right, mate. I really thought we might have convinced them. I tried. We'll have to come up with something else."

———

At the end of the plenary session, the delegates produced a document called "The Sydney Pact 2036," by which they agreed to "make note of the greatest challenge of our time." They emphasized a "strong political will to combat climate change in accordance with the principle of common responsibilities and the participating countries" respective capabilities." They also recognized "the critical impacts of climate change and that cuts in global emissions were required to reduce the potential impacts of global warming."

The most important aspect was their "target to stabilize greenhouse gas in the atmosphere at 500 parts per million by 2050 to limit global warming to 1.5 degrees Celsius." The agreement urged countries to reduce their use of fossil fuels rather than eliminate them.

As the last of the delegates left the room after the session and the event staff cleaned up the room, Dan, Zara, and Sandy sat to the side of the room, looking forlorn.

Dan reread the final version and threw the proposal on his desk. "This is a great disappointment. The major polluters have declined to commit to a timely reduction in greenhouse gas emissions and phasing out of coal-fired power plants. The terms of this document are far too weak in terms of action. They use a lot of words but don't commit to any significant change. We would reach these targets without this so-called accord. Some of the countries don't understand the urgency of what needs to be done to achieve a worthwhile reduction in emissions. As we are discussing the targets, some governments are granting further permits for oil and coal exploration."

Zara added, "In the medium-term, a six hundred parts per million concentration will lead to global warming of 2.5 degrees Celsius above the pre-industrial global average temperature level. These concentrations will be catastrophic for the Earth. These measures are *not* going to save the planet in the longer term. Why can't they see that?"

Sandy, who was sitting across from them, looked dejected. Slumped over, he was watching the delegates leave. Suddenly, as if a lightning bolt had struck him, he jumped up and said to Dan and Zara, "Wait for me here. I'll be back in a sec," and rushed off.

As Dan watched the delegates take their luggage out of the conference room, he sighed. "What a waste of time and energy. Let's get ready to head to the airport. Our flight is due later this evening."

———

Sandy came back into the room just as Dan was about to leave. "Great. You're still here. I've scheduled a meeting in the hotel's private conference room on the thirty-fifth floor in half an hour. Can you bring your notes and meet me there?"

Dan looked at his watch, baffled. "I have time, but what is this all about? Are you expecting anyone, Sandy?"

"Yes. Professor Isobel Löfgren."

Dan stiffened. The media coverage had gotten worse over the course of the conference. The phrase "Astrophysicist lives in the stars" had become the top trending line for all newspapers.

"The Swedish astrophysicist?" *There must be some mistake,* he thought.

"Yes." Sandy confirmed proudly. "Very punchy speech. By the way, do you know her?"

"Uh, I know *of* her. I'm not familiar with her work as an astrophysicist, but her research on climate change is well known in scientific circles, I believe and her sustainability campaign, of course, but Sandy, the reaction in the media?"

"Don't worry about the press, Dan. They're always looking for the next catchy headline. They're at the mercy of their editors and proprietors who support the big end of town, which resists climate change initiatives. Do you remember what we promised Dame Ngaire?"

"Sure."

"We need to evaluate all the alternatives; Dan. Isobel is an expert on space exploration."

"But Sandy, we all know there's nothing in the solar system that's suitable. Exoplanets are light years away. The technology to reach them just isn't there!"

"Agree. For the moment, it seems like 'mission impossible,' but we must make a start. We need to look at all the options for the long term, and see which ones are feasible even if the technology isn't available yet. Maybe it will be there in the next hundred years. That's what Dame Ngaire is expecting from us. I'll go to the lobby to meet Isobel while you get ready. See you in half an hour. The conference room is on level thirty-five. There'll be a sign with my name on it. Dan, be open-minded. Give her a chance."

When Dan told Zara, she was as bemused as he was, but she collected their presentation, her holoscreen, and a few copies of the report and followed him to the private conference room.

A few moments later, Sandy arrived with Isobel.

Sandy steadied himself. "Please make yourselves comfortable. Isobel, may I introduce my colleagues? This is Professor Daniel Robson, the director of the UN Office for Sustainable Development, and our chief scientist, Dr. Zara Naidu. They are both based in our head office in Incheon, Korea."

She shook hands with them both. Dan remarked, "I haven't had the pleasure, Dr. Löfgren."

"Call me Isobel, please. I'm delighted to meet you both."

After the introductions were out of the way, Sandy continued, "Let's get this meeting underway. Isobel, six months ago, Dan, Zara, and I met up with our Russian representative in Siberia. We witnessed the increasing deterioration of the environment in the Arctic Circle. The purpose of this meeting is to review our findings and try to reach a consensus opinion on what Earth's prospects in the future are."

His tone became business-like. "Despite all our efforts, national leaders won't achieve managed control of emissions in time. I'm afraid their governments don't grasp the magnitude of what is about to happen. As Greta Thunberg said, 'The most important facts given by the best scientists on climate change are ignored by politicians. They are unprepared for the emergency and paralyzed by short-term decisions, especially their obsession to stay in power.' She's right, of course. Our organization can warn the people responsible and give them reasonable guidelines, but we have no authority to enforce any measures to fix the problem. Say for instance, population is a critical issue for the preservation of the well-being of the planet. In most democratic states, citizens aren't prepared to accept necessary regulation of their family size to start with."

Sandy gestured. "Do you remember when China tried to solve the population problem several decades ago? They implemented their 'One Child Policy' for a few years. Their family planning policy prevented the birth of five hundred million children, but they had to abandon it, due to demographic distortion. Isn't that right, Zara?"

She gave a brisk nod. "Too many boys." Her casual remark generated a burst of nervous laughter in the room, easing the somewhat tense atmosphere.

"Now they allow three kids per family, I believe," Zara added.

Sandy paused and took a sip of water before continuing. "Isobel, the situation in East Siberia is changing fast. The massive release of methane from the Arctic permafrost shelves areas, which our team has been monitoring, is now self-generating at an exponential rate."

He turned to Zara. "Could you tell Dr. Löfgren the situation in Siberia?"

"Sure. A dangerous phenomenon has been triggered by the constant warming of the waters surrounding the Siberian shelf. A significant decrease in the ice cover is accelerating the melting of the permafrost around the entire Arctic Circle region and releasing methane that has been trapped for millennia. As you know Isobel, being a heat-trapping gas, methane is around thirty times more potent than carbon dioxide. The northern hemisphere climate is now getting out of control."

Zara brought up several 3D photos on the room's wall. "These are the latest pictures from our trip to Siberia a few months ago." She enabled the zoom function. "Isobel, you can see here that large columns of burning methane are bubbling up from the Arctic Ocean seabed, venting high into the air like jet streams. They are adding huge volumes of heat to an already dangerous accumulation of greenhouse gases in the Earth's atmosphere."

Dan continued, "Zara and I have projected that due to this sudden injection of methane, the concentration of greenhouse gases will increase dramatically. The degradation in the atmosphere will happen a lot faster than our earlier estimates."

Sandy looked at each one of them. "Thank you, Dan and Zara. We're now coming to the main purpose of this meeting."

He paused, looking serious and tense.

Sandy took a deep breath. "Based on the current state of the planet's accelerated degradation, will Earth be able to sustain the human species in the next few centuries?"

The question was blunt but complex. Silence reigned for the next few minutes.

Dan was the first to speak. He felt a lump rising in his throat. "My answer is NO, Sandy. We're running out of time faster than any previous prediction. Our conservative models have proven to be far too optimistic. We're entering uncharted territory. Global warming will rise more significantly than forecasted in any earlier modeling. As I mentioned at the conference, due to the rise in temperatures in the Middle East and North Africa, for instance, crop yields are projected to fall by 60 percent, exposing millions to mass starvation. World Bank economists have predicted that by 2050, over five hundred million people will need humanitarian aid on the African continent alone because of climate-related disasters such as floods, storms, droughts, heat waves, and wildfires. Of greater concern are the skyrocketing temperatures in North Africa and the Middle East. Going forward, they're only going to worsen and spread to most regions of the world. Temperatures above 40 degrees Celsius, or 104 Fahrenheit, cause the body's heat regulatory mechanism to fail. On the current path, I believe human civilization is heading for an alarming outcome in the next few hundred years. We're going to literally fry ourselves. Sorry. I know it sounds dreadful, but the facts cannot be denied. These are the dangers of global warming in a nutshell."

"Thank you, Dan. What do you think Zara?"

She glanced up from her screen, also looking devastated. "My answer is also NO. There is now compelling evidence of faster and irreversible self-degradation of our environment. My prediction is that the Earth's temperature will continue to increase by at least 3 degrees Celsius this century, and maybe 6 degrees Celsius in the next two to three hundred years with devastating effects on all ecosystems and therefore humanity. Taking the ice melting and the warming of the Earth's temperature into account, reliable scientific evidence concludes that within around five hundred years, our oxygen levels might become largely depleted. Our own Human Sustainability Report 2035 forecasts the gradual extinction of a high percentage of living species by the year 2200. Eventually, it could include our own."

"Thank you, Zara." Sandy looked at both in turn and then said in a low, serious tone. "I know that must be a dreadful conclusion for both of you to come to after all the effort you've put in."

Sandy turned to Isobel. "Dr. Löfgren... Isobel, based on what you've heard, I would like your opinion as well."

"Sure, Sandy. As a passionate conservationist, I regularly check the situation with my friends at The Stockholm Environment Institute. Also, I follow the NASA reports. They constantly measure land, sea, and atmospheric temperatures. Their current assessment is authoritative: global warming has reached a critical point. Due to our relentless need for economic growth, we are pushing the global ecosystem boundaries to a point of no return. Our civilization has tried to improve our lives by creating new products, but the existential quality of our planet has suffered in the process. We have been guided by good intentions, but our actions have always been motivated by short-term gains and not considered through for their effects in the future. Industries and transport are burning in a few centuries carbon reserves which have taken millions of years to form. In the process, our atmosphere has been polluted with massive amounts of greenhouse gases."

Isobel took a deep breath. "As I said in my speech, current trends indicate that, with time, large parts of the planet will become uninhabitable. There is no doubt in my mind that our current civilization is destroying itself due to its mismanagement of the planet's resources. I therefore have to say NO."

The room felt like the air had been sucked out of it. There was a stunned silence in the small assembly. Dan felt overwhelmed by his and the others' statements. *What does all this mean for us? What can we do?*

Sandy summarized their views. "We all agree with this assessment: environmental conditions are now at the worst we've seen and will deteriorate further and faster. Water, soil and in particular, air pollution, will reach catastrophic levels over the next centuries and the situation is irreversible. With combined population pressures and biodiversity conditions collapsing, the survival of humanity on Earth is under existential threat in the long term. We all agree that the chances of mankind surviving in the next few centuries are slim. Yes?"

Overwhelmed, they all nodded in despair.

Dan thought *There must be some way out of this*. He cast his mind back to the conversations over the past couple of days and shook his head. Very few of the delegates had taken any time to acknowledge the emergency. At most, they had rendered lip service and made vague promises.

The image of the Titanic came to his mind. Everybody had thought the ship was unsinkable. Despite warnings about icebergs, she kept sailing at maximum speed and due to her size, she was not able to turn around. *Was this going to be the Earth's destiny too?*

Sandy stood up. "Let's take a break and grab some dinner. Dan, Zara, can you stay in Sydney until tomorrow? I need to make a few calls and then we'll talk some more. I'll catch up with you in the hotel's private dining area in one hour."

———

Down in the hotel's restaurant, Dan ate in silence with Zara and Isobel.

At around 7:30 p.m., Sandy came down, looking like the weight of the world was on his shoulders. "I've just been in contact with the UN Secretary General. Dame Ngaire is very pragmatic. She is aware of our meeting and the conclusions we've reached. She is also completely supportive of what I am about to tell you."

He lowered his voice and eyed the door to the private room. "Here's the deal. From now on, the four of us will be part of a specialist team called 'Project Legacy.' We'll still be regarded as being part of the Sustainability Office, but we will be autonomous. Our mission is simple: to look for alternatives to maintain the survival of humanity in the coming centuries. To find a solution to humanity's looming crisis."

He continued, "Our research papers won't be mentioned anywhere. We cannot admit in public that there is no way to save the Earth's ecosystem in the future, otherwise we would spark general panic. We must continue to promote the current strategies in the public domain. All our research will be classified, and we will be bound by the Secrecy Act. Any concerns?"

Dan immediately saw a problem. "The systematic degradation of our environment is well understood by the scientific community. At some stage, Zara and I will face questioning about whether the actions that are being taken will be effective. How do we answer that, Sandy?"

Sandy nodded. "That's an excellent point, Dan." He gave a wry smile. "Look, I regularly deal with people associated with the intelligence community. They deny any association with these agencies and often detour the conversation. Perhaps we should take our cue from them. We can stick to standard statements even at the risk of being accused of 'All talk and no action.' For the well-informed out there, we'll involve them when necessary. I suggest we don't talk to the media on topics outside of our official roles. From now on, we won't take part in public interviews. When it comes to getting the support of important people, we might have to make some concessions, but I'll handle that aspect. Does that answer your concern, Dan?"

Dan agreed. He wasn't great at lying, he felt uncomfortable getting involved with the media. "Yes, that works for me. Zara and I will rehearse some standard answers."

Sandy turned to Isobel. "It'll be different for you, of course, since you're openly proposing a search for planet B and you're an expert in this field."

She shrugged. "Remember, I'm not part of the UN Sustainability Office. I'm an astrophysicist. I speak my mind freely."

Sandy laughed and patted her on the shoulder. "Well done, Isobel. Witty as usual." He straightened his tie. "As the Manager of Project Legacy, I'll answer directly to the Secretary General. She has guaranteed me that she will do her best to secure financial and diplomatic support for our project. We humans are a highly intelligent species, but we must ask ourselves whether we're intelligent enough to control our global destiny and save ourselves from potential extinction. This is the challenge for humanity in the future. The planet itself will adapt. It has done so many times before, isn't that right, Dan?"

Dan reflected on his early university lectures. "It's survived five major extinctions, Sandy. The Earth will keep on orbiting its star—the Sun—and travel through space like it's done for four billion years. Over time our planet will heal itself and create new forms of life in a different environment. But humans as a species might not be part of it."

Sandy went on. "However, as far as we know, in the immensity of our galaxy, we're probably the only life form capable of reasoning intelligently. Am I right, Isobel?"

Dan was surprised to hear Isobel burst into cynical laughter. "A few of us are that way, yes, Sandy, but look at the mess most humans are making of this planet. They aren't reasoning intelligently as far as I am concerned. Most of them are inconsiderate consumers. They just live on a day-to-day basis, taking whatever they can from their environment without any concern for the next generations."

Dan shook his head. *A bit unkind*, he thought.

Zara reacted quickly. "Not everyone has our knowledge of the situation, Isobel. Most individuals just want to get a good job, find a partner, buy a house, have a family, and enjoy the comforts of modern life. That's their scope. It doesn't mean some of them aren't concerned about the big picture. Quite a few ordinary people are actively trying to improve the planet's survival. They're joining conservation and lobby groups to get their voices heard."

Dan was pleased Zara had added her voice to his, and continued, "Well put, Zara. People just want to be happy, safe, and comfortable. There's nothing wrong with that, Isobel. They're normal aspirations of any human being. Even then, they're the lucky ones. The majority are basically struggling to stay alive."

Isobel smiled. "Sure, there are groups 'struggling to stay alive,' as you say. I agree, but there are also many who just want to keep filling their pockets. Industries producing energy from fossil fuels have constantly undercut the scientific evidence that greenhouse gases are driving us toward a climate catastrophe. It's greed pure and simple, Dan. They've made their fortune peddling non-renewables and want to keep it that way. If they had listened to the warnings from scientists over the years, we wouldn't be in this mess."

Dan rolled his eyes inwardly. *Time for Sandy's diplomatic skills.*

Sandy looked at them calmly. "Yes, you're right Isobel, and so are you, Dan and Zara. That's the problem we're facing as a group. We must balance the legitimate needs of individuals with the future of humanity. Is the comfort of today's generation going to be the nightmare of future ones? When we're looking at the big picture, as you reminded us, Isobel, there's no doubt in my mind that the best of our human characteristics must be preserved. Let's face it, individual governments won't act effectively. As climate analysts, we need to take a longer view. We must lay the foundations for a program to establish a sustained long-term presence of our species, whatever and wherever it may be. As we have determined, the damage inflicted to Earth is advancing irreversibly. We must act quickly!"

When Sandy paused, they all looked at each other, speechless.

Dan noticed that Isobel was calmer now. She broke the silence. "I have connections with people running projects to live in self-contained, self-sufficient structures. Some excellent work has already been done. We can learn from these ventures. The question for us is: what are the best long-term options? Eventually we'll have to consider the alternative of building a space probe to search for another planet like our own. Space technology has made enormous progress in this field."

Dan eyed her. *I still don't trust her judgment. She seems to be dismissive of practical ideas and is overly optimistic about untested options. I need to get Sandy to see the reality here.* He rose slightly from his seat. "I can see your point, Isobel, but do you really think the scientific community has the expertise to send humans to settle in space? Mass survival outside the Earth is an enormous challenge. Shouldn't we first have a look at solutions here? Places where we can preserve either some individuals or samples of our human DNA. That would be an easier goal to achieve."

He looked at Zara, who nodded and reinforced his stance. "I agree. We are saying that first an alternative for maintaining a human presence must be investigated on this planet. Surely, some populations and some individuals will survive. Space is an expensive way of saving humanity, and the know-how isn't there yet."

Isobel frowned. "Sorry, but I think we need to properly acknowledge the situation here. I believe that eventually, this planet will become uninhabitable for humans. Full stop! And that's not far away in the future. As the saying goes, 'It's not a matter of if, but when.' That's how we should look at our project. We must consider the space alternative. My research shows that with the constant advance of space technology, it's feasible in the not-too-distant future."

Again, Sandy tried to reach a consensus. "Point taken, Isobel. What we *will* suggest is to put in place foundations for several solutions within a reasonable time frame from the simplest to the more complex. It's important to have the necessary vision for this mission and to know where to find the expertise. I feel confident we can discover alternatives to save humanity from an uncertain fate. I look forward to your collaboration; ALL of you!"

A tall, blond waiter brought them the dessert menu. "Would you like coffee or tea?"

Dan felt emotionally and physically exhausted. He shook his head.

"Not for me, thanks." He turned to the others. "It's been a long day. I wouldn't mind getting some sleep."

Sandy rubbed his eyes. "Agreed. We can talk more tomorrow at breakfast time."

Zara joined Dan in the elevator, while Isobel and Sandy stayed and ordered dessert.

Zara hissed, "Dan, are you okay?"

"Yes. Thanks for backing me up. I'm not sure what to make of Isobel's ideas. They're too far-fetched at this stage, don't you think?"

The elevator doors opened to his floor. "Let's talk more tomorrow. I feel a bit confused and overwhelmed and above all, I need some sleep. It's been a long day."

———

Dan hadn't slept well. He needed to clear his head and opted to run on the treadmill at the hotel gym facilities rather than going for a jog outside. It was too hazardous outside in the polluted air. So much had happened in the past couple of days. He replayed Sandy's words, "The Secretary General's full support." After his shower, he got dressed and headed to breakfast in the private room. Sandy was already there.

"Morning, Sandy."

Sandy looked up from his tablet as he sipped his coffee. "Restless night? You look exhausted!"

"Yes, so much to think about." He thought, *What's the best way to phrase it?* "You know I have the utmost respect for you—"

Sandy grinned and interrupted, "You don't have to sugar-coat it, Dan. You doubt me, don't you?"

Dan hesitated, "Not you... Isobel. Sandy, I'm not sure about her ideas at all."

Sandy took another sip of his coffee. He looked at him kindly. "Dan, how long have we been working together? Nine, ten years?"

Dan recollected. "That's about right. Ava was just a baby when I started working part-time in the New York office alongside my lecturing post at Princeton."

"And in that time, we've disagreed a few times, right?"

Dan remembered. He'd come in, a brash expert in the academic world. *Not that dissimilar to Isobel*, he mused. He nodded, admitting, "Okay, a few times, but it was quite early on and that was mostly me... but Sandy, this is..."

"I know, Dan. I understand the significance of all of this. That's the reason why we must put all options on the table, no matter how unrealistic. You and I've fought for years to stop this catastrophe from happening, and you said it yourself—it now looks inevitable!"

Dan dropped his head wearily. "Inevitable, yes."

"Dan, you need to trust me. There are much bigger stakes here than we can even imagine. Our organization must lead this work. We are neutral, inspirational, and positive. We are well placed, but we must be open-minded."

"Sandy, I *do*. No question there. But none of us, besides Isobel, has the skill set to handle this. It's such an unknown venture... unchartered territory."

"I agree, but at this point, let's treat our project as a feasibility study. We'll gather intelligence, analyze the evidence to put together a case with no bias toward any option, for the future of humanity."

Dan could feel the caffeine and sugar starting to kick in. "I can do that, Sandy. So can Zara, I'm sure."

"Of course, you can. You're both brilliant researchers and analysts. More importantly, I trust you'll both weigh up all the options from an objective scientific perspective." He grinned again. "Dan, I promise you, if things get too loopy, I'll be the first to pull the pin."

Isobel walked in with Zara. "Morning."

"Do you want to order?" Sandy asked. He pressed a button. The tall, young blond man from the night before took their orders. "Continental breakfast and a cappuccino for me," Isobel said.

Zara raised her hand. "Same for me with Darjeeling tea, please."

Sandy resumed. "So, picking up on where we left off yesterday, we're interested in finding how to establish the infrastructure for a sustainable long-term human presence, be it here on Earth or in an extraterrestrial environment. What's the next step, Isobel? You're the expert."

"Well, most of the projects for future sustainable settlements outside the Earth's surroundings are carried out in the US. Let's see. I would recommend traveling to New Mexico first. We need to visit the self-sufficient habitats or biodomes which have been built in Albuquerque. Then we should go to Arizona to look at the Lunar Base Camp. I've got a contact there. These are the most advanced projects from a technical perspective I know of."

"Great idea," Sandy said. "Right now, I need to spend a couple more days in Sydney with some of the UN officials. After that, we can fly to the US and have a look at these facilities."

Dan gave him a thumbs-up. "Isobel, Zara, and I will

prepare an itinerary and organize some visits and meetings with the officials responsible for these facilities."

"How long should I allow Isobel?"

"I would say a week. Both projects are located around the Southwestern region, not far from each other."

"What do you think, Zara?"

"One week sounds about right. Dan, how long is Melanie staying in Indonesia?"

"Around ten days. I'll be talking to her tonight and confirm the dates with her."

Zara started laughing. "Luckily, I packed enough for a longer trip. Not sure about you."

ALBUQUERQUE, NEW MEXICO

As their flight from Salt Lake City began its descent, Dan watched a spectacular sunrise on the colorful Sandia Mountains with the oasis of Albuquerque in the New Mexico desert nestled at their feet.

Sandy turned to him from across the aisle. Folding his newspaper, he asked, "So, tell me, Dan, what are we looking at today?"

"The biodomes on the grounds of the Botanical Gardens. They're located near the banks of the Rio Grande."

"Is it far from the airport?"

"No, half an hour, give or take. Albuquerque isn't a large city."

"And who's the meeting with?"

Dan flicked through his notes until he found the name. "Tiwa Sandia, the Director of the biodomes."

"Sandia like these mountains?"

"You're right. Unusual name. He's made himself available to our group to explain the technical details of the biodomes."

"Do you know much about him?"

"This fellow has had an interesting life. The son of an indigenous tribesman, he was adopted by a local mining entrepreneur who became wealthy from the profits of gold operations. He was educated as an engineer at the University of New Mexico. Being a local man, he was familiar with the history of the environment and became involved in conservation. I'm sure you're aware the original forest in New Mexico was depleted by logging as early as at the end of the 1800s?"

Sandy interjected, "Yep. Typical of what went on at that time. Straight out plundering of the local resources without any concern for the future. Shocking! It's still happening everywhere now—current examples are the Amazon, Africa, and Indonesia."

"Sure is. We've improved our thinking in the twenty-first century, but that's about it. It's too late to do anything now. Here in New Mexico, only 2 percent of the forest remains today. Having witnessed the damage caused to the original plants and trees, Tiwa Sandia became a devoted environmentalist. His main goal has been to replicate the local ecosystem inside an artificial habitat to preserve the plants for future generations."

Sitting next to Dan, Isobel chimed in as she typed away on her holo, "NASA became interested in his project for different reasons. The conditions replicated in the biodomes were, in a sense, like what would be required in a space colony: self-sustainability."

"Right, Isobel," Zara said. "With the help of the University of New Mexico, the three parties created a trust to build these biosphere domes."

———

They were provided with a van and a personal driver as soon as they arrived.

Rounding the banks of the Rio Grande, a dirt road led them to the outskirts of the botanical gardens. Dan spotted three white structures covered in numerous panels of glass that resembled large-scale beehives. *Fascinating*, he thought, already chomping at the bit to view the inside.

As they stepped out of the van, a statuesque, well-built man in his fifties with a dark, sun-tanned face approached them. He wore a large black hat with a bright red feather in the hatband, a cream-colored shirt rolled up at the sleeves, well-worn jeans, and dusty brown boots. He smiled as he greeted them. "Hello. My name is Tiwa Sandia. I'm pleased to meet you all."

Sandy extended his hand first. "Thank you, Mr. Sandia."

"Please, call me Tiwa."

"I'm Sandy Fraser. Call me Sandy. May I introduce my colleagues? Dr. Isobel Löfgren, Dr. Zara Naidu, and Professor Dan Robson. We're all members of the UN Sustainability Group."

"Welcome to our complex. I'll get someone to take your bags. Please follow me."

Dan passed his bag to a small man, who scurried off. Tiwa took them down a well-signed path on their right and pointed to the domes.

He explained the setup with enthusiasm. "These green-houses were constructed ten years ago. The original aim was to replicate New Mexico's natural environment with their own water cycle and control of the oxygen levels. As you can see, the three biodomes are interconnected. They've been built to demonstrate the viability of closed ecological systems to support and maintain human life in a sealed environment."

"Is it okay if I take some photos?" Zara asked.

"Yes, of course. Go ahead." Tiwa continued, "As I said, the biodomes were designed to mimic New Mexico's ecosystem. Now, with NASA's help, the current purpose of the biospheres is to investigate the application of sealed, self-sufficient systems here on Earth and in space. In a way, the domes are like what we'd expect in a space colony. There, the astronauts will encounter different conditions such as gravity, atmosphere, and temperature, to name just a few."

Sandy nodded. "That's exactly what we are interested in, Tiwa."

Dan put up his hand. "May I ask you what materials were used to construct the buildings?"

"The structure of the domes, including the glazing, has been sourced from local materials. NASA insisted on that. I can't tell you the exact composition. Sorry. We still haven't finalized the process of registering the various patents."

"Sure. I understand. Maybe at a later stage?"

"No problem. I can tell you the panels also produce the electricity supply for the domes."

"So, there's a fair amount of silica?"

"Correct. The structures have been 3D-printed and assembled robotically like they would need to be in a foreign environment. NASA insisted on that aspect as well. The university's Department of Engineering worked out the material composition and designed the robotic printers and the computer program. Let's start with the first dome."

He took them up to an external platform. Dan leaned on the outside rail and peered through the glass panels. As he looked out over the railing, he felt the morning heat already building up. He swiped beads of sweat from his head.

Tiwa smiled, tapping his hat. "You need one of these."

"Yes, please," Dan said with relief. He saw the practical benefit of Tiwa's outfit.

"I have a spare one in my car. I'll call my assistant, Pedro, to bring it."

"Thanks."

"Glad to help, Dan."

The three biodomes were each about forty-five meters wide and shaped like elongated semi spheres. *Like giant beehives*, Dan thought. They were all connected by a short passageway.

"See. No doors, no windows like a true pueblo." Tiwa gestured with pride. "Sorry, I can't show you inside right now, Dan. A crew of ten people are working there, but we can look at the systems from the outside platform."

"No problem. I'm sure we can get a good idea from the exterior."

Tiwa pointed out, "Here in the first one, we've replicated a natural local environment. That's the original structure."

Dan peered inside and saw a woodland of low-level shrubs.

Tiwa continued, "We've used a variety of small creosote bushes, which can retain more water. These are evergreen plants prevalent in this region."

"I can also see a stream running through it. How amazing!" Zara enthused.

"That's the recycled water supply."

They all studied the scene for a few more minutes.

"Have you seen enough?"

They all nodded. Dan was sweating profusely now and was keen to move forward.

"Let's walk to the second dome?" Tiwa invited.

They continued on the paved pathway surrounding the domes.

"What do you think of this one, Dan?"

Dan leaned in and saw crops, with a couple of workers in white overalls tending to them. "It's like an agricultural area.

From what I can see, it's equipped with a hydroponic installation."

"That's exactly what it is. The crew members use this dome to produce food and to recycle nutrients and waste. This dome is a little bit larger than the other two."

Tiwa motioned for them to gather around him. "The hydroponic area starts over there with the blue tank. See? The water flows through these white conduits right up to the end of the third dome and is then forced back to the first dome through the green pipes near the ground. Pumps powered by the solar cells circulate and condition all the air and the water in the three domes. The big issue is the control of the temperature variations between day and night, especially in this region. Of even greater concern for us is the level of oxygen. Over time, there is a certain amount of depletion. At this stage, it must be regularly replenished from an external source. We're still working on the problem."

"Is there a leak to the outside?" Sandy asked.

"No, no. It's an internal issue. The crew is using more oxygen than the plants can produce."

"These are the very same problems we're likely to encounter in a settlement on a foreign planet," Isobel remarked, looking up from her hologram tablet for the first time. "The buildings would probably be on a smaller scale, and we would have to select plants that produce the right amount of oxygen."

Tiwa guided them down the final path. "Let's move to the last dome. These are the living quarters. They're furnished with a galley kitchen containing a refrigerator/freezer and a table. The electronic control center is located in a restricted area accessible with pre-programmed key passes and can only be operated when two people are present. All the electricity needed to keep the equipment running is produced by solar panels. The sleeping cabins are in the amenities section with a shower/toilet/washbasin area and compact fitness equipment. I've prepared a dossier for each of you. As I mentioned, ten crew members have been living inside the domes in isolation from the external world for nearly fifteen months now. It's the fifth team so far."

Sandy's eyes gleamed. "May I ask you about the relationship between the team members, Tiwa?"

"Uh... Apologies, Mr. Fraser, but the board of directors is clear about not invading the privacy of the crew members."

"I understand. What I meant is could you just give us a general idea about the group interaction? Nothing specific about individuals."

"That, I can do. As we have reported in the media, the teams normally consist of five men and five women. They're qualified in different fields of expertise: engineers, botanists, dieticians, medicos, physiologists, fitness instructors, and so on. Like what you would expect in a space program crew. At the start of their confinement, they don't really know each other. That's deliberate from our point of view."

"Any special issues?" Sandy pressed.

Again, Tiwa appeared cautious. "We've noticed they tend to get on well together for the first few months, but factions soon emerge. In fact, we had to stop the first team halfway through their time. Stronger personalities wanted to take control of the decision-making process and tried to establish some sort of hierarchy."

Sandy queried, "How did you deal with that?"

"Learning from experience, we've instituted a chairperson rotation system—but even that doesn't solve all the problems."

Isobel looked up from her computer again. "What about more intimate relationships?"

Tiwa started laughing. "That's even more sensitive, Isobel. Let me put it this way. Nobody got engaged or married. Nobody got pregnant. Nobody changed their sexual preferences. A team of psychologists constantly monitors the team members during their stay. After the experiment, most participants keep in contact with each other."

Admiration flashed in Isobel's eyes. "That's a wonderful result." She continued her questioning. "Do you use libido suppressants during their stay?"

Tiwa was amused. "It isn't necessary, no. In terms of food, the crew eats a strict vegetarian diet from the produce they cultivate. No meat. That makes them less aggressive, and we don't keep animals in there for fear of bacterial contamination."

"I'm a vegetarian," Zara quipped.

Sandy checked his blue Rolex, "Thank you, Tiwa. Both the technical and psychological aspects will be useful for our research."

"Good. I will make available to you a summary of our observations over the past ten years. To maintain their anonymity, the crew members are identified as A, B, C and so on in the report."

"We look forward to reading it. Thank you."

"By the way, the current team is coming out in a fortnight. If you want, I can make the facilities available to your team for a couple of weeks—"

Sandy's reaction was immediate. "Thank you, Tiwa. That won't be necessary. I don't think we'd last more than a couple of days," he added laughing.

Dan wiggled his eyebrows humorously, eyeing Isobel. "We're all alpha personalities." He clarified his comment. "No seriously, we're getting on fine, but we need our space, if you know what I mean."

Tiwa nodded. "I understand." He looked at his watch. "By my reckoning, it's just about lunchtime. Are you people hungry?"

One after the other, they accepted his offer. Dan's stomach growled. The cereals and juice on the plane seemed like a long time ago.

"Let's walk to my house. It's only a few blocks away. My wife Paloma has prepared some blue corn tortillas with beef and chicken."

"That's very generous of you, Tiwa. Yes, we'd love to share a meal with you," Dan said.

"For you Zara, I'm sure she will share a salad of local vegetables. My wife is vegetarian as well."

Zara smiled. "Good on her."

"Will we be able to try the famous red chili sauce?" Sandy asked.

"Homemade this morning. The best in Albuquerque."

———

Dan noticed the dust getting on his shoes and the bottom of his trousers. He wasn't dressed for the desert like Zara. He decided to shed his jacket and roll up his sleeves like their host. He folded his coat carefully and put it into his satchel. They cut across the parking lot and headed down the street back toward Tiwa's house.

They soon arrived at a cream clay house. In the front yard, Dan noticed a tiered garden with sandstones interspersed with a variety of succulents. A rocky path in the middle led up to the single-story house. From the outside, Tiwa pointed out the pueblo adobe architecture style of their house. The front pavilion was tiled on both sides with a slanted red terracotta roof. The two other rooms consisted of large, rectangular chambers.

"I wanted to maintain the building tradition of my ancestors. This pueblo has been constructed from sundried clay bricks mixed with straw for strength, then covered with additional protective layers of mud. The flat roofs are supported by a network of long beams whose ends protrude through the outer facades. However, being a designer of houses of the future, I've installed an array of solar panels on the middle pavilion as you can see. It's a necessary compromise."

Dan was impressed. "Perfect eco-friendly combination, Tiwa. You're utilizing the sun as an energy source and the Earth as an insulation material."

They sat down in the front lounge. To Dan's surprise, the interior was light and airy. Zara chose a couch decorated with lavish bright red cushions. Tiwa introduced his wife, Paloma. She was petite and round-faced. Her long, black hair was tied in a traditional knot. She wore a turquoise dress, an aquamarine necklace, and several stunning silver bracelets, which Zara openly admired.

Paloma invited Zara to the kitchen. "Come with me, Zara; we will prepare lunch together. Let's organize for ourselves some antojitos on corn tortillas with a variety of beans and vegetables I've grown in my garden. I've also prepared some grilled pepper strips, cactus flowers, squash blossoms, and guacamole, of course."

Dan overheard the conversation. "Are you growing all this yourself?"

"Well, with the help of my husband, of course." She squeezed Tiwa to her side. "He's installed a hydroponic system in a large greenhouse in the backyard."

Dan's eyes glinted. "Like in the biodome?"

"Yes, based on the same model. This way, we're able to harvest fruits and vegetables year-round."

"That's impressive. In my twenties, I built a self-sustaining garden. I know from experience just how difficult this is to achieve."

They chatted over drinks and food. Being fluent in Spanish, Dan was also able to make appropriate comments in Tiwa's language.

After lunch, Tiwa suggested, "Dan, why don't we try to put a video call to your wife so that Paloma and I can meet her? I've got excellent equipment with a fifty-five-inch holoscreen."

"*Buena idea. Muchisimas gracias*, Tiwa. I'll call Melanie ahead to check if she's free. Let's see. It should be around eight a.m. in Kalimantan. She starts early most days, but I don't think she would've left the hotel yet."

He dialed her. "Hi honey... How are you? Did you have a good night's sleep? We're having lunch at a friend's place in Albuquerque. His name is Tiwa, the director of the biodomes we're interested in. His wife's name is Paloma... If you've got a few minutes, can you set up for an incoming video call? We'll dial in a quarter of an hour... All good? Thanks." Dan turned back to Tiwa and Paloma. "Melanie should be able to take our call in fifteen minutes, Tiwa."

"Excellent. Now as a little surprise, I will play a couple of Mexican songs on the guitar. That will be a nice way for her to start the day. Do you know any songs in Spanish or English, Dan? More importantly, do you have a good singing voice?"

Zara started laughing. "You've asked the right guy, Tiwa."

"Why? It's not that difficult. All you need is an average voice."

Zara laughed even louder. "You'll see."

Isobel raised an eyebrow at the conversation. She looked at

Sandy for an explanation of Zara's comments. "What's going on?"

Sandy lifted his hands and shook his head hopelessly, quickly shooting Zara a covert wink. "Beats me."

Dan offered, "I tell you what. In recognition of your wife's fantastic lunch, I'll sing a Spanish song, perfect for the occasion. It's one of my favorites. 'Una Paloma Blanca.' Do you know the chords, Tiwa?"

"Yes, I certainly do."

"Can you play it in a classical style rather than rock, at an easy pace?"

"Sure. No problem."

"Wait a minute, wait a minute," Paloma intervened. "Why don't we have a real party? I'll fetch some ponchos and sombreros for the guys, and for Zara and Isobel, some of my colorful traditional Mexican dresses. Tiwa, can you get the lyrics on the screen so we can all sing together?"

A few minutes later, Tiwa put the call through. He stood in front of the group with Dan, who wore a beige and gold mariachi suit with a matching sombrero. Paloma and the others were standing behind them. Zara wore a stunning long, red Mexican dress with golden sequins, and Isobel wore a green topcoat and pants embroidered with a floral design. Sandy had borrowed a dude gunslinger costume and managed to draw a big black moustache with charcoal to look the part.

Melanie's face appeared on screen and Dan announced in a Mexican accent, *"Hola, mujer hermosa!* Let the show from Albuquerque begin. Our famous artist, Mr. Tiwa, will entertain you on the guitar with a song called 'Una Paloma Blanca.' I will accompany him with our fabulous choir, 'Los Sustainos.'"

Melanie burst into laughter.

Following the guitar opening, it was time for the team to sing the refrain, which appeared on the karaoke text generator.

Tiwa called, "*Uno, dos, tres!*"

After the first quatrain, Tiwa, Paloma, and Isobel stopped singing and gaped at Dan, astounded by the depth of his voice.

Tiwa stopped playing and asked, "Hey, senor, where did you learn to sing like that?"

Zara quipped, "He's just a natural."

At the end of lunch, Sandy voiced the group's appreciation. "Tiwa and Paloma, thank you for a delicious meal and a wonderful time."

Zara hugged Paloma. "Many thanks for the vegetarian dishes, Paloma. I look forward to receiving the recipes by email. Thanks for the suggestion."

———

As he walked them back to their car, Tiwa gave Dan a friendly slap on the back.

"I've really enjoyed your company, Dan. We have a lot in common. Our background, our interest in nature, and our perception of the environment. Let's keep in touch."

"I'd love that, yes. Video calls are the way to go."

"Excellent idea. So where are you heading after this?"

"Flagstaff. We want to have a look at the moon base."

"You'll find it interesting, especially the recreated site. It's like our domes but all underground. On the way, may I suggest you visit the Petrified Forest National Park. I've studied the fauna and flora of the region. Around two hundred million years ago, some conifers were buried so quickly in the area that they became fossilized. All these trees are now extinct as well as some of the smaller dinosaurs who lived there."

"Any known reason for that?"

"Probably the fall of volcanic ash. Please keep in touch, amigo. Again, I really enjoyed your company today."

After their excursion to the Petrified Forest National Park, the team went to the Painted Desert Visitor Center for some refreshments.

Dan was impressed by the park, but it also got him thinking. "I hope the entire planet won't look like this region in a few hundred years. It's so desolate. I know it's hard to believe, but this area would have been subtropical millions of years ago when the dinosaurs ruled the Earth. The weather was vastly different then. The poles were tropical, despite still being dark in the winter, and the tropics were unlivable."

"Makes you wonder," Sandy said.

"Yes, parts of the planet can change their microclimate features over geological periods. During that interval of time, some habitats disappear, and new ones are created. With the onset of massive climate change, it will be the case in most regions on Earth. However, this time it will be caused by human interference, not by geological or astronomical events, and it will be a lot faster."

"Let's keep driving to Flagstaff," Sandy suggested. "We should be able to compare the merits of the two projects. How far away is it, Dan?"

"Just a couple of hours. We're scheduled to meet our contact at the local airport, where we'll return this rental car."

FLAGSTAFF, ARIZONA

On the way to Flagstaff, Isobel explained the purpose of their visit.

"NASA restored the Cinder Lake Crater Field a few years ago. It was originally used in the sixties as a training ground for the landing on the moon. A new international project is underway. The European Space Agency has now constructed a 'Moon Base' on the reconditioned site. They've created a 'Moon Village' with the financial backing of commercial partners as a model to be used on the lunar surface. This will eventually allow a semipermanent human presence on the moon."

Sandy briefed the team on the historical significance of the interest in visiting the moon again. "Several crews of American astronauts first set foot on the moon in the second half of the twentieth century. Most people don't know the moon landing contest between Russia and America had its true origin in the ballistic missile arms race during the Cold War, rather than the conquest of space. The capability of the delivery vehicles was the real challenge for the two superpowers. The US was caught out by Gagarin's first flight around the Earth, so they were determined to demonstrate their technological superiority by sending a man to the moon before the Russians, which they did in July 1969. Their last mission ended three years later."

"Any reason for that?" Dan asked.

"Well, after the Apollo missions, the Americans had proved their ballistic superiority to the Russian leaders, albeit at a considerable financial cost. The race to the moon wound down as strategic gains were no longer sought by either of them. The national prestige of America had been restored. Most importantly, humanity had pulled itself from the brink. At the time, the competition between the two superpowers, which took place during the Cold War, prevented an open conflict that would've probably resulted in World War three."

"Thank God for that," Zara exclaimed. "The devastation would have been incalculable."

Isobel added, "Times have changed in this area. Today, rather than replicating the Apollo missions, space agencies have focused on establishing a sustainable settlement on the surface of the moon. But Sandy is right. There's still a strategic value in sustaining a human presence on the moon."

"Such as?"

Sandy answered, "The control of the space between the Earth and the moon, Zara. That's the area where all the military satellites are positioned."

"But what's our main area of interest in Flagstaff, Isobel?"

"Well, Zara. A key part of the current mission projects is the establishment of lunar base habitats to house crew members. This involves new technologies which will allow them to conduct short and medium-term journeys across the lunar surface. In Flagstaff, we'll meet up with the director of the European Space Agency, Beatrix Van Hamelen, a Dutch planetary scientist. She's mapped regions where different mineral crystals are distributed across its surface by studying how light reflects off it at various wavelengths."

"Do you know her?" Dan asked.

"I met her a few years ago at a conference at the Max Planck Institute for Solar System Research in Göttingen, Germany." Isobel smiled fondly. "I still remember our conversation while looking at the moon in the sky at the first evening's pre-dinner session. We were talking about its brightness and its changing shape, and about how humanity had tried for centuries to unravel many of its mysteries from the Earth. Since the dawn of mankind, cultures have believed it was just a motionless flat disk—which is what it looks like— but in fact, the moon does rotate at the same speed as its motion around the Earth. This has fooled various civilizations over millennia. Consequently, they believed the sun was also an unmovable flat disk. We know so much more about our natural satellite and our main star since the advance of modern science. Beatrix is passionate about knowing all its secrets."

A strongly built, blonde woman wearing bright pink glasses greeted them enthusiastically at Flagstaff Pulliam Airport. She wore a pink blazer matching her glasses over a white shirt and tailored gray pants along with bright pink high-heel boots.

Isobel accepted her hug with delight and introduced the team. "This is Professor Dan Robson and Dr. Zara Naidu. I believe you know Sandy Fraser, our director."

Beatrix answered in a heavy Dutch accent, "Yes, we've met at a conference once."

She gave him a handshake and a solid hug. "Nice to see you again, Sandy."

She greeted Zara and Dan with a hug and a kiss on both cheeks.

Dan always found this very awkward. He knew this was the way Europeans greeted each other, but it was out of his comfort zone.

"So, what can I do for your visitors, Isobel?"

"We're keen to find out what strides have been made at Cinder Lake crater field number three to improve life support systems on the moon."

Beatrix grinned. "No problem. I've hired a four-wheel-drive vehicle to get us to the site. It's half an hour away but let me warn you: the terrain around the moon base is rough!"

Dan eyed her shoes. "Will you be all right in... ah, those?"

She smiled, hitting him surprisingly hard on the back. "Don't be silly. I'll change them in the car for my pink sneakers."

As they drove, Isobel sat in the front with Beatrix. They chatted and laughed the entire way to the site of crater field number three. Dan hopped out of the car and immediately began to lose his balance on the steep mounts of shifting porous gravel.

Beatrix grabbed him by the arm as he was about to fall, "Steady there, big man!"

"This looks like the slopes of an extinct volcano," he said as he regained his footing.

"Well spotted, Dan. That's exactly what it is. It last erupted around one thousand years ago," Beatrix confirmed. Sure enough, she had now changed into pale pink sneakers with a prominent Gucci logo. She continued, "It forms part of the San Francisco volcanic field, but the craters you can see everywhere are man-made. NASA carried out a series of deliberate explosions to simulate lunar depressions. They tested their first lunar rovers on this pothole field to establish the reliability of their vehicles."

Beatrix walked them over to where the moon base buildings had been constructed. This time Dan trod carefully. He was used to hiking but not in his business shoes and his suit. He hadn't packed his mountain shoes, and this time he was really missing them.

"Can you see them, Dan?" she asked, moving his head in the right direction.

Dan looked around. "Not sure. Are they buried under some layers of ash?"

Beatrix took him by the hand. "Come with me."

Oh, awkward again, he thought. *She's a bit too friendly.*

She pulled him close to her and pointed out to an area a short distance away. "Over there. Can you see now?"

He could smell her rather overpowering floral perfume, but he tried to concentrate on where she was pointing and peered out. "Yes, I can sort of make out the shape of four mounts. That's about it. Their outline is just perceptible. I mean they don't look at all like the biodomes of Albuquerque," he remarked to the team, looking for support.

Beatrix explained the reason. "This is a replica of what some astronauts are currently building on the moon. On this site, a team of robotic machines first assembled hard-shelled modules with all their sub-system units. Then, to protect the astronauts from what would be intense cosmic radiation, the structures were covered with a blanket of basaltic cinders. The rigid material life support system modules are completely buried under three meters of ash."

Dan nodded. He didn't know a lot about the technology involved, but he understood the components. "Three meters. That's a lot. A necessary shield to survive lunar radiation?"

"Yes. It's essential. Even the airlock access tunnel to the living quarters has been sheltered that way. Come with me, guys." Again, she grabbed Dan's hand.

"You wouldn't find it by yourselves. To start with, we had to develop new excavation and construction techniques."

Sandy's eyebrows shot skyward, "Very impressive."

"Yes. We also built an entire support infrastructure using robots: lightweight nuclear power systems and an advanced external solar collection grid. On the moon itself, astronauts can use the domes as a base, mine the local surface for minerals, and process ice into water. Our intention is for the lunar missions to rely on sustainable operations without the need for constant supplies from Earth. Fuel, water, and oxygen will be produced from local sources. There is a host of useful material on the moon, especially noble gases of various kinds."

Dan inquired, "Is the intention for the astronauts to settle permanently?"

Beatrix smiled warmly at him. "Great question Dan, great question. Officially, the authorities have said, and I quote, 'For an extended but unspecified period.' The various agencies have developed new technologies that have enabled the first astronauts to live in the extreme environment of the lunar polar region for a few months. They will test the weather, measure the radiation, and conduct extensive geological surveys. This should help future missions to validate a permanent settlement and will act as a model for deep space operations," she concluded.

Isobel explained, "These initial lunar missions will also gather valuable information for a future trip to Mars. Settling on the moon will test significant technical aspects before sending humans on a journey to the red planet. Landing crafts and humans on the surface of Mars will be the next step in humanity's quest to explore space."

Beatrix added, "People may be living permanently on Mars in a hundred years' time. However, sending people to Mars will require a different level of technological complexity."

Dan was skeptical about the feasibility of Mars missions for their purpose. "The distance from the Earth to the Moon is relatively manageable, Beatrix. In contrast, a trip to Mars would take what? A minimum of seven months?"

"You're right again, Dan. It's a far greater distance. The exact time frame depends on suitable launch windows when Earth and Mars are both aligned." She took his hand and matched it to her hand, drawing an imaginary ellipse. "Like this. The most efficient route is called 'The Hohmann transfer orbit.'" She now squeezed his hand. He was becoming uncomfortable again and coughed slightly.

She let his hand go and continued. "The difficulties of the missions to the red planet are compounded by these distances but also by more dangerous levels of radiation. A stronger gravity than the moon makes landings more problematic.

Finally, Mars' atmosphere with its lack of oxygen and extreme weather conditions presents enormous challenges for getting humans to its surface and living on it safely."

Isobel concluded. "That leaves us with the option of an exoplanet."

Dan raised his eyebrows and guffawed out loud. "That's even a more complicated prospect, Isobel. First, we'll need to discover an exoplanet which has the essential characteristics to sustain human life: water, an atmosphere, and a livable temperature. Then, we'll need to build an unmanned vehicle to survey it and confirm its suitability for human settlement. And the distance—"

Zara once more came to his help. "Dan's right, the hardest part of a space option will be constructing a probe capable of reaching this—so far unknown exoplanet—within a reasonable amount of time. Under current technology, we wouldn't be able to get to a suitable one for several millennia."

Beatrix looked amused at their disbelief. "It's a lot more complicated, I admit but—"

Dan was happy to make the final point. "And of course, humans wouldn't survive the long journey there."

Beatrix smiled back, squeezed his shoulder, and then winked. "Well, anything is possible if we just put our mind to it, Dan."

After that rather awkward encounter, Dan was keen to get going with the team, but Beatrix insisted on waiting for their flight with them at the airport.

Once they'd driven back to the airport, they waited in the private meeting room of the business lounge for a plane connection to New York. Zara was curled up in a massive red armchair in a green blouse and canary yellow pants, along with the green high tops, trying to get some sleep. Dan was talking to Sandy about their next visit. Beatrix was chatting nonstop with Isobel about exoplanets, but every so often she'd look over and catch Dan's eye.

Finally, the call was made for their flight to Las Vegas, where they could connect to New York. Beatrix farewelled the team, giving Dan a long hug and two kisses. Holding both his hands gently, she whispered, "Call me, Dan."

Then she waved them goodbye and went back to her car.

———

Zara turned to Isobel, who was sipping lemonade while she worked on her computer. "Did you see Beatrix's shoes? Oh, my goodness they're to die for. She said she had them handmade by a designer in Amsterdam and she would send me the details."

Dan watched Isobel nod, but she didn't look at all interested. "Yes, yes, her shoes are unusual. Do you have the photos of our trip, Zara? Are you able to run through a summary?"

"Absolutely, I took lots of pictures and Beatrix gave me a few leads, which I've been following up." She sighed. "She's so brilliant and beautiful." She poked Dan in his side. "I think she liiiikes you!"

Dan rolled his eyes.

Sandy grinned. "Well, she's an extraordinary woman and extremely friendly." He paused for a second as if remembering something. "Anyway, onto more practical matters. From what've seen so far, what do you suggest we should tell Dame Ngaire in our report, Dan?"

"Well, we all agree the fate of the human species will be under existential threat sometime in the future. Overpopulation, global warming, biodiversity collapse, food and freshwater shortages will all lead to a general emergency that could threaten the existence of humans on Earth in the next centuries."

Sandy agreed with this assumption, "That's confirmed by our recent UN reports. These signs indicate the health of our ecosystem will reach a level of deterioration from which there might be no return."

Isobel added, "The path for safe living will narrow every century. Sooner or later, we will have consumed all our resources and polluted all our environment. One day, we will no longer be able to live safely on our planet. A time will come when some of our descendants will realize they are the last generation that can survive under such harsh conditions. This will be the end of humanity on Earth." She shivered. "Gosh! That's sounds dreadful, doesn't it?"

Sandy summarized, "It does. But our mission is to make sure that we, as a species, don't get totally wiped out. We'll inform Dame Ngaire that the aim of Project Legacy is to find and establish several 'safe storage areas' across different locations here on Earth or in space to preserve humanity's genetic material, therefore ensuring a continuing human presence in the universe. Our team will investigate various options by creating 'human DNA preservation vaults' first in safe locations on Earth, then aboard low orbit stations, followed by storage in artificial domes on the moon, Mars and according to you, Isobel, on a suitable exoplanet when it's feasible. Our hope is that with time, the Earth's ecosystem can heal itself and that humans will be able to return. Is this possible, Dan?"

"Based on our current scientific knowledge of Earth's evolution, I estimate this restoration process would take between twenty thousand and fifty thousand years. In the meantime, humans might be able to find a safer and more suitable environment somewhere in space. That's your domain, Isobel."

———

On board the plane to Las Vegas, while waiting for takeoff, Zara showed the pictures of their visits to Albuquerque and Flagstaff. "I think the moon is a good starting point. A lot of effort has been put into developing new technologies, which have been successfully tested. Astronauts have landed on the lunar surface and established a semi-permanent base there. That's positive for our mission. There are a few issues still to be resolved but anything else, like Mars or an exoplanet, is speculative at this stage—"

"It's not speculative!" Isobel interjected. "The technology isn't established yet, but the potential is definitively there. We have sent robots to the red planet that we can control accurately from Earth. That's just the beginning."

Dan retorted, "Personally, I can't even foresee a sizable colony on the moon or Mars. I mean like hundreds of people. The moon is averse to human life. It's a dead body without any atmosphere, high levels of radiation, and a sterile surface. That would be a tremendous challenge for a large human settlement."

"All very pertinent, Isobel and Dan," Sandy said. "But from what we have learned so far, I'm thinking that at this stage we should start by investigating suitable places here on Earth where a significant human population can survive in the types of artificial constructions, we have visited both in Albuquerque and Flagstaff. When we arrive in New York, we'll get in contact with an expert on survival in terrestrial shelters recommended to me by Dame Ngaire. I'm sure you've all heard of him,

General Makemba, the commander of the UN Peacekeeping Forces."

Showing serious concern, Sandy added, "But there's a bigger problem on the horizon." He grimaced. "When I spoke to the Secretary General yesterday, she said she's worried about the cost of extraterrestrial alternatives such as living in space. She was throwing around words like astronomical."

Isobel sat bolt upright. "You said we have her full support!"

Zara grinned. "Astronomical. How appropriate. We all knew that from the start."

"Well, I think she's realizing the overall cost of a space project. We'll need to consider some additional funding sources."

"Sorry Sandy, I'm broke." Zara pulled out brightly patterned pockets from her trousers.

He laughed. "I think we might need a bit more than any of us could afford. Let's put our heads together and find some solutions."

NEW YORK

New York was still recovering from the springtime hurricane, but the United Nations headquarters' buildings had received priority status for clearing the area. Sandy introduced the team to the UN Commander of the Peacekeeping Forces, General Makemba, a well-built Sudanese career officer with a friendly, outgoing personality. The general was wearing civilian clothes but proudly displayed the insignia of the UN Peacekeeping Forces on his lapel.

He explained the purpose of his presence at the meeting. "Dame Ngaire has asked me to help you investigate whether we could find suitable sites on Earth where some ethnic groups can be safeguarded or alternatively, where their genetic material can be preserved under cryogenic conditions. We would also keep the DNA of animals and plants."

As a biologist, Dan was supportive right away. "Compelling idea, General. Have you found any appropriate areas yet?"

The general brought up a world map on a screen showing several worldwide locations all highlighted with a green zone. "Some areas have already been chosen by expert members of our dedicated unit. The genetic material can be stored in vaults in locations in both the Arctic and Antarctic and in mountainous regions to take advantage of their ideal cold climatic preserving conditions. They'll eventually be administered by a team of scientific contractors but will be guarded by our own UN forces. These chambers, unfortunately dubbed 'doomsday vaults,' will be constructed in such a way that they are disaster-proof, including from a nuclear attack. Should the worst happen, and... let's hope it doesn't, we will still have a bank of mankind's genetic makeup to draw on at a later stage."

Sandy whistled. "Impressive. Thank you, General. That's a very interesting alternative."

Dan wanted to explore the idea more. "Will these sites have a similar purpose to the various governments' emergency command centers?"

"Same idea. As you allude to, Professor Robson, most advanced nations have constructed shelters for their government's essential services personnel. We're still negotiating with them to allocate some areas for storage of human DNA inside these facilities. They're open to the idea but are opposed to any outside interference. In one word, our role would be to supply them with cryogenic material, and they would take charge of it from there on. Not entirely satisfactory from our point of view."

"I understand. All pretty secret, I imagine, General. These

matters would be handled at a high state and military level. This would give us a backup, but we'd lose control of our material in the process."

General Makemba continued, "The US and some wealthy countries have built entire underground cities capable of being sealed off for several years. The construction of these bunkers has been financed by their respective governments as an evacuation point for their key decision makers. Here in the US, these structures have been dug through the Rocky Mountains. Some are also located in Alaska. They're outfitted with massive blast doors that can withstand the impact of nuclear bombs and can host several hundred personnel and their families. The UN has asked for some of their personnel to be included as well. Most of their representatives exert considerable influence. So, I feel confident we'll be able to keep a modicum of control over our material."

Dan's eyes widened. "Did you say they'll host families as well, General?"

He nodded. "Absolutely. Entire cities have been built inside these bunkers. These chosen people could start a new civilization underground until it's safe to emerge back to a secure environment on Earth."

"Interesting," Sandy remarked, "but how long will they have to hide for? A hundred years, a thousand years?"

"I'm not privy to that information, unfortunately."

"What about the common people?" Zara queried. "How will they face the threat of global destruction, General?"

"Well, they can buy individual doomsday bunkers from companies that specialize in this type of structures."

Zara retorted, "Not affordable for the average person, though? You'd need a lot of money to purchase one."

He gave her a pitiful look. "You're right, Dr. Naidu. Only for the very well-off, I'm afraid. I can tell you that right now, some individuals with substantial wealth are purchasing these expensive, concrete, steel reinforced bunkers and having them constructed in strategic locations. These buildings are designed to last for years and hold food supplies, power generators, even their own sewage treatment plants. Alternatively, a well-off person can buy a decommissioned missile silo with functional blast doors and then retrofit it."

"Is there really a market for that?" asked Zara, incredulously.

"Absolutely! I can recommend one not far from New York. It's on the market for fifty million dollars," the general added, tongue in cheek.

Zara laughed and then questioned him further, "Why would these wealthy people buy such expensive structures if they claim climate change doesn't exist, there's no danger, and it's all media hysteria?"

"Well, it's true some political leaders and industry super-rich publicly deny the reality of climate change, but I can tell you that privately, they're preparing themselves for the deterioration in our living conditions and the inevitable implosion of our society. For the moment, a favorite escape destination is New Zealand."

Dan sat up abruptly. "They can't be bothered to fix the problem they're creating now, but they come up with a backup plan instead! What a joke!"

General Makemba suggested several locations to build shelters to preserve human DNA. "For your objectives, Mr. Fraser, I'd recommend the northwest of Tasmania or Macquarie Island. It's a lot more stable geologically than New Zealand, which is prone to regular earthquakes."

Sandy put up his hand. "Being Australian, I can help with finding suitable sites. I know the Tasmanian region well from my younger years, when I was hiking near the King River.

There are several disused gold mines in the area which could be retrofitted." He continued, "Talking about nuclear shelters, General, do you believe we could eventually be heading for a nuclear confrontation?"

General Makemba's tone became serious. "I think some medium-sized nations may well be tempted to use nuclear weapons as a last resort once local conflicts have escalated to a point where conventional weapons aren't giving them any further strategic advantage. Our organization cannot stop them." He sighed. "We monitor these activities and report them to the Security Council. This is where international diplomats like you come in, Mr. Fraser."

"We're trying hard, General, believe me. Personally, I'm not convinced some countries would go to the brink of nuclear war and jeopardize the existence of a large part of their populations. The superpowers will intervene through negotiation. They will have to find a peaceful solution. History shows us that eventually they'll reach a compromise. A war at that level must be avoided at all costs. Can you imagine the destruction?"

"I agree, Mr. Fraser. Diplomats should do everything to avoid a nuclear weapons confrontation. Our troops can help relieve the tension by keeping belligerent nations apart. There's always a need for a massive deployment of our Peacekeeping Forces. We already have comprehensive plans in place to cope with these eventualities."

Dan was skeptical about the goodwill of some nations.

"Sorry, General, but what will happen if they don't want peace and some desperate megalomaniac foolishly escalates the hostilities with the use of nuclear weapons?"

Zara concurred. "In the conflict between India and Pakistan for instance, both nations have a large arsenal of nuclear weapons. They can destroy each other several times over. If the superpowers don't intervene, it will be literal Armageddon."

The general's answer surprised them all. "I don't think it will happen, Dr. Naidu."

"Why not?" she said, raising her eyebrows.

"The simple fact is that the superpowers don't want their own territories to be contaminated by nuclear material fallout for centuries."

"But—?"

"They will use powerful non-nuclear weapons like neutron bombs to defuse the conflict in a 'clean way.' Then, they'll disarm the fighting medium-sized countries of what is left of their so-called 'dirty weapons' and carve up their territories between them."

"Clean neutron bombs?"

"These are what we call 'contained area weapons' without the presence of dangerous radioactive material like uranium 235."

"No nuclear fallout?"

"Just massive instant neutron radiation."

Isobel, who hadn't said much during the meeting, chimed in, 'From a technical perspective, Zara, these bombs produce a powerful level of neutrons rather than heat and blast. The neutrons destroy the cells of living organisms but barely damage property. For instance, army personnel in a tank or sheltering in an underground bunker would have their bodies fried by neutron and gamma rays. Their vehicles or surrounding structures would be affected to a lesser extent by the heat and shock blast. Then, after the initial intense radiation flux, the neutrons would disappear from the environment. The radioactive level and the contamination period of tritium—a radioactive isotope of hydrogen which is used for this type of weapon—is a lot shorter-lived compared to uranium 235 bombs. No long-term contamination."

Sandy asked another question, "General, you said the superpowers will carve up their territories between them. What do you mean by that?"

"Our strategists believe the US and Canada will take control of all the American continents. That is North, Central, and South America. China together with India will annex most of Asia. Russia will reassemble the old Eastern Bloc and Europe will take over most of the Middle East and Africa. They'll have to agree between themselves, obviously."

Sandy gave a contemptuous laugh. "Bloody hell, so much for international law and diplomacy."

Dan expressed their common feeling. "Eventually human population density will reach unbearable levels. With their insatiable appetite for energy, humans will deplete the Earth's resources and damage its ecosystem. Subsequent lack of basic commodities and resources will damage it beyond repair and create massive conflicts. Over their history, humans have always been competing for control of territory. I am afraid this could be the outcome for our world if we can't find a solution to overpopulation, overexploitation of resources, and climate change. This prospect is terrifying."

After a moment of reflection, Sandy broke the silence. "It's beyond belief how people on Earth have been dealing with each other. The whole history of mankind is littered with wars and destruction. Humans have seldom risen above their basic instincts. They have failed time and time again to accept they were one people, one species, in the beginning. Most individuals are short-sighted and driven by their own interests. They don't consider the long-term risks of their actions. They should seek peace and focus on the survival of mankind as a whole."

Dan agreed, "All humans are related in their biological ancestry. That's why our project is so important."

After a lengthy silence, Sandy asked the group, "Any other issues?"

Dan felt drained. It had been a morning packed full of depressing information. He didn't know what to think. It seemed the others felt the same way.

"Time for lunch, then," Sandy declared.

Zara looked up. "I'm not hungry."

"Okay, maybe a bit later. Let's go to my office first."

———

They headed up to Sandy's office. As Isobel, Dan, and Zara sank into the brown leather chairs dejectedly, Sandy paced.

"So, what do we have?"

Zara shrugged. "Prospect of total annihilation!"

Dan threw up his hands. "What's the point? I've been fighting my whole life for what? For it all to be destroyed and for us to live in underground cities... I don't even know what to say."

Isobel's eyes lit up. "I do. Based on what we heard in New Mexico and Arizona, this is what I'm suggesting for our report to Dame Ngaire."

Sandy leaned forward. "Yes?"

"As I recommended, among other options, our effort can include the search for a potentially suitable planet to sustain a human presence. The way I see it, the exploration effort will extend over many decades and will involve space agencies from many nations, the most important being the United States of America, the Russian Federation, the People's Republic of China, India, and the European Union. We'll seek assistance from high-tech private companies as well. Once an exoplanet has been located and ascertained to have potential, we'll initiate the construction of an exploratory probe to further examine its viability for human habitation."

"Excellent suggestion, Isobel," Sandy said. "It's going to require the creation of an international body under the authority of the United Nations. Together with a 'Human Space Evaluation Agency,' we can create an exploration program to foster human habitation of the closer star systems across our galaxy."

CHAPTER 3
YEAR 2037—SONGDO, KOREA

It had been three months since Dan and Zara returned to Korea after their whirlwind tour. Their attention was suddenly drawn by an online call.

Sandy was beaming as his face popped up on the holo screen.

Dan answered him, "Morning, Sandy, you look rather pleased with yourself."

"I am, indeed, Dan. Hi, Zara. Guess what?"

They remained silent, trying to think of some outstanding issue.

Sandy raised his arms and pumped his fist.

"Are you ready for this? You both need to pack your bags. We've all been invited to Kensington Palace."

Zara's eyes went wide. "As in London?"

"Yes."

"To meet the prince? Oooh... Maybe I'll get married after all."

Dan laughed. "He's too young for you, Zara. What's this all about, Sandy? We know the King is interested in—"

Sandy shook his head. "No, No. Well, we may see some

royals, but I'm not sure whether we will meet them. We've been invited by William Wei."

Dan racked his brain. He'd heard the name. "Can you refresh my memory?"

"You know, Billy Stargate Wei."

Dan's eyebrows rose. "The Chinese billionaire?"

"Yes. That's him. His group is organizing a special meeting near Kensington Palace."

"What do you mean by 'his group'?"

"Have you heard of 'the Billionaires' Club'? 'Billios' for short."

Zara nodded. "I have. Many of their members are ranked in the top two hundred richest families in the world." She now wiggled her eyebrows suggestively. "I could definitely find a husband there."

"You're right about the wealthiest families, Zara. Best of luck with the husband hunting." Sandy smiled and continued, "In order to qualify for membership in 'The Billios' Club,' apart from their monetary wealth, the billionaires are required to financially contribute to scientific research to help humanity. That's the positive side of their group. This year they've chosen the field of space research."

Dan remembered. He'd heard about their commitment as well. "Wait, don't members pledge 10 percent of their fortune to worthwhile humanitarian causes?"

"Something to that value," responded Sandy.

Dan's eyes widened. "That's—"

"Yes," interrupted Sandy. "A lot of money."

"That sort of money could make an enormous difference to the project, but how could we arrange a meeting with this group? It's not like we could just use the holo and call them."

Zara was curious as well. "Do you know them, Sandy? Are you a secret billionaire?"

"Ha-ha, not even close. Hang on. Isobel is here. She'll explain."

Dan watched the screen as Isobel's form filled the screen. She was wearing her silver glasses and, as usual, seemed distant. She raised her hands, palms up, at Sandy, confused.

"What do you want me to tell them?"

"About William Wei, your friend."

She continued to look puzzled for a moment and then after some gesturing to the screen by Sandy, she nodded. "Oh, yes. Hi Zara, hi Dan."

Dan got straight to the point with Isobel. "You have some powerful friends, Isobel. How do you know William Wei?"

She shrugged, "Oh that? Well, about a year ago, I was watching a documentary where Billy was being interviewed. From memory, he said something like, 'We face risks the dinosaurs never saw... not an asteroid but catastrophic global warming. Humankind evolved over millions of years, but in the last hundred years, climate change has created the potential to extinguish us. Sooner or later, we must expand life beyond this green and blue ball or... go extinct.' As you know, that's precisely what I think."

Dan scrubbed his hand over his face. Getting information from Isobel was always a slow process.

Sandy smiled at her in a kind manner and gestured with his hands, prompting her. "And... go on, Isobel."

"Well, I contacted him through a friend of a friend and praised him for his foresight. He had of course heard of me and my work, and we talked extensively. When he and his wife, Lillian, were in Stockholm, we met up and we've become good friends since. As I said, his views are in line with mine. He's extremely intelligent, not quite at genius level, but still highly intelligent. It's a little surprising for someone who hasn't done any postdoctoral study, but nevertheless refreshing."

"So, you just called a billionaire to thank him for his foresight?"

"She peered over her glasses at him. "Yes, that's what I said, Dan. Why not? He's a very approachable fellow."

Dan glanced at Zara. "Isobel, you're amazing. So, what sort of meeting is this?"

Sandy interrupted her, "Not too clear about that. It's hush-hush but connected with supporting space projects, and we've put our bid in."

"And who's going to be there?" Dan queried.

Sandy answered, "Mainly his fellow billionaires, I would imagine. Some of the Billios are already connected through their involvement in the space industry. These entrepreneurs have filled the void left by governments, which had cut funding to space missions due to their lack of vision. Ironically, the Billios' companies are now securing lucrative contracts with them."

Isobel looked up from her screen and added, "William Wei is the chief designer and supplier of advanced technology spacecraft vehicles. The super heavy multipurpose launch vehicles, or SHMLV... you know how the Space Industry likes acronyms. Billy's private endeavor is to contribute to settlements on other worlds, starting with the moon and then Mars. Colonizing Mars is his big dream."

"So, in a sense his aim would be like that of Project Legacy?" Dan questioned.

"Very similar, I suppose yes."

Dan was starting to become concerned. "So, he'd also understand what we're trying to achieve, Sandy?

"I am sure he does. The members of his club are well informed. They're aware the days of human beings populating the Earth are numbered and are positioning themselves accordingly. Look at how many billionaires are involved in space research in one form or another. That's the reason for their interest in our work."

Dan hesitated. "Isn't that a bit too close for comfort to deal with them, Sandy?"

"Fair point. The Billios group is going to look after their members, not humanity at large like we do. I'm aware of that, but we must take this opportunity."

Isobel interjected, "We've got no alternative, Dan. We need William's expertise and… money. His manufacturing corporations are now the primary producers of space rocket engines. They've been selected as the providers of reusable spacecraft by most national agencies around the world."

Dan still expressed some concern. "What is he likely to ask in return, Sandy?

"We'll find out soon enough. We'll tell him as little as necessary."

"Or do a deal?"

"More likely. All right, Dan. I'll send you the invitations, and Zara don't forget to wear your tiara."

She grinned. "You mean the plastic one?"

KENSINGTON PALACE, UK

Four days later, Dan found himself walking through the King's Gallery at Kensington Palace, which was being set up for an elaborate dinner. Fine China and crystal glasses adorned the table. Wait staff were bringing out more pieces.

Zara admired the gallery of gold gilded paintings on the ruby red wall. "Wow, I never thought I'd see this in real life. Look Dan, that's Van Dyck's portrait of Charles the First on horseback."

They followed Sandy and the courtier through to a smaller

room with dark paneling decorated with more large portraits adorning the walls.

Dan leaned in for a closer look. "The opulence is unbelievable, Sandy."

Further along, a small oval table had been set up with coffee and tea, along with trays of biscuits and an assortment of cakes.

High tea at the palace. This is surreal, Dan thought, laughing inwardly.

At the end of the table, he noticed two people sitting and facing each other. On the left was an immaculately dressed Asian man in his mid-thirties with cropped dark hair wearing a midnight blue suit and a matching tie. His face was chiseled, giving him the appearance of a magazine model. Dan recognized him as William Wei. Across the table sat a stunning woman wearing a pale blue satin dress. She also had cropped hair, which showed off her enormous diamond earrings. They were both on calls on their holoscreen.

The courtier bowed slightly to them. "Sir, your guests have arrived."

William finished up his conversation and turned toward them.

"Isobel." He came over and welcomed her with a kiss and hug as if greeting a long-lost friend. "So good to see you. These must be the friends you spoke about. Lillian, please, meet Isobel and her friends."

She joined him, greeting Isobel warmly and kissing her on both cheeks. "You look well, darling. Is this a new outfit?"

"Not really," Isobel said slowly.

"Oh darling!" Lillian laughed. "I'm just teasing. I know you think clothes are just for comfort and practicality. Oh, I've missed you." She drew Isobel to her in another hug.

Dan could feel his eyes bulging out of his head, and looking at Zara's face, he could tell she was taken aback as well. *Isobel, friend with billionaires. It just baffles the mind.*

"So, Isobel, your friends?" William prompted.

Sandy leaned over and introduced himself. "Sandy Fraser, sir, ma'am. It's lovely to meet you."

"Ah! The head of the sustainability group himself. I've heard a lot about you, Mr. Fraser, from all quarters. All good things."

William shook his hand heartily. "And please, please, we aren't royalty. No formalities for us. Call us William and Lillian."

Lillian smiled warmly as she shook Sandy's hand, her left still wrapped around Isobel's waist.

Sandy indicated his companions. "May I present my colleagues, Professor Daniel Robson and Dr. Zara Naidu?"

"Wonderful to meet you, wonderful. Please sit down."

William gestured after shaking both their hands. "Would you like coffee, tea?"

Dan hesitated. "Oh um, coffee, thank you."

Zara said joyfully, "Darjeeling tea for me, yes please, and could I have one of those fantastic-looking biscuits?" She pointed at the plate displaying a mound of macaroons.

"Of course, oh aren't you delightful," Lillian said. "Do you know those are the King's favorites? They don't make them for anyone else besides him and us. Isn't that superb?"

A tall blond man dressed in an immaculate dark suit came over and poured coffee and tea and served them biscuits. Dan looked at him, intrigued. He seemed familiar. *No, no*, he thought, *why would I have met a butler from the palace before*?

"Anyway, please, let's get down to business. We have drinks down at our residence in Kensington Gardens with the other members in an hour."

"Yes," Lillian confirmed. "We'd invite you all, but unfortunately, the club is all a bit of a secret squirrel you know, no outsiders. A tad ridiculous but keeps the members happy."

"No worries," Sandy said. "We have our own plans anyway."

"Let's cut to the chase." William sipped his coffee. "Isobel has filled us in about the broad aims of your project in advance of the meeting. I've called your own Secretary General. Lovely woman, we go skiing every year in New Zealand together. She's given me the big picture. So, you're planning to store some human genetic material in facilities both on Earth and on the moon as a backup, just in case something goes terribly wrong on this planet?"

Sandy nodded. "That's correct. It's still in the early stages, mind you. We are looking at different options, William. Eventually, we'll need logistical support and finance."

"I understand. You mean access to cargo space on a spacecraft. I have the connections to help you with that."

"Thank you," Sandy said.

Dan couldn't tell if this conversation was going well or not. It didn't seem like William was getting a good deal.

"I've put a bit of a line out with our members, and they're interested. Lillian and I want to take part, of course."

Sandy looked pleased. "That would be very helpful."

"We can talk numbers and all that later as the project shapes up, but we thought we could start you off with say, one to two?"

Zara blinked, whispering to Dan, "One to two million will probably get us a small building team."

Lillian overheard her. She leaned over and squeezed her hand, laughing. "No darling, one to two billion. Nothing in aerospace apart from the theories comes in the millions."

Dan gasped audibly. *One to two billion to start off with...*

Sandy appeared calm but wary. "That's, ahh, very generous, very generous."

William half smiled. "Of course, we need quid pro quo. Nothing's free in the business world, as you know."

"Of course, William, and that would be?"

"Very simple. Just keep us informed, Sandy. Whatever and wherever your projects for humanity are heading for, let us know. We're all interested in what the future holds and are happy to pay handsomely for this information."

Lillian exclaimed, "We're Chinese. Our culture values family names, dynasties. Ancestors and descendants are everything to us. We want to be included."

Zara began to disagree quietly, "Sure, but that isn't quite—"

Sandy interrupted her, "As I mentioned, at this stage, we're still exploring various options but sure, we will update you on our progress. That shouldn't be a problem, Lillian."

William smiled warmly. "Excellent. I can tell I'm going to enjoy working with you, Mr. Fraser."

Sandy nodded. "Likewise."

After they had finished their high tea, Dan, Zara, and Sandy rose and shook hands again with Lillian and William. Isobel accepted their hugs.

"I'll ring you soon, darling," Lillian called as they departed.

————

Once they were outside, they headed for a traditional London black cab. Dan could feel some anxiety rising. He'd guessed what the Weis were thinking, and he didn't like it.

"Are you sure that's the way we want to go, Sandy?"

Sandy smiled, but his eyes betrayed his true feelings. "We must be pragmatic Dan, you too, Zara. We need money... big money, and this is the type of people who have it. They're interested, have expertise, important contacts, and the necessary financial resources. If it means we adjust some of our ideals slightly in the process, then we'll go along with it for the sake of the bigger mission. Without them... we won't achieve our objectives."

Dan shook his head. *This is far from ideal*, he thought. *We're already compromising our values. Where will our project head in the future with a group of billionaires funding a space program?*

As they were walking toward the cab, they noticed the smoke generated by a devastating fire in Chingford in the distance. This area of the Epping Forest had been burning for several days following a heat wave, which for the first time had pushed the temperatures of greater London above 40 degrees Celsius, 104 Fahrenheit. A new high of 42 degrees Celsius, 107 Fahrenheit, had been recorded at the Greenwich Observatory the day before. Key transport services officials had put the Greater London railway system in a state of emergency. Their fear was that some rail lines could start to buckle in the abnormal heat.

Dan pointed out several water-bombing helicopters and planes racing to extinguish the fires. "It's happening!"

"Indeed," Sandy said. "Record temperatures have been registered in major cities all over Europe, not just in the UK. These extreme events are, without a doubt, caused by climate change. We must fast-track Project Legacy!"

CHAPTER 4
YEAR 2038—SONGDO, KOREA

Dan was working in his office. He reached for his second cup of coffee as the holo buzzed. It was Melanie, calling from Jakarta.

He answered, "Hi honey, how are you?"

"Great. I had a pleasant flight and a good night's sleep."

"Where are you?"

"I'm about to have breakfast at the Jakarta City Hall. I met up with some influential people here yesterday and I'm seeing them again in an hour. I intend to stay here for another day, then I'll fly to the island of Borneo."

"What did they have to say?"

She rolled her eyes on the screen. "They made it clear Jakarta will continue to be Indonesia's commercial center. The majority of the eleven million residents will stay here, while the government administrative functions will be moved to Borneo... you know, like the new House of Representatives we're tendering for?"

"So, they're looking at building new government offices and homes for civil servants, this type of thing in Kalimantan, right?"

"Correct. They've cleared the land and put most of the

infrastructure in. Now it's a matter of waiting for the main buildings to be constructed."

He frowned. "But isn't the whole of Jakarta sinking?"

"You're right. The city is sinking fast, unfortunately. We're talking about a few inches every year. Yesterday I had a look at the levies with the officials. Jakarta is like a cork sitting on a freshwater reservoir. The residents keep extracting their drinkable water from the underlying aquifer. In the process, the freshwater table level lowers, and the land above it sinks in behind it. As the city is surrounded by the sea, the salt water slowly seeps into the suburbs, despite the seawall levies."

"Really? That doesn't sound good."

"No, not at all. In the meantime, they're still building apartment blocks and shopping malls, which just adds to the weight of the city. The hygiene is poor and they have an endemic pollution issue. Now that I've witnessed it firsthand, I realize the gravity of this environmental issue."

"They're already creating another one in Borneo with massive deforestation, hon," Dan said wearily. "Only one quarter of the original jungle remains today. The felling of valuable timber species and replacing them with oil palm plantations are the main reasons. Half of the timber species in the area have already disappeared. In the process, a high number of wild animals have also become extinct. The orangutan, the emblem of Borneo, is on the verge right now. Their population has experienced a sharp decline due to the loss of their natural habitat. There's no sustainability management plan. It's shocking."

"Dan, I'm starting to understand what you and your team are fighting for."

"Lanie, you know what John Lennon said in his song, 'Maybe one day you will join us?'" Dan started singing the famous words.

"You're right. One day, I might just do that: join your group. Right now, I'll need another week here, but I'll have to come back regularly to supervise the construction project. You should join me at some stage."

"Good idea. Talk to you later. Keep safe."

"Bye, darling."

He hoped she would indeed come back soon.

Dan, Zara, Sandy, and Isobel were flying to the state of Andhra Pradesh on the East Coast of India to visit their National Space Agency in Sriharikota.

It was a rather turbulent flight due to the remnant winds from a recent tropical monsoon. From their window seats on the Air India Boeing 888, Dan noticed how much damage had been caused by the constant heavy rains which had triggered floods and landslides. He peered closer and pointed it out to Zara. "Look at that large building poking out of the water."

She'd just finished watching the Indian news on the plane's holo. "They're reporting that one million people have been stranded or displaced and are now living in relief camps. Buildings, rail, and essential infrastructure are underwater. Hundreds have been killed by the heavy monsoon downpour."

Dan shook his head in despair. "I was reading the other day that by 2050, more than 70 percent of India's population will face threats from both heat and humidity driven by climate change."

"You're right. In the Bay of Bengal, many areas in the delta are now gone due to the rise in sea levels. The Sundarbans and the Ghoramara islands have now been completely submerged, displacing thousands of people."

After they'd landed at Chennai International Airport in Meenambakkam, Dr. Krishnan, the highest-ranking official of the Indian Space Agency, welcomed them. Zara had already filled Dan in on his background as she'd heard him speak on many occasions during her student years at the University of Madras. The son of a greengrocer, Dr. Krishnan had stood out even in his younger years due to his brilliant mathematical mind. He was an absolute visionary who had helped to develop modern space technology in India and was worshipped as a hero in the Tamil Nadu region, where he was known as "Rocket Man."

———

They were all airlifted by helicopter 200 kilometers north to the restricted zone of the Satish Dhawan Space Center, the launching area of India's GSLV MKX reusable carrier rockets.

Sandy briefed the team. "Since their Chandrayaan lunar probes have been launched, India has indicated its interest in mining for Helium-3 in the upper layers of the regolith of the lunar surface. They're also interested in the extraction of water. According to their estimations, millions of tons are present in the shallow craters of the polar caps. As both elements will be essential to the propulsion of a new type of space vehicle, our team should consider allocating the important moon base contract to their National Space Agency."

Isobel also explained the technical side to the other members. "Helium-3 is formed when streams of charged particles flow from the sun to the moon's surface. Lunar rocks retain these elements, as there is no magnetic field to deflect them like there is on Earth."

She went on to describe how it would be used for the project. "Fusing one atom of Helium-3 with one atom of deuterium under very high pressure and temperature will yield the enormous amount of energy necessary to propel an interstellar space vehicle."

Dr. Krishnan gave them the latest update. "India has sent several unmanned spacecrafts to the moon's south pole in the Aitken basin. We intend to complete a base for the extraction and processing of Helium-3 for the interstellar mission. Most of the infrastructure for a team of twenty engineers will be built on the ground. They will be living in sturdy headquarters, which will be assembled robotically over two years. The components of our pressurized mining vehicles will be constructed by a large Japanese company but assembled on site by an Indian team of engineers."

Isobel explained, "I've discussed this with William Wei. When the construction of a space probe has been completed in orbit 250 kilometers above the Earth's atmosphere, the best method to launch it into space is to first tow it into a lunar orbit. Around two hundred tons of the Helium-3 fuel will then be loaded aboard over several months by a fleet of shuttles based on the moon itself. Then the Space Explorer will be towed again to 1.5 million kilometers, where the nuclear reaction of the engine can be safely sequenced. That's the concept we're working on for the moment."

Dr. Krishnan announced with a flourish, "This evening, we'll launch a heavy lift vehicle rocket with a payload of forty tons of material. Let me tell you that our organization has managed to provide a more economical way of traveling to the moon. The Indian spacecraft missions take a lengthy and indirect trajectory to reach our satellite. It initially involves several revolutions around the Earth to take advantage of its gravity by performing a series of slingshot maneuvers. Once around the moon, it slows down by gradually circulating its orbit before descending to the surface. This compensates for the less powerful propulsion system of the launcher, but the journey takes longer."

He smiled at the team. "Zara, you and your colleagues have been invited to the Ignition Control Center as our privileged guests to witness the send-off."

They were all impressed.

"What an honor, thank you, Dr. Krishnan," said Zara.

"It's our pleasure, young lady. Before that, let's have a meal together. Our chef is famous for his biryani."

Isobel complimented their host. "Thank you for the invitation and your hospitality, Dr. Krishnan. We all wish you great success with your mining venture on the moon. As physicists, you and I know we're close to making the power of nuclear fusion here on Earth a reality. Power plants using Helium-3 could provide a high efficiency source of clean energy and bring an end to our dependency on fossil fuels."

Dr. Krishnan clarified her statement. "According to our recent calculations, three space shuttles could bring enough fuel to power fusion plants for all the energy needs on our planet for a year."

Isobel added, with a grin on her face, "It will also make your organization very wealthy."

"Why do you think we're working so hard, Isobel?" Dr. Krishnan winked.

CHENNAI, THE NEXT DAY

The air on the Coromandel Coast was hot and humid. Dan fanned himself with a magazine. Even Sandy had taken his expensive Armani jacket off and rolled his shirt sleeves up. They piled into the chopper to head back to Chennai. As they left the Satish Dawan Space Center, they passed over Pulicat Lagoon. A flock of flamingos was wading in the water, undeterred by the heavy noise above them.

Zara was in familiar territory. "Huge isn't it, Dan? The lagoon has been through a lot. In my time on the board of the Environmentalist Foundation of India, we tried to salvage wildlife habitats and encourage restoration in this region. Sometimes it felt like we were fighting a losing battle, though every three to five years the area experiences massive flooding with the monsoon. That causes natural desalination through the introduction of fresh water. We also had to deal with the damage caused by industrial pollution, but we kept fighting the fight."

She explained with enthusiasm, "I grew up in Adyar, one of the greener areas of Chennai. My father, who's a medical practitioner, had bought a house there. As you know, I studied at the nearby University of Madras for a few years."

She continued, "Urban development has encroached on the wetlands and has gravely compromised the city's sustainability. Originally, there were three rivers and numerous lakes spread across the district. Urbanization has resulted in shrinkage of their original flow. It's now causing severe water shortages."

Isobel looked out of the window briefly and muttered, "Won't matter soon, will it?"

Sandy hushed her, but Dan could see the frustration on Zara's face. She whispered to Dan, "Well, we must try, mustn't we? Every life matters." She turned back to the window and crossed her arms in front of her chest.

———

They checked into their hotel, located only a few minutes from the international airport. Dan stifled a laugh as the receptionist fawned over Sandy when he presented his "Gold VIP Guest" credit card.

After everyone had checked in, Zara said to the group, "How about we meet in one hour? I'll take you out for an early dinner of ambur biryani."

Dan looked at his watch. "Sounds good to me. That should give me enough time for a quick walk."

———

After breakfast, Zara offered to take them on a whistle-stop tour. "I'll take you to visit a famous landmark in Chennai: the Kapaleeshwarar Temple. In the afternoon, we will head to the beach and try some sundal. It's a popular snack served at the beaches in this area. This delicious snack, made from channa and spiced with local masalas, is sold by street vendors."

By the time their taxi arrived at the Kapaleeshwarar Temple shrine, the site was already crowded with worshippers. Dan carefully got out of the taxi and had to duck back in to avoid being run over by a bright yellow and green rickshaw.

As they entered the site, Zara started into full tourist guide mode. "Dedicated to the state's most popular Indian God, Shiva, the temple displays the main architectural elements of many Tamil Nadu shrines: an ornate, rainbow-colored monumental entrance tower called the 'gopuram' and several pillared pavilions."

Dan whistled. "Look at the size, the variety of the carvings, and the bright coloring of the east gopuram, Sandy. The whole structure is stunning!"

"Okay Dan, it's now a quarter to eleven," Zara said. "Uchi Kaala Pooja starts in fifteen minutes. It's a fascinating worship ritual performed by Hindus to offer devotional homage and prayers to one or more deities. It's intended to honor a guest or to celebrate an event. Worth a watch. I think you should start lining up before eleven and meet us back here."

Later, Dan moved through the temple, taking it all in: the smells, the burning incense, the rhythm and sound of the instruments, the offerings of food, and the sheer number of people. It was his first time to Chennai and there was something so unique about this place due to the mixture of Tamil and Hindu cultures.

He checked his watch. It was twenty minutes to twelve. *Better get back to the others.*

———

NOON

As he rounded the corner, Dan spotted Zara's red sari, which stood out like a beacon on her tall stature. He waved to her and stopped for a moment to take one last picture of the temple structure. But when he glanced back, she'd disappeared. He heard a scream and saw Sandy's enormous frame barreling toward a group of men.

Dan's eyes widened in alarm. He tried to push through the crowd, but he felt like he was moving against a tide. Everyone else was heading away from the commotion, while he wanted to head for it.

When he got to the spot, he saw Sandy on the ground, his head bleeding. He appeared to have been struck. Isobel was holding her scarf to his head with one hand and pulling out her holoscreen with the other.

She pointed to the left. "Quick, Dan. Some men took Zara that way, quick!"

Pushing through the crowd, Dan ran in the direction she'd pointed until he made it to the street. His heart was beating fast. He saw something red. It was Zara.

Two men were pushing her into a rickshaw. Dan leapt over a fallen bicycle and ran into the street, but the rickshaw began to speed away, veering around cars and out of his sight. After realizing he wouldn't be able to catch up with it, he headed back to Isobel and Sandy, who were now surrounded by a small, concerned crowd.

Isobel signaled him. "I've called the police. We need to get Sandy some medical attention too."

Even on the ground, Sandy kept his upbeat demeanor. "I'm fine. Did you see the guys who took Zara?"

Dan panted, sorting through his bag for his bottle of water. "Yes. They pushed her into a rickshaw. I got part of the number plate. What the hell happened?"

Isobel started talking rapidly. "Sandy and I were making our way back to Zara when we saw three men push her and start to drag her off. She fought back and screamed, and Sandy yelled at them. He tried to help her by throwing a few punches, but then one of them came up behind him and smacked him on the head with a cricket bat, I think."

Two police officers in their distinctive, light brown uniforms pushed their way through the crowd. Sandy turned to Isobel.

"Isobel, my wallet." She fished through his pockets and found it. He pulled out his UN credentials and spoke to the police officers while still on the ground.

"We are United Nations officials. A member of our team has just been abducted. I want to speak to a senior officer as soon as possible!"

The two police officers helped Sandy back to his feet and offered to take the three of them to their headquarters in their vehicle. They tried to reassure him, "It's only a few minutes away, sir. Should we call an ambulance?"

Sandy declined. "No thanks. I'll be fine, but our colleague was abducted by three men."

Holding his head, he said in a firm tone, "Please contact your superior immediately. Also, can the local police force start setting roadblocks on the main streets leading out of Chennai?"

———

Sandy and Isobel sat in the back of the police car, while Dan was to the policeman. Isobel held her jacket to Sandy's head as he called the representative of the UN Office on Crime in India.

Within ten minutes, they arrived at the police headquarters—a prestigious, white, classical heritage building. As they walked up the stairs, Sandy pressed the policeman who escorted them. "I want to speak to your most senior officer," he said again.

"Sorry, sir. The assistant inspector deals with abductions and missing persons. He'll handle your case. I'll take you to his office. His name is Inspector Singh."

Dan noticed Sandy's frustration.

They were introduced to Inspector Singh, a small, middle-aged Indian man with a large mustache. His line of questioning was methodical and slow.

"Who is the name of the missing person?"

"Miss Zara Naidu."

"Okay." He typed it into his computer with two fingers and then looked up. "Is she an Indian citizen or a tourist?"

"She has dual citizenship: Indian and British. We're here for a conference."

"Okay." He typed again.

Dan watched as he pressed each key.

The inspector glanced up again. "Do you have a picture of her?"

Isobel pulled out her holoscreen and pulled up a picture of Zara. She'd also taken a video of the confrontation.

"This was taken half an hour ago in front of the temple's entrance gate, sir." She scrolled through a couple of pictures.

Inspector Singh looked closely. "Oh, she's very pretty. Kidnappers are interested in these types of beautiful women."

Dan's frustration was rising. He also pulled out a picture of Zara taken during their recent visit to the Sriharikota Space Agency. "Here's another one, Inspector."

Inspector Singh examined the picture, paused for a while, and asked, "Isn't that Professor Krishnan next to her?"

Sandy's eyes lit up. Dan nodded to him. *Go Sandy, get him moving*, he willed silently.

"Correct, sir. We met him yesterday at the Satish Dhawan Space Center." Sandy became more insistent. "Inspector Singh, I beg you, this is no ordinary abduction. Our colleague, Zara Naidu, is a top scientist working on a classified project with—"

"You mean defense project?"

Sandy nodded gravely. "Yes, defense project."

Alarm showed on Inspector Singh's face.

Good one, Sandy. Keep going, Dan thought.

Sandy pushed further. He said with a tone of urgency, "Inspector, this woman has to be found quickly before her abductors manage to extract some top-secret information."

"Yes, yes. I understand."

Sandy's holo beeped, and he answered, "Yes, I'm Sandy Fraser. We are at the police headquarters, being helped by a very diligent officer, Inspector Singh. I'll put you on holoscreen and you can talk to him."

"Inspector Singh?"

"Yes."

"I am the representative in India of the UN Office on Crime. Inspector, Miss Zara Naidu must be found as soon as possible using all the manpower at your disposal. I've been in contact with your Minister of the Interior... He has assured me that the Army will give you assistance with the case. Your contact will be Captain Chandra Shah. He will get in touch with your superior. Could you please direct Mr. Fraser and his party to your highest-ranking officer at the station? It's a matter of national security!"

Inspector Singh sat taller in his seat. "Yes, sir. I will do that straight away."

"Inspector, we really appreciate your help."

Dan watched as Inspector Singh used the holoscreen to call the Deputy Commissioner of the Central Crime Branch, putting him on large screen.

"Good afternoon, sir. Inspector Singh from Chennai Missing Persons. Sir, we have a situation code red one. I have been informed that it will be handled by a Captain Chandra Shah."

"I know who he is, Inspector. I'll take charge of the case from now on. Please bring these people to my office. Thank you."

2:30 P.M.

After a few more questions and statements, Dan, Isobel, and Sandy went back to the hotel. Isobel had arranged, despite Sandy's protests, for the hotel's resident doctor to meet them in Sandy's suite.

The doctor reassured them, "He'll be fine. I've put in a couple of stitches. The printout from our portable X-ray machine appears to show just superficial bleeding. He's going to have a concussion headache for the next day or two, but the wound isn't deep. A cut to the head always bleeds profusely. He should recover quickly. He's quite strong for a man of his age."

"I'm not old!" Sandy retorted. He buttoned his shirt up, which still showed blood stains. He was now wearing a white gauze bandage over his head.

"I'll check in again tomorrow," the doctor said as she packed her kit up. "Make sure you keep on top of the pain, sir." She turned to Isobel. "Keep an eye on him. If his symptoms change or he becomes confused, dizzy, or complains of increased pain, call me straight away." She passed over her card. "You can call me on this number any time of the day."

"Thank you, Doctor."

After she left, a waiter accompanied by a taller, older man arrived at the door with a trolley loaded with food and coffee. "Can we come in?"

"Yes, sure, sure," Isobel said.

The waiter unloaded the trays onto the table. The taller man extended his hand.

"Good afternoon. My name is Aahil. I am the hotel manager. I'm sorry to hear what happened to you, Mr. Fraser, and to Miss Naidu. The police have spoken to us, and we're increasing our security. Let me know if you need anything else. Just press 'one' on the holo." "Thank you, much appreciated," Sandy said. "You are most welcome, sir." The hotel manager gestured to the waiter, and they both exited the room.

Dan grabbed a bottle of water off the tray and offered one to Sandy. Isobel poured herself a cup of coffee and they started helping themselves to the food.

Sandy slouched in the chair, holding his head. "Bloody hell, Dan. What a mess; it all just happened so fast. I tried to get to her. Why on earth would they want to kidnap Zara?"

Dan looked at him, puzzled. "Do you think this is related to the project?"

"Right now, it's hard to say. We need to let this Captain Shah do his job and see what he can find out."

Dan walked over to the window, looking out. "Maybe I should offer to help them."

———

Captain Shah was the commander of an elite hostage rescue squad called "The Black Cats"—a name derived from their distinctive, all black Nomex coveralls. He was tall, lean, muscular, and hyper-aware of his surroundings. After he had received the call from his commanding officer, he first thought it was just a case of tourists getting themselves into trouble, but when the photo of the kidnapped woman came through to him, he gasped to himself. "I recognize this woman, Zara Naidu, from somewhere. Her face looks familiar, but I can't quite place her."

3:30 P.M.

Shah's team had managed to trace the whereabouts of the auto rickshaw from the information provided by Dan. It had been abandoned a few kilometers away from the temple. Some locals had witnessed a young woman in a red dress being dragged out from an auto rickshaw and transferred to a waiting car.

Eager to follow the lead, Captain Shah had instructed the police to make house calls in the surrounding area and to advise the residents that a substantial reward would be paid to anyone giving accurate information about the getaway car.

4:00 P.M.

Answering a call at her door, a middle-aged woman spoke to the police and provided some valuable information.

"This morning, I see a black car... big car, in the street with the engine running. Three men inside," she informed the police officers.

"Did you see the number plate?" one of them asked.

"Yes, the plate was black. Yellow numbers."

A black plate indicated it was a rental car.

"Do you remember any numbers on the plate?"

"Oh yes, the last numbers were two-six-zero-eight."

"Are you sure?"

"Yes, twenty-six is the day and eight is the month my youngest daughter was born. I do not forget that."

Captain Shah called on his holo his technical experts. The best match was a vehicle from a medium-sized rental firm called Indicar, operating in the East of Chennai.

He dialed the rental agency.

"This is Captain Shah from the Defense Ministry. You will be receiving an email as we speak verifying my ID. I need to know who hired a large black car with number plates ending in two-six-zero-eight in the past few days. I repeat, two-six-zero-eight. I'm holding."

It took a few moments for the clerk to come back with an affirmative answer.

"Yes, sir. It's an MPV. According to our records, the person who hired it is Mr. Rajiv Bhandari."

"Have you recorded his place of residence?"

"Yes, sir. Just a moment. Here: number ten, in fifth street, Surapet."

"Thank you. You've been extremely helpful. What's your name?"

"Ramesh Kumar, sir."

"Mr. Kumar, please DO NOT contact this person... under any circumstances. Understood?"

"Yes, sir. I understand. I will also tell the staff."

4:30 P.M.

Captain Shah assembled his team of fifteen operatives. He took them through the details using his mobile holoscreen. "Surapet is a suburb near Puzhal Lake. The location of the residence gives us several advantages."

He displayed a map of the area and pointed to the address in question. "The house in Fifth Street is adjacent to a water treatment plant... here. Several vehicles, including an ambulance, can be parked in the nearby fenced area without drawing attention from the occupants of the house where the woman is probably being held captive."

He turned to his second in command. "Lieutenant, contact the manager of the water treatment plant to get access to the area. The perimeter will be fenced and gated. Tell him it's an Army exercise. Requisition the necessary vehicles, manpower, and equipment from our closest depot. We need an unmarked ambulance, one small troop carrier, and two all-terrain vehicles. Organize to have them positioned as soon as possible but with maximum discretion."

Finally, Shah addressed one of his senior operatives, "Rajiv, you need to pick up a black SUV with tinted windows from Indicar. Also, get a blank form of their standard contracts. This vehicle will be driven by Lakmé and will also carry four of our men."

5:00 P.M.

Captain Shah rang Dan at the hotel on his mobile.

"Is that Mr. Robson?

"Yes, I'm Dan Robson."

"Sir, my name is Captain Chandra Shah. I'm the officer in charge of the rescue of Miss Zara Naidu. Could you please keep your holo on? I'll need to contact you during the rescue operation."

"Of course."

"Thank you."

6:00 P.M.

Captain Shah pointed to one of his best operatives and nodded, mouthing, "You're on, Lakmé."

The number she'd been given by Indicar was working. She raised an eyebrow, questioningly. He gave a thumbs-up while listening to the conversation. "Mr. Bandhari?" she asked.

"Ah, yes," came the answer.

"Sir, my name is Lakmé from Indicar, the firm you hired your car from."

"Yes."

"Sir, we've been advised by the manufacturer of your rental vehicle that it contains a suspected faulty air bag. We're going to send you a new vehicle to replace it. Should be in say half an hour."

Mr. Bandhari protested, "There's no need to do that, I am quite happy with the vehicle. Forget the new car."

"Sorry sir, we're following the instructions of the manufacturer of this specific model. There is a serious risk that the driver's air bag could inflate without the vehicle being involved in a collision. The insurance company won't take responsibility in case of a mishap. We have a contractual obligation to replace your MPV."

Mr. Bandhari sighed, sounding somewhat reluctant. "All right then. Please make it quick. I'm a busy man."

Shah gave a thumb-up again, which afforded the operatives just enough time to get into position.

6:30 P.M.

Captain Shah was ready at the water treatment plant, his sharpshooter rifle next to him. He peered through his binoculars. An MPV was parked outside the house. He checked his watch. A similar model black MPV with tinted windows pulled up in the driveway, close to the front door. "Right on time."

A young lady dressed in an Indicar uniform came out of it and rang the front doorbell. She apologized. "My name is Lakmé from Indicar. I spoke to you half an hour ago to swap your vehicle. Apologies, Mr. Bandhari. As I explained to you on, it's a manufacturing default. To make up for the inconvenience, our firm will allow you to keep the new car for an extra week."

"Thank you."

"Here's the new set of keys and here is the new contract. Could I have your signature, please? Thank you." She then asked for the keys of the replaced vehicle and started to walk away. After a few steps, she walked back.

"Oh, I almost forgot. We need you to confirm the odometer reading. Could you come with me, sir? It's a brand-new car. It has barely 300 kilometers on the clock. There won't be any problem with this one," she added, laughing.

As Mr. Bandhari leaned forward to read the mileage, the hard muzzle of a pistol dug into his lower ribs. The young lady from Indicar said, "I have a gun pointed at you. Let's go back to the house. Don't do anything stupid. I won't hesitate. Act naturally."

She was holding a folder with the firm's emblem to cover her gun pointed at his flank. When they arrived at the porch, she asked him, "How many in the house?"

"Two."

"Where are they located?"

"One on this level, the other one upstairs."

"What about the woman with the red dress?"

"Upstairs as well."

Lakmé replied, emphasizing every word, "Okay, let's find her."

That was the agreed code signal for the rescue to start.

––––––––

Shah ordered the four commandos (Cats 3, 4, 5, and 6) who were waiting inside the new MPV to make their move. Wearing Indicar uniforms but fully kitted with weapons, they reached the porch.

Cat 3 grabbed Mr. Bandhari by the neck. "Open the door and leave it ajar!"

As soon as he did so, Cat 3 told him, "Call your friends one at a time. First the one on this floor. Don't say anything suspicious or I'll shoot you. Just call the first one!"

Mr. Bandhari did as he was told.

"Gopal?" Bandhari said.

A young man emerged from one of the rooms, a surprised expression on his face. "What?"

Cat 4 took a few steps forward and tasered him. He fell to the floor, convulsing from the electric discharge. Cat 4 jumped on him, handcuffed him, duct-taped his mouth, and dragged him behind a couch, pinning him to the ground.

"One down, Captain," he said into his mike.

Shah ordered over the holo, "Stay with him. Cat 3, secure the front door. I have you covered from the outside with Cat 7 and 8. Lakmé, go with Cat 5 and 6 and find the woman."

Lakmé pointed to the upper floor and whispered to Mr. Bandhari, "Take the three of us upstairs to where the woman is being kept. Don't do anything stupid."

Shah watched the screen, which showed the other two operatives in front of Lakmé. They crept up to the second level, stopping in front of the door where Zara was presumably being held hostage. Cat 5 spoke to Mr. Bandhari in a muted tone.

"Knock on the door and call your friend in a normal voice."

He complied. "Nay?" There was no answer.

"Call again louder."

"Nay?" he repeated. Still, there was no answer.

"Is the door locked from the inside?"

"No."

"Right."

Cat 5 pinned Mr. Bandhari against the wall and whispered to Cat 6, "Get inside on alert."

With his pistol in hand, Cat 6 slowly pushed the door open.

A middle-aged Indian man was asleep in a chair. An Indian woman was tied to the bed next to him. She had blood on her face and appeared to be unconscious.

Shah ordered over the line, "Neutralize the male!"

Cat 6 moved fast. He tasered the man, then used duct tape to gag him, tied his hands, then his legs together, and handcuffed him to a post at the base of the bed.

Lakmé entered the room and checked the pulse of the Indian woman. "We've located her, Captain. She's breathing but unconscious. I'll show her to you via my camera. The description matches the missing female, but I need to confirm her identity. Could you relay the picture feed to Mr. Robson?"

Upon seeing her, Dan exclaimed, "Yes, that's Zara. Oh, my goodness, she looks terrible; she's bleeding. Please help her."

Captain Shah took over. "I will, Mr. Robson. Thank you." Then he ordered, "Bring the unmarked ambulance to the front door."

Cat 5, who had pinned Mr. Bandhari hard against the wall, asked him, "What drug did you use?"

"I don't know; it was given to us. Don't hurt me."

"Did you interrogate her?"

"No. She was drugged in the auto rickshaw. We didn't get anything out of her after that."

The unmarked vehicle which had been stationed nearby with Cat 9 pulled in behind a bush. Zara was carried downstairs by Cat 5 and 6, then transferred to a stretcher in the ambulance by a couple of paramedics.

Shah spoke to Dan over the holo, "Mr. Robson, Miss Naidu is being driven to Chennai Hospital. I will contact you later. Thank you."

After the ambulance had departed, another MPV followed. Cat 3 and 4 bundled the two abductors who'd been tasered inside the van and took them to police headquarters.

Cat 5 and 6, who had handled Mr. Bandhari, were still inside the house with him.

Captain Shah entered the kitchen where Bandhari was now tied. He stood opposite him. The man was in his fifties—pudgy and unkempt. His shirt had been torn when he tried to pull away from Cat 3. Shah's upper lip curled in disgust. *This is the worst sort of offender, one who's aware of the despicable nature of his crime, yet indifferent to his victims.*

He started questioning him. "What were you going to do next with the woman?"

"I don't know."

Shah grabbed him by the neck and shook him hard. "Don't play games with me!"

"Okay, okay. The Major is coming to collect her this evening."

"Who's the Major?"

"I don't know. We just call him the Major."

Shah grabbed him again. "Don't lie to me, Bandhari!"

"I don't know who he is," he repeated, this time shaking with fright.

"All right, when do you expect him?"

"This evening."

"When?"

"Not sure about the time. He'll ring half an hour before he comes."

"Will he come alone?"

"Probably with two other men."

"We'll wait for them with you." Shah cautioned him, "Bandhari, we have enough charges against you to hang you. Cooperate with us and I'll put in a good word to the prosecution for you."

"Yes, please, please. I cannot die. I have a wife and children."

"When the Major arrives, let him in and act naturally."

Shah dialed out. "Send another three operatives."

7:30 P.M.

A car pulled in the driveway. As instructed, Mr. Bandhari acted naturally and let the three men in.

A tall, blond man asked him straight away, "Where is the woman?"

"Upstairs, Mr. Major."

They had barely taken three steps toward the stairwell when Cats 10, 11, and 12 burst out of their hiding place in the adjacent kitchen and tasered the Major and his two associates. Then, the three men were handcuffed and gagged with duct tape and marched to a nearby troop carrier to be taken for interrogation. Shah instructed his operatives to stay inside to search the house and gather further evidence.

8:30 P.M.

Isobel was typing on her computer. Sandy was sitting in a chair next to her, cradling a whisky and trying to make himself comfortable. Their half-eaten plates lay on the table between them. None of them felt like eating.

Dan couldn't sit still. He tapped on the side of the chair to distract himself. "Why haven't we heard anything yet?"

Sandy looked up at him. "Dan, we just have to—"

Out of the blue, there was a knock on the door of their suite. They all stood up anxiously.

Dan went to the door, his heart beating faster in his chest. A tall Indian man, clean-shaven with short black hair, stood in front of him. He was fully kitted out in black: black army jacket, black pants, and black combat boots. He carried a folder with him.

"Good evening, sir." He pulled his ID out and held it up for them. "Captain Chandra Shah. May I come in?"

Dan stood with his mouth agape. "Yes, yes come in. I'm Dan Robson."

Sandy tried to stand on his feet, looking worried.

"Zara is she—" Dan began to ask.

"Alive, yes, sir. Safe in a Chennai private hospital but still unconscious."

They all breathed out a collective sigh of relief.

"Thank God for that!" Sandy exclaimed.

Captain Shah continued, "May I sit?"

"Yes, yes, please. Would you like a drink?" Dan asked.

"Just some water please," he said, eyeing Sandy's whisky.

"Miss Naidu is safe. I'll take you through some of the details, but you need to understand she's been injured and drugged."

Dan felt his throat close again.

Captain Shah opened his file and read from the report, "She has three broken ribs on her right side, severe bruising on her face. The doctors say the effects of the drug will wear off in the next twenty-four to forty-eight hours, but she won't be able to receive visitors for several days."

"Does she have any family locally?" asked Captain Shah.

Dan gave a brisk nod. "Yes, she does. We tried to call her parents earlier but discovered they're overseas now. Her father, Dr. Chatresh Naidu, who has a practice here in Chennai, is attending a medical conference in the US."

"Probably for the best. She looks battered now. Does she have a husband or partner?"

"No, no, Zara is single. Although originally from Chennai, she works with us in Korea and holds a British passport."

He wrote the information down without a flicker of emotion. "All right. Thank you. I will let you know when you can visit her as soon as the doctors allow it."

Sandy asked, "Captain, is there any reason why she was targeted?"

"Too early to say, sir, but we've apprehended all the culprits. They are in custody. We're interrogating them to find out their motives for abducting Dr. Naidu."

"Captain, my name is Sandy Fraser. I am the director of an influential organization in the United Nations. If you need any assistance, please let me know."

"Thank you, sir. I am aware of your status. I appreciate your offer. I think we should have a fairly good idea of who is behind this reasonably soon. I will keep you posted the moment I know. Anything else I can help you with?"

Sandy hesitated. "This is more personal, Captain. Mmmm... when I was on the ground, someone stole my Blue Yacht Master II Rolex. It's not for the value, you know... My father gave it to me when I graduated and—"

Captain Shah smiled. "Well, I've got good news for you, Mr. Fraser. One of the culprits was wearing it. I thought it must have been stolen. That's one more piece of evidence against them. I'll see what I can do to have it returned to you quickly. In the meantime, could you make a statement? I'll send one of my officers to collect it. I can be contacted on this number. I wish you a full recovery, sir."

"Thank you, Captain." Looking at Isobel, he added, "I've got an excellent nurse." He smiled at her, patting her on the knee. Then he said, "Captain, congratulations for a well-run rescue operation. We're so relieved and grateful to you and your men. Well done."

THE NEXT DAY

Dan finished answering a holo call and headed over to the table where Sandy and Isobel sat. Both looked tired and were drinking black coffee to keep alert. Sandy had a fresh gauze bandage on his head, somewhat smaller than the one he'd sported the day before.

Dan brought a seat over. "That was the hospital. Good news."

Isobel and Sandy both looked up with expectant expressions on their faces.

"Zara has regained consciousness."

Sandy breathed out heavily as if he'd been holding in air for days. "What a relief. That's fantastic news, Dan."

"The doctors want her to stay under observation for another week at least. They say the drug used has left her disorientated, and the injury to her head needs to heal. She's also still extremely shaken from her ordeal."

Dan glanced at Sandy, who was still paler than usual. "What about you, Sandy? Are you recovering?"

"No worries, mate. Isobel changed my bandage this morning, and I took a couple of painkillers, which have dulled my headache. Don't worry. I'm a Queenslander. I've got a bloody strong head! Gee, I'm so happy to hear the news about Zara. I suggest we extend our stay in Chennai. What do you think?"

They all agreed. "Good idea," Dan said, "until Zara is feeling better. I'll let Lanie know about our change of plans."

A FEW DAYS LATER

Zara was well enough to receive visitors, so Sandy, Dan, and Isobel came to visit her at the hospital. Captain Shah was sitting in her room. Zara seemed to be in good spirits, despite the bruises on her face. She hugged each of them cautiously.

"I'm so happy to see you guys."

"Not as happy as we are to see you," Dan said. "You're certainly looking better than when I saw you during the rescue."

"I'm improving every day."

"Excellent."

According to the chatter at the nurses' station that Dan had overheard, the captain had been visiting Zara every day, bringing her flowers and fresh fruit.

Zara confirmed it. "Captain Shah has spent a fair bit of his time attending to my welfare and talking to me. Beyond the call of duty," she said with a wink. "We've found out we went to the same high school in Chennai, but he was a couple of grades above me."

As they were leaving the room, one of the ward nurses called out to them, "Excuse me, are you the friends of Miss Naidu?"

Dan answered, "That's us. We've just finished visiting her."

"Good. Dr. Patal, her physician, would like to keep you up to date. Please follow me."

She brought them to his consulting room.

Dr. Patal greeted them, "Good morning. I'm Dr. Patal. Are you Miss Naidu's relatives?"

"Not exactly," Sandy explained. "We're her colleagues."

"Miss Naidu is recovering well, considering the ordeal she's gone through. Her facial lacerations are healing without any infection. I put a few cosmetic stitches in just to help. Her ribs will mend over time, but she needs rest and no heavy lifting for a few weeks. That's the good news."

They all looked at each other anxiously.

"Now... medium to long term, the side effects of the drug she's been injected with could cause speech difficulties, lack of attention, confusion, lack of memory, and poor coordination. So, I would recommend two to three months off her normal duties. Would you inform her employer?"

"We will. Thank you, Doctor. When will she be able to travel overseas?"

"I would say in a couple of months or so."

"We will contact her father, Dr. Chatresh Naidu, to look after her."

"Oh yes, Dr. Naidu. I have had dealings with him professionally."

———

After leaving the hospital, Dan expressed everybody's feelings. "So, she won't be able to work with us for quite a while?"

Sandy raised his eyebrows in a conspiratorial manner. "Well, I think I might know the perfect person to replace her."

Dan looked at him, confused, and then it dawned on him. "Sandy... No. I don't think that's a great idea."

"Hmmm... it might be my best yet."

"Who are you two talking about?" Isobel asked.

Sandy just grinned, then continued more seriously. "I've spoken with Captain Shah. His preliminary investigation indicates that Zara's abduction wasn't a random one. It has international ramifications. Apparently, the so-called "Major" is a contract man. The Indian Interpol Branch has been advised that his orders came from a group called New Order. The lead has been confirmed by Interpol in Europe. They've instructed their agents to carry out further investigations."

He frowned at Dan and Isobel. "From now on, we must be more careful about our safety! Captain Shah has assigned a couple of his Black Cats as our bodyguards while we're in India. I'll talk to our VIP protection unit in New York and find out what measures they recommend following our departure from Chennai. Then I'll contact my intelligence community contacts to gather information about this New Order mob. Too much of a coincidence if you ask me."

Dan dropped his satchel on the counter. He spotted Ava on the couch, video conferencing with her homework group. She was wearing jeans frayed at the bottom up to her mid calves, a blue and white striped top which tied in the middle of her stomach, and bright yellow converse high tops.

I'll never understand teenage fashion, he thought as he gazed down at his gray suit. She turned and smiled at him, putting herself on mute. "Hey Dad, how was work?

"Good, sweetie. Is your mum around?"

She pointed upward. "I think she's in her study."

"Thanks." He took the stairs two at a time and knocked on her door.

"Come in," she called. Melanie lit up when she saw him. She looked at her watch. "You're home early. I've got a client tele-call in half an hour, but we can chat till then."

She ushered him to the couch. "A big client. I mean potentially. A new port in Abu Dhabi. We've drawn up some plans, which they like, but they want it to be even bigger. We need to talk through the specs today."

She grabbed her tea off her desk, pushed some of the cushions aside, and sat next to him on the big gray couch.

"What's going on at the office?"

He felt that lump in his throat rise again. He pushed it down and cleared his voice.

"Zara formally put in her resignation today."

She studied his face. "Well, that was to be expected, wasn't it? After what happened to her. What a dreadful ordeal, Dan."

"Yes, I know. I still feel terrible about it all." He hesitated. "Responsible, somehow."

"It could have happened anywhere, Dan. It wasn't—"

"My logical side says you're right, yes, but it was on my watch, hon. I still—"

"Maybe you should talk to someone about all this. I know it was distressing for everyone, but it's been a month now. You don't seem to be getting over it. Have you heard of post-traumatic stress disorder?"

"Yes, of course, but there's no point talking to a shrink when I already know the answer. Here's the rundown. Zara is still in Chennai with her family. She's recovered from her injuries and... oh... wait for this, that's the news, she's seeing someone."

"Fantastic. That's the best thing that can happen to her."

"Yes. She said it's still early days but get this—it's the special agent who helped rescue her. They're becoming an item."

Melanie raised her eyebrows, then let out a delighted laugh. "I knew it. I knew it! The handsome Black Cat?"

"I never said he was handsome."

"These guys are always handsome, Dan. Don't you watch TV soaps?"

Dan thought back and conceded. "Okay, he is actually quite a handsome man."

"Seeeeee, well, well, that's wonderful news. That's the solution to your worries. Life is full of happy surprises as well,

Dan. It's not all gloomy news. Not the end of the world, like your group predicts."

He corrected her, "Not for our generation, anyway."

He suddenly felt less tense. "You're right, Lanie. There are still plenty of happy days ahead for all of us."

"See. It'll make her family happy, even if it's early days. We mothers know these things. Wasn't she looking for Mr. Right?"

"Well, she joked about it, sure, but obviously she wouldn't talk about it at the office. She is not the type. She's a career woman, Lanie. That's the way I saw it, anyway."

She looked him up and down and said with mock indignation, "Excuse me, Professor Robson, I'm also a 'career woman' and happily married with three wonderful kids. These days we're allowed to have it all, you know!" She elbowed him and continued, "Everyone's looking for happiness. I know she was helpful to you, but you'll find someone else. Try not to worry."

"I won't really need to, not right now."

"What do you mean?"

"Well, Sandy's taking me offline for a while to work on—"

"Another project?"

"Another aspect, anyway. We're moving on."

"Will you be able to tell me more about that, Dan?"

"Not yet. Sorry, honey."

"Hmm." Her eyebrows furrowed. "I don't like us keeping secrets from each other."

"Neither do I, but it's part of the job." He hesitated. "Actually, Sandy's coming to Songdo next week to discuss the project. He wants to talk to both of us."

"Both of us? He probably wants to apologize for taking my husband away all the time!"

He stood up, cutting the conversation short. "I'm going to get dinner started while you have your tele-conference. Do you need me to get the boys from soccer?"

"Yes, please. In half an hour. Wait a minute, wait a minute..." She grabbed his hand. "Before that, let's sing, 'Oh happy day' together—"

"The one with our own words?" He smiled. Singing together was always a joy. Melanie had a powerful alto voice and had been in her own church's choir growing up.

"Yes." She hugged him. "The one where I sing, 'Oh happy day, when my man comes home.'"

YONG SE UNIVERSITY

Melanie fidgeted in her seat as the car headed over to the university.

"Dan, this is ridiculous; you need to tell me at least something before we go and meet with Sandy."

He shook his head. "I honestly don't know why he called both of us together."

"Uh," she groaned. "Daniel Robson, you are the most stubborn man when you want to be. Just like leading a mule—"

He finished her sentence. "To water."

He grinned. "You know that isn't the correct saying."

She grinned back. "I know, I know, but it still applies to you."

He watched her. She was tapping her fingers on the side panel of the car. She kept playing with her lip before catching herself and stopping. Then slowly her fingers would creep back up again, a bad habit of long forgotten youth. He smiled to himself. He was usually the nervous one, while she was always self-assured, the boss lady of the second biggest infrastructure firm in South Korea. He put his hand on her shoulder.

"You don't have to worry. It's just going to be Sandy and us."

"Just Sandy!" She rolled her eyes at him. "I know you talk

about him a lot, so it seems like we are old friends, but I think I've only met him twice. The first time at the Ericsons' in New Jersey and at a Christmas party a couple of years back when he dropped into the office."

"Why are you so nervous? You've influenced Saudi princes, presidents, and billionaire property moguls."

"None of those big shots happened to be my dear husband's direct boss."

He laughed. "Don't worry, Sandy is a great guy. You'll get along very well with him. He also loves romantic comedies."

She poked at his ribs. "Stop trying to make me feel better."

———

When they arrived, he watched her get out of the car, smooth out her favorite red skirt, and put her silver jacket back on over her crisp, white blouse. She looked like the consummate professional with zero sign of nerves. As they rode up in the elevator, he began to feel his own nerves rising. This was ridiculous. He and Melanie had never worked together before. If he was honest, he wasn't sure it was the best idea. He felt a lot more comfortable keeping family and work separate.

"Honey?" He held the door open for her. He smiled. "Are you coming?"

He led the way to the conference room. Sandy was already there and... damn it, Isobel was there, sitting on the far right, busy at her computer. Sandy walked over to them, extending his hand to Melanie.

"Melanie, I thank you so much for coming in. We really need your expertise."

Sandy introduced Isobel. Melanie looked over at her. "You're the famous astrophysicist? I'm very honored to meet you."

Isobel glanced up and smiled politely. "Not sure about famous. I'm pleased to meet you too, Melanie. Dan speaks a lot about you, especially when he's away from home. You're lucky to have such a caring husband."

Melanie smiled warmly. "Oh, I definitely miss him, too, when he travels."

Sandy, always the diplomat, intervened. "Well, Melanie, I have the perfect solution to this. Why don't you join us and travel with us? I'm not sure how much Dan has told you?"

"Nothing," Dan interrupted hurriedly. *I don't want Sandy to think I've been pillow talking.*

Melanie looked over at him. She shook her head and turned back to Sandy. "Dan has told me next to nothing, only that you're all working on a special project."

Sandy's mouth twitched. "All right, then. Let me take you through the generalities and some of the details."

He spent the next hour taking her through everything from the environmental dilemma to their concern about future generations to the search for a suitable planet and the prospect of the construction of a space probe. When he'd finished, he studied Melanie's incredulous face. "Any questions?"

"So let me put all the pieces together," Melanie said. "You're all planning to send a probe, which has never been built before, to a yet undiscovered planet located light years away, hoping it may be able to sustain human life?"

"That's the gist of it," Sandy said.

She shook her head. "I'm sorry. This is plainly impossible."

Isobel stood up from her chair. "No, not theoretically."

"Yes, theoretically sure, Isobel. But you are an astrophysicist, and I'm a project engineer. I'm looking at this from a practical point of view. Sorry." Melanie gazed back and forth between Isobel and Sandy. She raised her voice as if slightly annoyed. "You're asking me to manage a project where the key elements don't exist yet and may not be in place for several decades."

Sandy raised his hand. "If I may? I know what you're saying, Melanie. A lot of the pieces are either only partly developed, missing, or don't even exist yet, but we need your help to develop them."

There was silence in the room. Dan felt that he should say something, but he didn't know how to break the tension. Melanie always brought the practical side to a situation. He knew that Isobel had been theorizing and Melanie's reaction confirmed to him how much speculation lay in her thinking.

"Can I be frank, Sandy?"

"Please."

"What you're proposing has never been done before. It's going to cost billions of dollars, and I would estimate just off the top of my head it will take around fifty to one hundred years to achieve this sort of scale. Even in my world, this is unheard of."

Sandy said slowly, emphasizing every word, "I understand what you're saying, Melanie, but we must make a start. The future of mankind is at stake. If we don't act, our species will be wiped off the face of the Earth as if it had never existed."

"That's very dramatic. You can't be serious?"

"Very serious. Ask Dan."

"Sandy's right, Lanie. We are systematically destroying life on Earth. We'll soon reach a point of no return. There is no solution to fix it, no way out. We face the extinction of our own species on this planet in the future. That's the terrible situation."

Isobel added, thoughtfully, "If you think about it, it's probably quite a common cycle in the universe: planets evolve, create intelligent life forms, get over-exploited and eventually their ecosystem becomes exhausted and collapses."

Melanie gaped at her explanation, and then turned back to Sandy.

"How much money have you got?"

"You mean the budget for the project?", Sandy asked.

"Let's start with that and then we can talk about my fee," she replied jokingly. "How much do you estimate the budget for such a venture?"

"What's the price of human civilization, Melanie? What's the price of our species being kept alive in the future?"

She threw up her hands. "You don't have an indication of the costs, do you?"

Sandy replied firmly, "We're still negotiating that aspect, Melanie, but I can assure you money won't be a problem. Substantial funds are on the horizon."

"I'm assuming secrecy is of the utmost."

"Essential. The fewer people who know, the better. That's the reason we want to keep it in the family, so to speak," he said ironically.

"So, you're literally talking about multiple components being designed, manufactured, and semi-constructed in complete isolation from each other."

Isobel chimed in, "It's quite common practice in space projects."

Melanie was silent for a few moments. "Okay. Let me think about all this. It'll probably take me a good four... no more... like six months to even get something resembling a plan and to sound out the right people."

Sandy replied enthusiastically, "Take a year if you want."

"Isobel, I will need your help here."

"Sure, I know a lot of people in the space industry."

Melanie pulled out her folder, ripped out a page, and started writing.

"I'll send you over a contract, but this is an indication of my sign-on fee and the cost for six months of work. I am forewarning you. I could do the scoping work and it may come to nothing. As I said, this has never been done before."

Sandy took the paper and glanced at it. Again, he spoke slowly, "Melanie, this will be a job for life, well paid, working close to your husband and for the only project worth being involved with right now: saving humanity. If we succeed, the whole of mankind will be indebted to us. Think about it and let me know."

He then approached Dan. "Can we get together tomorrow? I want to talk to you about something that's come up. Highly confidential."

"Sure. Let's meet at my office. I'll ask my secretary to book a conference room where we won't be disturbed."

———

In the car on the way back home, Melanie put her head on Dan's shoulder. "No more secrets from me, okay."

"You have my word."

INCHEON CAMPUS, UNIVERSITY BOARDROOM

Dan and Sandy sat in the conference room at the back of the Incheon Campus.

Dan's assistant brought them coffee and some Yakgwa—a traditional Korean cookie flavored with honey and ginger. Dan had a feeling she was trying to impress Sandy. He seldom got delicious pastries with his coffee.

Sandy settled into the black swivel chair at the head of the table and looked outside, slowly sipping his coffee. "Mmm, just what I need."

Dan eyed him. "What's going on, Sandy? What's with all the cloak and dagger? Why couldn't we meet in my office?"

Sandy sighed and hesitated. "Ahhh. This is related to Zara's abduction, Dan."

Dan stiffened, remembering: the red dress, the men dragging her away, the terrifying hours not knowing what had happened to her. After Zara's ordeal in Chennai, he hadn't heard anything further about Interpol's inquiry. Then Zara left the organization. His chest heaved as he snapped back to the conversation. Panic began to rise in him. "Is she okay? Has something else happened?"

Instinctively, Sandy lowered his voice, calming him. "No, she's fine. No worries there. Sorry mate, I should have been clearer. The thing is... I've received some information on a possible motive for her kidnapping. The breakthrough came from an unexpected source, an old friend in the World Health Organization's Early Detection Unit. This is what they've discovered: some researchers unknown to them have developed a biological process to render certain ethnic groups completely sterile—"

Dan put his coffee cup back down. "What? That's crazy."

Sandy nodded. "There's more. It appears their research has been financed by an international group of eco-terrorists identified as 'NEO,' which we know stands for 'New Earth Order.' Now Dan, do you remember Captain Shah mentioned Interpol had traced 'the Major' to a European organization called 'Neu?'"

"Yes. I recall him saying that. Also, that Interpol was going to investigate further. 'Neu' means 'new" in German, am I right?'

"Correct. Same mob."

"So, you think that there's a connection there?"

Sandy continued, "Yes. According to the World Health Organization's Early Detection Unit and Interpol, 'Neu' or 'NEO' is convinced the only way to stop the deterioration of our planet's environment is to cut down its population drastically, by any possible means. In their eyes, the main cause of the Earth's destruction is the excessive number of inhabitants on the planet. Now, do you also remember your conversation with Franz Jürgen in Bonn?"

Dan's eyes widened. "You're right! That's precisely what he was advocating. His exact words were 'to cut the world population by half.' But Sandy, there have always been conspiracy theories regarding these types of solutions before. Let's face it. It's hard to develop a new disease in a lab without being noticed by the scientific world. To start with, it involves a lot of sophisticated equipment like electron microscopes, biohazard labs, and protective gear. Where's the evidence?"

They had had some good debates about Dan's demand for scientific proof.

Sandy continued, "This time, Dan, there is evidence. The Detection Unit of the World Health Organization has convincing reports that some tribes in the Republic of Congo haven't seen a single new child being born over the past ten years. Ten years! The villagers believe a curse has been cast on them. However, the circumstances raised a red flag in the Intelligence Branch of the World Health Organization."

Dan scratched his head. "No births for a decade... that certainly does sound suspect. Have they been able to carry out any tests?"

Sandy nodded repeatedly and passed him a folder. "Have a look at this. Although this part of Central Africa is remote and unsafe, the Detection Unit of the World Health Organization has managed to obtain blood samples of some of the villagers.

They've detected a mutant of the Zika virus, ZKV/Lisala, in the blood samples of these ethnic groups. When pregnant women are infected with this virus, the embryo becomes contaminated as well through the placenta. Genomic analysis tests carried out have revealed that this specific strain attacks the brain of human embryos in their early stages of development inside the womb. It results in premature termination of pregnancy in 100 percent of the cases."

Dan flicked through the case file, perusing the results from over one hundred blood tests and pictures of shriveled fetuses.

"What do you think?"

"This is the first time I've seen this file, Sandy. I would need to do more reading, but at first glance, I'd say that they're right."

Dan took a sip of his coffee before continuing, "Although the Zika virus originated in Central Africa, a mutation of that significance couldn't have happened naturally. To have such a different effect on humans, it must have been engineered in a lab. Some amino acids of the virus's DNA would need to be artificially altered."

He shook his head, pensively. "That's exceedingly difficult to achieve even with today's technology. Some top-class virologists must have been able to genetically modify the DNA of the Zika virus and release the mutant in these targeted regions of Africa."

Sandy agreed, "That's pretty much what my source told me. More alarmingly, the World Health Organization believes the epidemic is now getting out of control. They have information that the disease is currently spreading rapidly in some of the tropical and subtropical regions of the globe."

Dan's eyebrows raised. "Sandy, the implications are shocking. If these figures are correct, a pandemic could easily wipe out entire ethnic groups within a few decades." He flicked through the papers again. "These figures are worrying. Honestly, I don't believe it could have occurred naturally."

He looked up at Sandy. "So, do you think that's what Franz was referring to in Bonn? You think he's linked to all this?" He gestured at the pictures of the empty maternity wards and crying women.

Sandy stood up and gazed out the window. "It's highly likely he would've been aware, if not been part of this type of research, Dan. Do you remember? He appeared so damn sure of himself."

He smacked his hand against the window. "If he is involved, the bastard must be held accountable. You won't believe what he is up to now."

"No idea."

"As I predicted, he has gone into politics. He has managed to get elected to the Luxemburg Chamber of Deputies and is now, get this, Assistant to the Minister for Science and Technology."

"Isn't their government leaning to the far right?"

"Exactly. It's a perfect spot for his ideology."

Dan's mind suddenly shifted back to the beginning of their conversation. "And sorry Sandy, you said you now believe Zara was abducted by this NEO group?"

Sandy turned and sat back down, leaning forward with his hands on his knees, anger in his eyes. "At this stage, I have no proof, only a strong suspicion. I'd say they wanted to extract information about our own activities and the best way was to obtain it from a member of our team under interrogation. They tracked us and grabbed Zara at an opportune time. God knows what would have happened to her if Captain Shah and his men hadn't been able to rescue her!"

Dan's face fell. "It's my fault. If I had been closer to her, I could have..." his voice trailed off.

Sandy reached out to squeeze his shoulder. "Dan, if it hadn't been there, it would have been somewhere else. They could have grabbed any one of us to extract the information they wanted."

Dan's clenched jaw reflected his internal struggle to take in all this new information. He leapt up, grabbed another Yakgwa, and took a bite. As he chewed, his mind whirled. "Zara was bad enough, Sandy, but what about Melanie or the kids? Are we... my family... Melanie, the kids... are they in danger as well?"

"Dan, it's okay. Don't worry, mate. They'll be safe. I've made sure that this mob won't get to us again. I've obtained extra funding from the UN diplomatic security unit. Your family, and especially you, have been protected twenty-four-seven. It's been discreet. Here's the number of the security agency. Mention my name and ask for Mr. Mendez."

"Thanks, Sandy. I feel a lot more reassured now."

Sandy continued, "You'll need to get some training in weaponry as well."

Dan's eyes widened in shock. "Hey, this is getting damn serious, Sandy! This NEO group sounds extremely dangerous. What else do you know about them?"

"We're still gathering information. According to my sources, this organization is very secretive. They use almost impenetrable communication technology. All their contacts are made through the dark web, using the most advanced encryption systems. There is no known hierarchy. They operate through independent cells. At this stage, they appear to be mainly active in northern Europe."

Still thinking of his children and his wife, Dan asked almost in a whisper, "Are they supremacists?"

Sandy rubbed his chin, pondering. "It's a strong possibility. One cell in Scandinavia is under surveillance by Interpol. It's a covert association of scientists who share their knowledge to —according to them—save the planet by any means, including, I would say, reducing the world's population. They use coded knowledge through a scientific platform to exchange information. This is very smart and confusing for intelligence agencies."

Dan looked at Sandy. A nagging thought prompted him. "I'm not sure whether I'm overreacting, Sandy, but I noticed quite a few blond people when we were traveling."

Sandy grinned. "I saw them too, mate, but we were in Germany, England, and Australia. Lots of fair-haired people there."

Dan wasn't going to be dismissed that easily. This thought had been at the back of his mind for months, and he felt it was finally coming to the surface. "Do you recall, even in the hotels and restaurants in India, we saw blond men. Many more than there normally would be. Do you think these guys have been shadowing us? Seems too much of a coincidence."

"You're right." Sandy chewed his own pastry thoughtfully. "It makes sense to me as well, Dan. They could have been monitoring us. Mind you, these guys would've operated at a lower level of decision-making. More likely to be foot soldiers, so to speak."

"So, what else are the NEO members up to that you're aware of?"

"Well, as far as I know, they have also unleashed cyberattacks on IT systems of industries involved in producing or using fossil fuels. A lot of finance companies now refuse to lend funds to known polluting industries for fear of reprisals. Allegedly, more aggressive members of NEO have been held responsible, among other things, for blowing up oil refineries and tankers in the Middle East, Europe, and North America. Some of their hard-liners are more aggressive in their tactics. Radical fanatics, you might say, Dan. They've been classified as 'eco-terrorists' by several government security agencies."

"I can see they have a totally different approach, Sandy. They won't hesitate to get rid of some of the people who don't fit in with their ideology. That's clear. They are determined to continue living on this planet, but with a reduced population. The problem is: who stays and who doesn't?"

"Obviously, they want to stay," said Sandy. "I'm afraid this type of radicalism is likely to manifest itself a lot more widely than we expect when entire populations start running out of food, livable space, and resources. These populists will have an open field for their ideology and tactics."

"Totally agree. We could see the re-emergence of lethal infections. It would be tempting for rogue fanatic groups to release cheaply produced, genetically engineered diseases such as deadly bioweapons. Highly contagious infections such as smallpox, typhus, anthrax, and Ebola could also be reactivated or engineered. Frozen stocks of viruses and bacteria have been kept by various laboratories around the world; determined groups could acquire them easily. The virus pandemics of 2020 through 2023 and 2030 through 2033 were a warning of the devastating effects that viruses can have on populations. Some scientists are aware of the damage they can inflict by manipulating viruses of zoonotic origin."

"You're right, Dan," said Sandy. "When it comes to the crunch, climate-change disasters will act as triggers for extremism. The habitable areas of the Earth are shrinking rapidly. There will be increasing conflicts to have access to them. People will become desperate and resort to violence. Several ecological collapses such as loss of agricultural land and subsequent food shortages will also multiply the risk of conflicts around the world. They pose a serious threat to international security. That's something we'll have to watch very carefully. In the meantime, regarding Franz Jürgen, I have some contacts in Berlin. I'll ask them to dig in his past and see if they can find some dirt on him."

Isobel talked them through the visit in the business lounge of The Indian Space Research Organization in Bengaluru, India. She was in full professorial mode.

"The hunt for Earth-like candidates outside our solar system has been ongoing. Observatories around the world have been searching for these planets for a while, resulting in the discovery of numerous exoplanets orbiting a star like our sun."

Dan asked, "How many, Isobel?"

"The tally, so far, is around ten thousand exoplanets, but more will be found. To be in contention, the planet must be within the habitable zone: not too close and not too far from its star, not too cold but not too hot, just like the Earth is at the right distance from our sun."

"The 'Goldilocks principle' where the temperature variations allow water to be present in its three forms: liquid, vapor, and ice, so that it can harbor life as we know it?"

"Correct, Dan. It must also be made of rock and not gas. The filtering process has reduced the likely candidates to a few."

"There is of course the question of distance, Isobel. How far from the Earth is the closest exoplanet?"

"Thanks for asking. Today, this is the single most challenging issue. The closest exoplanet is at least four light years away from our solar system. That's already a huge distance."

"But is it suitable for human life?"

"Unfortunately, signs are this particular one isn't."

"So how do we find one that is?"

"Many of the worldwide observatories and agencies have been trying to locate a suitable planet for decades. For our team, it's an attractive aspect of this first challenge. They're doing the work for us. One good example is India. Surprisingly, India has made enormous progress in the space research field over the past twenty years. Bengaluru is the center of its high-tech industry. The Indian Space Research Organization is now capable of handling complex space missions. My suggestion is that we now consult with Professor Kumar Alkim. He's an exoplanet expert at this newly built Bangalore Convention Center. Professor Kumar Alkim has a brilliant mind, the best in his field, but he's a bit of an eccentric and an occasional joker, I believe."

———

Professor Alkim introduced himself to the team as they arrived. Dressed very casually with a shirt decorated in colorful planets and bright yellow stars, he started his introduction in a serious tone.

"My task is to coordinate the findings of several space-based monitoring observatories. The James Webb Space Telescope—JWST—is currently analyzing the atmospheres of several known exoplanets and will determine whether they are capable of sustaining life as we know it. JWST has been designed to detect whether ozone molecules are present in the atmosphere of a planet. This is a sign oxygen and possibly water may also be present. It can detect water in the infrared band, and hopefully that will be on a rocky planet. Other vehicles such as PLATO and E-ELT will complement its results by probing its atmosphere. I feel confident we will find a suitable candidate soon. It's just a matter of time and, as Albert Einstein would add... space."

He paused for effect. Nobody seemed to catch his drift. His mouth twitched. "Matter, time, space... Einstein." He laughed at his own play on words.

The team members stared at him, their brows furrowed, clearly not understanding his joke.

He continued, "More seriously, we will let you know as soon as we have confirmation that a suitable planet has passed all the selection criteria. Sounds like a job application, doesn't it?" Again, he laughed to himself. "My understanding is that depending on its discovery, an international engineering team will go ahead with the design of a probe to further analyze its characteristics. The plans of the spacecraft are already in place and its construction will start as soon as I'm able to give them the green... or blue... or red light."

Once more he laughed awkwardly, and this time got some smiles from the team.

"Okay, okay, that's it from me," he concluded nervously. "Thank you. Thank you." He left the conference room with a huge smile, waving expansively.

Dan remarked softly, "I think he's already on another planet."

From Bengaluru, the team flew to Chennai for Zara's wedding.

Dan looked up at the large, elegant white house. Melanie and the others had headed over to the gardens for the pre-wedding buffet and celebrations, but he had something he needed to do first. He rang the doorbell. He could hear a lot of noise inside. A small, elderly Indian woman opened the door.

"Are you Zara's mother?" he asked. She didn't react to the question. He assumed she didn't understand it, but she gestured him in. Dan bowed respectfully and was immediately hit with an overload of people, colors, noises, and smells. There must have been twenty people in the front room alone. There was a group of young women painting their hands with henna, small children playing with blocks on the ground, and several waiters carrying trays of samosas out the side door. None of them were paying any attention to him. The small woman had disappeared into the throng.

Dan had texted Zara that morning saying he wanted to pop in before the wedding, but he couldn't see her anywhere. He walked further in. Two young men passed him as though he wasn't there, speaking in Hindi.

"Ah excuse me..."

They ignored his attempt to connect and walked out the front door. A bit bewildered by the fact that no one was attempting to help him, Dan kept heading through the house, passing more and more people. He finally reached the kitchen, where an assortment of colorful Indian sweets was being prepared.

He spotted several that he recognized from his last trip: Balushahi (Indian donuts), Gulab Jamun (fried milk balls), and his favorite, Kulfi (cardamom ice cream). He felt some pride that he was able to put a name to them and at the same time, his mouth watered at seeing them. This was going to be a well-catered wedding.

"Hello, hello." Finally, somebody was acknowledging his presence. He looked up and noticed a tall, stylish Indian woman wearing a deep burgundy and gold sari with a bindi on her head. She wore large gold earrings and was a carbon copy of Zara with a few decades added on. The resemblance was uncanny.

She perused him from head to toe, sizing him up, before asking in impeccable English with a slight British accent, "You must be Professor Robson."

"Yes, I am." He knew straight away who was talking to him.

"I am Meera, Zara's mother. It's wonderful to finally meet you, Professor Robson. Zara always speaks about you with great respect."

"Thank you. It's great to meet you as well."

She waved her hands around expansively. "Welcome to my house. Sorry for all the noise and chaos, but Indian weddings preparations are always frantic like this."

"Most pre-wedding activities are."

"Zara is my youngest child." With a wink, she confided, "We thought she'd never get married. I suppose you want to see her before the ceremony. It's all right. I know you Anglo-Saxons have reservations about that, but in Indian custom, it's not a major issue. I prefer not to see or talk to her as per our family tradition. She is upstairs. Take these stairs at the back there, then it's the third door on the right."

"Oh great, thank you." He hurried upstairs, leaving the noise behind but entering a new type of squeals and giggles and high-pitched chatter. *Third door, third door on the right.* He knocked on the door. Another woman, shorter this time, opened the door.

"You must be Professor Robson. Mami texted me you were on your way up. Come in, come in."

He walked in and was struck by the scents of perfume, incense, and flowers. He estimated there were another fifteen women in the room. Some small girls were getting into stockings, some doing makeup in front of mirrors. Loud Indian music was being played through the room. They all appeared extremely excited for their little Zara. She was at long last getting married.

"Aieeee, I love this song," a woman squealed.

Another woman introduced herself quickly. "I am Aesha, Zara's second sister," and ushered him through the chaos.

"Oh, she has two sisters?"

"No, no! I am number two. There are six of us." She pointed them around the room.

"This explains the number of dresses," Dan exclaimed.

She brought him to a large white chair where an older woman was carefully doing makeup. "Here she is."

Zara was sitting in the chair with her back to him. He knew it was her as he could spot her colorful braids, this time with gold and white ribbons woven on her head, interspersed with white orchids.

Aesha tapped her on the back. "Zara, your friend Professor Robson is here."

Zara turned around in her chair. "Dan!" She laughed. She was wearing a gold dressing gown with the word "bride" emblazoned on her chest. He looked at her in awe. She looked so different, so glamorous. She saw his hesitation, leapt up, and gave him a long hug. Cheers went around the room.

"Aiiieee, your makeup," yelled the older woman, berating her.

"Sorry, Maasi."

"Welcome to my wedding, Dan," Zara said, her eyes sparking.

"Yes, well, it's certainly something." The number of dresses in the room seemed to be closing in on him. Was it possible to drown in dresses?

"Please come here, Dan!" She drew him toward the balcony, but the older woman yelled after her, "Five minutes only, Zara. We've got to get your makeup on."

"Yes, yes, Maasi."

The warm breeze on the balcony helped to clear his head. They sat on two wicker chairs that were positioned to the right of the door. The grounds were teeming with wait staff ushering food to large tents. He gestured to the throng of people near the frangipanis.

"Major event!" Zara beamed at him. "Yes, we have invited more than two hundred guests. I'm so glad you could come."

"I am too, and so is Melanie. Sandy and Isobel are down there somewhere as well."

"Isobel came? I have to say I'm surprised. She's barely spoken to me since the incident."

"She's not an extrovert like you are." He wiggled his eyebrows. "I'm not always great at reading situations, but I think she has come as Sandy's date."

"Nooooooo." Zara laughed. "So, it *was* flirting on the plane?"

He grinned widely. Then his tone changed.

"Zara, you lost your ruby necklace in the... um, incident."

"Yes, my great-grandmother's necklace." Her face fell.

He searched for something in his pockets. "I had something made for you. It's not the same, but..." He passed her a jewelry box. Eyes sparking with anticipation, she opened it. It contained another ruby pendant with a triple row of red gemstones. She looked up at him in awe. "Dan, it's stunning."

"I wanted you to have it, Zara, I was so—"

She shook her head resolutely. "Dan, you've apologized so many times. It wasn't your fault. It happened and because of it, I have found a man I truly love, and dozens of Indian women are happy for me."

He smiled. "Yes, but you're not—"

"It's fine, Dan. I don't know if you have heard, but I've been made Chairperson of the Bengal Tigers' protection task force." She grinned proudly. "I overlook the management of more than thirty reserves all over India. Shah is a great help to combat poaching with his military experience. There's plenty of work for both of us and we share a common goal. It's not as meaningful as Project Legacy, but I'll still be contributing to preserving an endangered species. Every life is precious, even if it's only on a smaller scale." She gave him a reassuring smile. "Don't worry about me, Dan. I'm happy."

"I can see that. I'm so pleased for you, Zara."

"I need to get ready now, sorry." She walked over to the door. His throat began to tighten at the thought of going back into the chaos of the house. Watching him, she threw her head back and laughed. "Don't worry, Dan. There's another exit at the end of the balcony, which goes straight down to the gardens. You can escape down there."

He gave her a thumb-up, relieved. "That's much better. See you at the ceremony."

———

As Dan made his way to meet the others, he took his time wandering through the gardens of the large estate. The scent of frangipani filled the air. It had been an eternity since he'd literally taken the time to stop and smell the flowers. He had been so absorbed by his work. Now, he breathed deeply and took in all in the beauty of the rose garden beds, the sounds of the Indian instruments, the colorful clothing of the guests, and the pleasing atmosphere.

He realized he had been carrying the fate of humanity on his shoulders for too long and tried to reason himself. *Maybe my vision is too pessimistic? Some things will be saved, surely. Some species will be preserved until the time is right for them to emerge again.* He knew that his group was on the right mission. They had to save this beautiful world in some form somewhere. If the team could just salvage the basic building blocks of it, all the time and energy they were spending trying to find a solution to the unfolding catastrophe would be worthwhile.

The sound of laughter snapped him out of his reflections. He kept walking toward the growing crowd of people. Next to the wedding tent, he passed by a pond with new blue lotus blooms emerging on the surface. Colorful water birds were swimming and feeding.

In the lawn, next to the pond, multiple rows of white and gold chairs were quickly filling up with guests. The altar at the front looked spectacular, with a large pink and gold canopy held up by four pillars. The front was adorned with eight bunches of red roses, pink lilies, and two golden thrones. Zara had said it was going to be a combination of a classic Indian wedding with modern elements, and the venue was stunning.

He recognized his group seated toward the front. Melanie wore a long silver dress with her hair held up with tiny crystal pins. As he approached, she patted the seat next to hers for him to squeeze past. He shook Sandy's hand and gave Isobel a kiss on the cheek. She blushed slightly but looked pleased.

Sandy turned in his seat. "I love a good wedding, particularly one with great food!" He wiggled his eyebrows excitedly. Dan laughed.

Melanie shushed them. "Sssh! I think it's about to start and..." Her voice rose in pitch. "Oh, wow!"

In the distance, they caught sight of Captain Shah riding a white horse decked out in red and gold brocade, slowly making his way toward the assembly. Dan was impressed. This was certainly fancier than the weddings they were used to.

As he came closer, Captain Shah was the epitome of an Indian prince, dressed in a long white coat emblazoned with gold sequins over a white traditional suit. He was wearing a red turban braided with gold and adorned with a large ruby in the center. Showing his army training background, his posture was impeccable—his back and shoulders straight—as he rode toward them. A group of his friends and family began dancing and singing in a large circle, celebrating his arrival.

He dismounted, then escorted by his mother and father, he came down the red carpeted aisle toward the front. There, he bowed and greeted the priest.

Isobel exclaimed, "Whoa."

"It's the stuff of fairy tales, isn't it?" Sandy remarked.

The musicians increased their tempo, led by the rhythm of a two-headed hand drum.

Dan turned and saw Zara arriving with her female friends, singing loudly.

Melanie exclaimed, "Wow! She looks stunning in that sari."

Dan nodded. Zara was indeed dazzling, so different from the quiet, professional woman he knew. She wore an elegant white and gold sari with large pearl earrings and a necklace of rubies. Her hands were covered with henna and there seemed to be an endless row of golden bracelets on both her arms. She was escorted by her mother, who Dan had met in the kitchen, and her father, the doctor—a tall, imposing man with a trimmed beard.

Zara was all smiles as she walked down the aisle. Dan

caught her eye on the way past, and she winked at him before joining Captain Shah. First, he bowed to her parents, giving them flower garlands. Then he escorted Zara to the golden thrones in front of the altar, where they exchanged white flower garlands.

Then the priest lit a fire in front of them.

Sandy leaned over and whispered, "That's the *agni*. It symbolizes the witness of the divine. Any commitments made in front of it are made in the presence of God."

As usual, Sandy has done his homework, Dan thought.

Dan whispered to Melanie, "Do you remember when we lit a candle together at our wedding?" Melanie squeezed his hand and kissed his cheek.

He smiled. "I love you too."

The next part of the ceremony was celebrated in Hindi, and Dan found it difficult to follow, but he understood that her parents were "giving her away" to Captain Shah. He knew Zara had always been respectful of her parents. Dan watched as Zara and Captain Shah joined hands and circled around the fire seven times.

Sandy whispered again, "They are circling around the four pillars to a happy life."

He pointed to the pillars holding up the canopy on the altar. "The pillars represent duty to each other; family and God; prosperity, energy and passion; and finally, salvation."

"That's so meaningful," Melanie murmured.

Suddenly, as a further surprise, Zara and Captain Shah stopped circling and raced back to their seats. Zara arrived back in her seat first, and the audience cheered. She picked up her sari and showed a pair of shoes to the guests. Dan recognized them as her favorite Adidas green pumps made from recycled ocean plastic.

"What's going on?" Dan exclaimed, totally baffled.

Sandy leaned over. "Zara won. I knew she would. It is believed that whoever is the fastest to sit will hold the dominance in the marriage."

Dan's mouth twitched. "That sounds about right."

Then Zara and Captain Shah rose from their seats and began to take large steps, seven in total. Sandy explained, "Each step represents a sacred vow the couple will make, symbolizing a happy, faithful, and prosperous life."

Finally, Captain Shah began to apply a red powder to the center of Zara's forehead and tied a black and gold beaded necklace around her neck.

Melanie whispered to Dan, "Don't get any ideas about helping me with my makeup." He stifled a laugh.

Sandy murmured, "It symbolizes her new status as a married woman and his vow to always protect her."

"That's super sweet. I love that," Melanie said.

The priest then raised his hands over them, and a big cheer went out across the rows. Captain Shah leant over and kissed Zara. This caused laughter among the crowd.

"They are now married," Sandy said.

The four of them stood up and applauded loudly.

At the completion of the marriage ceremony, they and the rest of the guests filed out and headed to the tent, which was now adorned with even more flowers and red, white, and gold decorations. Dan's stomach rumbled. He hadn't eaten since early in the morning, and he was starving.

A massive buffet had been laid out along the far wall with a variety of curries, naan, many different types of biryanis, and a whole separate table for cakes and desserts.

Zara had organized the seating with consideration for the interests of the guests.

The four of them sat at the same table with several of the Indian scientists they'd met during their previous visits. Dan couldn't believe his eyes: as Isobel settled into her seat, she had also brought out her holoscreen on the table. Together with Professor Kumar Alkim and Dr. Krishnan, she spent most of the evening talking about the latest details of newly discovered planets, inputting mathematical formulas, calculating launching orbits, and the feasibility of an exploratory mission.

After the opening of the bridal waltz, Sandy invited Isobel to the dance floor and the two of them proved to be the perfect dancing partners: waltz, foxtrot, cha-cha-cha, tango, modern; you name it, they knew the steps as if they'd danced them many times together. They were even improvising to Indian traditional music.

Natural partners, Dan thought, amused.

Suddenly, he was reconciled with the world. *This is the best that human life has to offer: celebrating the love of two friends, enjoying delicious food, and sharing meaningful conversation in interesting company. Surely, this is as good as it gets.*

He invited Melanie for a few twirls as well and told her, "I'm so lucky to share my life with a beautiful, intelligent woman."

At the end of the dance, she whispered to him, "Ready for our performance?"

They walked to the stage. Dan asked to be given a microphone.

He announced to the audience, "Zara, Captain Shah, my wife and I would like to make a little contribution to this wonderful wedding."

To everybody's delight, they sang the famous duet "Endless Love" and, as a further surprise, a few verses in Hindi of a well-known Indian wedding song.

Toward the end of the evening, Captain Shah and Zara came up to the table. Sandy and the captain had a lengthy discussion and Dan saw them exchanging numbers.

Melanie spoke extensively with Zara as well. When the time came for the bride and groom to say their farewells, Melanie hugged Zara. Dan could see tears in their eyes.

As the new couple was leaving, Dan heard Isobel telling Zara sternly, "No more than two kids, all right?"

Melanie laughed when Dan told her what he'd overheard.

On the way back to their hired car, she reflected out loud, "I'm so happy for her. It's important to have the right companion to travel the journey of life."

"He certainly appears to be Mr. Right."

Melanie smiled, bemused. "As long as he's not Mr. ALWAYS Right, Dan."

He feigned indignation. "Hey! Why are you looking at me like that?"

They laughed.

"We'd better get a good night's sleep, honey. Sandy has scheduled an important meeting tomorrow to discuss the future of the project. I'll have to prove I can earn my keep.

KÖLN, GERMANY

Isobel, Dan, Melanie, Sandy, and William Wei were picked up at the Cologne-Bonn Airport by Beatrix Van Hamelen, the Director of the moon project in Cologne.

Isobel embraced Beatrix. "You know Sandy and you remember Dan, don't you?"

"Of course I do." She shook hands with Sandy and hugged Dan. "I'm so pleased to see you again, big man."

Then Sandy introduced William Wei.

"All right. Let's drive you to my office at the Luna facility, which is part of the European Space Agency. The building is right behind the airport, but I must go the long way, unfortunately. We had torrential rains last week, which caused a lot of damage to some of the roads. I'll keep you up to date with the moon project."

———

The Lunar Mission Center—shortened to LUNA—hosted the operations for the moon resources exploration and extraction for the European Space Agency (ESA). Beatrix was the current director.

"Now Dan, what do you know about Helium-3?" she asked.

"I understand it's very rare here on Earth, Beatrix. Although emitted in big quantities by the sun, our atmosphere prevents it from reaching us. The lunar soil, in contrast, has been absorbing this gas for millions of years. It's plentiful on the moon."

She smiled at him warmly. "Brilliant. You should come and work with me. We've estimated there is around one billion tons on the lunar surface. The extraction of Helium-3 is a relatively simple process. It can be released by heating the lunar soil to around 600 degrees. But it's been an expensive undertaking to get the miners and their equipment to the lunar surface and provide them with accommodation."

"How did you achieve it, technically?" Sandy asked.

"We modeled our construction on what we saw in Flagstaff. We started by installing inflatable domes and covered them with 3D-printed layers using lunar volcanic rock minerals, and finally, we protected them with a two-meter layer of soil. We've kept a crew of engineers on the lunar surface—around thirty people—in these purposely built lunar modules. They have been sourced mainly from India and Japan, with a few Europeans and Americans. The current team has been rostered for two years. They have another twelve months to serve. Then they'll be replaced. As you would expect, they hardly leave their shelters—"

Isobel interrupted, "The radiation?"

"Exactly. We monitor the danger of cosmic rays. Their health and safety are paramount, of course. There's also a high risk of bone density loss due to the weaker gravity. Most of the operations are activated by remote control from the domes. The vehicles and machinery used for extracting the Helium-3 are also operated robotically. The regolith processing finally reached the production stage six months ago."

Isobel gave further details. "A spaceship would require a large amount of Helium-3 to fuel it on its journey to an exoplanet. Most of it would be spent to create the initial energy burst needed. The prime acceleration will propel the vehicle to its required interstellar cruising velocity. Tell me, Beatrix, how long will it take to produce a suitable quantity?"

"We estimate another five to ten years to process enough Helium-3 for our purposes. One of the advantages is that there's no requirement to transport the final product back to Earth in this present phase. That'll save a lot of time. It will be stockpiled in situ in purpose-built containers, which can then be transferred later to a space probe by specialized shuttles after the vehicle has been towed in orbit around the moon."

Beatrix gathered them around her. "Please, follow me. Let's go to the Control Center. We have a constant feed on a large screen, I can show you what's happening in direct time."

———

Beatrix swiped her security card, and they entered the Control Center. It was a large room with around thirty personnel busy at their individual consoles.

"Okay, here we are. Please bring your seats in around me.

The chief mining engineer is online right now. I'll introduce you. By the way, there's a three- to four-second communication gap between conversations. Take your time when you speak... and the sound can fade at any time... ready? Isobel?"

"Yes."

After an initial delay, the picture of a middle-aged Indian man appeared on the screen with some interference noise in the background.

"Hi Prakash, this is Beatrix. My guest today is—"

"I know. Professor Löfgren."

Isobel furrowed her brow. "Have I met you before?"

"Yes. You probably don't remember me. I was introduced to you a few years ago in Chennai."

"One second... at the Indian Space Agency in Sriharikota? The launch of the Chandrayaan probe, right."

"Correct. You have an excellent memory, Professor. I'm the nephew of Dr. Krishnan, the director of the Space Agency."

"Rocket Man!"

They both laughed.

"So, what type of work are you involved with, Prakash?"

"I specialize in the development of mining methods, rock formation mapping and storage... and analysis of soil samples... and telerobotic vehicular activity. There's plenty to do, Professor Löfgren."

"Please call me Isobel, and this is Sandy and Dan."

"Hi, Sandy."

"*Kaalai Vanakkam, Prakash. Eppadi irukkindriirgal.*"

"Oh, you speak Tamil?"

"I watch documentaries about Indian space exploration."

"That's more than I do!"

They all laughed again.

Isobel asked, "More seriously, Prakash, what is life like where you are?"

Prakash took his time, seemingly hesitant about what to answer. "Uh... Interesting technically, but lonely and claustrophobic, Isobel. The landscape is featureless. No trees, no animals. No fresh air, no smell. I'm basically confined to a computer room. My bedroom is nearby. To tell you the truth, I can't wait to go back to Earth."

Beatrix leaned in, listening closely. "I can see that."

"Yes. It's getting to me." Prakash scrubbed his hand over his face. "Talking to someone I met in India brought this sudden nostalgia."

Isobel's expression softened. "I'm sorry."

To their surprise, Prakash started to sob. "I find it difficult to go on every day, sorry... sorry."

Beatrix intervened again. "Would you like me to bring you back to Earth earlier, Prakash?"

He nodded, wiping his face. "Yes. Yes, please."

Beatrix whispered to Isobel and Dan, "Quick, say something, but not goodbye."

Isobel complied. "Nice to talk to you again, Prakash. Keep safe."

Dan added, "Courage, Prakash," and Sandy said, "Good luck, my friend."

Beatrix concluded the conversation. "I'll work something out, Prakash. Don't worry. I'll talk to you again soon."

She turned the live feed off. They were all shocked by what they'd witnessed.

"Let's go and grab some coffee downstairs, everyone. "They serve a fabulous apple strudel with fresh cream."

———

As they were enjoying their coffee break, Beatrix reviewed the live feed event. "That didn't go as expected. I'm sorry. Prakash is the third moon astronaut to react like this in the past few months. Something must have triggered—"

Isobel suggested, "Do you think that a two-year stay is too long?"

"You've just summed up the problem, Isobel. When we started, we originally suggested a two-year crew rotation, but we've had problems with adaptation. We thought they could progressively get used to the lunar environment. This is not an isolated incident. I can see it's not working well for some, especially the scientists. At a later stage, a long stay would bring more mental stress for the astronauts."

"There is a big issue at stake here, Beatrix."

"I'm aware of what you're going to say, Isobel. The permanency of a human settlement on the moon is now in question."

"Let's face it, Beatrix. The moon is such a hostile environment. There's no breathable atmosphere, no vegetation, nothing like what they've experienced on Earth. It's a totally alien world. We can transport people to the moon, house them in safe accommodations, and build all the necessary support systems—but we can't alter the human mind element. I think for the present time, we should only contemplate a stay on the lunar surface from an energy supply point of view. The moon is not going to be a second home for humanity, I'm afraid."

"You're right, Isobel. The moon should only be considered as a refueling base and an observation post. Not as a place for a permanent human colony. However, as far as your group is concerned, the 'Lunar Ark backup plan' is making progress. A lava tube has been selected for that purpose in the 'Sea of Tranquility.' It measures around fifty meters in diameter. The lava tube will give better protection from radiation and meteorite strikes and will be a more suitable location to install cryogenic modules. Priority has been given to the storage of human DNA."

Isobel clarified, "Eventually, all buildings, including human habitats, will be in lava tubes. They just require complex excavation work after they've been assessed by lidar scanning. We need to get this right before we can even contemplate sending astronauts to Mars. It's a hell of a long journey—six to seven months just to get there, compared to three to four days to go to the moon."

Isobel turned toward William Wei, who was sitting next to her. "I hope these problems aren't going to compromise the future of a settlement on Mars. What's the latest with the red planet project, William?"

"We're making progress, Isobel. I believe Mars is a better place for a longer-term settlement. Our company has now perfected the technology of reusable boosters. It allowed us to land our spacecraft 'Eagle 10' on the Martian surface and use it again to return to Earth."

"That's a major breakthrough."

"Indeed. Control of the spacecraft trajectory and all the onboard subsystems have been thoroughly tested several times. At present, we're still sending a variety of robots, but we've also started to build the components of our first Martian base in the Jezero crater. It's not a one-way ticket anymore, but it will take a while before we send a human crew there. As you indicated, we can only launch a mission every twenty-six months when the Earth and Mars are aligned in a way that allows the most energy-efficient voyage. We must be methodical and patient. Any mishap would set us back decades. You know how cautious the various space agencies are. So, sending humans to Mars won't happen in my lifetime unfortunately, but I'm sure my son Walter will witness it."

"You'll live to see it, William. You're still young."

"Thanks, Isobel. I hope so. I've spent a lot of time and money to achieve this ambition. I hope these problems with adapting to the moon don't compromise the future of a settlement on Mars. The red planet is definitively a better place for a longer-term human settlement. We'll obviously have to terraform some regions by planetary engineering to conform the existing climate to our requirements."

BALTIMORE, MARYLAND, U.S.A.

The Webb Science and Operation Center, a world class scientific research center located in Baltimore, U.S.A, is dedicated to the analysis of the data generated by the James Webb Space Telescope scanning program. Isobel had contacted them, flown back to the States, and asked for their help with a key part of the project.

It was 10:00 a.m. and Professor Kumar Alkim and Isobel were analyzing the latest data, which had been transmitted to Earth by Webb. The signals had been received a week earlier through large radio antennas that formed part of the NASA Deep Space Network, one of them being at the Canberra station. Most of the information had been relayed to Baltimore by dedicated optic fiber lines. Then the processing had been calculated by conventional super-computers.

Suddenly, Kumar pointed at his screen. "Look! Look!" he shouted frantically.

Isobel rushed over to him to peer at the pictures on his monitor, mesmerized. She gasped and pumped her fist in the air, "Yes, yes, yes!"

Kumar jumped up and started singing a famous Bollywood tune, "Chabba, Chabba," grabbing Isobel and dancing energetically in pure exuberance until they both collapsed on their chairs.

They had just discovered not one, but two exoplanets that

ticked all the right boxes. All of them showed traces of liquid water, which was key to mankind's survival.

Isobel took several calming breaths. "We've got to call Melanie."

She brought up her holo. "Melanie, it's Isobel... we've found it! Yes, we've found the right planet. Sure. I'm positive. Kumar concurs."

Still half singing, he danced in front of the holoscreen "We've found it.'

Isobel was now recovering from the excitement. "Melanie, we've found not one but two planets, both with liquid water around the Epsilon star in the constellation of Eridanus.

"I have heard of it. One of the first stars examined for signs of intelligent life, I believe."

"Correct. The star has been observed by humans for more than three thousand years. I'm very familiar with the constellation. I presented my Ph.D. thesis on Eridanus. Historically, it takes its name from the original Babylonian constellation known as 'the Stars of Eridu.' Eridu was an ancient city in the extreme south of Babylonia whose main river was held sacred in their culture as being the world's freshwater reservoir below the Earth's surface."

Kumar jumped in the conversation with further technical details. "Melanie, Eridanus is a G class star with the right mass and luminosity. A rocky planet in its midlife cycle, very stable, similar to our own solar system... the position is right too: About 10.3 light years from the Earth. Its atmosphere is composed mainly of hydrogen and helium. This time, the specialized detectors on the James Webb telescope have been able to eliminate a lot of background noise in the radial velocity of Epsilon. Aegir, the largest planet of the system, similar in size to Jupiter, was hiding these two smaller ones.

Oh my God, I can't believe our luck. Not one but two planets that fit our criteria!"

Sandy, who was standing near Melanie, asked the important question, "Are these two exoplanets suitable for human habitation?"

Isobel confirmed they were. "They fit all the criteria of the Similarity Index, no question. Both rocky planets, within the habitable zone, and comparable in size and mass. The data show that all the necessary ingredients are present: water, oxygen, nitrogen, carbon dioxide, and methane."

"Which one is the better prospect?"

Kumar intervened to give the answer. "Probably the third planet in the system, Sandy. It's at an ideal location: 100 million kilometers from Epsilon. It also shows the right mass. Very similar to our own Earth."

Melanie beamed. "Great work, guys. Is it reachable?"

"It's ten light years away," Kamar said. "That isn't far in astronomical terms, but it will require a new type of vehicle to reach it." Then he gave her additional data. "This planet is around 85 percent of the mass of Earth. It completes its orbit every two hundred and fifty Earth days and according to our calculations, it would receive about 75 percent of the stellar energy we get from the sun."

Isobel piped in as well, "We'll run further double-blind tests and ask other telescopes around the world to confirm our findings. Then we can go ahead with the project."

Kumar appeared confident. "From now on, I think that we should focus entirely on this specific planet. There is no need to search any further, in my opinion. We'll put a full report together in the next few weeks with all the available data."

Sandy clenched his fist in a congratulatory gesture. "Well done, team. You'll be remembered in the history of astrophysics. Cigars and champagne on me. What should we call the planet?"

Dan, who'd been quiet on the call, lit up. "What about Thera, the sister of Earth?"

Isobel was pleased right away. "I like it. I'll check the name with the International Astronomical Union. Leave it with me, Dan."

Kumar, still quivering in excitement, closed the holo, did a few more steps of his Bollywood dance, clicked his fingers in the air, and roared, "Unbeee... lievable!"

CHAPTER 8
YEAR 2043—MOSCOW, RUSSIA

As they were driven from the Alexander Pushkin International Airport to the city of Moscow, Melanie gasped at the extensive damage caused by a recent severe thunderstorm in the region two days earlier. The destruction was widespread.

She pointed it out to Dan. "Do you see? All these trees have been toppled and there… most of the electrical cables have been severed." She wondered what weather event had been so powerful to cause such damage.

Dan peered over her. "Absolutely devastating. The news on the plane reported strong winds in excess of 150 kilometers an hour hitting Moscow a couple of days ago. Their Bureau of Meteorology has described these storms as exceptional. Apparently, they've caused extensive structural damage to buildings, including some parts of the Kremlin."

———

As the car approached the main building of *Zvezdny Gorodok* (Star City), they slowed to a virtual snail's pace to navigate through multiple units of emergency workers in bright orange protective gear, clearing up the debris strewn around.

A low-lying, beige building appeared: the Yuri Gagarin Cosmonaut Training Center.

They were welcomed by a tall, strongly built Russian Air Force officer with white hair, who introduced himself in a measured Slavic accent, "I am General Alexei Titov, Director of Roscosmos. I am aeronautical engineer in charge of construction of new Space Explorer. It is great pleasure to welcome you to Star City Center. This Center named to honor Comrade Yuri Gagarin, the first man ever to go in space in 1961. He brings everlasting glory to our nation."

Melanie laughed to herself. *This is going to be an interesting meeting. So much formality.* She recalled Gagarin had been selected because of his height. He was only five foot two inches tall. Anyone taller wouldn't have been able to fit in the capsule. Perhaps she should share that detail with her guides. No, she needed to maintain a respectful attitude.

———

General Titov invited them to a conference room.

As they entered, Melanie noticed a memory plaque on the door written both in Russian and English. It read, "Yuri Gagarin's Flight Briefing Room."

The building itself hadn't changed since its original construction. Historically significant for the achievements of Russia's space discovery, it also reflected the construction style of the former Soviet Union architecture.

William Wei was already seated at the table. They went over and shook hands with him. William moved around the table and kissed Isobel, then declared to the group, "Nice to see you all again." Melanie noticed Dan's eyebrows rising. She knew he wasn't William's biggest fan and had spent several conversations with Isobel discussing how the project's values would be compromised by the intervention of big money.

As they settled around the table, Melanie referred to her notes and then opened the discussion. "General, can we start by reviewing the role of International Space Station 2?"

"*Da.* Good idea. ISS2 has been joint venture now between Russia and US components built by many countries. We also send crew members from many nations to operate station. Successful cooperation between us. This is good."

"I understand it will be used as a technical model for the new deep-space exploration vehicle Explorer 1, General?"

"Correct, Mrs. Robson. Like ISS2, many countries will construct new vehicle in low Earth orbit. We will build Explorer 1 during extra-vehicular activities, module by module."

"How many trips will be necessary, General? Do you have a rough number in mind?" asked William with pen in hand, ready to write down the key figures.

"I think we need around five hundred trips over many years. We improve payload capability of Proton 4, Soyuz 3, and Angora rockets. Shuttles and rockets from America will also be used to assemble various modules. Other vehicles come from European, Canadian, Japanese, Chinese, and English aerospace centers to be used to deliver additional payloads. Most launched from our new Vostochny Cosmodrome on East Coast but also still from Baikonur and some international places."

"Could we inspect the Russian launching areas at some stage?"

General Titov hesitated. Melanie could tell he was calculating. They had been asking for months to visit Vostochny but to no avail. It had been Dan's idea to use William to ask the question as he was well invested in Russia and the Russians needed to keep the relationship productive.

The general finally accepted. "I can arrange visits to Baikonur, no problem, but Vostochny still security area. More difficult. You can only visit launching areas for heavy lifting rockets."

Eyeing his advisors, General Titov carefully asked William Wei, "America to speed up production of Shuttle 3 model, yes, Mr. Wei?"

Surprisingly, William answered him in his language, "*Da, General, pravil'nyy.*"

Melanie understood a few basic words of Russian herself to recognize what he was saying: *Yes, General, this is correct.* Melanie was impressed. William was proving to be a vital asset. He knew just how to appease the general. It had been his idea to hold off on Shuttle 3 to use it as a bargaining chip at the right time. They had been obliged to use the Russians as the lead builder on the Explorer 1 due to their role in the space station, but it had taken intense negotiation to even get to this part of the project development stage.

Turning now to the team members, William explained the current state of development. "My understanding is that the US currently has six fully operational Shuttle 3s. Another five are in various stages of construction or repair. We intend to subcontract some of the payload lifting using our own Eagle 5 rockets. They have proven to be very cost-effective, reusable, heavy lift launch vehicles."

Isobel added with a gleam in her eye, "These are the launchers William's group has recently developed."

Melanie put up her hand to get everyone's attention. "When the Explorer is fully assembled, how heavy will it be, General?"

"Two hundred tons, approximate. Size of large crude oil tanker."

Melanie had guessed this figure based on the elements going into the Explorer. However, Dan and Sandy's eyes widened at the news.

Noticing their reaction, General Titov continued with a laugh, "Don't worry. Probe will not look like petroleum carrier. Looks like this."

He got up and unveiled a scaled model on a large table. The prototype consisted of a series of six individual spheres interconnected by a central tubular passageway.

"Please, come and see."

They crowded around. The general explained, pointing at the different parts, "Front module, larger size, contains all guidance systems. Modules 2, 3, and 4 used for scientific measurements equipment. Second last is power plant. Then rear section is nuclear fusion propulsion system."

Melanie had seen several online simulations of this over the years, but it felt good to have a tangible, scaled model prototype right in front of them.

William winked. "The Explorer has been nicknamed 'The Skewer.' No surprise."

His comment brought laughter to the room. Melanie felt the earlier tension begin to dissipate. Yes, William was a key ally.

Isobel inspected the prototype with great attention. As they sat back with the model now carefully moved to the front of the room, she said, "What you must remember is that the probe doesn't need to be aerodynamic. It won't be exposed to air friction around the Earth, as it will be built 350 kilometers up there... outside the atmosphere. Then it will travel through the void of space for hundreds of years. When it finally reaches the new planet, it will be in a permanent orbit 300 kilometers above it. So, there won't be any friction there either."

Melanie elaborated further, "As discussed, General, I have suggested that most of the hardware components should be built here in Russia, and this will be outlined in the final proposal."

He smiled. "Good, Good. Our government will be pleased, *spasibo*."

She added. "China and India will be involved as well. The electronic support systems will be assembled in the US and Britain. The secondary exploration vehicles will be built by Japan and Korea. We're also calling for tenders from international ventures for the development of some of the specialized equipment to be used aboard the Explorer."

Isobel came to the next point. "Talking about the engine, researchers in Vancouver are still testing the efficiency of a new type of nuclear fusion-based engine. So far, the design and trials are proving, well... challenging."

General Titov interrupted, "This means... problems?"

Isobel swallowed, looking down for a second. "Let's face it, General, nuclear fusion is an incredibly complex challenge to solve.'

"That's the summary of our role with the Explorer at this stage," Melanie noted.

Isobel intervened swiftly ahead of her concluding remarks. "Before we complete this initial meeting, General Titov has requested we crunch a few numbers."

Melanie shifted in her chair. When had Isobel spoken to General Titov? She eyed the general, who also seemed strangely hesitant.

"I ask clarification about speed of space vehicle, but what does 'crunch' mean?"

Isobel paused for a while and smiled. "Sorry, General.

English expression. It means summarize complex calculations."

"Okay. Correct. I ask you about figures."

"I am pleased to oblige, General. Here are the numbers. With the current technology available, the fastest speed reached by liquid fuel rocket is still around 100,000 kilometers per hour. Agree?"

Melanie nodded along with the general's advisors.

Isobel continued, "This is with conventional propellants and after taking advantage of all the planetary slingshot accelerations. Fast…but nowhere enough for interstellar space travel. At this stage, we're aiming to design a vehicle which could reach—at least—1 percent–of the speed of light or approximately 10 million kilometers per hour. How does that compare with the current speed?"

She paused momentarily before answering her own question, "One hundred times faster. The planet we've discovered is located ten light years away. If we can increase the power of an engine with one hundred times more thrust and therefore speed, it'll still take a probe traveling at 1 percent of the speed of light a minimum of one thousand Earth years to reach its destination. This is in a straight acceleration mode. The vehicle needs to first accelerate then decelerate progressively, which adds a factor of two. So, we're looking at a minimum of two thousand Earth years of space travel for the probe. It will then take a few years to receive and process all the data transmitted by the Explorer. These are the numbers and the timing."

It dawned on Melanie why General Titov had gone directly to Isobel to get this information.

The general turned toward Isobel. "*If* we reach manned mission status, how can crew members survive journey of two thousand years?"

"A very important question indeed, General," said Isobel.

"At this stage, as we all know... we're working on an unmanned exploratory mission only, a probe. But I agree, eventually the problem you are referring to will need to be resolved."

Melanie eyed William and Sandy. They hadn't discussed how to approach this with the Russians. She had to step carefully. "Obviously, the issue hasn't escaped our attention, General, but right now it's a long way off. Isn't that right, Isobel?"

"Yes, yes, of course. It will be an unmanned vehicle."

Melanie continued, "By the time people get some feedback on whether this new planet is suitable, and that's two to three thousand years away, we feel confident the issues of manned long-distance travel for a human crew will have been satisfactorily resolved. Some researchers are already working on the problem. Right, Isobel?"

"That's correct. I've been told a team of French astrophysicists is investigating the possibility of a multi-generational project. This would involve astronauts raising successive families aboard the space vehicle. The main issues with that approach are the production of food for several centuries and the size of the spaceship to accommodate thousands of people."

General Titov endorsed her comment in his usual forthright manner. "*Da*. Our government has heard also."

CHAPTER 9
YEAR 2043—PARIS FRANCE

After their arrival in Paris, Sandy, Melanie, and Dan were contacted by the Deputy Mayor of Paris, Madame Francoise d'Orleans, who oversaw the environment and sustainable development of the city. Paris had adopted a "Climate Action Plan" together with several large cities in the world—known as "the C40 climate action group"—to reduce their carbon footprint to zero by 2050. The authorities of the world's leading cities, like Paris, were focused on fighting climate change in their own urban areas.

She invited them into her private apartment in the "Hotel de Ville," a striking neo-Renaissance edifice housing the City Hall, to give them details of the purpose of the plan. A dedicated environmentalist, she explained, "Paris has chosen to confront the main reason for climate change: the carbon-based economy. We've involved the local communities and businesses so they have a role in making Paris a more sustainable place to live. To date, by controlling emissions, we have already reduced our greenhouse gas levels by 50 percent since the implementation of the plan. Our aim is to reach a carbon neutral target by 2050 and to rely completely on renewable energy to power the city."

Dan queried, "I take it this includes urban planning and building codes?"

"Absolutely. Our suburb of Clichy-Batignolles is a good example of our biodiversity plan. It's the showpiece of our urbanization projects of the future. The area used to be a neglected railway yard, and we saw the opportunity to build a model for a sustainable agglomeration. It implements our objectives of energy-efficient buildings and renewable energy production together with the provision of green spaces and affordable housing. We have also reduced the use of cars by providing cheap, reliable public transport. We can visit the suburb this afternoon if you have time, Dan?"

"Sure, this sounds fascinating. You've piqued our interest."

Madame Francoise d'Orleans suggested, "Why don't we have brunch together first? I'll get some food brought in and we can talk more. After that, I'll give you a lift around Clichy-Batignolles in my all-electric Renault Zip2 van. I'll drive along the Seine, head toward Place de la Concorde, and show you the Palais de l'Elysée, the official residence of our president. When we arrive in Clichy, we can walk through Martin Luther King Park, which is a feature of the new suburb. Then I'll drop you back at your hotel. Where are you staying?"

"Aux Ducs d'Anjou."

"It's not far from here."

———

Back at the hotel after their tour of Clichy, they discussed their individual appointments for the next day. Sandy had a meeting with UN officials who were monitoring the achievements of the Paris Agreement. He explained, "Nation signatories are invited to participate in a transparency framework to verify the implementation of their initial commitments. The agreement stipulates that this assessment is crucial to the success of a pledge-and-review system. We need to evaluate the performance of the participating countries and monitor how well the various stages designed to lower emissions are working. As you're aware, the countries have been asked to submit progress reports every two years to demonstrate they're achieving their targets."

"And if they're not?" Melanie asked.

"We bring the technical experts in to review the reports. If some nations aren't reaching their targets, we provide them with technical or financial assistance. We also encourage them to be more ambitious going forward. One of the current issues is advanced nations switching to electric vehicles, then selling their old petrol models to third world countries at bargain prices."

"I see what you mean. It's just shifting CO_2 emissions from one part of the world to another."

"A far from ideal outcome. What about you, Dan? What do you have on your plate tomorrow?"

"Melanie and I are going to catch the TGV from Paris, Nord, to Lille, Europe, to visit a group of geneticists at the Institut Pasteur. The question of multi-generations for a future human settlement on the moon or Mars, or eventually on an exoplanet, needs to be investigated. If ultimately a spaceship needs to travel for a minimum of two thousand years, the matter of the crew's survival becomes critical. Under today's state of scientific knowledge, there is no tested solution for keeping a crew safe and alive for such a long period aboard an interstellar mission. We must address the issue to justify the purpose of Explorer 1."

"Is it feasible?"

"Different solutions have been proposed. Suspended animation is the most widely mentioned, but mainly in the realm of science fiction. As a biologist, I'm certainly not in favor of that option."

"What's the problem there, Dan?"

"Even when using the best-known methods, it's still impossible to preserve mature human beings under suspended animation and hope to wake them up fully functional after a long hibernation. It can't be done. Once thawed, the bodies will be clinically dead. The difficulties of recovering individuals from a frozen state are well documented. Massive tissue degeneration occurs upon thawing the bodies, especially at brain level. All neuroscientists agree that what makes the brain work is contained in its delicate anatomical structure. With the cryo-preservation process of a mature body, it's impossible to effectively preserve the synoptic circuitry of the brain and then restore it to a functioning state. Ergo, suspended animation is clearly unsuitable."

Melanie tilted her head. "Hon, what about all these people who have had their bodies frozen under cryogenic conditions expecting that the advance in health science in the next centuries will cure their illnesses?"

"Absolute waste of money!"

"Really?"

"The participants should ask these firms if they've woken a person or even an animal after cryogenic treatment and successfully brought them back to life. They haven't."

"Because it doesn't work. I see. Is there any other option?"

"A multi-generational crew has been suggested in some quarters. I've had a look at the theory of successive multiple generations living on board a spacecraft until they have arrived at their destination."

"What did you find out?"

"This option presents many challenges, the main one being how large would a spacecraft need to be to sustain such a crew for two thousand years? The provision of food and water, for example, is huge. At this stage, I don't believe there are any feasible solutions to guarantee their survival on such a long journey. The science is not there yet."

"So, what's left, Dan?" Sandy asked.

"I think the best option for preserving a human footprint is the storage of genetic material for delayed fertilization. IVF was developed many years ago and is a reliable technology used routinely with an extremely high success rate. It's improving all the time, providing the embryo is implanted back in a female body within a few days."

"Would it work in space? Like storing the embryos on a satellite or on the moon or Mars?"

"Cryo-preservation of human genetic material, either sperm and eggs or already fertilized embryos in an outer space environment, has already been tested by various agencies. The studies have shown there is no detectable damage when the cells are brought back to an ambient temperature under normal terrestrial gravity conditions."

Sandy exclaimed, "So what will happen, say in a few thousand years, assuming everybody on Earth is dead and the only remnants of the human species are some bits of preserved genetic material frozen in a container stored somewhere?"

"I'm not sure, Sandy. That's the reason I want to have a talk with the geneticists in Lille."

"I hope you can solve the problem, mate. What's the point of developing a multi-billion exploration project if humans are unable to reproduce somewhere in one form or another?"

"Exactly. As you said yourself, we need to investigate all

options, should Explorer 1 produce positive results. I feel confident that, in the future, scientists will find a solution to achieve the continuity of our species. Many labs are working on the issue. It's a question of getting a breakthrough, but I hope for humanity's sake that we don't run out of time."

LILLE, NORTHERN FRANCE

Melanie and Dan arrived on the TGV from Paris in the historic city of Lille at the northern tip of France near its border with Belgium.

They were welcomed at the Lille-Flanders train station by a chauffeur of the Institut Pasteur and driven to a nineteenth-century building. Melanie gazed in awe at its red brickwork and arched windows. The two symmetrical wings gave it the appearance of a French aristocratic palace.

The Institut Pasteur of Lille, under the former leadership of Professor Henry Dutrant de Montville, had consistently been rated one of the best in the world for its research in assisted reproduction and neonatal intensive care.

Professor Henry Dutrant, an old-fashioned aristocrat with gray hair and silver glasses, welcomed them. *"Bienvenue à Lille, Madame et Professeur Robson."*

"It is an honor to meet you, Monsieur Dutrant."

Melanie reached out to shake his hand, but instead he kissed the back of hers instead—the aristocratic *baise-main*.

He shook hands with Dan. Then he escorted them to his office decorated in Louis XVI furniture, renowned for its neoclassical straight and regular lines, and showed them to seats close to his own.

"I am delighted you contacted us. We believe a solution to long-term survival in space could be worked out from development in reproductive science conducted right here at the

Institut. I'm convinced some human cells... how can I put it... can potentially be stored in space for many years and brought back to life when required."

Melanie was paying rapt attention.

Professor Henry Dutrant leaned toward Dan and said in a low voice, "What I am going to tell you is highly confidential."

Dan was now almost whispering himself. "One of your colleagues at the Biomedical Center in Paris contacted us discreetly. She knew we were looking for a solution to our predicament to the survival of a crew on a space mission. Your name came up. She said you're the best-qualified person to talk to on this matter."

Henry Dutrant inclined his head, acknowledging the compliment. "*Merci,* Professeur Robson. I will do my best to help you."

Dutrant explained, "This is what we achieved here in Lille many years ago. Put it simply, some of our embryologists under my guidance managed to create human lives from conception to birth entirely under artificial methods. We developed the technique but at the time, it was... how do you say... kept under the wrap... in view of ethical and religious concerns. No one, except for the scientists involved in the project, knew about our experiment. We never published the results of our research."

Henry Dutrant touched Melanie's arm. "I tell you, madame, this is what our own team of reproductive physiologists achieved in the past. It all happened here in a restricted area of our Faculté de Médecine. I was involved with the project and much younger. Look at me now, gray hair and all," he said light-heartedly.

Melanie and Dan smiled at his self-denigration.

He continued, "Forty years ago, two embryos were nurtured in specially designed artificial wombs for nine months, right up to their full term. Now, this is the important point." He paused. "The embryos had been frozen for several years beforehand."

He became more animated, gesturing with his hands. "Then they were reawakened. We used a very precise thawing method. Afterward, they were transferred to artificial uteri... not implanted in a human womb. *Non, non.* All artificially nurtured in synthetic bio monitor bags."

He now took on a very reassuring tone, almost paternal. "The two children, they are now adults and doing well." Then he dropped the bombshell. "You will meet them later. They are my own sons, André and Michel."

Melanie and Dan were flabbergasted by his candid admission.

"Specialists from this university continue to monitor them. No problems," he said. "They are healthy. No sign of early degeneration. At the time, to avoid any concern, the children's births were registered as being from natural parents, my wife and myself. It all looked legitimate."

Dan pursed his lips at this last comment.

Professor Dutrant reassured him, "I can see the question in your eyes, Professeur Robson. Don't worry; the authorities had cleared it. We had received top level approval from the Ministère de l'Intérieur for our research. As you know, we are now restricted to keeping the embryos for no more than fourteen days unless special approval is given by the International Society for Stem Cell Research. This experience cannot be repeated any longer. This is how far our research is controlled these days."

He turned toward Dan. "Now, tell me, Professor Robson. Do you think this technique of ours could be useful for your project?" He smiled charmingly, with a twinkle in his eyes. It was obvious he already knew the answer to his question.

"In one word, Monsieur Dutrant, yes. Some aspects will. Should a larger human colony be envisaged on the moon or especially on Mars, our concern is that natural childbirth will be too demanding for the initial settlers. It would put female astronauts on hold, could be harmful to their health, and would require considerable medical resources like a fully operational maternity ward. All the information you've given us today is as an option for population growth, at some stage. But it's still a long way off and only one option our team is considering."

Dan asked Dutrant a technical question now, "Professor, when you started this procedure, why did you decide to progress with the fertilization first, then freeze the embryos after three days rather than freezing both male and female genetic material?"

Dutrant explained, "At the time, I reasoned that to be successful with the cryo-preservation of humans, it would be necessary to first initiate the fertilization, then give the cells sufficient impetus for their multiplication going forward. However, we had to freeze as little material as possible to avoid cellular deterioration. With that in mind, I conducted the research. I concluded optimum results would be obtained when the embryos were three days old at the morula stage. It is now the accepted, standard procedure for all IVF techniques. I have several diagrams with pictures of fertilized egg stages and statistical probability calculations of embryos maturing to full term. Just give me a second to pull them up."

Dan examined the computer screen with rapt interest.

Dutrant pointed to areas of the charts and pictures. "As you can see, here and here the tests show that when the cells have reached thirty-two divisions inside the egg, they bind firmly together in the process called compaction, as you know, before they start to differentiate significantly. This is the optimal condition for cryo-preservation. Can you see?"

Dan remarked, "Yes. It's very noticeable. Thank you. As you said, it's now standard practice. You and your team were the pioneers of embryology, Monsieur Dutrant. It's an absolute honor to speak with you."

"Do not mention it, monsieur," Dutrant said, placing his hand over his heart.

Melanie then asked him, "Now, Professor Dutrant, is it possible to see the artificial wombs you used for your experiment?"

"Unfortunately, the equipment has been removed from the research center due to the change in embryo legislation. Legally, it couldn't be used any longer, and we were ordered, discreetly mind you, to dismantle them. However, we have kept all the technical documentation. At the time, we had also developed a computerized program to copy the artificial gestation of the fetus in the womb during the nine-month cycle. You are welcome to access all this material."

"I'm grateful for your offer. I am aware synthetic wombs have added major developments in neonatal intensive care."

"Correct. They mimic the uterine environment of a human being. Being a sealed system, they prevent the risk of any external infection. In the latest modern version of this equipment, miniaturized pumps provide the constant exchange of amniotic fluid with a calculated amount of water and nutrients to the bloodstream. The oxygenator guarantees a sufficient, constant level of respiration. And stable blood pressure. I can provide you with some documentation on this as well."

"Thank you so much. We'll study your papers."

"Could you explain how you intend to use our expertise for your project, Professor and Madame Robson?"

Dan glanced at Melanie. She nodded. "Sure. Our intention

is to eventually collect genetic material here on Earth from various sources and grow the embryos up to a period of forty-eight to seventy-two hours like you have done. Once they've undergone the cryopreservation process, they will be saved in secure containers with liquid nitrogen under a temperature of minus 196 Celsius. These containers will then be stored and preserved in determined locations, such as in a vault on Earth or aboard a space station orbiting the Earth or on the moon, and at a later stage, on Mars. If, for instance, tests prove the environment can safely sustain the artificial creation of humans on Mars, the decision to go ahead with the conception of a new generation there could be made at an appropriate time."

Dan shrugged. "Of course, we wouldn't be able to justify the creation of humans if the conditions proved adverse."

"I understand. It would be a waste of human lives. Now, tell me Professor Robson, how can we be of assistance in the future?"

"Your research team could be vital to our project, Professor Dutrant. I'm sure you're aware the International Society of Stem Cell Research has relaxed its strict fourteen-day limitations. The question of growing human embryos beyond that period is now considered on a case-by-case basis. Our legal team has done comprehensive research on this complex issue. The Institute could try to obtain an exemption on the basis that the current fourteen-day prohibition applies to countries on Earth and that you're looking at the potential survival of a human colony outside a terrestrial environment?"

Dan paused for a second or two to gauge Dutrant's reaction. "That's where you could help us, Professor. Please, let us know if you could get a favorable answer from the International Society."

"*Bien sur*. My sons and their colleagues would be happy to

contribute to the project. It's a relatively simple technique. These days it's used extensively in agriculture for the reproduction of farm animals. Plenty of data is available to confirm its effectiveness. The question is how far our research can go with human embryos?"

"Precisely. We want to keep this project confidential, Professor Dutrant. Die-hard leaders of some countries would not be pleased with our intention to give birth artificially to humans outside the Earth. Several heads of conservative government and church leaders have already issued strong warnings to scientists not to contemplate such research. Our legal team has warned us that if our intentions were divulged, we could face withdrawal of funding for our project. In the case of the US, it would be disastrous. The new Secretary to the Office of Science and Technology has been anything but welcoming of any such proposal. So, we've issued a statement saying we aren't contemplating any research about artificial human conception in space ourselves... but you could, with your history of studies in this field."

"Monsieur, we are keen to contribute in any way we can. I am convinced this is the only way to protect humans from potential extinction in the future."

"I agree entirely with you, Professor. However, many politicians don't understand the Earth will become a contaminated place for mankind in the next few centuries. They still refuse to accept the reality of climate change and its frightful consequences for life on Earth."

Dutrant made a sound of mild disgust. "These politicians, they are the mouthpieces for influential vested interests. Fortunately, we aren't bound by political pressures or religious prejudices. We are better informed and can see the future ahead more clearly from a scientific viewpoint." He gripped Dan's arm firmly. "Try not to worry. Politicians come and go.

There will be a change of public opinion. Slowly but surely, people from all nations and beliefs will realize that humanity has a dangerous future ahead of it if it continues in this way."

"Our concern, Professor, is that it might be too late then. We're trying everything we can to inform the relevant authorities about the dangerous future ahead of humanity. A lot of them ignore our advice or, worse, refuse to acknowledge it."

They all fell silent for a moment. Then, Dutrant stood up slowly and smiled at Melanie and Dan. "Follow me, Monsieur and Madame Robson. Let me invite you to my favorite restaurant in Lille for lunch; *déjeuner*, as we say. Some of our scientists will meet us there, including my two sons. Let me tell you we French take our time to enjoy our food. We'll probably be there until late in the afternoon. It will be a working lunch, of course. There will be plenty to talk about. That means apéritif, entrée, main meal, dessert, and pousse-café. Let's not forget the cheeses. They are top quality in this region."

XICHANG PREFECTURE, SICHUAN PROVINCE, SOUTHWEST CHINA

China had become the largest space building industry in the world. Xichang was the launching facility of the long-range heavy lift rocket "Flying Dragon 3," and had been designated as one of the manufacturing centers for some of the Explorer 1 components.

Melanie had brought together an international team of scientists and lead engineers to the project scope meeting at the Chinese Aerospace Manufacturing Center. They were all experts in the technological challenges of interstellar travel.

She folded her arms and mock-frowned at the participants. "Best and brightest, right."

William Wei grinned. "Absolutely."

Melanie identified the fundamental requirements. "The probe needs to be built from scratch, ground up. It's an enormous technical challenge. Basically, it is the most complex technical space project mankind has ever attempted. We are now working on the premise that the vehicle must be capable of reaching a cruising velocity of around 1 percent of the speed of light on its journey to the Constellation of Eridanus. It needs to travel ten light years or approximately ten trillion kilometers. That's a long journey. Let's examine the engine first."

A short film about the blueprint of the nuclear propulsion system was projected in 3D to the attendants.

Isobel gave more details of the nuclear reaction elements. "This nuclear fusion-based engine design is currently being trialed at the National Ignition Facility in California. A scaled-down prototype fusion reactor driven by plasma injection contained in a strong magnetic field is also being tested in Vancouver. They both use the fusion of Helium-3 atoms as a power source method for the propulsion. As you know, Helium-3, an isotope of helium with two protons and one neutron, can be fused with Deuterium in the probe's reactor to expel propellant out the back of the spacecraft. The vehicle will harness this thermonuclear reaction to generate thrust. It will receive its energy from minute pellets of a deuterium/Helium-3 mix ignited in a reaction chamber by inertial confinement using electron beams. Being a rocket that relies on a nuclear reactor, this concept offers advantages as far as fuel efficiency and specific impulse are concerned. Scientists have studied the technology extensively over the past few years, and a similar model is currently being tested right here at the Xichang Space Research Center."

Isobel paused, leaning forward. "Unfortunately, at this stage, the exhaust velocities we're getting on the prototypes peak at only 1,000 kilometers per second, or approximately 0.3

percent of the speed of light. This is a phenomenal thrust but not powerful enough for the requirements of this mission."

Turning to the engineers present, she asked, "Any suggestions? Your input would be much appreciated.'

A well-respected physicist from the United Kingdom, Dr. Olive Kettigreen, raised her hand. "If anti-protons are injected into the nuclear fuel mass to start the reaction, the resulting energy release can be used to provide additional acceleration in space through very high specific impulses. It will also reduce the volume of fuel supply. I've prepared a document on this improvement design, and I can submit my research papers to the panel. It still needs to be tested, obviously."

Isobel's eyes sparkled with interest and a measure of relief. "Thank you, Dr. Kettigreen. This is excellent, excellent. Sure, please forward your research papers to Melanie and me. Our engineers will test your theory and try to improve the velocity of the engine with the anti-protons."

Also joining them were representatives from two of the largest aerospace companies in the world, one British, the other American. Together, they'd completed a new testing facility plant at Culham, Oxfordshire, to develop the concept of the interstellar probe.

Isobel explained the progress made so far to the team of aerospace experts. "A scale model of the Explorer 1 has been constructed in a large hangar. A detailed blueprint of the various working parts has also been prepared and is available in computer-assisted design files. Explorer 1 will consist of six main interconnected modules and the reactor. In the engine, nuclear fusion produced by confinement in a magnetic field will release ionized gases under the appropriate temperatures and density.

"Ideally, the engine will progressively accelerate the space-craft to 1 percent of the speed of light. It will incrementally reach its optimum velocity after two hundred years. After that, Explorer 1 will enter an eight-hundred-year cruising mode, during which it will maintain its momentum. Over the following eight hundred years, the spacecraft will start to slowly decelerate. Eventually, it will reach the orbit of Eridanus and lose more momentum during a one-hundred-and-fifty-year deceleration period. Finally, it will orbit closer and closer to the planet Epsilon, deploying solar sails to further retrograde its speed.

I invite you to have a look at its projected trajectory on our computer modeling program here."

———

After the morning break, Mr. Yip, the Director of the Agency, led Sandy, Melanie, Isobel, and Will together with a group of engineers through the clean room modules assembly. They all wore pure white cleanroom suits and their eyes were covered with protective goggles as they entered the gigantic, deconta-minated hangar.

Mr. Yip, an MIT graduate, explained the reasons for the extreme precautions, "In view of the sensitivity of the mission, the aim is to reduce the bioburden to a zero-tolerance level. A maximum sterilization level is necessary to avoid any contami-nation of the new planet. All the manufactured components need to be sterilized. The heat tolerant components will be treated for forty-eight hours at a temperature above 110 degrees Celsius (230 Fahrenheit). Sensitive electronic compo-nents will be cleaned with alcohol wipes during assembly and then vented through high efficiency filters in a sealed room." Mr. Yip then showed them the various components which were being assembled in the rooms.

Melanie explained them to the group, "The interstellar

spacecraft will be the largest vehicle ever built. No rocket could currently pull a craft of this size out of the Earth's gravity. Therefore, Explorer 1 will be constructed in orbit four hundred kilometers above the Earth. The six module shells will be produced here in Xichang, in Russia, and other factories around the world. They will be assembled by Chinese and Russian astronauts during extravehicular activities. The engine will be constructed through a joint effort of the US, the UK and Canada." She nodded at each of the representative countries.

"Shuttles, rockets, and other vehicles from China, US and Russia, European, Indian, and Japanese aerospace agencies will be used to deliver the payloads. First, all the external parts of the modules, the shells, then all the internal components. Once the assembly of all components is complete, the Explorer will be towed near the moon to load the fuel of Helium-3."

Feeling she'd covered the basic ground, Melanie turned toward Isobel with a demanding tone in her voice, "Isobel, the moon? Can you explain the reasons for a stopover in orbit around the moon?"

"Sure. As you know, there is little Helium-3 here on Earth, but it is present in high concentration on the lunar surface. It has been embedded in its upper layers over billions of years, as there is no atmosphere. Various projects are already well underway to establish a base on our natural satellite. A consortium of Indian, Japanese, and Chinese companies will be mining enough fuel for the interstellar mission, thus turning the moon into a refueling steppingstone for any future interstellar destination project."

She elaborated. "The preferred location for the lunar base will be near the polar regions where there is constant sunshine and a high chance of water being present. The Indian engineers have informed us the station will be powered by a variety of energy sources: electric, nuclear, and solar. We also intend to build a radio telescope there to track the trajectory of the probe in the solar system. After the fuel has been loaded, the probe will be towed a second time by several tugboat shuttles approximately 1.5 million kilometers away from the Earth to a stable area of the solar system where the nuclear reaction can safely be sequenced."

———

After the visit to the factory, they talked for several hours while unpicking and refitting the technical elements.

"All right on the engineering side," Melanie announced. "Now there are two other key questions. First, timeline. How long is it going to take to build the probe? Second, budget. How much is it going to cost? Let's talk about the timeline first. How long will it take to build this new type of probe? Any idea?"

Mr. Keto, the lead Japanese engineer, cleared his throat. "If I may… according to my calculations, around fifty years."

Melanie's brow furrowed at such a long timeline. "Fifty years is a good estimate, Mr. Keto, but I am afraid it's not going to be fitting for us. We would like to fast-track the completion of the project and launch Explorer 1 by 2085. So, our target timeline is forty years, but we need to do parallel construction, engineering layout, functionality, physics, and operations. We require six core teams to design and build the major modules and the engine. If we achieve all that and with minimum hiccups—which is a big if—forty years to launch status is feasible. What do you think?"

By the skeptical look on the engineers' faces, Melanie knew they had concerns about the length of the timeline. The majority shook their heads in disapproval. After a few convincing arguments from their side, Melanie decided. "I understand timelines are difficult to establish, especially on that scale, but let's agree at this stage that forty-five years would be a feasible compromise. We'll do our best to achieve it. We will review our progress yearly. I have worked up a plan based on the following timetable. Let's do it with six core teams: one here in China, one in the US with Canada, one in Russia including the Eastern European states, one in Japan with Korea, one in India, and one in Western Europe with the UK. The US and our own team will be based at NASA headquarters, where the engine is to be tested and assembled. We will also coordinate the development and the construction of the probe with the other teams from there. The next stage will be for each team to subcontract the construction of some components. International aeronautical engineering firms have already been asked to submit their tenders."

Melanie then introduced the next topic. "Now, Sandy and I will briefly talk about the budget."

Sandy first asked the audience for some input, "As you can imagine the budget is going to be literally... astronomical. How much is the whole project going to cost? Anybody?"

An engineer volunteered, "Five hundred billion dollars?"

"Not a bad guess," said Sandy. He paused before revealing the number, "At this stage, a conservative estimate by our team is around five trillion US dollars." He added with a grin, "In today's money."

There was a collective gasp among the group of engineers.

"I know." He jokingly opened his pockets. "Who's going to pay for this?" Then he explained. "It will be a public/private investment. We already have commitments from several of the contributing countries. They intend to redirect part of their space exploration budgets and, would you believe it, some of their defense budget as well. That still leaves a lot to be financed by private investments."

Smirks, eye rolls, and coughs of derision came thick and fast from most of the audience.

Sandy raised his hands slightly in the air. "Wait, wait. We've been busy. We have contacted major private and corporate donors. Multinationals, billionaires, and philanthropists. Mr. Wei has a lot of contacts and has been very generous with his contribution to the technology."

The engineers applauded William.

"Well deserved. William has been an outstanding supporter of the project. Still, the budget will require a lot more cash. For this reason, we've arranged for the best-known international merchant banks to approach high wealth individuals and conglomerates to raise additional funds. They have offered their services free of charge."

Sandy continued, "As well, numerous countries have been asked to run national lotteries. The Board has approached the best advertising agencies in various parts of the world. The promotion material will be designed by a conglomerate of the top names in the business in London, New York, Paris, Moscow, New Delhi, and Tokyo. We hope these various sources will help build the coffers of 'Project Explorer 1.'"

———

Back at the hotel, the team gathered in the coffee shop.

Dan looked at Melanie. "What's next on the list, boss?" he asked her with a grin.

She rolled her eyes. "Cheeky. All right. Let's see what we've achieved here. The agenda for the construction of the spaceship itself is coming along well. So far, the Chinese government is being more cooperative and open than the Russians are. The only thing that concerns me is their request to manufacture replacement parts of all the components of Explorer. They argue that if some components are proven defective once installed in orbit, they can remedy the faults in their workshop here in Xichang and dispatch the new parts without delay. What concerns me is that potentially, this would give them the capability to build another Explorer for themselves in the future without any international supervision. Highly worrying, to say the least!"

William added, "That's a strong possibility, but let's face it, there isn't much we can do to stop them."

LILLE, NORTHERN FRANCE

Dan and Melanie, along with Sandy and Isobel, were back in Lille. When they arrived, the city was covered in a haze of smoke, blown by a wildfire that had raged for a week across the Forest of Saint-Amand, a few kilometers south of the city.

Henry Dutrant, accompanied by his two sons, welcomed them with the traditional two kisses on the cheeks. "Lovely to meet you all again," he said. He introduced his guest. "Please meet my dear friend, Dr. Karli Reinhardt from the Munich Institute of Genetics. We have invited her to share her knowledge on reproduction planning."

They all moved to Mr. Durant's office to review the agenda for future population policy.

Dan asked, "Dr. Reinhardt, we'd like to discuss the generational guidelines of artificial fertilization we previously investigated with Mr. Dutrant. Our specific interest is in how to create future crew members for the moon and Mars seeding projects. The process itself."

"Sure. I'd be glad to help. I think a scientific approach to population planning must be the fundamental rule of any potential human settlement outside Earth. These are the hard facts. Here on Earth, the population has grown almost 500 percent in 130 years, from about 1.65 billion in 1900 to eight billion plus now. This increase has exceeded the safety margin for the sustainability of our planet. Our assessment is that poorly managed population growth without any compulsory family planning and the resulting uncontrolled depletion of Earth's natural resources will bring about the destruction of human civilization."

Raising her voice, Dr. Reinhardt reiterated, "I strongly recommend that on any new settlement outside our planet, family sizes should not be left to the casual decision of individuals as it has been here on Earth. We cannot make the same mistake ever again. Any population expansion must be scientifically controlled. These are the conclusions of our Department of the Future of Humanity in Munich. We're still trying to have this approach implemented here on Earth, but with little success. We get the same answer from all quarters: any control of family size in democracies is politically unsaleable."

Sandy nodded. "No government is prepared to tackle this issue, let alone legislate on it. It appears to be political suicide, but in the long term, as you say, this is going to be the main cause of humanity's downfall. Pity the pollies and the public can't see it—"

Dr. Reinhardt wrinkled her nose and pursed her lips. "But... this methodology is imperative for the success of any human colony in any new surroundings. In an extra-terrestrial environment, births should only be allowed by assisted reproduction methods. The number and the diversity of the human embryos must be strictly determined on a scientific basis!"

Her analysis was exactly what Isobel wanted to hear. Dr. Reinhardt then reviewed the related topic of the succeeding generations. "Once settlement has taken place in a new environment, the process of artificial fertilization must be continued for all the following generations, whatever their source. The follow-up population strategy will be implemented by the existing astronauts according to a sustainable demographic plan. Our department at the Munich Academy has devised an elaborate interactive computer selection program, which will be made available to the first settlers of any new territory. According to the proposed plan, after an initial colony has been established by the 'First Fleet,' the pool for the following human generations will be chosen from a selection of all the ethnic groups identified on Earth based on their genetic uniqueness. I believe researchers have categorized around fifteen hundred types so far. Is that right, Professor Robson?"

"Correct, Dr. Reinhardt. I've been in contact with Professor Spencer Walsh, the famous anthropologist who has dedicated his life to this field of research. His team has been able to identify all the ethnic groups currently living on Earth by their genetic individuality. The latest modern DNA sequencing techniques have been carried out in every part of the globe by specialist geneticists."

Dan had a delighted smile on his face now. "According to their criteria, an ethnic group is a unique category of people who relate to each other based on common ancestry and share a similar gene pool. This genetic genealogy has been determined by DNA testing and the analysis of the markers of the Y-chromosomes and certain mitochondrial variations. The prospective pool of genetic material will be chosen for preservation from these various sources. As well, another fifteen hundred candidates will be filled by the countries involved in the project, based on their contribution to the development, financing, and technical input."

Dan added, "With the help of our own team of geneticists,

we've also devised a program to screen all the DNA material for any hereditary diseases or defects."

"Thank you, Professor Robson. We obviously don't want to compromise the health of any future generations."

Dan clarified. "Every candidate will have to be cleared through a complete genomic sequence analysis." He then took the opportunity to review another issue. "While on this topic, Dr. Rheinhardt, I'd also like to raise the matter of genetic adaptation. To survive in any new environment, the crew might need corrective genetic improvements to their DNA so that they can adapt to the different environmental conditions present on the planet. For Mars, for instance, we will have to improve the skeletal and muscular performance necessary to adapt to a different gravity and modify some physical characteristics, such as a better resistance to ultraviolet and soft X-rays. Mars exerts a much lower gravity pull than Earth—around 38 percent comparatively. A person who weighs one hundred kilograms on Earth would weigh only thirty-eight kilograms on Mars. This technology will be designed by a specialized English lab using the latest expertise to improve specific genetic alterations in the DNA of humans."

Dr. Rheinhardt added, "Our research has shown that here on Earth, the best approach to maximize the chances of success of artificially generated population is to store a minimum of five embryos per individual, allowing for potential miscarriage."

Isobel clarified, "After they are conceived, the new humans will be raised and educated by androids which are being developed in Japan specifically for the Mars mission."

With a grin on her face, Dr. Reinhardt introduced her next topic.

"This is an interesting one: Sex in Space."

The other members smiled at her light-hearted approach.

"It's actually a serious matter," she told them. "The seeding program calls for batches of a mixed gender crew of men and women to be conceived in situ. An equal representation of the genders is the best option to preserve our species. We strongly believe in a monogamous society, where couples are paired for the duration of their reproductive lifespan. On the procreation side, the matching of genders can create difficulties. It is anticipated that if the conditions are like on Earth, the new crew members will probably reach puberty by the time they are twelve to fourteen years old and become sexually active by around age sixteen. Under terrestrial conditions, they would have started experiencing an increase in their hormonal levels and noticed changes in their bodies, especially the women. Our study has recommended the young crew members should be totally focused on their technical tasks in their most productive age period. Isn't that right, Dr. Löfgren?"

"They must be, Dr. Reinhardt. No romance allowed. That would distract them from their mission and cause jealousy and irrational behavior. We all know what love can do to some people."

"It's a dilemma, Dr. Löfgren. On the one hand, the young astronauts shouldn't be distracted by their sexual impulses, while on the other, sexuality is a basic need. The crew will consist of young people loaded with hormones, and frustration should be avoided as well because it could eventually lead to aggression."

"So, what's the solution, Doctor?" Dan asked.

Dr. Reinhardt tried to ease their concerns. "As a solution to this problem, we have planned to include hormonal suppressants in the astronauts' diet over time to control their emerging libido. We can block their bodies' ability to produce excessive levels of hormones to a large extent. For the female crew members, we have developed a new 'A_r inhibitor' drug. It will block the production of the enzymes which the female body uses to make estrogen. For the males, we can use current testosterone suppressant drugs. They've proven to be quite effective."

Isobel insisted, "We should make sure the astronauts aren't aware of these measures."

"No problem," Dr. Rheinhardt reassured her. "It will be included in their daily rations when they start puberty, but without their knowledge."

Dan inquired, "Can they still tolerate these supplements once they have passed puberty?"

"Unfortunately, Professor Robson, we cannot use these drugs for more than five years. After that, there is a serious risk of an increase in cell mutations, especially with the added radiation on Mars."

"I understand. Thank you, Doctor."

Sandy asked the participants, "Any further questions?"

No one came forward.

"Time for lunch then," Professor Dutrant declared.

———

As they were leaving the building, Dan noticed a couple holding a poster. It read, "DON'T PLAY GOD!" He saw Isobel approach the pair, seeking an explanation for their claim, when the man suddenly shoved her in the shoulder, screaming, "Don't play God!"

Dan reacted in an instant and restrained the man with the help of their bodyguard, who dialed security.

Sandy came to Isobel's assistance as well. "Are you alright?" She was pale but otherwise unhurt.

"I'm okay," she replied bravely.

Surprised by this violence against her personally, she asked the group, "What was that all about?"

Sandy's face twisted. "Our group is going to attract increasing protests from radical individuals. From now on, Isobel, if you see anyone acting suspiciously, don't get involved."

"I will be careful, sure." Isobel pointed at the couple. "Don't press charges against them. They don't realize what we're trying to achieve."

Dan and Melanie arrived together with Sandy and Isobel at Kansai Airport, on the man-made island in Osaka Bay. It had been recently flooded by a powerful typhoon, but thanks to the efficiency of the Japanese Transport Ministry, accelerated replacement work began quickly, and the airport became fully operational again within a week.

Their contact, Mr. Isawa, was waiting for them in Terminal 2. He directed them to a black limousine parked in the VIP area and sat in the back, facing them. He explained, "This high-tech electric car is our latest automated technology vehicle. It will self-drive us to Osaka University. I just need to input our destination coordinates and hand over control of the vehicle to the pilot assist system, which has in-built self-steering, accelerating, and braking features."

———

One hour later, they pulled into the School of Engineering at the University of Osaka and proceeded to the Office of the Director of Systems Innovations to meet Professor Roshi

Shigora, the renowned international expert on android robotics.

Dan recognized him straight away by his long hair, an unusual feature for a Japanese academic. Professor Shigora greeted them with traditional Japanese courtesy, "Konnichiwa," bowed formally, and showed them to the conference room. He pointed to four vacant seats around a large oval table and sat near his secretary, who was dressed in a black floral rose-print-layered kimono. She had perfect facial features and wore a traditional, styled black wig tied up in a chignon with an ornate hair comb.

Like a beautiful display doll, thought Dan.

"Her name is Keika," Professor Shigora explained. He then introduced three engineers who were also sitting around the table, explaining their qualifications and their role in the construction of the androids to be used in space. They all bowed and greeted the members of the team one by one. The atmosphere was quite relaxed.

After the formalities, Sandy confirmed the purpose of their visit. "Professor Shigora, we would like to find out the progress made on the design and construction of the androids, which are going to raise and educate the young astronauts when they are eventually born on Mars or—"

Suddenly, the door of the conference room flew open. A person in a white coat and hat burst in and pointed at Mr. Shigora, shouting, "This man is an imposter!"

Dan, Sandy, Isobel, and Melanie gaped at each other, stunned. They turned toward the Japanese engineers for an explanation, who were unusually calm during the fracas. After a few moments, the intruder burst into laughter.

He removed his hat, and putting both hands on his chest, he declared, "It's me, me Roshi, the real Professor Shigora."

Then, pointing at the chairperson, "This is an android copy of myself, my geminoid."

The Japanese engineers then started laughing politely. One of them whispered to Dan, "Professor's favorite party trick."

"Do you like my joke?" asked the real Professor Shigora.

Recovering from their initial shock, they started laughing nervously. "This is hilarious," Isobel admitted gingerly.

"*Ki-do-ai-raku*! Great sense of humor, Roshi." Sandy said.

Professor Shigora turned toward his geminoid and gestured. "Go back to your room, you naughty boy." Then turning to his secretary, he said, "You can stay." He whispered to Dan, "She's a robot as well. Very pretty, don't you think?"

Dan agreed. "What a wonderful traditional Japanese makeup and costume."

"All right." Professor Shigora cleared his throat. "Now, onto serious matters. Since you contacted us, we've been busy. Our robotic section refocused its work at your request. We receive financial support from both the government and our manufacturing leaders: Honda, Mitsubishi, Toyota... and more. Japan is high-tech economy."

He focused his gaze on the team. "Many people interested in your project. Huge amount of support. We built a new wing at the Maternity Hospital on the university campus. Entirely modeled on the conditions on the Mars habitat modules. The room soundproof, lit only by artificial light. Area free from outside interference and contamination. Some of our students, new parents, offer to have their babies raised by our robot nurses."

He projected a picture of the androids on the conference room screen. "We call the robots 'nursoids'. Nursoids programmed to perform all functions required to raise newborns: feeding, changing, bathing, putting to bed, health monitoring. For better maternal contact, we develop special temperature-controlled skin to cover the robots. It can adapt to baby's temperature and give almost human tactile sensation. Nurses can apply correct force when handling babies. Different programs also designed by our IT specialists for various demands of babies when they grow up."

Dan remarked, "The nursoids look almost human, very maternal, but they appear to be quite small. How tall are they, Professor?"

"One meter only. Babies are small. No need for nurses to be bigger otherwise take unnecessary space. Nursoids can even teach children how to walk. How to talk is another program, right, Sandy?"

"Correct, Roshi. Space Technical English will be the language spoken outside Earth. It will also be used for technical training in all the scientific disciplines: physics, computing, mathematics, space engineering, all the skills which will be necessary for astronauts to perform their mission. This part is currently being designed in Seattle by an American/Canadian team. Sorry, Roshi. I got a bit carried away. Please continue—"

"*A so desu ka.* Thank you for information." Professor Shigora went back to his explanation. "Yes, maternity wing. We try to replicate conditions encountered outside Earth environment. Ward is catering for twelve babies. All same age. We monitor them and register progress of development in foreign environment."

He raised his hands apologetically. "I cannot show you inside maternity wing. Area has been isolated. Fear of contamination. Sorry."

"We understand," Dan answered politely.

"We can show you room from external observation platform. I can also run video when we finish."

"I would love that," Dan said.

Professor Shigora bowed in agreement. He turned to his colleagues and invited him to present the next topic. "We also develop other types of robots."

Professor Matsu, who'd been trained in the UK, had a much better command of English even with a strong British accent. "Thank you, Professor Shigora." He bowed and then turned to his audience. "Our department is working on robots we call 'NGnoids A.' They're programmed to carry out engineering work, including maintenance and repairs, but ultimately under human supervision. They have a more typical robot appearance. However, what is unique to these robots is their inbuilt mechanical features, which will multiply their physical strength and capabilities. A second version, the 'NGnoids B,' will be capable of building accommodation and vehicles utilizing 3D printing technology. *Arigato*, Professor."

Pointing to his colleague, Professor Shigora continued, "Professor Matsu and his team, all experts in artificial intelligence. They develop new prototypes of quantum computers. They can create their own program, make their own decisions. Minimum human input."

Professor Matsu agreed repeatedly with the statements by bowing his head and gave the team further information. "We call them 'Masterminders,' or Master Ms. They can assist astronauts with education and decision-making during mission. They can develop solutions to new problems."

Melanie chuckled. "They will encounter many of those."

Professor Shigora concluded the session, "We organize Gala reception tonight in honor of your visit so we can support your project. Many scientists and financial backers invited. We also have short theater performance by nursoids. They show their skills at raising babies. You will enjoy it."

"Sounds like a lot of fun," Isobel said. "We're looking forward to it."

Sandy bowed and joined his hands like a local. "*Arigato gozaimasu*, Roshi, Professor Matsu, and your colleagues. Your contribution has been outstanding."

———

That evening after the reception, Melanie stood in the bathroom, washing her face. It had been a productive, if rather bizarre, day. She'd seen lots of robots in the construction industry but not ones that appeared to be almost human with distinctive faces.

She dressed in her favorite silk pajamas and climbed into bed. Dan was doing Sudoku as she sat there. She looked up at him. "Can I talk to you now, hon?"

He smiled at her. "Of course."

"Wasn't today strange?"

"That's exactly what I was thinking."

"Honestly, I'm feeling really uncomfortable setting up this fake family scenario."

He started, letting the Sudoku fall onto his lap, "What do you mean?"

She could feel her thoughts churning, processing. She jumped out of bed and started pacing. "Well, it's pretty awful, isn't it? The way these new kids could be brought up: no parents, no family, just intelligent semi machines. I understand why it would have to be that way, but it's not... how can I say... emotionally healthy."

She stopped and stared at him. "You and I, we've worked hard to raise our family, to bring up our kids well. I mean, family is important. We cherish them. We love them."

"You're right, you are totally right. But I don't think there is any other way, hon." He sat there, thinking. "The issues around sending real generations are just too enormous. Practically, I can't see any way around it. This is the only solution. Welcome to the families of the future."

She nodded. "Fake nursoid parents? Come on Daniel, it feels wrong for the kids. Almost sickening. Like some awful sci-fi cartoon joke. Is that the way future human generations are going to be?"

He looked at her quizzically. "But Lanie, what's the alternative? There isn't one."

"Okay... but what if we didn't send a probe to discover an alternative way of living?"

His eyes widened. "Lanie, that could mean...?"

"Yes. It could eventually mean the end of human civilization. This is ridiculous, Dan." She raised her arms in exasperation. "Why are we even having this conversation?!"

He patted the bed next to him. "Come sit."

She sighed and sat down next to him. He had a bottle of wine on the side of the bed and poured her a glass. "Here, nightcap." Then he said, "Cheers" and raised his glass to her.

She smiled sadly as they clinked glasses.

He looked at her. "I think this project is getting to you."

"I know. It's insane and wonderful and critically important all at once. Normally I'm making big decisions, but these are just..."

"Out of this world," he offered.

She leaned back on the array of gold-colored pillows. "Literally, yes. The whole venture is overwhelming. It's like I'm kissing goodbye to our own children and replacing them with androids. That's the way I'm starting to see the future for humanity."

"I understand, Lanie. I've been there as well. But you must keep going."

She shook her head, tears welling in her eyes. "Dammit!" She angrily dabbed her eyes.

He put his hand on her shoulder. "Lanie, it's okay… you can cry."

She turned to him; her eyes blazing. "I don't want to, Daniel. This…" she waved her hand furiously in front of her face, "is not me. I'm a proud, intelligent, black woman. I was the first senior vice-president of my company. But I'm also a mother. I nurtured our kids the moment I could feel them in my womb." She placed her hands on her belly, remembering the feeling. "They weren't pieces of biotechnology engineering. They were real, living human beings."

He put his hand on her shoulder, "I understand, hon."

"Let me finish. It was my choice. But so much of it's out of my control in this venture, and I don't like it."

He studied her carefully. "Then, maybe you should consider leaving the project."

Melanie's mouth fell open. "Leave?" She couldn't believe he was even suggesting such a thing. Did he think she couldn't handle the pressure?

Dan repeated, "If you hate what we're doing, then, maybe you should leave."

"But—"

"We'll find someone else. Sandy has other possible—"

"Like?" She was curious now.

"Well, he's mentioned Isaac Lawson."

She shouted, outraged, "Isaac Lawson?! That idiot!"

Dan nodded.

"Come on! I'm better than him."

"Lanie, of course you are, but if you're not comfortable…"

She felt heat rising in her chest. "Comfortable? It's not about being comfortable. It's about having to deal with the concept of saving this damn planet by creating half-humans to replace us. Getting rid of real motherhood. Producing children who won't have any love from their parents. That's what's getting to me. Do we have to resort to that, Dan?!"

He remained silent and put his hand on her shoulder. "I understand."

After a few moments, she settled down. "Isaac Lawson!" She shook her head in disgust, then tumbled down on the mountain of pillows, groaning. "Fine, you're right. There is too much at stake. The future of humanity and all that."

"Love you," he said as he kissed her on her cheek and turned out the light.

"I love you too. What a mess mankind's heading for."

CHAPTER 11
YEAR 2045—RUSSIAN CONSULATE GENERAL, N. Y.

The Russian Consulate General was on East Street, about a fifteen-minute cab ride from the UN building on a good traffic day. Sandy and Melanie had opted to walk. They both enjoyed walking in New York and, given that it was on the other side of the park, it was a good opportunity to get their morning miles in.

The dark-haired receptionist sat behind a tall glass panel and was rather frosty when Sandy introduced them. After that, she barely spared them another glance.

They'd received a summons late in the evening the previous day to be at the Russian Consulate at 8:30 a.m. sharp and been given few details other than General Alexei Titov was in town and had requested their presence.

They had already been waiting for twenty-five minutes and there was still no sign of the general. Melanie tapped her fingers on the side of the mission brown couch. She had rescheduled her early morning meetings, but at this rate, she'd have to reschedule others.

Sandy leaned over and whispered, "Psychological power play."

Sandy was right: the late request, the waiting, even the

ambience was meant to intimidate them. After another twenty minutes of waiting, a tall blond-haired man in a green army uniform approached them. Sandy recognized him as one of the general's aides. He gestured at them to follow him.

As they went up in the lift to the fifth floor, Melanie could feel the slow but steady onset of a tension headache. She eyed Sandy. He also seemed unusually concerned. Neither of them knew why the general had called them. Russia's involvement at this stage was critical to the mission, and negotiations with General Titov had been relatively cordial since their meeting in Moscow.

The elevator opened to a floor with a row of doors on both sides. They followed the aide-de-camp to the end of the corridor, where yet another receptionist sat. She gestured for them to sit down.

"General Titov won't be long."

You got to be kidding me, Melanie thought. She tried to message her assistant to reschedule an appointment, but her holo wasn't working. The receptionist pointed to a glass case.

"All electronic devices must be left in here."

Sandy objected. "We're high-ranking UN officials."

"Regulations."

They reluctantly handed over their devices to the receptionist, who put them in the case and locked it. She handed them the key. "Your devices will be safe there."

Melanie took the key and put it in her pocket, knowing it was all for show. As soon as they were inside, the techies from the consulate would be remotely scanning through their files. They had brought their burners on the advice of their cybersecurity expert when they had heard of the meeting.

General Titov came over to shake their hands. "Hello comrades. Melanie, Sandy, apologies for my delay. I had a meeting run over."

Yeah, right! Melanie thought. The excuse was obviously made-up. From her information, the general was a late starter and given that his hair was still damp, she assumed he'd just arrived from his apartment.

In their late-night discussion the previous day, Melanie had agreed to let Sandy lead the conversation. It was a pity that William wasn't present to act as the go-between. They had called on him unsuccessfully over the last few days to play a peacekeeper role. The Russians' participation had proven consistently difficult. They were demanding more and more money, missing deadlines, and being opaque about where they had achieved progress.

The general ushered them inside a large gold wall-papered office with several bookshelves, an enormous desk in the middle, and a few armchairs in the left corner.

"Please sit down." He pointed to the seating area, with three club seats arranged around a small marble table.

The general offered them coffee and once the receptionist had left, he faced Melanie. Sipping his black coffee slowly, he watched her with bright blue eyes over the cup. After a few exchanges regarding the state of play of the project, he stated firmly, "Comrade, I thought we had an understanding. Do you remember the Russian proverb I told you about, 'You cannot take a word out of a song'?"

They both took a sip of their coffee, waiting for him to clarify his thinking.

The general eyed Melanie. "You promised to be honest with me, Mrs. Robson."

"Excuse me? I've been entirely honest, General." She shot a confused look at Sandy.

General Titov put his coffee cup down and raised his voice. "Not entirely, Mrs. Robson."

Melanie was taken aback. "General, I'm not sure what you

have heard, but I haven't kept any information from you about the project."

Sandy leaned sideways toward her and said softly out of the corner of his mouth without looking at her. "Please let me handle this, Melanie."

He was entirely focused on the general. "Forgive me, Alexei," Sandy started calmly. "Tell us what you've heard and the things we haven't told you. I promise, we will try everything we can to fix it."

The general smiled in a way that unnerved Melanie. *Like the cat about to get the cream*, she thought.

General Titov picked up his coffee cup and firmed his back in the chair. "I've always liked you, Sandy. You're direct. A problem-solver. Unlike others. You remind me of myself: a powerful man, one of influence and calculating. Like someone playing a game of chess."

Irritation rippled through Melanie; she knew he was being dismissive of her.

Sandy nodded, leaning in. "Alexei let's fix the problem. That's what men like us do: we fix things."

Melanie groaned inwardly.

The general gazed triumphantly as he sipped his coffee. Raising an eyebrow at Melanie, he said slowly, "I know about embryos. You did not tell me."

Melanie couldn't help it. She inhaled sharply. "It's only a feasibility study."

"Melanie is correct, General. At this stage, it's only a remote possibility. We haven't got any authority to deal with that right now. The technique is highly regulated, controversial, and still a long way off." He laughed. "Even the Americans aren't up to speed on this, Alexei."

The general relaxed. "Thank you, at least you are honest, Comrade." His smile did not reflect in his eyes, which remained calculating. "When this technique is ready, my country wants to participate in decision-making about selection for Russia. I want to be *personally* informed."

Sandy reassured him, "Sure, General. I will contact you myself directly. No problem."

The general puffed his chest out. "I... we want full control over who will be selected for Russia."

Melanie interrupted, "Providing the health requirements are met, you will have full control. But I repeat, *nothing* has been decided yet."

"No problem, Alexei." Sandy confirmed, still not looking at Melanie.

"Excellent. Wonderful doing business with you, comrades." After a small pause, the general put his hands on the table and leaned forward. "What we discuss here, Sandy, Mrs. Robson, is only between us. Nobody else!"

Sandy confirmed, "Sure. Only between us, Alexei."

Melanie gritted her teeth, but she knew how to play the game.

Sandy stood up, followed by Melanie, who said, "Thank you for the coffee, General."

General Titov also rose, patting Sandy firmly on the back. After he shook hands with them, he retrieved an envelope from his pocket and handed it to Sandy.

"These are four tickets to concert at Carnegie Hall next week. Ivan Pavlovich, Russian baritone famous for vocal range and soprano Anna Vasilia. They sing Russian songs together. I know your husband likes good singing, Mrs. Robson. Beautiful voices. You will enjoy also. You and partners sit with me in front row of balcony of Weill Recital Hall. I also invite William Wei and wife. After concert, we have dinner together back here at Consulate. We talk more."

Melanie was astounded by his change in attitude.

However, Sandy said, "That's very generous. Thank you, Alexei. I will check with Isobel. We'll let you know as soon as possible, General. Thank you again."

They picked up their briefcases, collected their phones, and headed downstairs to the lift. As they exited the building, Sandy turned to Melanie. "Alexei is, at the best of times, a crafty character to deal with, but this was something else. I believe the general is acting for himself, not for his country. I'm sure of it."

"Agree, and he doesn't want to be found out." She almost growled with anger.

"In a way, we have something on him, Melanie. Although he'd probably deny it. But from now on, let's play the game his way. Russia's participation is critical to the project. I get a feeling that from here on, General Titov will be more cooperative. He wants to form a special bond with us for obvious reasons. Who's passing him this stuff? There must be a mole in the organization, or their Federal Security Service has taps on us?"

"He was so disrespectful."

Sandy put his hands up defensively. "Hey Melanie, I'm just playing the game according to his rules. If I hadn't smoothed him over, we would have lost his support. I'm used to dealing with Russians. Not an easy mob. Rumor is Titov will run as candidate for the next presidential election. You know what that means, don't you?"

She gawked. "He's likely to become the next president of the Federation."

"A cunning, ambitious fellow and extremely dangerous," said Sandy pointedly.

Melanie mulled over what Alexei had asked. She shook her head. "Are we sure we want his selection in the genetic pool?"

Sandy breathed heavily. "We won't have any control in the matter, I'm afraid. Thankfully, it's a long time off."

UN HEADQUARTERS, NEW YORK

It had been a busy morning full of meetings. Melanie had just finished a two-hour consultation with Dr. Reinhardt, evaluating social dynamics and preventing psychopathic tendencies in groups.

Isobel popped her head into her office. She looked mildly panicked, something Melanie had never witnessed before. "Are you free for lunch?" she queried.

Melanie's eyes narrowed. Isobel wasn't one to just call in for lunch. Sandy, sure. William, yes. Dan, of course, but Isobel? She struggled to remember the last time the two of them had even had a casual conversation.

"Yes, sure. Hang on." She grabbed her clutch.

"What about that Italian place a couple of streets back? They make a good risotto."

"Yes. That's a good choice. Let's go."

————

They settled into the booth and ordered the lunchtime special. The waiter poured them some sparkling water, Italian, of course. Isobel looked at Melanie furtively.

Melanie sat back in her seat. "So?"

"I wanted to talk to you about something," Isobel said in a shaky voice.

"Okay," replied Melanie just as cautiously. "Is this about the Russians? Has the general been talking to you again?"

"I'm pregnant."

Melanie's eyebrows shot skyward. She took a sharp breath

in and reached for her glass of water. "What? what?" She rubbed her face. "Um, hang on." She took a long sip of her water. "Isobel, you're pregnant?!" This news just seemed beyond belief.

"Yes," Isobel replied resolutely.

Focus, Melanie thought. *Don't say anything controversial. Congratulate her.* "Congratulations, Isobel."

Isobel looked almost grateful. "Thank you. You're the first person I've told."

Melanie's eyes almost bulged out of her head, "What?"

Isobel spoke more slowly now, as if she was speaking to a total disbeliever. "You are the first person I've told."

A million thoughts ran through Melanie's head. *Take it slowly, Melanie. This is Isobel, it is going to take a while.* "Ahh, thank you, I'm flattered."

"You're welcome." Isobel grinned broadly.

Melanie took another sip of her water. It just wasn't doing it for her. She signaled to the waiter, "Can I get a glass of pinot grigio, please?"

"Absolutely, madam. And you, madam?"

Isobel nodded. "I'll have one too."

Melanie slapped her hand softly. "Isobel you can't!" she hissed, "you're pregnant."

The waiter offered. "How about iced tea? Non-alcoholic," he reassured.

"Yes, that's fine."

Okay… details, Melanie. Ask her questions. "How far along are you, Isobel?"

Isobel smiled warmly.

It's strange to see her smile so much.

"Fifteen weeks." She rifled through her bag and handed over an ultrasound picture.

Melanie examined the black-and-white picture, making

out the outline of a fetus. "Wonderful news, Isobel; wonderful."

The waiter brought the wine and the iced tea.

Melanie reached for the wine.

Isobel laughed. "I did one of those tests, of course, to make sure. And it's a girl."

Melanie reached for her hand. "I have a girl and she's amazing. Yours will be too."

The risotto arrived. The smell was amazing.

As Melanie took her first bite. Isobel continued, "I've chosen the name already: Sandra... after her father."

Melanie began to choke on her food. As she coughed and spluttered, Isobel patted her on the back, concerned.

"Are you okay? You really must be careful how fast you eat."

The waiter brought Melanie more water, which she sipped slowly. Once she had settled herself, she asked hoarsely. "Is the father... Sandy?'

"Yes of course. I thought you knew about us."

Melanie had suspected, of course, but Dan had dismissed her thoughts, saying Sandy was friendly with everyone. She didn't buy it as Sandy had been more than friendly toward Isobel. In fact, he had been consistently attentive to her.

"Well. That's wonderful... amazing... fantastic news. He must be thrilled."

Isobel frowned. "He doesn't know."

Melanie wasn't eating this time. She closed her eyes for a second and breathed in. Most conversations with Isobel were like this: convoluted and surprising. "Sorry. Why not?"

"You're the first person I've told, remember?"

"I thought you meant outside of the father, Isobel?"

"Well, then I would have said you're the second person I've

told or the first besides the father. Logic. You really need to listen better, Melanie."

Keep asking questions, Melanie! Be patient. She breathed in deeply. "Isobel, why did you tell me before Sandy?"

"I need your advice."

Finally, Melanie thought, *we're getting somewhere.* "About what?"

"I have to tell Sandy, but I don't know whether he wants to be involved."

Finally, we're getting to the reason why she came to seek my advice, Melanie thought. She decided to be constructive. "Getting involved is a good thing, isn't it?"

"No."

"Sorry I'm not following here, Isobel. Tell me. Do you like Sandy?"

"Yes, of course."

"So why wouldn't you want him involved?"

"I don't want to impose on him. He is too busy with his work. I can raise the baby by myself."

"Yes, of course you can, but if you like Sandy, and he would like to be involved, then that would be wonderful for both of you."

"Do you think so?"

"Yes, Isobel of course." Melanie ate a mouthful of her risotto. *It seems safe now*, she thought as she chewed and swallowed. *Okay, I need to think like Isobel.* "Babies are hard work, Isobel, especially by yourself. They require a lot of attention, and they restrict your professional life."

"Really?"

"For a few months, anyway. Obviously, we need you on the project. With your knowledge of astrophysics."

"Yes. I see what you're getting at. My contribution is critical to the success of the project, isn't it?"

"Certainly. Help is easily available with the feeding and the changing, to make sure you're at your best for work."

Isobel nodded. "Couldn't I just get a nanny?"

"A bit early. Eventually, yes, but not yet. You don't want the baby to bond so early on with someone else outside of her parents. The parental bond is critical for the future success of the child." *Thank goodness for the two-hour lecture this morning.* "You need to get Sandy involved."

Isobel's face lit up. "I think you're right. I should tell him. Thank you, Melanie." She stood up.

"Where are you going?"

"To tell him."

"Now?"

"Yes. He has a 3 p.m. appointment with the Secretary General. I'd better catch him beforehand."

"But—"

"Don't worry, I'll pay before I go."

"That wasn't—"

Isobel leaned down to kiss Melanie on the cheek and left some money on the table. "Thanks, Melanie. I really appreciate your advice. Little Sandra will be so lucky to have you as her godmother."

As she left, Melanie signaled to the waiter. "Another wine, please, and make it a large one."

UN PRIVATE CONFERENCE ROOM, NEW YORK

Several weeks later, Melanie, Dan, and Isobel were preparing for a status update to the Secretary General in one of the UN private conference rooms. Dame Ngaire was due to arrive in New York from Geneva the next morning.

Dan got up. "Must be the IT guys."

As he opened the door, Sandy strolled in. "Hi Melanie, Dan, Isobel."

Isobel started to move away, but Melanie put her hand across to stop her.

"Stay, Isobel."

"I have nothing to say to Sandy."

Sandy eyed Dan and Melanie.

Melanie spoke first to Sandy, "Hi Sandy. Isobel was just telling us how upset she is… that you think she can't handle the pregnancy and the baby by herself."

Dan gave Sandy a complicit wink. "Very upset."

Melanie sighed inwardly.

Sandy sat next to Isobel, taking Dan's seat, and reached out for her hand, which she immediately pulled away. "Iso." He looked at her. "I love you. You know that don't you?"

Isobel said nothing.

"I think you're an amazing scientist and an incredible woman."

She lifted her gaze and half smiled.

Sandy took her hand again. "I want to marry you and live with you by my side and raise our child together—"

"But—"

"Not because you need help, Isobel. You're extremely capable, and you can handle this pregnancy all by yourself. For the child's sake. I want us to be a family, and functioning families live together."

"I guess, but…"

"I don't want you to do anything you would be uncomfortable with."

"Okay."

"Okay what?"

"I'll come and live with you. I told you I didn't have the sort of functioning family everyone talks about, and I want a safe environment for our child."

He smiled.

She continued, "I want her to experience something I never had... a loving family, caring parents, a mother and a father. I'll marry you after she is born, and I don't want an over-the-top wedding because it's a waste of money."

Sandy's mouth was the one now agape.

Isobel placed her hand on her belly. "But I'm not taking your last name alone. Our daughter will have both our names. Mine first because I'm doing all the hard work."

He smiled. "Sandra Löfgren-Fraser. What a beautiful name. It has a nice ring to it."

Suddenly realizing what he'd said, he patted his pockets. "Talking about rings, I don't have the engagement ring with me. I left it at home—"

"After I walked out on you, obviously. Sorry about that."

To lift the atmosphere, Dan said, "Congratulations to you both."

Melanie gave Sandy a big bear hug and Isobel a kiss on both cheeks.

"Wonderful news. We're so happy for you. You can call on us any time, day or night." Dan elbowed her in the side, "More day than night, but absolutely; we're here to support you two... ahh... three."

CHAPTER 12

Melanie had just finished a two-and-a-half-hour online meeting with a Russian project manager. She felt a great sense of satisfaction. It hadn't been easy, but she'd managed to secure a guarantee for their financial contribution for the next three years.

She checked her watch: 8:30 p.m. *Is Dan still in the building, or has he headed back to our New York apartment?*

As she locked up her office, she happened to glance out the window and notice the snow hitting the windows with force. The blizzard that had been expected to come in overnight was already here.

Her holo beeped. It was Dan. "Hon, where are you? Tell me you're at home."

"I'm so sorry, Lanie. I got caught up with the Russians. Wait. Aren't you at home yourself? I thought you said you were going to leave early and pop to the shops before the blizzard?"

"I've been stuck in meetings myself. Have you seen the weather outside? It's come early. Are you still in your office?"

"Yes. I'm starting to walk to the elevator."

The lights blinked, and the floor went dark.

"Hey! What's going on? The lights have gone off. Dan, are you still there?"

"I'm just outside my office on the fifteenth floor." He paused. "Wait for me."

She remained in the dark, purposefully slowing her breath. She didn't want anxiety to overwhelm her. "Breathe, Lanie, breathe," she told herself. *He's on his way. It's okay.*

As the emergency generator kicked on, Dan appeared from the fire stairs.

"Oh, Dan! Thank goodness." Relief flooded over her. She hugged him.

"I'm glad you're okay."

"Let's head downstairs and see if we can drive home. It's not far."

They picked their way down the fifteen flights of stairs. The emergency lighting was low and dull and blinked on and off, but she preferred some light to none.

As they came into the foyer, the burly middle-aged security guard who manned the front desk stopped them. "What are you two doing here? Didn't you hear the warnings?"

Melanie shook her head. "I've been in meetings all evening."

Dan nodded. "Me, too."

"We sent everyone home an hour ago. All the roads are blocked. You can't go out. The blizzard." He narrowed his gaze at Dan. "Excuse me, sir. I saw you on the TV. You're one of those guys working on climate change, aren't you? Tell me. How come we get hit by these crazy blizzards and they're talking about global warming? Don't make sense to me."

Melanie rolled her eyes. *Here we go,* she thought.

Dan peered at the security guard's name tag and went into full professorial mode. "Good question, Henry. Let me quickly explain. The overall rise in the temperatures affects the ocean's temperature. It creates more evaporation of the sea water. Just like hot steam coming out of a kettle. Therefore, the atmosphere holds more moisture in the form of thicker clouds. In the cold countries in winter, this moisture in the clouds eventually falls as snow but with more intensity as a blizzard because…" He looked at Henry for an answer. "Because?"

"Because there is more water in them clouds?" Henry said hesitantly.

Dan beamed. "Excellent answer, Henry. So, it's because global temperatures are on the rise that we get more intense snowstorms."

"Now I understand. Thank you, sir. You explained this very clearly."

"You're welcome, Henry. That's what I do for a living. Now let's see if this storm is that bad." Dan tried to push the doors open, but the strength of the wind slammed it closed. "Huh, I see what you mean."

Henry shook his head. "I told you, sir; it's crazy out there. Worst storm in over a hundred years, they say. There's no one going in or out."

A voice came from behind them. "Who's not going in or out?" Isobel emerged from the side door.

Henry's face fell. "Oh, my goodness, another one. Didn't you hear the warnings?"

Isobel waddled over, eating an apple. "What warnings? I didn't hear anything. I was in the library listening to a podcast."

Henry gripped the side of the desk and briefly raised his gaze heavenward. "There were at least several warnings over the loudspeaker ordering staff members to leave."

"Oh, is that what that was? I had my earphones on. I assumed it was a drill."

Henry slapped his head in disbelief.

"Hmm, looks like we are going to be here for a while," Melanie said out loud.

Out of the blue, the lights flicked back on. The elevator dinged and out stumbled Sandy, looking worse for wear. "Didn't anyone hear me? I was waving at the camera," he groused, looking at Henry.

"Sorry, sir. Nothing came up on the system."

Sandy looked around, registering that he wasn't alone. "Dan, Melanie, Iso? Iso, what are you doing here? You're supposed to be at home."

Now eating a bag of pretzels, Isobel tried to justify her presence. "I was home in the morning, but then I came back in to use the digital library. Do you know it also holds over four hundred thousand physical books? Absolute heaven." She exhaled happily.

"Isobel, you're supposed to be on maternity leave. You are due in two weeks."

"Yes... yes... but I got bored. So, I came in. I thought we could grab dinner together."

"Darling, there is a massive storm outside."

She appeared distracted. "Anyway, let's go up to the conference room. They have food there, right? I want to sit down. My legs feel heavy."

In the conference room, Sandy gestured Isobel to the visitors' armchairs.

"Here, sit, sit. Dan and I will check the cupboards for food."

The wind gusted outside. All Melanie could see outside was covered in white snow powder. "Wow, the storm has really picked up."

Isobel was struggling to settle. She moved from side to side in her chair, clearly uncomfortable.

"Are you okay?" Melanie asked.

"I just can't get comfortable."

Melanie pondered the chair next to her. "How about this footstool? That might help."

She got up and pushed a large, tan leather ottoman over to Isobel so she could put her feet up.

"Ah that's better; I think I was sitting too long in the library. I'm all crampy."

Melanie's mind went immediately on alert. "Crampy?"

"Yeah, uh... there's another one, uh... hang on." Isobel paused, grimacing. "Uh, it's gone."

Melanie stared at Isobel. "Isobel how long have you had these cramps for?"

"Let's see." Isobel furrowed her brow. "I got to the library just after lunch, around one. I think they started around two. I was consulting a fascinating book on the dynamics of—"

Melanie interrupted her, "How regularly are these cramps coming?"

"They were coming every ten minutes, I guess, but now every two to three minutes. I did eat some Thai food yesterday. Maybe that's playing up on me. Oh, hang on, here's another one—" she groaned. "Ahhh, they seem to be getting worse."

Her face scrunched up in agony. She was sweating.

Melanie jumped up in alarm. "Isobel, you're in labor!" she exclaimed.

"What? No, I can't be. I'm not due for another two weeks! This isn't supposed to happen so early!"

Melanie stared at her. "Isobel, babies don't come on the mother's command."

Isobel shook her head. "I've got a booking at Mt. Sinai in two weeks to have a caesarean. Quickly out. That's what I want." She groaned. "Ahhh... Oh god, maybe I should go to the bathroom?!"

Melanie put her hand up. "Isobel, we need to—"

Dan appeared out of nowhere with supplies from the cabinets. "Here you are, mother-to-be. I even have a mini pizza."

Isobel growled at him, "I don't want food anymore now. Ahhh—"

Dan dropped the food on the conference table. "What's going on?" he asked.

"Sandy, help me out of this damned chair... nooowww!" Isobel closed her eyes again, her knuckles turning white as she gripped the wooden arms.

Sandy did as she asked, but she collapsed to her knees with a loud "Ahhh!" as she leaned on the ottoman. He knelt and put his arms around Isobel, rubbing her back gently and whispering in her ear. "We're all here to help you."

Melanie said in a rush, "She's definitely in labor. She's been having contractions since two o'clock."

Sandy reacted. "Eh? Since two? That was several hours ago!"

Melanie nodded. "And they've really intensified."

"I'll call the doctor."

"No doctor, Sandy. I'm fine," Isobel said, breathing heavily. "It's just... oh, here comes another one. Ahhhh!"

Melanie pulled another chair next to Isobel. "Iso, it's happening. You need to breathe slowly. You've been to the classes, right? Just breathe." She rubbed her back.

Isobel shook her head. "I didn't go to classes. I told you. I want to have a caesarean in two weeks."

Melanie inhaled sharply through her mouth. "Okay, okay." Forcing herself to calm her racing thoughts, she turned to her husband. "Dan, find some towels. Sandy? What's the hospital saying?"

Sandy shook his head. "They might be here in two hours. It's total chaos out there."

Melanie eyed Isobel, who was panting heavily, obviously

experiencing another contraction. "I don't think we have two hours."

Sandy's eyes went wide, slightly panicked. "You're right. We need medical assistance right now." He was sweating now.

An idea came to Melanie. "The medical services on the fifth floor."

"Brilliant. I'll give them a call and see if anyone's there."

"Hurry."

Sandy kissed Isobel on the head. "Hang on, Iso. I'll be back with someone, okay?"

She nodded, slightly teary and panting. "Okay."

Sandy rushed off to the elevator to get the doctor, a man on a mission.

Dan emerged from a side door with a bundle of sheets and towels. "Hit the jackpot. Supply closet."

Melanie wrapped her arms around Isobel and heaved her up. "Isobel, can you stand for a sec? I'll help you." She signaled to Dan, "Make the ottoman like a bed."

He placed a sheet over the ottoman. "Done."

"Iso, do you want to lie down?"

———

Fifteen minutes later, Sandy emerged from the elevator with an armful of medical supplies, followed by a small Asian woman in a white coat wearing a stethoscope around her neck. Melanie recognized her as Dr. Li, the head of the Medical Services Division.

Dan and Sandy started clearing his desk and setting up the medical equipment.

Dr. Li eyed the makeshift bed with Isobel under the sheets.

"Ahhhh," Isobel groaned.

Dr. Li went into professional mode. "Let's see how far

along you are." She squatted down and examined Isobel. "Ten centimeters dilated already."

Isobel blew out a breath. "I've got ages still, right? I should be able to go to the hospital."

Dr. Li blinked at her, bemused. "No, Dr. Löfgren. Ten centimeters is fully dilated. You are ready to start pushing."

Isobel's breathing was quick and shallow. "But... I..."

He squeezed her hand. "You can do this, Iso—"

"But this wasn't the plan. I was going to go to the hospital and have a Caesarean..." she trailed off as she moaned again, this time long and loud. At the end of it, she looked up at Sandy. "This is happening, isn't it?"

He nodded at her, smiling, "Yes, darling, it is."

Dr. Li glanced around the room. "Mr. Fraser, can I get you down this end and Mr. and Mrs. Robson, can you hold her hands?" They moved to do her bidding.

"Dr. Löfgren, when you feel the next contraction, I want you to push long and hard. Okay?"

Isobel's eyes were hooded with pain. She gave a jerky nod. "Okay, it's coming. Ahhh." She screamed long and hard.

"Great! Really good."

Isobel pushed for around thirty minutes, then slumped in Sandy's arms, her face shiny with sweat. Melanie could tell that she was nearing exhaustion.

Dr. Li smiled reassuringly at Isobel. "We're not seeing the movement we need to see. Next one, really long and hard. Okay, Dr. Löfgren?"

Isobel shook her head. "I can't, I can't!"

Melanie knew what this was like. "You are so close, Isobel," she whispered, wiping her forehead with a towel. "You can do this. You're an amazing woman, a world-renowned physicist, and you are going to be an amazing mum very, very soon. You just need to get this baby out."

Isobel got a bit teary. "I can do this. I can do this." She gritted her teeth, "Let's go." She pushed long and hard, letting out a growl of effort.

"I can see the baby's head. Blonde hair," Sandy exclaimed gleefully. "Keep going, Iso."

Her eyes scrunched close in concentration; Isobel bore down hard again.

This time, Melanie heard a small cry.

"Head's out," Dr. Li reported. "Well done. Now, next push about half that strength, okay?

"Mmmm... Ahhhh," Isobel answered.

With the next push, Dr. Li cried out, "She's out!" and signaled to Dan to bring a towel. She cleaned the baby's face and put the wriggly, crying bundle onto Isobel's chest.

"It's a girl and a good size."

"Well done, Mama," Melanie whispered.

Isobel sobbed, now holding Sandy's hand and cuddling the baby with her other. "She's here, she's here! Our little girl."

Melanie leaned on Dan. "The miracle of life."

He smiled and kissed her on the head. "Exactly what I was thinking, love."

———

The ambulance arrived one hour later. As the paramedics transferred Isobel onto the stretcher, Sandy headed over to Melanie and Dan. "Thank you so much. I'm so grateful to both of you. I'll go to the maternity with Isobel. Here, take the keys to my apartment. Feel free to stay tonight while the storm is letting up. It's closer than Brooklyn."

Melanie nodded. "Give us a call tomorrow, Sandy. We'll come to the hospital for a quick visit."

It was still snowing outside, but gentler now. As they exited the building, they waved at Henry.

"Exciting night," he said. "This job is certainly never boring."

Thankfully, the snow ploughs had been doing their job, so the roads were now relatively clear. The streetlamps were back on too.

"It's like walking into a winter wonderland." Dan turned to Melanie. "You were incredible in there, honey."

She shook her head. "Crazy circumstances. I can't believe she had been in labor all day and didn't realize it."

Dan laughed. "Really? Are you surprised Isobel didn't explain what was happening to her?"

Melanie laughed and took his gloved hands in hers. "I love you."

"I love you too, honey." He paused. "You know, Mel, as a biologist, I understand how the creation of a new life works, but I still don't understand why. Why is there life on this planet? Where did it come from and why does it manifest itself in intelligent creatures like us? More importantly for us, will the Earth still sustain this wonderful process in the future, or will it eventually disappear forever?"

"That's what we are fighting for, Dan. To keep the miracle of human life going."

CHAPTER 13
YEAR 2046—MIAMI, FLORIDA

After the aperitifs had been served, William Wei tapped the side of his glass to call for attention. He cleared his throat and addressed the audience. "Dear friends, it's good to see you all again. George, thanks for making Freeland available to us for our meeting. Our purpose today is to pledge further support for space exploration, and more specifically, the research into potential settlement by humans on the moon and later Mars. As you know, I'm personally involved with the Mars project. I am also aware some of you are already devoting substantial resources to the exploration of the red planet. Jeffrey, you have several projects in the pipeline where your focus is on colonizing the solar system, and you strongly believe in a new civilization."

He turned toward another attendee. "And you Noel, you've helped us considerably by establishing a base on the moon, and this will happen soon on Mars.

"Friends, today only twenty-five financial pledge commitments to project 'Moon and Mars' will be auctioned in this room. You have all been invited to participate. As outlined in the briefing material, families can bid as one. The donors will, as usual, be registered in our golden book roll of honor. Once the hammer has fallen on a final price, the last bidder will be asked to wire 10 percent of the money in cryptocurrency to the club's trust account. Details have been provided in your individual information pack. Larry, our treasurer, will take you to a private room to undertake the transfer. Once it is confirmed, you will receive a notified certificate and a request to remit the balance within thirty days. Are there any questions?"

The audience remained silent, feeling a bit nervous but, as usual, maintaining the poise of their social rank.

William Wei continued, "Thank you. You are now invited to bid for entitlement number one. As explained in your invitation letters, this first right will be given 'Gold Status' in our roll of honor.

"Let's start the bidding at fifty million US, with increments of a minimum of fifty million." He paused and glanced around the room. "Yes Adrian, one hundred million to you... one hundred fifty million to Nick in the white suit. Should we take it up to two hundred million? Yes, back to you, Adrian."

The bidding continued in a calm and dignified atmosphere, slowly raising the value of the first entitlement.

William called the final bid of 1.17 billion dollars for the first pledge to Mr. Adrian Bedrock, a renowned e-commerce products and services proprietor. "Thank you, Adrian. Please follow Vanessa in the blue coat." He smiled at the audience. "Friends, we are off to a good start. Let's proceed with the auction."

A short time later, William wiped his brow discreetly. The Dalton family conglomerate had just bought the second seat for 900 million, while the third had gone to a Saudi Prince.

The remaining twenty-two seats all sold quickly at record prices.

William Wei concluded the auction. "Friends, on behalf of the Trustees of the Club, I thank everyone for joining us this morning. Our next auction for the project 'Moon, Mars, and Beyond' will take place in the main boardroom of our Rockefeller Plaza Office in New York on Wednesday the sixth of December. Could you please make your way to a lunch service in the President's Gallery Room now."

CHAPTER 14
YEAR 2048—ALEXANDRIA, EGYPT

Dan and Sandy were scheduled to attend the last Paris Agreement consultative meeting at the Bibliotheca Alexandrina Conference Center. From the US, they first flew to Cairo. Sandy wanted to take advantage of their stay in Egypt to have a closer look at the great pyramids on the plateau of Giza, the oldest of the ancient wonders and the only one still in existence. He was keen to experience the true size of these monumental structures in real time. He firmly believed the pyramids would still stand for thousands of years more after the collapse of human civilization.

Dan, on the other hand, was looking forward to visiting the Tutankhamun Gallery at the newly constructed Grand Egyptian Museum. He had always been fascinated by the gold-plated coffin and funeral mask of the young king. The fortunate discovery of his intact tomb had given the young pharaoh international fame, and indirectly his sought-after eternal life.

———

Leaving the infamous Cairo traffic behind, they settled for a visit to the Giza plateau by horse and carriage early the following morning.

Looking at the massive size of the pyramids, Sandy asked, "Now Dan, can you understand why the pharaohs needed to have such massive memorials built to preserve their mortal remains?"

Dan came up with his own explanation. "Sure. The pyramids were a fortress to protect the remains of the pharaohs, but at the same time, they were gigantic time machines. Not only would the pyramids protect their physical bodies, but they were also designed in such a way to be a conduit to eternal life. Since the dawn of civilization, the biggest question mark for humans has been what happens after death. The pharaohs didn't accept they would disappear forever once their earthly life was over. They wanted to come back once more; to have a second chance. That's why they had their bodies mummified in expectation of a new life once they'd passed away."

Dan shifted on the carriage seat, trying to make himself more comfortable. "Some shafts cut from the king's chamber pointed directly to the circumpolar stars, a symbol of permanent stability. So, the Egyptians believed the stars of the northern sky were associated with an eternal afterlife. As I said, in the pharaohs' culture, a pyramid was a gigantic time machine to eternity. Various instructions on how to reach immortality were written on the walls, and their favorite objects were included in their funeral chamber. As you know, Sandy, most religions are based on the hope of a resurrection of the body or reincarnation of the soul."

Sandy added pensively, "In a way, our project is not dissimilar to their beliefs, Dan. Instead of a pyramid, we want to construct a space vehicle to reach a perfect world. But we want to save the human species from extinction, not single individuals. Don't get me wrong. I can understand the pharaohs' need to survive their physical death. First, they had privileged lives and wanted more of it, but also, they thought of themselves as gods and gods are not subject to the common rules of time. Now, tell me, Dan. If the consciousness of an individual comes out of nothing and goes back to nothing, what is the purpose of a short-lived awareness about the world? Isn't that a cruel game by nature?"

"Who knows? There's no logic or sense of purpose in the laws of nature, Sandy. We humans always look for a purpose in the way our lives unfold and the universe works, but logic doesn't apply to nature. Nature doesn't reason. It doesn't have a purpose for its own sake. Consciousness is the ultimate gift for an individual and it is to be appreciated for as long as it exists. That's all there is to it. It's a great marvel to be aware of the world we live in, if only for a defined period. After death, our brain stops processing information. We're gone. Full stop. That's how I see it as a scientist."

"Makes sense to me, Dan."

"By the way, the irony of it all is that during the process of their mummification, the pharaohs had their brain removed, which effectively took their consciousness away forever. At the time, the Egyptians didn't know that."

Sandy laughed. "They weren't aware of the consequences of interbreeding either, mate. All their incestuous relationships were bad news for their genetic pool. Do you know the Australian aboriginals had worked that one out a long time ago? They never married into the same clan."

————

The following day, they landed at Borg El Arab Airport, located to the west of the old city of Alexandria, and headed for the Bibliotheca Alexandrina Conference Center.

The Bibliotheca Alexandrina had been a beacon of knowledge since antiquity. The pyramids were a symbol of the power and glory of a handful of egotistic individuals millennia ago, but libraries were the repository of human intellectual research, and that was Dan's preferred environment. He firmly believed human civilizations had progressed through scientific discoveries and not by warfare or conquests.

The port city of Alexandria was the chosen the venue for the forum to encourage Egypt to put more resources into fighting climate change and to spread awareness globally about the risks of rising oceanic waters in the Mediterranean. Over the past fifty years, the sea level on the Middle East shores has risen by twenty-five centimeters. In Alexandria, all the beaches had disappeared. Wave barriers had been erected in the lowlands, but the foreshore was prone to frequent inundations. North Africa was one of the regions hardest hit by the impact of climate change. It faced rising temperatures and ever-worsening aridity of its land.

The aim of the conference was to review the progress of the 2050 objectives of the Paris Agreement—the key date of the Treaty, only two years away. Europeans had been trying hard to reach their targets and were getting close. Unfortunately, some countries were still a long way from achieving net zero, especially the larger emitters like China and the US.

To start his speech at the Forum, Sandy apologized to the audience. "My own country hasn't been proactive, unfortunately. Too much cheap coal in the ground in Australia. The US, China, and Russia are looking at 2070 to achieve net zero... maybe. Africa and Asia have had major economic issues. They're now talking about 2100 to attain this goal. We understand the main reason for the delays. Let's face it: transforming a country from a fossil fuel-based economy was always going to require a tremendous effort at all levels. Some countries haven't had sufficient time or money to restructure their power generation sources, production techniques, agriculture methods, and consumption patterns. To reach the 2050 targets demands unprecedented action. Worldwide, the temperatures are now already close to 2 degrees above pre-industrial measurements. This level of warming is confirmation all of us need to increase our efforts to further reduce our dependence on fossil fuels. Now, what is happening in this region, Professor Robson? You've been following the developments."

"Thank you, Mr. Chairman. Ladies and gentlemen, this is our latest assessment of the effects of climate change in this region. Due to the increased desertification and the subsequent loss of productive land in North Africa, many countries are experiencing endemic poverty. Some are in a deep recession with unemployment rates of over 50 percent. Several civil wars are ongoing and social order has become uncontrollable in some areas. Their populations are desperate and have been crossing borders into Europe for several decades in hope of a better future, resulting in massive migration and resettlement problems."

Dan tapped on the forward arrow of the software presentation program. There were gasps and loud exclamations from the delegates as they viewed scenes of street riots, queues spanning several blocks for essential supplies, and people drowning at sea in overcrowded dinghies.

Sandy concluded, "Thank you, Professor Robson. This is an appalling situation. The regions of North Africa and the Middle East are still relying too much on demand for their oil and are resisting the transition to renewables and green technologies. Climate change is leading to reduced precipitation. This is putting pressure on water resources, demand from rivers, and aquifers. Rainfall is forecast to decrease by half by the end of the century. Low-lying regions are expected to face serious problems due to sea submergence. It is expected that 5,000 square kilometers of the most fertile Egyptian agricultural land will be lost. About half of Alexandria's population now lives below sea level."

CHAPTER 15
YEAR 2050—WASHINGTON SQUARE PARK, N. Y.

Dan and Melanie eyed the green building with the vertical gardens covering its outside walls.

"Is this the restaurant, Ava?"

"Yes, Dad. It's called 'Sustain.'"

"How appropriate."

She smiled. She was happy he liked it. She knew Sandy's birthday party was a major event for her father to manage. "Well, you have invited Zara. You told me she's vegetarian."

"Yes, she is. Good thinking."

"This restaurant has an extensive vegetarian menu. Like their name indicates, they offer healthy cuisine that also takes care of the planet."

"I'm sure Sandy will like the concept. But the menu?"

She smiled. "He will, Dad. I've made sure there is a good mix of dishes. Something for everyone."

Dan was excited to reunite with the original "Project Legacy" group. It had been a long journey for all of them since its creation in 2035.

"I can't believe Sandy is going to retire as the Under-Secretary-General after the last plenary session of the Paris Agreement."

Ava looked at him as if reading his mind. "I'm sure he'll want to talk about lots of issues with you guys. I've booked a private room so you can chat alone."

"Well done, Ava, and great choice of venue. Thank you."

"The private room has been booked for six p.m. We're a bit early. Our guests should arrive soon. Let's see what it's like inside. Come in, Ava, and you too, Melanie. We can sit down and wait for them. Hmm. The aroma. I can smell traces of herbs and garlic. I like the place already."

Zara and Chandra Shah were the first guests to arrive. As usual, they were a striking couple. Zara was wearing an elegant navy blue printed long kurta with large red earrings that swept over her shoulders. Her hair was decorated with elegant braids shot through with silver threads. Chandra was dressed in a printed-art, gray-silk Indian suit.

Dan shook hands with Chandra. His handshake was firm, indicating the soldier's continued strength.

"It's Colonel Shah now, I believe. Congratulations on your promotion."

Shah was taken aback. "Thank you. Who told you? I was promoted to the rank only a few days ago."

Dan pointed to his ears. "Ears to the ground, Colonel."

He hugged Zara. "Look at you; you haven't changed a bit. How are the children?"

"They're well, thank you. We left them with my family in Chennai. We thought they were still a bit young for such a long trip. Lakmé is seven now and Chandra junior four. I'll show you some pictures and a video after we sit down."

"Yes, please. I'd love to see them."

Dan gestured to their seats. "I'm so thrilled to see you both again. Come in and make yourselves comfortable while we're waiting for our guest of honor."

Five minutes later, Sandy arrived at the restaurant with

Isobel and their young daughter, Sandra. Sandy was wearing a light blue Italian suit and a blue bow tie to match. Isobel looked glamorous in an haute couture dress. Ava was rendered speechless for a moment as she'd never seen Isobel in such a fashionable dress. As they entered the room, the guests clapped to welcome them.

Dan stood up and kissed Isobel and Sandra. "You both look so elegant." He gave Sandy a bear hug, slapping him on the shoulders in a friendly way. "Good to see you."

"Good to see you, mate. You're going to apply for my job, aren't you? You're the best qualified by a mile and we need to keep the project moving forward."

"Thanks. Yes, I will, of course."

"Hi, Melanie. Hi Zara and Chandra. It's great to see you all. Ava, I hear you've helped Dan to organize this evening's get-together. Thank you. How's the job going at the UN?"

"Very interesting, Uncle Sandy. I work with amazing people."

"I'll talk to you about it during the evening. Is there anyone else coming?"

She checked her mobile. "I've just received a text message. William and Lillian will join us soon with their eldest son, Walter. They're caught in a bit of traffic. They should all arrive in a few minutes."

As the master of the ceremony, Dan organized the seating. "Let's sit down while we are waiting for the Weis. We have plenty to discuss, especially the latest on the project, but we can start by looking at the menu. Ava dines here regularly, and she can recommend a few dishes. Ava?"

She came to help. "Sure. The menu is wide-ranging. Obviously, they can prepare a large variety of unique vegetarian dishes, Zara, but seafood is also available. It's procured from sustainable fisheries and harvested without jeopardizing specific ecosystems. May I recommend the pan-seared salmon and the sustainably harvested shrimps? Organic chicken breast is also a possibility."

Sandy asked gingerly, "Is there any meat, Ava?"

She laughed. "Yes, Uncle Sandy. I've spoken to the chef. He has indicated he will prepare an all-organic, grilled New York strip steak for you."

"Beauty!"

"For drinks, I've pre-ordered a few bottles of 2035 Cabernet-Sauvignon from a regenerative vineyard in South Australia."

"Great choice, Ava. I'm impressed. That's the date of the start of our team. Excellent year for a vintage wine, I can tell you. I've always loved Australian wines. They're so mellow. Plenty of sunshine when the grapes are ripening. That's the secret, you see. It's how I've acquired a taste for good wines. Hmm, is there whisky available by any chance?"

Sandy had just finished his sentence when the Wei family arrived. Lillian was wearing a stunning white feathered dress. She went straight to Isobel to admire her dress.

"I've been helping Isobel with her 'chic-classic dressing,' Sandy. We went to Lorenzo di Milano together and each chose a special dress for this evening's occasion."

Lillian hugged Sandy, and with a grin and giggle, said with a forced Australian accent, "Congrats, mate."

William waved to the assembly. "Good evening, everyone."

Their son, Walter, presented Sandy with a silver bag wrapped in golden ribbons.

"Ta-daaa! This is from all of us, Sandy."

Sandy unwrapped the present carefully. He read the label on the bottle out loud. 'Clan Fraser Special Reserve, triple distilled scotch whisky.' Wow! Thank you, everyone! It's a thoughtful present. I will open it to start this evening's meal and enjoy its contents later in my retirement."

They all greeted each other. Dan showed the Weis to their seats.

"Friends, this is going to be a fabulous evening. Let's be proud we had the foresight—especially you, Sandy—to understand what was ahead for humanity. That's what we're celebrating tonight. Let's raise our glasses to your incredible contribution, Sandy."

They all rose and called out, "To Sandy."

Sandy rose with his own glass. "Thank you, my friends. It has always been a collective effort. On the one hand, I'm proud all of us have sought solutions. On the other hand, I am concerned the generations to come will have to deal with challenging issues. Ava, it will be up to you to continue our work to save humanity. The road ahead will be arduous."

Ava headed to the outside room. Her parents loved talking shop with Sandy and, after living the theory all day, she needed a breather. She went to one of the outdoor tables. Above her was a canopy of vines with twinkling lights threaded through.

It seemed surreal that Sandy would be retiring following the Paris 2050 session. After she had finished university, he helped her get an internship at the New York office and started mentoring her. He used to invite her out for coffee and talk to her through some of the issues he was facing and how he was addressing them. He had taught her some of his tactics for building relationships with difficult clients. He had been an exceptional leader in the UN, respected even among the senior staff. She heard laughter explode inside. She looked in to see Sandy gesturing with both hands. She smiled.

She started to text her brothers. They were due to arrive in town the next week on a soccer tour. They were coming to stay

with her but hadn't provided any details about their flight. *Typical!*
She was just pondering how to tell them not to bring any surprise
teammates with them when Walter sat down in front of her.

"Am I interrupting?"

"No, not at all." She tilted her head toward the room. 'They
seem to be having a good time."

He grinned. "Indeed. My dad has just started impersonating a Russian guy. I thought it might be a good time to check out the rest of the venue, when I spotted you here."

"I still can't believe Sandy's retiring. He's part of the institution."

"My dad speaks very fondly of him. Do you know him well?"

"Yeah, he's been somewhat influential in my career."

"You work at the UN too?"

She nodded. "Certainly do. My dad's been training me up for a while, but Sandy has introduced me to a lot of influential people."

"Sounds like my dad."

"So, what do you do, Walter?"

"Let's call it corporate finance. My dad has fingers in a lot of big pies."

"Your mum seems nice too. Very fashionable. So classy."

He laughed. "She would love that compliment. By the way, I like your dress as well."

"Thanks, I made it."

"What? You made it?"

"Yes, I chose the material—"

"And turned it into a dress?" He whistled in admiration. "Incredible. My mother would never think of this. She'd take you straight to her favorite haute couture designer and pay a fortune for the dress."

Toward the end of the evening, Melanie asked Sandy, "What are you going to do in your spare time? Life is going to be a bit boring without international travel and conferences."

He winked at her and took a sip of whisky. "I don't think I'll completely retire, Melanie. I'll spend more time with Isobel and Sandra in our home in the Hamptons, where you're all welcome any time. I'll also continue to be involved in sustainability projects by helping Dan. I still need to introduce him to most of my contacts."

While they were still all sitting at the table, Ava ventured, "You're a bit of a mystery man, Uncle Sandy. You seem to have lots of connections with the intelligence network."

"Ava, our mission is to protect humanity from an uncertain future. To achieve that goal, we have no choice but to connect with the best informed and most influential people. It would be foolish for us to think we can achieve this on our own, even with all the resources of a large international organization. I can help your dad and you to connect with the appropriate networks. That will be my undertaking in my retirement years. Now tell me, what does a sustainable retirement dessert look like?"

"Your favorite, of course, Uncle Sandy: Pavlova with pineapple and passionfruit. Still a true-blue Queenslander."

———

As Ava escorted her mother and Isobel to a cab, Walter turned to her and asked, "Do you think you'd be interested in having a drink next week? I'd love to talk more about your work and what else you've turned into outfits."

She laughed and peeked at him under her eyelashes. "That sounds great."

As she waved the ladies goodbye, she felt like she was riding on a cloud. "I'd better stay with dad and help him with cleaning up and packing the presents. We'll take Sandy home."

Ava helped her dad tidy up while Sandy chatted to the restaurant owner.

By the time they walked outside into the street, the air had cooled markedly. She pulled out her jacket from her bag. As she did, she eyed Sandy, who was visibly drunk and struggling to stay upright. She laughed to herself. He had certainly enjoyed the wine she had selected.

Dan gave Sandy a concerned look. "Sandy, could you wait in front of the restaurant with Ava while I get my car? I won't be long. I'm parked a couple of minutes away." He headed off down the street.

Ava turned to Sandy. "It was a fantastic party, Uncle Sandy. You spoke so well. That story about you negotiating with the Russians over vodka shots was incredible."

He laughed, slurring his words, "Ah, I've had an amazing career, Ava. Amazing. I'm sure you will too."

She agreed but was uncertain. She loved working with refugees. It was important and meaningful, but she also felt like she was navigating a never-ending situation.

"Thanks for organizing the evening, Ava. It was fabulous. So good to see Chandra and Zara. What a nice surprise. Oh, and did you try the dessert? Just the way I like it and the wine wow... superb." He hiccupped.

A black SUV slowed down on MacDougal Street and moved closer to the curb. Sandy moved forward. Ava looked alarmed and shouted, "Wait, Uncle Sandy, that's not dad's car! He drives a blue—"

Out of nowhere, Ava saw three flashes of light and heard a yell. She saw Sandy fall heavily to the pavement, holding his chest. Ava screamed, "Uncle Sandy!"

She ran over to him, throwing herself to her knees next to him. His white shirt was already stained with blood.

He grasped at her, struggling to breathe.

She screamed, "Help, help, I need help! Someone call the police!" She whispered in Sandy's ear, "Hang on, Uncle Sandy... hang on!"

The owner of the restaurant, Terence, had heard the commotion and came out, his eyes bugging at the sight before him. "Mr. Fraser, Mr. Fraser!" He signaled to his wife. "Jodie, call the police!" He ripped his apron off and wrapped it around Sandy's chest. Blood was now streaming from Sandy's mouth. He was trembling in spasms.

Ava pulled back from the road, frightened, as Terence was trying to stop the bleeding by pushing some towels over the wounds. Dan's car pulled up at the curb and he leaned out, his eyes bugging. "Ava. What's going on?"

He jumped out of the car, leaving the door open. "Ava, are you okay? What in the hell happened?"

She sobbed. "Sandy has been shot." She pointed to the ground in front of her. "Uncle Sandy has been shot and is bleeding badly."

"Oh, my God! That's awful!"

Ava could already hear the wailing sound of the ambulance's siren in the distance.

Terence had quit trying to stop the bleeding. Dan leaned toward Sandy, put his arm around his head, and whispered, "Sandy, Sandy, can you hear me?" There was no answer. Dan repeated over and over, "Sandy, can you hear me?"

The paramedics pulled up behind Dan's car. Ava watched as they headed over to her dad and Sandy. It was like an unreal nightmare unfolding in front of her.

Dan heard a loud voice behind him. "Excuse me, sir, we need to assess the condition of the victim. What's his name?"

Dan struggled to speak. "Sandy... Alexander Fraser."

"And you are?"

"Daniel Robson. We work together."

"Okay, thanks. Once we stabilize him, follow our vehicle to Mount Sinai Hospital, sir. Once there, please wait in the ICU lounge for an update. One of the doctors will talk to you."

Dan overheard the paramedic call into his mike, "Identification: Name, Alexander Fraser. Male, Caucasian, over sixty. Initial assessment. High-level trauma. Gunshot wounds to the chest, abdomen, and neck. Substantial blood loss. Patient unconscious. No palpable pulse. Blood pressure, nil. Transporting patient to ICU. Starting intravenous saline transfusion, epinephrine, and oxygen. Calling for full team response. Patient's status critical."

As they moved away, Dan called to the restaurant owner, who was also smeared with blood. "Terence, Ava and I are going to follow the ambulance to the hospital."

Terence shook his head, ashen faced, "I tried, I tried." His voice broke. "He wouldn't respond—"

"Thanks for your help, Terence. This is terrible. Here's a couple of my business cards. My contact for the police when they arrive. Tell them Sandy is a high-level UN diplomat. Thanks, Terence. Ava and I are going to follow the ambulance to the hospital."

Terence and his wife held each other and started sobbing.

The paramedics worked quickly. Ava watched as they

wheeled Sandy on the stretcher into the ambulance, Terence's bloodied apron tails streaming off the bed.

Dan signaled to his daughter. "Let's go, we'll follow them."

She struggled to move, hearing her father as if from a distance. She felt like she had ice in her veins and was wading through concrete. She got into the passenger seat jerkily... like a marionette. Dan reached in the back and grabbed his coat. "Here, put this over you. You're in shock, honey."

As they left, they saw several vehicles from the NYPD pull in.

MOUNT SINAI HOSPITAL, FIFTEEN MINUTES LATER

Once they arrived at the hospital, Dan and Ava walked through several corridors to locate the ICU lounge. Ava was now wrapped in her dad's large, brown winter coat, yet she still felt cold and couldn't stop shaking.

The receptionist acknowledged their presence.

"Good evening, sir. You are?"

"Daniel Robson. An ambulance brought our friend, Mr. Alexander Fraser, to the ICU."

She looked at her computer screen. "That's right. Mr. Fraser was admitted a few minutes ago. Gun shots. Dr. Friedman is overseeing the unit this evening. She should be able to talk to you soon. Please take a seat."

They sat silently. Multiple thoughts swam in Ava's mind. She asked her father to give her some answers. "Dad, who shot Sandy? Surely this is a mistake."

But Dan kept shaking his head, repeating, "I don't know, I don't know, Ava."

Finally, a middle-aged woman in a surgical gown and mask entered the room and looked at them. "Are you here for Mr. Fraser?"

Dan stood up. "Yes."

"I am Dr. Friedman. Are you the next of kin?"

"No. His wife is. She went home before the incident. She normally switches her holo off during the night. She has a small child, you see. Mr. Fraser is my superior. My name is Daniel Robson, and this is my daughter, Ava." Dan retrieved his wallet and showed his UN credentials.

Dr. Friedman examined his identity card and waited a few moments as if looking for the appropriate words. "I'm sorry, Mr. Robson. Mr. Fraser was clinically dead upon arrival at the hospital. There wasn't anything we could do for him. His injuries were too serious. One bullet went straight through his heart. Another severed his aorta near the neck. The third one damaged the right lung. It's likely he died instantly."

The world started to close in. Ava sat down, pulling Dan with her. They were both speechless. She couldn't stop shaking. She began to weep; she hadn't had the space and now there was nothing else to stop her. Her father held her close, and she cried in his arms.

Dr. Friedman put her hand on Ava's shoulder and turned toward the receptionist.

"A glass of water for the young lady, please, Wendy."

"I could do with one as well," Dan said, who had begun to cry too.

Dr. Friedman continued, "Two detectives from the NYPD will arrive shortly and talk to you about the incident for their report. They will be in interview room two. When they've finished, a member of our team will put you in contact with our post-traumatic counseling team and discuss the collection of Mr. Fraser's body. That's all I can do for the moment. I will issue a full post-mortem and send it to the coroner. If you have any other questions, please raise them with our counseling team. They can talk to you after you've spoken to the police, if you wish. I'm so sorry for your loss, Mr. Robson, and yours, Ava."

"Thank you, Dr. Friedman."

The duty receptionist stood up and brought over two glasses of water. "When you're ready, I'll take you to the interview room."

"Here, honey, sip this," said Dan, wiping his eyes with the sleeve of his other hand.

Ava drank the water slowly. "Sandy's dead." She repeated, "He's dead, he's dead."

"I know honey, I know." He hugged her tight as she sobbed into his shoulder. She lay in his arms for what felt like an eternity as he patted her hair.

As her sobs began to subside, Dan said softly, "It's time to talk to the detectives, Ava." She followed him.

As they walked toward the interview room, Ava leaning on her father, Dan whispered, "Tell them everything you saw at the scene this evening. But when it comes to motives, let me handle it."

"Okay, dad."

As they entered the room, two officers in plain clothes were waiting for them. They showed them their badges.

"I'm Captain Peter Moor and here is my colleague, Lieutenant Joanna Bryce. We're both detectives with the crime squad."

Dan extended his hand. "I'm Daniel Robson and this is my daughter, Ava."

"Thank you for leaving your card with the restaurant owner, Mr. Robson. The NYPD have secured the area as a crime scene. A team of detectives has already started to gather evidence."

He opened a holoscreen in front of him. "So, from the

details on your card, Mr. Robson, you're the Chief Scientist and Director of the Sustainability Unit of the UN in Korea?"

"Yes, I am, and Mr. Fraser is... uh, was my superior: the Under-Secretary-General of the department based here in New York. We were celebrating his birthday. Nothing official. Just dinner with family and friends. He intended to leave his post after the 2050 Paris Agreement review session."

"So technically, he was still an employee of the United Nations?"

"Correct. He hadn't resigned yet."

"In which case, the inquiry might fall outside our jurisdiction, Mr. Robson, but we'll do all the preliminary investigatory work. The file might be referred to another law enforcement body. Most likely the United Nations Department for Internal Safety and Security."

"I understand. Mr. Fraser was also a foreign diplomat with dual Australian-American citizenship."

"Then, the Australian Embassy will be involved as well. All right. Who witnessed the shooting?"

Ava gulped. "Me, sir. I was with Sandy... Mr. Fraser when he was shot."

"Could you describe what you saw?"

"We were waiting in front of the restaurant for Dad to pick us up. Uncle Sandy was a bit drunk." She shook her head. "We'd bought him some expensive Australian wine. I hadn't seen him drunk before. Sandy was saying how much he enjoyed the party." She sniffled. "When he saw a car slow down, he thought it was Dad's, but it wasn't." She felt the sobs starting to rise again.

"Take your time, miss. It's okay."

She breathed in, trying to compose herself. "I saw three flashes... shots, I guess, and Sandy fell. He yelled and just fell straight down, and the car left."

"Did you see the person who fired the shots?"

She tried to remember, but all she could see were the flashes and Sandy's body falling in her mind's eye. "No, no. I didn't. It was dark. I was watching Sandy. It wasn't Dad's car. Why did he go to the wrong car?"

"What kind of car was it?"

"A black SUV, I think. I wasn't paying much attention. I should have gotten the license plate number, right? But I didn't. Dad, I didn't." She began to sob again.

He patted her hand. "Shh, it's okay, honey. It's okay."

Captain Moor continued, "Have you seen this car before?"

She thought for a moment. "No. Why would I have seen it before?"

"Any distinctive features?"

"No, no, sorry. I wasn't looking at the car. As soon as I realized Uncle Sandy had been wounded, all I could think of was trying to help him."

"I understand. Did you hear sharp gunshots, like ah... the cracking of a whip?"

She shook her head, "No. Not really. It was more the light I saw, but yeah there was noise. It was more like a cork popping. A muffled type of sound."

The detectives looked at each other.

"What does that mean?" asked Dan.

The captain shook his head.

Dan asked louder this time, "What does that mean?!"

"They probably used a silencer... professionals."

Dan stuttered, "Was... was it a contract killing?"

Captain Moor ignored his remark and resumed his questioning of Ava. "At what time did all this happen, miss?"

"I'm not sure, but we left the restaurant a bit after midnight, and then Dad went to get the car."

Dan interrupted, "I arrived back at 12:17. I checked the car dash as I was pulling up."

"We'll check the CCTV before and after midnight. Keep going, miss. What happened after the shooting?"

"Umm. Uncle Sandy was bleeding on the pavement. I ran to him, but then the restaurant owner ahh…" She looked at her dad for help.

"Terence."

"Terence came out and tried to stop the bleeding… but there was so much blood and then… Dad came and then… the ambulance. Terence has a wife and…" she trailed off.

"Thank you, miss. Your testimony has been very useful. You'll need to sign a statement later." Captain Moor then directed his questioning to Dan. "Could you tell us what line of work Mr. Fraser was involved in?"

"Our role is to monitor climate change and make recommendations to reach a zero-carbon emission level."

"Did Mr. Fraser have enemies in that capacity?"

"No. No threats have ever been made directly to us, but obviously we've been confronting powerful lobbies."

"Such as?"

"Well, the whole fossil fuel-based industries: petroleum, coal, and gas companies as well as their related manufacturing companies: steel, aluminum, cement. The list is extensive."

"But none of these have made threats?"

"Nobody would do that openly, sir. We're part of an international organization. But over time, some climate deniers have expressed strong disagreement with our policies."

The detectives looked at each other again. "We'll ask you to provide specific names later. This is a preliminary inquiry, you understand. What about specific threats, unrelated to his work?"

"No, sir. Sandy was a skillful diplomat. He never made specific accusations or confronted individuals."

"Thank you, Mr. Robson. That gives us a start for our inquiry."

The captain gazed at his colleague. "Anything else, Joanna?"

"Who's the next of kin, Mr. Robson?"

"His wife."

"And what's her name?"

"Dr. Isobel Löfgren."

"How do you spell that?"

"L-o with a double dot on top of the o... f-g-r-e-n."

"We'll need to talk to her."

"I'll give you her number, but she switches her phone off at night. She has a young child. I'll go by tonight once I get my daughter home."

Inspector Moor concluded the meeting. "Sir, miss, it's been a traumatic night for you both. You will probably need counseling, miss. The hospital offers this service for free. Please contact them later. In the meantime, try to have a good rest."

"Thank you."

"Oh! One more thing, Mr. Robson. Mr. Fraser's body can only be released after all the forensic examinations have been done by the NYPD. The coroner will inform the next of kin."

"I understand."

Dan and Ava stood up. "Let's go home, Ava."

BROOKLYN, ONE HOUR LATER

As they headed home, Ava stared out the window, watching the lights pass by, the image of Sandy's body falling to the pavement playing over and over in her head.

They arrived at their condo in Brooklyn. Her parents had

bought it when they were living in New York when she was growing up. She borrowed it from them now. It had two beds and two baths, which was perfect. When her parents were in town, they insisted on staying with her, even though they could afford to stay much closer to their workplace.

They parked up the street and walked to her building. Her father still held her close. As they climbed the three flights of stairs, she felt her heart heaving.

"Dad, what are we going to tell Mom?"

Dan shook his head and sighed. "I'm thinking about the best way to break the news, sweetie."

As he unlocked the door and dropped the keys in the bowl, Ava noticed the lights were on. Melanie came out of the bathroom in her yellow robe, drying her hair with a towel. She smelt like peaches and cream from her recent bath.

"Oh, you're up, Mom?"

"Wow, did you guys have an after-party? It's three-thirty!" She looked at Ava's pale and stained face and the towel fell from her hands. "Something's wrong!" Her eyes suddenly widened as Dan took off his jacket. "Daniel, is that blood?"

He nodded, slowly. "Lanie, please sit down, I have some bad news."

Melanie fired off questions in quick succession. "Were you two in an accident? Is that why you're so late? Whose blood is that?"

Dan interrupted her, "Honey please just sit down, I'll explain."

She frowned but sat down on the gray couch, hands clasped in her lap. Dan positioned himself in front of her near the wooden coffee table, while Ava stood awkwardly in the corner near the front door, unsure of what to do.

"Honey," he explained slowly, "Sandy was shot outside the restaurant as we were leaving."

"What!" Melanie screeched. "What... oh my God, oh my God!"

Dan spoke quickly. "Ava was with him. A car pulled up. Sandy thought it was me. He was shot three times by a passing car. The ambulance came and took him to the hospital, but he didn't make it. They couldn't save him. We've been at the hospital talking to the police."

"The police?" She breathed heavily, repeating his words robotically.

She turned to look at Ava. "Ava, honey, you were with him?"

She nodded and sobbed. "I wasn't hurt, but Uncle Sandy died in my arms."

"Oh, my poor girl!" She got up and rushed over to Ava, sorrow on her face. She grabbed her. "Oh honey, that must have been terrible."

"It was." Tears welled again, and Ava let out a wail. Her mother held her now.

Melanie looked at Dan. "Has Isobel been informed?"

"Not yet. She doesn't have her holo on during the night." He stood up. "I'm going to head over there. I just wanted to get Ava home and..." he grimaced at his shirt, "... get changed."

"Are you okay to drive?"

"I'll shower and then go. I need to tell her. The place will be swarming with reporters in the morning." He headed to the ensuite bathroom.

Melanie turned her attention back to Ava. "Honey, how about I make you some tea?"

"That would be good, Mom." She sat on her sofa in her dad's jacket watching her mom make her tea. *How can any of this be real?*

Her mom brought two mugs over. Her favorites with blue

waves, which she'd received for her twenty-first birthday. She held her mug of tea close to her face.

"You're cold, sweetie?"

Even though it was warm, Ava agreed. The fan was on, but she still felt like it was freezing. Melanie reached into a basket next to her and pulled out a blanket, placing it over her, rubbing her back.

Ava looked at her mother. "Why would anyone want to kill Sandy, Mom?"

"I have no idea. It's completely beyond me."

Ava breathed in the scent of the peppermint tea and asked the question on her mind since the interview room. "Is all this because of what you and Dad are working on?"

Melanie's eyes widened as she sipped her own tea. "I don't think so."

Dan wandered out dressed in a light brown jumper over a tan shirt and khaki pants. His face was ashen.

"What do you think, Dad?"

"Sorry, sweetheart... about?"

"Was Sandy killed because of the project you and Mom are working on?"

He sucked in a sharp breath, took his glasses off, and began to clean them on his shirt—something Ava knew he did when he was nervous. "Maybe. I don't want to get into too much detail, Ava. As I said, there are things the police aren't supposed to know. Our work is top secret."

"I want to join the team."

"Ava, this isn't the right time."

"Dad, I want to join," she insisted.

"Honey, you're in shock. We all are. Let's get through the next few days and then we can talk. Okay?"

She nodded. "If you say so, Dad."

"I'm so sorry, but I've got to go. Thank goodness Isobel is

staying at their city apartment and not at the Hamptons, but it's still going to take me half an hour to get there. I'll probably hit the early morning traffic on the way back, so don't wait for me. Lanie, there are some pills in Ava's bag to help her sleep. The hospital gave them to her and—" he hesitated, "when she's ready, she will need a clean-up too."

Melanie stood to hug Dan. "Be safe, my love."

"I will." He closed the door behind him.

Ava had forgotten about what was under the coat. It was still wet with Sandy's blood. No wonder she was freezing. She showed her mother.

Melanie looked at Ava and exclaimed, "Oh, good God, your dress is covered in blood." She sighed deeply. "Okay, honey. Let's see what's the best way to clean this mess."

They walked to the bathroom. Melanie helped Ava peel off first the blanket she had wrapped herself in and then the jacket and placed them on the floor. She gasped as she saw Ava's dress completely red with blood. Some parts had dried up, and given the warmth of the evening, the dress was stuck to her body. Smelling blood, Ava gagged. Melanie came behind her.

"I'm just going to cut it off, honey. Okay?"

Ava nodded. Even if the dress could be salvaged, she knew she could never wear it again.

"Close your eyes, okay?"

Ava did as she was told.

Melanie snipped the dress off with care. She brought in a large rubbish bag from the kitchen, bundled the dress and the coat in the bag, then threw the blanket in the hamper.

She turned the shower on for her. "Have a warm shower. You'll feel better."

Ava followed her mother's instructions and stepped into the shower. The warm water stung her body at first but then came as a welcome relief. She watched the pink water circle in the drain. She sobbed and tears started to fall down her face. *It's Sandy's, Sandy's blood.*

After her shower, she slipped into her green bamboo cotton pajamas and got into her parents' bed. No way was she sleeping alone tonight. Her mother came in with a glass of warm milk and a tablet. "Here, Ava. This will help you sleep."

Normally, she hated medicine, preferring herbal remedies, but she knew her mom was right. She swallowed the tablet and curled up. "Mom, could you leave the light on? Tell Dad to sleep in my bed when he comes back?"

"Yes, of course." Her mom smoothed her hair back. Thoughts merged in her head, pictures, noises. She wept and eventually fell asleep.

———

The next morning, Ava woke up feeling groggy. Her head was spinning. Her eyes adjusted slowly to the light. The curtains were drawn, but bright light peeked in from the top. She opened the curtains. The light hit her, and she fell back on the bed. What time was it? She gazed at the clock on the side of the bed: eleven in the morning.

She rubbed her eyes—this wasn't her room—her parents slept there... what was she... oh... the memories of the previous night, Sandy, the car, the blood, the hospital, the police, her parents, it all came flooding back. She reached for the rubbish bin and threw up.

Afterward, she wiped her mouth and drank some water. She carried the bin out to the kitchen where her mom was watching the news while eating a bagel. She quickly turned the TV sound off when she saw her daughter. Ava showed her the bin. "Sorry. I woke up and couldn't help it!"

"Don't worry, I'll take care of that."

When she returned, she kissed Ava on the head. "How are you feeling now? Are you up for a bagel and some coffee?"

Ava nodded. She needed something in her stomach. Melanie passed her a plate with a plain bagel on it. She slowly picked at it. "Is it on the news?"

"It's everywhere. They are suspecting terrorists."

"Hah."

Dan emerged from the hall, still in his pajamas. His face looked ragged with thick bags under his eyes. He kissed Ava and Melanie on the cheeks and sat down. "Any coffee for me, Lanie?"

"Yes, and your favorite blueberry bagel from Sam's. How was Isobel? What time did you come back?"

He sighed. "Around six-thirty. It was awful, of course. She didn't believe me to start with and then she just stared at me for a long time. I said we'd come by again today and that the police would want to speak to her. I told her not to mention the project. Also, I've been instructed by the Director of the UN Security Department that Sandy's papers are not to be disturbed. They will send a specialist team to sort them out. What was strange is that she didn't seem more upset. More like stunned. Then she started talking about her suspicions. She mentioned something about things escalating too fast, nothing specific. It was hard to make out; I think she was referring to..." He glanced at Ava.

"You can say it, Dad. I'm going to join the team, remember?"

Dan hesitated. "She said that Sandy had something on Titov."

Ava's eyes widened. "The Russian general? The one who was mean to Mom?"

His mouth fell open. "You know about that? Yes, that's him, but now Titov is head of State. Anyway, he liked and respected

Sandy. He said several times they were cut from the same mold. So, I don't think he would've been directly involved."

"You never know. Perhaps somebody in the apparatchik found something, got overzealous, and decided to protect Titov?"

"It's possible," Dan said, "but personally, I suspect the 'Neo' group and that snake, Franz Jürgen."

Melanie reared back in surprise. "You think so? Again?"

"Again," repeated Ava, "what do you mean *again*?"

"Well, Sandy was well connected with the intelligence community. At the time, they had a strong suspicion Jürgen's group was responsible for Zara's kidnapping in India."

"I didn't know about that either."

"What is this guy Jürgen doing now?" Melanie asked.

"Sandy told me a few months ago that he now lives in Berlin and is Head of the Conservation Department in the German bureaucracy."

Dan took Melanie's arm and looked sternly at them both. "Listen, you two, don't mention any of this to anyone. These are my suspicions. I haven't raised any of this with the NYPD, except for the fossil fuel lobbies. I want them to conduct their own inquiry with an open mind, but I'll run my thoughts by Chandra Shah. After all, he was involved with Interpol when Zara was abducted."

"Zara was abducted! Why is all this bad stuff happening, Dad? The project you're working on, what is it exactly?"

"In due time, darling. All you need to know is that climate change is a very confronting issue. There is a lot at stake for some very important people and organizations. The problems are getting more threatening every day. The way we will live in the future is at stake."

"Well, at least Uncle Sandy died doing what he loved, right?"

Dan and Melanie turned to stare at her.

"Well, he said, in the restaurant before he..." she sucked in her breath, "before he was killed, he was telling me how amazing his career had been."

Dan agreed. "His career really was incredible. Sandy was a special person."

Melanie dusted off her hands. "Are you two all right? I'm going to visit Isobel." Melanie kissed them both and went to get her car.

UNITED NATIONS PLAZA, NEW YORK CITY, THREE DAYS LATER

Ava looked in the mirror and adjusted her hair; she just couldn't get it the way she wanted. She started to tear up. Her mom came up behind her and hugged her shoulders. She leaned in and whispered. "Ava honey, I think you're ready. It's time to go."

Ava wiped the tears from her face. It was time to say goodbye to Sandy.

———

The official memorial service was held at the Chapel of the United Nations, located across the street from the UN headquarters. Many delegations and officials were expected to attend.

Ava walked in with her parents. The chapel was packed. Had it been a normal event, she would have glanced at their outfits, but her eyes were focused on the front of the church. The coffin lay in state, draped in an Australian flag. On the altar, among all the flowers, a picture of Sandy was displayed in a Fraser clan tartan frame.

She began to tear up again.

They took their seats up the front next to Isobel and little Sandra.

The former Secretary of the UN, Dame Ngaire, approached the lectern. "Ladies and gentlemen, your excellencies, we have lost one of our top diplomats: Mr. Alexander Fraser, the Under-Secretary-General for Social and Economic Affairs. He wasn't just a colleague but also a valuable friend to most of us. Sandy, as we called him, dedicated his later life to the preservation of the Earth's ecosystem. Over the past few years, his group has worked to encourage countries to mitigate the deterioration of our environment by establishing guidelines to protect the state of our planet. In the true spirit of this organization, Mr. Fraser was fighting for the future of all living creatures. We will miss his foresight and dedication to the environmental cause. Our sympathy goes out to his wife, Isobel Löfgren, their daughter Sandra, and his extended family."

The Australian Ambassador then rose to say a few words. He was similar in build to Sandy but with dark brown hair and a large mustache. "Ladies and gentlemen, your excellencies, Sandy was born and studied in Queensland, Australia. He worked in the Department of Foreign Affairs in our National Capital of Canberra for a few years. Thanks to his skills as a negotiator, he soon embarked on a career at international level in the United Nations. Gifted with a brilliant intellect and problem-solving skills, he contributed to the resolution of several major conflicts in the Middle East. In his later years, he dedicated his life to the preservation of our most precious resource: the planet we all share. Isobel and Sandra, Sandy was a dear friend, and he will be missed by many, especially my own family. Sandy, farewell, mate."

Dan was invited to sing the Australian anthem: "Advance Australia Fair." His powerful voice resonated in the chapel. At the end of the rendition, the Russian ambassador approached Isobel. He faced the audience and announced, "The people of the Russian Federation wish to present Mr. Sandy Fraser posthumously with the 2050 Milankovic medal in recognition of his outstanding contribution to the research of long-term climate change."

The ambassador also presented Isobel with flowers and handed her an envelope, telling her, "Personal letter of sympathy from our Leader, President Alexei Titov, who was a great admirer of your husband's work."

Melanie and Ava concluded the brief ceremony by singing "Amazing Grace," accompanied by two pipers in full ceremonial Clan Fraser regalia.

After they finished their performance, Ava announced, "Refreshments will be available in the Chapel Hall."

As they were mingling around with the mourners, Dan was approached by a tall gentleman of Mexican appearance, who introduced himself. "My name is Emilio Sanchez. I am the Director of the United Nations Department of Safety and Security."

He gave him his card. "Here is how you can reach me. May I have your contact details as well?" Dan gave him his card. The gentleman had a close look at it. "Mr. Robson, from now on, our agency will oversee the investigation into Mr. Fraser's murder. He was a trusted friend. I relied on his advice on some matters, including your protection, Mr. Robson.

"Now may I ask your help with the following: Mr. Fraser

owned two holoscreens and a computer which were supplied to him by our agency. The latter contains highly classified information. You are a close friend of Mrs. Fraser, and you will see her soon, I would imagine?"

"Yes, we're having a gathering of relatives at her place this afternoon."

"Fine. Mr. Robson, would you ask Mrs. Fraser not to disturb Sandy's papers, documents, and his communication devices?"

"Of course."

"I'll be in touch soon and we will go through his belongings together. I'll meet you at Mr. Fraser's residence. The sooner, the better. Is tomorrow convenient?"

"Actually, it is. I'm free in the morning."

"Perfect. Say nine o'clock? Mr. Robson, I can assure you we will apply all our department resources to find out who's responsible for this dreadful act."

WESTHAMPTON, LONG ISLAND

In the afternoon, they headed to Sandy and Isobel's house in Westhampton. As her father drove, Ava looked out at the familiar countryside. She shook her head pensively. *From now on, it's just going to be Isobel's house.*

She remembered how they'd spent a couple of weeks each summer at the Hamptons in recent years. The house was located a few streets back from the ocean. They passed a series of massive residences next to the beach. The past decade had seen the ones closest to the sea, multi-million-dollar properties, being relentlessly eroded by the rising water. They now lay empty behind protective metal fences. The roads leading to them had been permanently closed to traffic. During their beach walks, Sandy had focused on these houses. He would point out the residences to Dan. "So much money has been spent on these houses and they'll eventually be washed away. That's the reason I bought on higher ground."

Dan had frequently quoted the Bible verse, "A wise man builds his house on a rock and a foolish man builds on the sand," and they had both laughed.

Ava recognized the name of the street. Isobel's house was the third one on the right, the pale brick one with a well-designed garden. In springtime, azaleas and camelias in the front yard blossomed in a riot of color.

She remembered last summer. Little Sandra had been running under the sprinkler in a bright yellow swimming costume, her father chasing her. She kept him young at heart. The three of them were so happy.

She closed her eyes and clenched her fists to force back a wave of grief.

They knocked on the door. Isobel answered, red-eyed, looking drawn and tired. Ava studied her. She was still wearing the black dress from the memorial service but had covered it with a pastel yellow apron. Her hair was twisted back in a messy knot, and there were traces of flour on her dress.

Ava sniffed the air. *Something's burning.*

"Hi, hi, come in, come in," she said, forcing a smile. She ushered Melanie and Ava into the kitchen, while Dan parked the car in the shade.

Ava loved their kitchen. It was spacious, white and yellow, had a large bay window, and an in-built herb garden. There was a large island bench in the middle surrounded by wooden stools. Together with her mom, she'd helped Sandy and Isobel prepare many meals there over the years.

Today it was covered in dirty pots everywhere. The mixer

was going, the tap was flowing, and suds were piled high in the sink. Most surfaces were covered with flour and smoke was coming out of the oven.

Ava noticed that little Sandra was also seated at the island, still dressed in her black dress with small white pearl detailing, licking a beater. Her face was covered with chocolate. She grinned at Ava, who kissed her and said, "What a good girl to help Mommy. What are you cooking?"

"Cake for the guests."

Melanie's hugged Isobel. "Hi Isobel, what are you doing?"

"The wake. I'm getting ready. I started making a chocolate cake, Sandy's favorite, and uh, I also made some hors d'oeuvres. They're cooking right now." She looked at the oven, suddenly registering that smoke was pouring out, and ran over it.

"Isobel, don't!" Melanie screamed. It was too late. Billows of gray smoke spewed out of the oven into the kitchen as Isobel took it off and flung open the door. The fire alarm began to beep. Melanie shouted, "Ava, open the back door. I'll do the windows."

"Okay." Ava ran over and opened it wide, while Melanie opened the windows and went over to the far wall to turn the fan on. As the smoke subsided, the alarm stopped beeping.

Isobel slumped to the floor next to the oven. "I can't do anything right," she wailed. She slid down the cabinets and began to weep into a soiled tea towel. Melanie and Ava eyed Sandra, who appeared oblivious to the commotion. Melanie sat down next to Isobel and put her arm around her. "Don't worry, Isobel. It's perfectly normal for you to be upset. You've been through the ringer the last few days."

Isobel covered her face. "Help."

Melanie held Isobel and asked her, "How many guests have you invited?"

She tried to concentrate. "His ex-wife, Elizabeth, and their daughter, Amia... oh, and their two sons, Ray and Lachlan. I wanted to do some of my own cooking for them. Then there is your family, and I've also invited the Weis and Zara and her husband, the Colonel, and us. That's about it."

Melanie calculated out loud, "You two, us three, the Shahs two, the Weis three, Sandy's family, say four or five. So, all together, fifteen, I'd say." She looked Isobel in the eyes, trying to reassure her. "Don't worry. I'm going to call my friend, Cassie. She runs a catering business not far from here. We can rely on her to provide for the wake. She'll put something wonderful together if I give her the numbers. Your guests start arriving mid-afternoon, right?"

Isobel nodded.

"Perfect, that still gives us a few hours." Melanie went to call the caterer as Dan walked in.

He surveyed the kitchen. "Holy heck!" He went over to the mixer, which was still beating, and switched it off. Ava sighed. She felt a sense of relief. Her senses were getting overloaded. "Thanks, Dad."

Dan loosened his tie, took off his jacket, and placed them on the back of a chair. "Let's get to work, Ava. Where are the plates and cutlery, Sandra?"

"I'll show you, Uncle Dan."

"Do you want to help, darling?"

"Yes, Uncle Dan."

Melanie's entrance interrupted them. "All sorted. Cassie's looking after the food and drinks. She'll be here around three."

Isobel blew her nose noisily. "Thank you, Melanie, Ava. You're all amazing," she said and burst into tears again.

Dan gave her a hug and whispered, "It will all be fine, Isobel. Don't worry. We'll help you."

THE VISIT

A few days after the funeral, Ava woke up in the middle of the night, experiencing a wonderful feeling of tranquility. She sat up in bed. She recalled her dream: she was lying in a warm bath, her body felt weightless, and her mind was at peace. This was a wonderful relief after all the restless nights she'd experienced since the dramatic events of the previous week.

She noticed that the TV monitor was still switched on, but the sound had been turned off. *I must have fallen asleep while I was watching the evening news*, she thought. She could now see the images of an old movie. Ava checked the digital display on her alarm clock: it was 12:30:20. The seconds were ticking; the numbers kept moving. She switched off the TV using the remote control that she kept on her bedside table.

As her eyes adjusted to the change of light, she noticed a human shape near the entrance to her bedroom. Then, she saw him. Sandy was standing near the door, radiant and serene. He wasn't looking at her but appeared transfixed... as if in a daze.

Sandy didn't speak to her, as if he only wanted her to be aware of his presence.

For a while Ava remained speechless. She couldn't believe Sandy was meters away from her, when just a few days ago she'd witnessed his violent death in a city street.

Recovering from her initial shock, she muttered, "Is that you... Sandy?"

Sandy didn't reply but grinned his famous smile at her and waved goodbye. He then faded away and she fell back asleep, at peace at last.

CHAPTER 16
YEAR 2050—U. N. DEVELOPMENT GROUP

It had been four weeks since Sandy's death. Dan had relocated to the twenty-fifth floor in the office previously occupied by Sandy. The Secretary General had appointed him interim Deputy Secretary General of the Development Group while they formally advertised the position. Dan knew he was well placed to eventually take on the job on a permanent basis.

His secretary, who had been eager to follow him from their office in Korea, notified him that Mr. Emilio Sanchez, the Director of the Department of Safety and Security, was in the waiting room.

Dan shook his hand. "Nice to see you again, Mr. Sanchez. Please come in."

"Good morning, Mr. Robson."

The tall, well-built man sat down in the visitor's chair across from him. Dan noticed a sidearm under his gray jacket. Mr. Sanchez appeared to be a serious, task-oriented official who had little time for small talk. Dan had met him several times over the past few weeks as his team sought further details about Sandy's killing.

"I believe you have some information for me, Mr. Sanchez."

"Yes, sir. There's been an interesting development. Our

team of experts has analyzed the data from Mr. Fraser's electronic devices, and we've come across something."

Dan fidgeted in his seat. Although he had been waiting for some progress, he wasn't sure it would clarify the reasons for Sandy's murder.

"We have discovered that Mr. Fraser had been trying to track the origin of a number of overseas financial transactions."

"Really? Please carry on."

"Am I to understand he hadn't mentioned anything to you?"

"Correct. It must have been something recent."

"Sir, Mr. Fraser had hired a private IT contractor in Amsterdam to track some transactions involving a group called 'Neo.'"

Dan sucked in a breath. "I'm familiar with that name, Mr. Sanchez. Neo is an extremist eco-terrorist group. Mr. Fraser had a strong suspicion they were responsible for the failed kidnapping of a staff member when we were traveling in India a few years ago."

Mr. Sanchez nodded. "Right. Thank you for confirming that incident." He continued, "We've managed to locate this contractor in Amsterdam, and he has given us some additional information. What attracted our attention was the form of financing Neo used: cryptocurrency. These transactions are difficult to identify. We passed it on to our specialist IT team in Silicon Valley. They applied the latest quantum computing technology and have managed to decode some of the encryption key information on the blockchain. Some of the payments associated with this group definitively came from a person based in Luxemburg."

Dan muttered, "Franz."

Mr. Sanchez looked surprised. "We weren't given any

names. The participants in such transactions are very hard to trace. However, our experts have been able to determine the origin of some of the payments, their amounts, their destination, and the dates. Large sums have been transferred over several years. This individual has been financing a laboratory in South Africa involved in genetic mutation research. I have prepared a full report with this information for you."

"Yes, yes, thank you, Mr. Sanchez. This information makes a lot of sense to me. I have a pretty good idea of his identity and what this money was used for."

"Would you care to enlighten me, sir?"

Dan drew in a deep breath but didn't answer.

Mr. Sanchez continued. "Rest assured this information will be kept strictly confidential."

"Oh, I have no doubt. I'm not calling your discretion into question, Mr. Sanchez. It's just that only a handful of people are privy to this information. I need to speak with them first."

"I understand."

"Anything else?"

"Yes. This individual also paid a substantial sum to a scientist in Germany involved in a classified government contract. There is even a reference: 'M-br-10.'"

Dan reacted immediately. "Could you repeat that reference, Mr. Sanchez? I need to write it down."

"Sure. Capital M, b r in lowercase, and then the number ten."

Dan had a look at the reference on the piece of paper, repeated it several times, and suddenly understood its meaning: embryo.

He exclaimed, "Damn it! He's managed to..."

Noticing Mr. Sanchez's reaction, he calmed himself.

"Mr. Sanchez, I appreciate your help and input. I can't divulge more for the moment. But I will personally brief you at the appropriate time. You have my word. If further information comes to light, could you inform me?"

"Certainly."

"Thank you."

As Mr. Sanchez left, Dan rang his secretary. "Please get Melanie to call me urgently." Closing the holoscreen, he reflected, *we have a serious issue with the selection protocol for Project Legacy. I also need to call Colonel Shah.*

CHAPTER 17
YEAR 2051—BERLIN, GERMANY

The International Union for Conservation of Nature (UCN) had organized a world conservation congress in Berlin. More than 1,500 state and agency members from 170 countries had assembled to review the most urgent issues regarding the ever-increasing extinction of animal species. The conference had been planned by the German Ministry of Environment and Climate Change. On the program, its permanent head was listed as Franz Jürgen.

The IUCN Director General, Naomi Chen, introduced the first guest speaker of the day for the session on the preservation of big cats. "Ladies and gentlemen, tigers, lions, cheetahs, and leopards are among the most spectacular animals our organization monitors. Unfortunately, the survival in the wild of these big cats is worse than ever. Lions have now become extinct in forty countries. Cheetahs have almost disappeared from their natural habitats. However, India has managed to not only preserve but also increase the numbers of the Bengal tiger in the wild. It's a true success story. It is therefore my great pleasure to introduce to you Colonel Chandra Shah, the Director of The Indian Bengal Tiger Preservation Project."

"Thank you, Madame Director."

"Colonel, could you please explain how your institute has managed to conserve this big cat species in India?"

"It would be my pleasure, Madame Director. Ladies and gentlemen, tigers are indeed beautiful animals. I see them at close range regularly. Their deep orange coats and black stripes are stunning. Let's have a look at some of them." Colonel Shah projected several pictures taken in their various reserves.

"As you can see, tigers are magnificent animals. But, ladies and gentlemen, let me remind you that in the wild, they are also very dangerous. Tigers are the largest cat species in the world. A mature male weighs around two hundred kilograms and is more than three meters in length. They are carnivorous and require a lot of meat on a regular basis. If we hadn't confined them to specific parks, they would still kill Indian villagers and their cattle due to the decline in their natural prey. The villagers would still hunt them. And that's where the threat to the survival of big cats resides. The main cause of their extinction is the loss of their habitat due to the clearing of land for agriculture and urban development."

Shah placed both hands on the lectern and swept the room with his gaze. "For us, the dilemma has been to keep the tigers and villagers away from each other. India is a vast country. So, we decided to use some of our existing parks to create reserves where these animals could subsist in their natural environment and could be safe. The local state authorities took some persuading, but we managed to obtain several leases in suitable areas. We then had to secure the parks with proper fencing.

"Unfortunately, it wasn't the end of the tigers' demise. These big cats continue to be illegally poached for use in traditional medicines. In several of our reserves, tigers were hunted ruthlessly by criminal gangs in the past. Poachers killed all our tigers in two reserves in 2040. Now, let me state this in front of this forum and to the world at large: the ingestion of tiger bones does NOT cure cancer. We have therefore had to organize armed patrol teams to protect them. That's where my military background has been of particular use."

Colonel Shah then introduced two of his rangers. They wore their full patrol uniform. "Ladies and gentlemen, may I introduce Mickey and Ali: two of our patrolmen. Let me say that in India, we are very proud of them. They are the true guardians of our wildlife. Every day, they risk their lives to not only protect the tigers but also several other threatened species like leopards, the Kashmiri red stag, and the Indian bison.

"As you can see, this is their standard equipment: camou-flage weather resistant jackets and pants, backpack with their survival kit; food, drinks, tents, sleeping bags, binoculars, two-way radio, and rifles. Thank you, guys."

The audience applauded loudly.

Colonel Shah resumed his presentation. "Of the nine subspecies of tigers, four have already gone extinct in the last one hundred years: the Balinese, Caspian, Javan, and, recently, Malayan tigers. Only five subspecies of tigers still survive today. From these five, the South China and Sumatran tigers are now considered critically endangered. The Siberian or Amur and the Indochinese tigers are classified as endangered. A century ago, there were as many as one hundred thousand tigers in the wild. Today, fewer than two thousand persist in their natural habitat. In India, we have managed to increase the local population. As you said, Madame Director, ours has been a success story because we have made every effort to analyze the situation, find solutions to the problems, and implement them. Even when things became extremely dangerous.

"So, I would encourage all nations whose wildlife is in decline to create and maintain reserves where threatened creatures can live in a secure habitat. Not only the famous ones like the Bengal tiger and the snow leopard, but also the lesser-known ones, like some frog species which are unique to our country. I know several nations have already put in place similar programs for the preservation of gorillas, rhinoceros, pandas, and elephants, to name a few. These efforts are commendable and encouraging.

"Ladies and gentlemen, we are presently witnessing the sixth mass extinction of wildlife on our planet. We need to protect these species by increasing game reserves in their natural habitat. I thank you for your attention."

———

The Berlin Conference was a great success in reinforcing the need to take concrete steps to improve the preservation of endangered wildlife species worldwide. However, it was marred by a serious criminal act on the last day of the conference. Franz Jürgen, the permanent head of the Ministry of Environment, was killed in a car bomb explosion. Nobody claimed responsibility. The German Police's initial investigation was focused on a terrorist group.

Colonel Shah had already flown to the US the previous day.

His first visit was to Isobel.

It had been two years since Sandy's death and Ava felt like her life had changed direction in a positive way. She was now working part-time with her parents on Project Legacy. Under her mother's guidance, she'd also commenced further study in mechanical design engineering. At least that horrible night at the restaurant had brought one positive outcome into her life: Walter. She smiled just thinking of him. He'd been amazing in the aftermath, so calm and steady. He had decided to move to the US to help oversee the financial side of the project and, well—as they say—they discovered soon enough that they were perfect for each other. Her relationship with Walter was progressing well. Her days were full but happy.

Walter had asked her whether she was free for the weekend.

Secretly delighted, she said, "Yes. What do you have in mind?"

"It's a surprise."

———

That weekend, he picked her up from her parents' place early in the morning, then drove to LaGuardia Airport to his own private jet, a Gulfstream VII Gold Class. As she entered the cabin, she noticed the cream leather seats and the mahogany paneling throughout.

Moving toward the end of the plane, she asked, intrigued, "Why do you have so many computers and monitors here?"

"It doubles as my office and my gaming lounge."

Ava laughed. "So, you're still addicted to computer games, even after all these years?"

SHANGHAI, CHINA

As they began their descent, Ava looked out and, in the distance, saw enormous buildings poking through the clouds.

"Walter, where on earth are we?"

He grinned. "Shanghai Pudong International Airport. I thought I'd take you to visit my hometown."

She felt a wave of excitement. She'd lived in Korea most of her life and had visited Japan, Hong Kong, and Southeast Asia, but had never been to mainland China.

The hot, muggy air and the smell of the town invaded her senses. As they made their way to a limousine on the tarmac, the pollution stung her eyes. Walter passed her a face mask, which she put on eagerly.

Then Walter grabbed her hand. "This way." He gestured toward the surrounding fog. "We will only be outside for short bursts. Most of Shanghai's center is now connected underground."

———

They exited the limousine and made their way out of the Jing An District underground parking garage. Shop after shop of designer wear lined the arcade. On the ceiling, screens made it look like a starry night. Her jaw dropped. "I thought you were taking me to the place where you grew up?"

He smiled. "I have. I spent a lot of time in this sector with my mother when I was young, but it has changed a lot since."

They went into a range of shops. He insisted she should try on different clothes, while he sampled assorted delicacies offered by the merchants. To her embarrassment, as soon as she liked a garment or a piece of jewelry, he bought it for her.

By the sixth shop, she was getting flustered. "Is this fun for you, watching me shop?"

He nodded. "Sure, whatever you enjoy, I enjoy. Do you want to go further up the street? There's a lovely little boutique."

"Actually, I'm famished. Could we get something to eat?"

"Sure. I'm taking you somewhere special for lunch."

"Your old stomping grounds?"

He laughed. "Something like that." He picked up his holo-screen and dialed for reservations.

———

They pulled up next to an enormous skyscraper and took the lift to the forty-second floor. The restaurant was already packed. A single table on a raised platform was set aside from the main crowd. It overlooked a picturesque scene of Shanghai with blue sky. She was puzzled. They had just come from the polluted ground floor.

He whispered in her ear as he noticed her staring, "All fake, but it looks incredibly real, doesn't it?"

She nodded. He pulled out a chair for her to sit. The table

was set with gold cutlery and wine glasses. She had been expecting chopsticks and cups of green tea.

He grinned. "You are now in the multi-hatted, award-winning 'Walter's Restaurant.'"

She snorted. "Named after you? You are joking, right?"

"One hundred percent serious. This used to be my favorite restaurant when I was growing up. For my twenty-first birthday, my parents bought it for me and renamed it."

Her eyes widened. "For my birthday, my parents bought me a nice coffee mug."

The banquet courses were a delicious mix of fusion cuisine, accompanied by expensive European wine. Halfway through the fourth course, she heard a couple of loud bangs and the lights blinked, as did the screen of the "Shanghai scenery."

Ava's heart was beating like a drum in her chest. "What's going on?"

He looked up at the lights that were dimming and then increasing. "Oh, this happens regularly. Don't worry, the lights will be back on soon."

"But what is it?" she insisted.

"A brownout."

"What?"

"The city uses so much power that occasionally the system gets overloaded. They usually divert the power within the hour."

She started to get hot and fanned herself with her napkin. "Walter, I don't like the lights flickering. It's kind of scary."

"Just think of it like a dance club, sweetie."

She shook her head. With every flash of light, she was brought back to that moment in Washington Square Park when Sandy fell on the ground covered with blood.

She fell back. Her chair flipped over. Waiters rushed to help her. She pushed them back. "I'm fine, I'm fine!" She was sweating now. She turned to him. "Walter, I need to leave. The bursts of lights. That's what I saw when Sandy was shot. It's brought it all back!"

"Darling, the lift is out of order until the power…"

She got up and grabbed her bag. "Sorry. I'm having a panic attack. I heard these noises and saw these lights when Sandy was… the stairs. Where are the stairs? Quick."

The waiter pointed to the corner of the room where a green and white emergency exit sign still glowed. She pushed past the diners, who were gawking at her and taking photos on their mobiles.

Walter ran after her, grabbing her hand. "Ava, it's forty-two floors."

She shrugged, took off her shoes, and started picking her way down the stairs. The light was dim on the stairs but wasn't blinking. Relief washed over her that she was out of the restaurant, but her dress was hampering her movement. She looked down and tore off the bottom, shoving it into her bag. Her legs were now free.

He caught up to her on the landing at the thirty-fourth floor. Her face was wet with sweat. He grabbed her and held her. "It's okay, Ava; it's okay. I'm here. Let's go down together."

He took her hand and kissed it, and they walked down hand in hand.

"You know you're showing me a new part of my hometown? I've never been here before."

They walked down another flight together, more slowly now.

"Is this really where you grew up?" she questioned.

He laughed. "Well, not these stairs but this district, yes."

She eyed him. "The shops, the restaurants?"

"That's where my father grew his business, which he had inherited from my yéye."

"Where did your family actually live?"

"We lived all over the world. My brother and I flew every-where with our parents: Paris, Rome, London, Hong Kong, New York. When we were here in Shanghai, we stayed in a pent-house a couple of blocks away, but my parents upsized a few years ago. They're always buying and selling real estate."

"In one way, that sounds amazing."

"It was. I got to see lots of different things, and I ate in top class restaurants; it was incredible, but—"

"But you were always moving; you didn't really have anywhere to call home?"

He shook his head. "Not really. Now that I think about it, there is this one place in Shanghai I'd go to get away from it all."

"Show me when we get to the ground floor."

"Okay."

After many more flights of stairs, they made it to the ground floor. As they exited the stairwell, he kissed her on the forehead. "I love you."

It was the first time he'd said that. She smiled at him "I love you too."

———

They drove for about fifty minutes to Zhongshan Park. In front of them, she could see a large dome. "Come. I want to show you this place."

He took her through the main pavilion and then through a smaller door to a much smaller dome. It was almost empty. It felt serene. Azaleas and camelias bloomed throughout. Birds and butterflies floated through the air. He took her down a small path to a willow tree, where a small boat was tied.

"Hop on." She carefully placed one foot on the boat and

stepped in. He rowed out to a little island in the middle of a small lake. She climbed up the rocks behind him. On top, she noticed another willow tree and a small bench. They sat and surveyed the gardens in front of them.

"This is beautiful, Walter."

He nodded. "This is where I would escape to when I needed to breathe. Now, breathe in deep." She did so, and she tasted the sweet-smelling air.

"No idea how they do it, but it's the closest to nature you can get."

She inhaled again, closing her eyes in pleasure. "Walter, today was lovely, but…"

He interrupted. "It's not you."

"Right. I love clothes but I don't need to shop for hours, and you buying me all those dresses… I didn't feel comfortable."

He laughed. "Most girls would love that."

"I'm not most girls."

"Definitely not." He leant over and kissed her. Her lips were soft and gentle. As he pulled back, he studied her. "I meant what I said at the tower. I love you. I love you like I've never loved anyone before."

She stroked the side of his face. "I love you too."

He put his arm around her, and they watched two white butterflies fly up in the dome.

Ava stared out the window of her apartment. She sipped coffee from her blue wave mug, breathing in the aroma. It had been three years since Sandy's death and her life had taken a new path. She was now working full-time on Project Legacy. She felt a duty of loyalty to both families. Sandy was gone and her parents weren't getting any younger. She was now the one who needed to carry the project through.

She played with the enormous ring on her left hand. Walter had surprised her six months ago on a trip to the UK, inviting her for the legendary afternoon tea at the Ritz, which he'd managed at the time. This one was one of the most prestigious of the Weis' hotel chain. He had proposed in the "Palm Court" with a fifteen-carat, rectangular cut, pink diamond ring. She had almost fallen over when he opened the box. She had protested at the size and the expense, but he had shrugged, saying, "I wanted to choose something as rare and as beautiful as you."

———

She surveyed her apartment, a world away from the classy Louis XVI interior of the Ritz. She had tried to convince Walter to come and live in it, but his parents had insisted it wouldn't be appropriate for the heir to the Wei financial empire to stay in a two-bedroom condo in Brooklyn. So, William had bought them an apartment on Fifth Avenue in the same building where his parents lived.

Boxes lined the floor, all labeled in clear black pen references. She was going to miss the place. She had so many fond memories here, and that bakery down the road was to die for.

Her holoscreen buzzed. Walter was downstairs and told her they were heading over to the compound. After Sandy's death, William had insisted the project should move to a secure building. He had organized a purpose-built site just outside of Princeton, which could be reached by private jet at Trenton Mercer Airport. The chosen fifty-acre estate was surrounded by secure fencing and electronically monitored 24/7.

———

As they entered the compound, a person dressed like a gardener double checked their IDs at the boom gate. Ava rolled her eyes. She came here once a week, yet they still scrutinized her as if she was America's most wanted person. They drove past the unassuming home at the front to a steel barn at the back, where they parked their car and used the lift to descend into the underground space. They scanned their fingerprints first and then their retinas.

The underground space was massive. William had spared no expense for the internal furnishings. They met her parents at the logistics center. Dan had taken over Sandy's role as the Under-Secretary-General since his death. This meant she hadn't seen a lot of him in recent months as he undertook his official duties, and she focused on the project with her mother.

They had also invited William and Lillian to join them for the session. Once every six months, the Weis attended their meetings. Today they were going to get some wide shots of the project. It was complicated from a technical perspective.

They sat down at the conference table. William and Lillian sat to the left, with Isobel opposite. She had brought Sandra with her.

Dan came up and kissed her on the cheek. "Ava, honey," he said, and then he shook hands with Walter.

She smiled. "Dad, I'm so happy to see you. Come sit down next to me and Walter."

"Good timing honey, the connection is just coming together."

Melanie spoke first. "Here's the latest update. The engineering construction of Explorer 1 is proceeding according to plan, albeit with some delay. India and China have refurbished the International Space Station 2 and connected two additional specialized habitat units. They consist of workshop elements where the engineer astronauts can build parts of the modules which are brought from various parts of the Earth but mainly China, Russia, and the US. The components have been assembled with shuttle lifting arms during extravehicular activities. They've been able to complete the entire first section, including the internal fittings. Protection against stronger cosmic radiation requires more resistant materials that are normally used in low Earth vehicles. NASA, the Canadians, and the UK are still testing the nuclear fusion propulsion system. All in all, depending on a breakthrough in the construction of the engine, we are still looking at twenty to thirty years before completion of Explorer 1."

William tapped the table. "Mmmm. Behind schedule, but I

suppose a few years won't make a lot of difference to the overall project."

Isobel interrupted, "Sorry, we're just connecting now."

A young man saluted her on screen. "Morning, ma'am."

"Hi Patrick, how are you doing today?"

"Well, thanks. I'll patch you through to the external probe. As you know, the outer hull is now just over 65 percent completed."

A structure came into view. Patrick spoke over the screen. "What you are seeing here is the first module, which is where all the guidance systems will be fitted. Modules two and three house most of our survey equipment: the high-resolution cameras and sensors in one compartment and all the rovers to be deployed on the planet in the other. Modules 4 to 6 are still being assembled. Number 6 will house the Helium-3 and other propellants."

The half-built structure was impressive. Ava had seen parts of the modules while under construction but hadn't seen the various stages coming together.

Melanie declared, "Thank you, Patrick. We're impressed with your progress. Keep up the excellent work."

Ava checked her appearance in the mirror and smiled. She had styled her hair back and wore a red kimono, reminiscent of her days in Korea.

As she walked into the foyer of the Weis' apartment on Fifth Avenue, she stopped in front of at a water lily painting and peered at the signature: Claude Monet. She didn't think these rare paintings were displayed outside of museums. William interrupted her inspection.

"Isn't this scenery tranquil, Ava? You know, we Buddhists like to meditate. When I gaze at this painting, I'm overwhelmed by a feeling of peace and beauty. I look at it every morning and it sets me in the right frame of mind for the whole day. That's the reason I bought it. For its spiritual one. What about you, Ava? What type of paintings do you like?"

She pondered. "French impressionist art is wonderful, but I prefer the depiction of the human body."

"Like Degas?"

She nodded. "Yes. I adore his ballerinas. They are so gracious and convey such a sense of beauty and balance."

Lillian interrupted them, "Darlings, so good to see you." She kissed Walter first, and then Ava. "Your parents have already arrived, Ava. I have also invited the delightful Isobel. Her daughter, Sandra, is away at a science camp. With your parents, there will be seven of us."

She ushered them into the lounge room, which radiated with vibrant colors. The first time she came to the Weis' apartment, Ava had expected the color palette would be restrained and refined. Instead, when she entered this room, she had needed a moment or two to take it all in. Numerous pieces of artwork hung across the deep red walls.

She had learned from Lilian that the founder of the Han Dynasty was known as the Red Emperor. Since then, in the Chinese culture, red symbolized authority and wealth. Heavy red doors with gold studding opened into the dining room. Lillian told her they were a replica of the gates of the Forbidden City. Gold drapery framed the windows, which were expansive and showed a view of New York from multiple angles. The dining table was enormous and gilded. The piece of furniture was large enough to fit at least fourteen guests. Pink roses and yellow dahlias dotted the room, and an arrangement of orchids covered the middle of the table.

Lilian invited them to the table, and her staff served the entrée.

The evening was going well until Lillian said, "And when you have children, of course…"

Walter interrupted her and glanced at Ava, hesitating for just a moment. "Mum?" Ava shook her head almost imperceptibly and then shrugged.

Walter cleared his throat. "Ahh, actually, we aren't planning on having children."

An ominous silence filled the room.

Lillian laughed. "Oh darling, we all say things like that early in marriage. Just enjoying the bliss of each other's company. I understand. You'll change your mind later. Just you wait." She lifted her glass to her lips.

Isobel nodded. "You're right, Lilian. I felt the same when I was younger, but we had Sandra, and I changed my mind about children. I'm so happy I did."

"Is that how it happened, darling? You changed your mind?" Lillian said teasingly and then laughed heartily at her own joke.

The conversation restarted.

Ava shook her head and sighed. She spoke louder, "Walter and I have had an in-depth discussion about parenthood. We don't think we should bring children into what will be a decaying world."

She could see her father giving her a disapproving look and glancing at her mother. Dan coughed. "Ava, honey, we don't need to talk about this now."

William almost growled, "Sorry, Dan. I think we should talk about this now. What's this all about, Walter?"

Walter almost seemed to melt under his father's stare. "You heard right, Father; Ava and I have decided not to have children."

"You can't be serious, son. Lillian, talk to them." He glared at her and gestured at them. Lillian dismissed the issue with a wave of her hand. "Oh, William darling, I wouldn't worry; they're still young. They'll come around. As Isobel said, they'll change their minds."

Walter looked at Ava, who was feeling like she didn't belong at this table. He took her hand in his and kissed it. "No, Mother, Father, we won't."

William and Lillian's eyes both widened in alarm.

Ava looked at them sternly. "We can't."

Lillian extended her arm across the table. "Oh, honey, I'm sorry. I had no idea."

Ava tried to clarify her misunderstanding.

"No, I mean, we can, but we don't want to."

She looked at Walter for help.

"Mother, Father. You should understand. The Earth. We are now on countdown. How could we bring a child or children into this uncertain world? A lot of young couples we talk to feel the same."

Shock and reality dawned on their parents' faces. Ava sipped her wine. This wasn't how she'd expected to break the news.

William stared at them both and then pulled up from the table and announced, "I'm going to get some air. Lillian, call me when the main meal is served."

They watched him leave. It was the first time Ava had ever seen Lillian lost for words. Dan sipped his beer nervously, while Melanie gazed into her white wine, biting her lip. After a while, Isobel gave them all a quizzical look. "Have I missed something?"

Melanie whispered, "'Isobel, William is looking forward to a male grandchild to continue the Wei dynasty."

"Ah. Now I get it. You two have explained this is your choice because of the situation on the planet." She folded her napkin carefully in front of her. "Totally understandable."

Ava felt a rush of gratitude. Thank God Isobel had saved the situation.

Lillian wiped a tear from her eye with her napkin. She sniffled slightly. "You're right darling, of course. It's just a shock for William and me."

Isobel looked confused now. "Really? But you knew their work."

"Yes, of course, but..."

"But?" Isobel asked, prompting an answer. A voice came from behind her.

William had quietly returned to the room. His anger had dissipated, but his face now appeared old and sad. "But we never thought it would affect us. We thought we could keep on with our own family traditions. Denial on my part, I admit." He walked over to Walter and Ava and put a hand on both of their shoulders. "I apologize for my outburst earlier."

"Father."

"Let me speak, son. I went on the balcony and prayed to Buddha for guidance. My own father started a company in a small office in Shanghai. With constant hard work and wise business decisions, he created wealth. Over the years, and with the same spirit of enterprise, I had the good fortune to develop the business to an international conglomerate level. I was so proud when I passed it down to you, Walter. You have the right professional acumen, and I am sure you will also carry on successfully. I was expecting you'd hand it over to your own son, but I understand your thinking about the future of this world." William paused, squeezing the bridge of his nose.

"Although... I still ask you to think about your decision. I'm convinced the end of humanity is not going to happen in your children's time nor their own children's. But no matter what you decide, I am proud of both of you, and I want to give you a special gift, Ava."

He moved toward a large painting of a "Shan Shui" Chinese landscape and swiveled it on its hinges. Behind it, Ava could see the heavy door of a safe. William pressed a code and retrieved a parcel wrapped in fabric. He turned back toward Ava and asked her, "Can you guess what this is?"

She shook her head. "I have no idea, William."

"Turn around and when I tell you, you can have a look."

"Sure." She turned, uncertain of what would happen.

He unwrapped the parcel. "Ready?

"Yes."

"Okay."

She spun back and couldn't believe what was in front of her.

"It's a ballerina!" She gulped. "Is it a Degas?"

He grinned. "'*Danseuse en blanc.*'

I bought the piece six months ago. Isn't she beautiful?"

"Absolutely gorgeous, William. It's like, I suppose, somebody new."

"Exactly. A new life coming into your world. Well, Ava, I want you to have it."

Her mouth fell open in shock, "I couldn't, William. It must be worth a fortune."

He insisted. "Ava, I want you to have it for its emotional value." He glanced at Lillian, who smiled. "It will do for you what the Monet does for me. I want you to hang it in your bedroom and enjoy it every day when you get up and when you go to sleep. No other conditions attached. I hope the painting will guide your daily life."

She rose and hugged him. "Thank you so much, William. I will treasure your fabulous gift."

Walter eyed his father, who smiled back at him conspiratorially.

"I think it's time for our main meal," Lillian announced. Then she whispered to Melanie, "Isn't he a crafty old devil?"

Dan raised his beer. "William, Lillian, a toast perhaps?"

William smiled and took the glass that Lillian offered him.

"Of course. Let's all raise our glasses to the good fortune of our families."

They clinked their glasses. Lillian smiled with tears in her eyes.

"May we all be blessed for ten thousand generations."

———

Ava smoothed on night cream in the mirror, preparing for bed. Things hadn't gone as she had expected, but outside of William's outburst, both sets of parents had eventually been prepared to accept their decision. She chuckled to herself. She never thought she would be grateful to Isobel for her intervention.

Walter came up behind her, ready for bed in his blue satin pajamas embroidered with his initials, WW, on the pocket. "What's so funny?" he asked.

"Oh, I was just thinking how grateful I am to Isobel for taking our side."

He chuckled too. "Indeed, she's an interesting one that Isobel. My parents adore her even if she is an eccentric genius."

She turned to face him. "Something bothers me though, Walter."

"What is it?"

"Well, your dad was upset, but my parents weren't. That's strange."

"I think your parents aren't concerned about dynasties like us Chinese. In the end, they've accepted we are adults. We can make our own choices."

She raised an eyebrow at him and put her arms around his neck. "Really, Mr. Wei. Tell me who chose the pajamas you're wearing?"

"Fine, fine. My mother bought them for me. I get your point, but the Wei dynasty is all about name, heritage and—"

She finished his sentence "Future generations."

He kissed her on the head and went to get his toothpaste to brush his teeth.

She watched him meticulously brush each individual tooth. "I'm going to see if my own parents are still up."

She wandered into the lounge area. In contrast to the bright colors of Lillian and William's, their apartment was a mixture of muted blues, subtle sages, grays, and whites. She had redecorated some rooms after they arrived. Together with Walter, she'd spent many pleasurable weekends searching the internet for the perfect pieces to suit their taste.

She found her father seated on a teal-colored, velvet vintage settee, wearing his dressing gown and sipping tea as he read one of his favorite books, *A Life on our Planet*, by David Attenborough, his hero.

"Hi, Dad."

He looked up from the book. "Oh, hi honey, you're up late."

Her mother came through the door. "Hey, Ava. Did you want anything? A cup of tea?"

She shook her head.

Melanie settled into her favorite wingback chair. Ava sat opposite her, next to her dad. Melanie studied her face. "Are you okay, honey?" Her mother looked concerned as she sipped her tea. "This evening was rough going with William's outburst. I've never seen him like that before."

Ava thought through her next words carefully. "I've seen him worked up before. I've overheard business deals when we've gone over for dinner. I know he doesn't back down easily. In fact, he doesn't give up until he gets his way. This time, William cooled down rather quickly and then he even gave me this valuable painting." Ava tapped her fingers as she gazed fixedly at her parents. "But it's your lack of reaction that surprised me. You and Dad didn't seem upset about our decision not to have children. That's what bothers me." Silence filled the room. She looked at her parents. "How come?"

Melanie's eyebrows rose. "Let me understand. You're worried we aren't more upset about your decision not to have children?"

When she put it that way, it sounded absurd. Ava tried a

different tactic. "Family has always been very important to both of you, hasn't it?"

"Absolutely, our number one priority," Dan said.

Melanie confirmed his thoughts. "You kids are everything to us."

"You once told me you were devastated when you thought you couldn't have more children after me; that's why you went for IVF."

Melanie smiled. "It was a painful process, but I ended up with my two beautiful boys." Narrowing her eyes, she asked, "Honey, what are you getting at?"

Ava breathed out heavily. "If family is so important to you and it's paramount to the Weis, why have you accepted our decision not to have children so... easily?"

Melanie glanced at Dan for a second before answering calmly, "Well, you're both adults. You make your own decisions and maybe our boys will have children. Harry is seeing that lovely Ellie. You never know." She bit her lip.

Ava pointed at her. "That!"

"What?"

"Biting your lip. You did it at dinner too... you never bite your lip unless you're worried about something."

"Honey, you're being ridiculous."

Ava could tell that her mother was getting annoyed now.

Melanie continued in an even tone, "Your father and I are trying to be supportive of you and Walter in your decisions, whatever they are. We accept both of you are making a tough choice. How can we not support that?"

Ava nodded. *Maybe they're just super rational, wonderful people.*

Hesitant, Dan interrupted her thoughts. "Maybe it's time to tell her, Melanie."

Melanie bit her lip again. She rose from her seat and looked at him questioningly. "Dan?"

"They are making a massive sacrifice for their future. We should tell her."

"Are you sure?"

"Yes."

Ava frowned. "Mom, Dad, what's going on?"

Dan turned to face her. She'd rarely seen him so serious. "We support you, 100 percent, darling. We love you and we appreciate everything you're doing for the project."

Melanie chimed in, "The reason we aren't more concerned about your decision not to have children is that over the years, we've discussed this as a possibility. The more we got involved in the project, the more we realized that, even though you kids are everything to us, we believe eventually the fate of future generations—"

Dan finished her sentence, "—won't be on the Earth."

No one said anything for a few seconds. Ava's mind was racing now. *How could the future of their family be anywhere else but here?*

Dan's professorial mode kicked in. "Ava, in the next few centuries, the last option for humanity will come. We can choose to focus on an uncertain life here on Earth or we can prepare ourselves for a future out in space."

Ava nodded. "I'm aware of all this. That's what Walter and I are working on."

Dan continued, clearing his throat. "When they were preparing the embryos for storage, we included some of our own... material."

Her jaw dropped. She knew they'd been hiding something, but this, this was just unbelievable. She was utterly shell-shocked. "You guys have some of your genetic material stored?"

Melanie smiled. "Yes. We produced some embryos. I had some spare eggs from the twins' IVF, and we worked with Professor Dutrant's team to make it happen."

Ava got up and tried to steady her breathing. She couldn't believe her parents. "How could you? You're jeopardizing the whole Legacy Project. You've tainted the experiment. It's supposed to be an objective process, 'best and brightest,' and you just put your own baby Robson embryo in the humanity genetic pool!" She roared with anger. "Dad, how could you? You're a scientist. How could you even countenance this?!"

Melanie gritted her teeth. "Sit down, Ava, before you say something you regret."

Ava knew that tone and sat back down, still seething.

Her father spoke with a firmness in his voice that she hadn't heard for many years. "Ava, Project Legacy isn't just a scientific experiment."

"But—" she interrupted.

"Shhhh, let me speak."

Dan continued, "This is about the future of humanity, yes, but you're naive to think it's simply a project about the best and the brightest that humanity has produced. Yes, fifteen hundred candidates will be selected through Project Legacy, but on top of this, we also have room for another fifteen hundred embryos chosen from the contributors to the project on a merit basis. These are the ones we are talking about."

Ava put her hand to her head. Her entire view of the project was imploding. "The mission is going to be filled with the children of billionaires sold for the highest price, politicians vying, uh... " Her face filled with revulsion. "The child who is going to be selected from the States could be the great-great-grandson of slave owners. His 'parents' are probably oil tycoons who are polluting our planet in such a blatant manner it's been discussed in Congress. Is that the type of person you want representing humanity in the future?!"

Melanie leaned forward, putting her hand over Ava's. Her voice softened. "Honey, you're right, we tipped the odds. We want to give the mission the best chance of success, but we also want to give our own family an opportunity to survive in the future. We are extremely qualified for this project. It wasn't a straightforward decision."

Ava looked at her father. "What do you think, Dad?"

Dan closed his book, running his hand across the cover. She watched his face. His liquid brown eyes began to fill with tears. She rarely saw him show this type of emotion.

He pointed at the front cover. "Do you know why I love this book?" His voice shook as he stared at the cover. "Because it gives us hope. It tells the truth, but at the same time, it tells us there is still a chance, a chance of salvation for the planet and for humanity. I've spent my whole life fighting for that hope. I just can't accept our survival is going to end with its total demise sometime in the future. We must make sure the human genome survives in the universe."

His voice stronger now, he turned to Ava, steely resolve on his face. "We're *not* going to hide underground for centuries, waiting for things to magically fix themselves. It won't work. I'm sure the planet itself will survive. It will eventually heal over millennia despite all the destruction we have caused. But the human species might not unless we take out some form of insurance policy. Project Legacy is the insurance policy, and we want to be part of it!"

He said more slowly, "The diversity of the flora and fauna might not survive either. The environment will become toxic to most forms of life. So, our only hope is to start again. We must do everything within our power for it to succeed.

EVERYTHING, Ava! Otherwise, the emergence of an intelligent species like ours will become just an event for the geological record."

Dan closed his eyes and took a deep breath, as if the weight of this revelation had been resting on him for a long time. "Now, I understand if you disagree with us or feel we have deceived you. I'm sorry about that, but I don't regret our decision. Just like I don't regret marrying your mother and having you kids. Those are the best decisions we have ever made. We've loved every moment of our family life. As far as you are concerned, let me tell you this. This is my professional opinion. My forecast is that humanity's last call will come... but not for another few hundred years. It's still a long way off. You and your children, if you want them, will be all right and their children too, probably for up to twenty generations. So, you and Walter can safely enjoy the wonders of parenthood. I strongly suggest you do."

Dan rose and took his wife's hand. "Come on Melanie, let's head to bed. We've got an early meeting tomorrow. Good night, Ava. Just remember we love you and always will, whatever you think of us."

"Good night, Mom and Dad."

She listened as her parents walked down the hallway to their bedroom.

She sat on the couch and tears poured down her face as she stared out of the window at the moon.

Then she turned her gaze to the Degas painting hanging on the wall.

"My little ballerina, you will be safe!" she murmured.

"I'll look after you."

CHAPTER 21
YEAR 2065—SHANGHAI, CHINA

Ava and Walter had received a call just after lunch and had flown out immediately to Shanghai. William's health had deteriorated rapidly over the last few months. He was now pale and weak, his skin looked sallow. The monitoring equipment in his room beeped loudly

Ava walked over and hugged her mother-in-law. Lilian's hair was a mess, indicating she had slept yet another night at William's side.

Walter grabbed a chair and sat next to his father. "Hi, Dad. How are you feeling?"

"I've been better, son. I want to talk to you about a few things."

"Sure. Are you comfortable?"

William winced. "My whole body hurts. Dr. Tsai told me it's time to start some pain-killing treatment. You know what that means, don't you?"

"It means you won't feel any pain?"

"Also means everything's going to start getting blurry in my mind. I want to discuss a few things before this happens."

Tears welled in Ava's eyes. William had been so kind to

them over the years. A unique source of knowledge and wisdom.

"I'm listening, Dad."

"When my earthly life is over, and when it's practicable, I want my ashes to be placed on Mars near a small statue of Buddha. The planet has been a big part of my professional life and that's where I wish my spirit to be laid at rest."

"I can do better than that, Dad. Right, Ava?"

She smiled through her tears, "Oh, yes."

"You're going to be pleased, Dad. As a contribution to your extraordinary support for the exploration of Mars, we've been terraforming a small area in the Jezero crater to house a memorial for you. Our scientists believe the environment would have been favorable to life 2.5 billion years ago. I've got some pictures. Have a look."

"Wow. Beautiful. What's it made of?"

"It's a glass dome, two meters in diameter, with prayer plant greenery growing in a climate-controlled environment. All built robotically. There's already a shrine with a statue of Buddha and next to it a niche for your ashes. Can you see?"

"Very impressive. Thank you. You're a good son. My soul feels a lot lighter already. I can now face the end of this life with serenity."

"I love you, Dad. You've achieved so much and given me the opportunity to carry on with your work."

"We have been extremely fortunate, son. Good deeds lead to good karma."

Sitting on her chair, Lillian coughed discreetly and said softly, "I'd like to keep some of your ashes as well, William. So would the rest of the family. We could have a shrine at our apartment on Fifth Avenue."

"Of course, my love."

William rose slightly on his bed. With a grin on his face, he asked Walter, "Will I be able to find spiritual peace by being in different locations?"

"Yes, Dad. You've contributed so much to so many places in your lifetime. Every location is significant. Conditions have improved for the locals wherever you've worked. That is what Buddha preached: leave the world a better place. I will also send some ashes with a memorial plaque to the Billios' Club, the Weis Emperors' tomb in China, where our ancestors come from, and one to each charitable organization you have created or sponsored."

"Son, you'll need to hire a chemist to sort out all these parcels of ashes."

They all laughed.

William was looking more relaxed now. The worry in his eyes was gone.

"How's the Mars project going, Walter?" he asked.

"We've assembled the best team of astrobiologists and planetary engineers to look at potentially replicating some of the life-sustaining conditions existing on Earth. Their ultimate goal is to recreate the same planet conditions where mankind can survive."

"Good. Do they think it's possible?"

"Yes, but it's going to take time."

"Great, what are the next steps?"

"We first need to warm up the planet and start rebuilding the atmosphere. Scientists confirm all the elements to achieve this warming are present."

"Good."

"Curio3 rovers have discovered large reserves of water held in hidden glaciers. The rovers have also been drilling for carbonate minerals and found copious supplies. Together, they can be used to produce super greenhouse gases, which can be released into the atmosphere to warm up the Martian surface, especially in summer. The ground will then emit its own gases and water vapor once the process has been initiated."

"Then it will start raining. Wonderful. Water is the source of life. Are we ready to send a crew of astronauts?"

Walter shook his head. "Not yet, Dad. We still need more time. You might have the place to yourself for a while."

William became agitated. "But it's going to happen, son, isn't it?"

"Oh yes, it will happen, Dad. First, we must install the type of infrastructure used on the moon base. Accommodation for the astronauts is crucial. The problem is, it's a lot of trips to bring the requisite equipment. Mars is a hell of a distance away."

"I understand."

"We've already started constructing some of the domes, but it will take time"

"So, what are we looking at? Thirty, forty years, a hundred?"

"More like fifty."

"So, it's no longer a dream?"

"Not at all, Dad. It will happen for sure."

William lay back with a gentle sigh. "Thanks, son."

Walter kissed him on the forehead, with Ava at his side.

"Don't worry, Dad. You rest now; everything will be sorted. I'll make sure of it. Before we go, Ava has something to say."

"Yes?"

Ava took his hand. "I'm expecting. It's a boy. We've already decided to call him William, after you."

William squeezed her hand, sobbing.

"Come here you, two. This makes me so happy."

CHAPTER 22
YEAR 2075—THE HAMPTONS, LONG ISLAND

Ava had been dealing with the UN monitoring of zero carbon targets, the position previously held by her father.

Together with Walter, their young boy, William, who was now nine, Ava's mother Melanie, and her father Dan, they were visiting Isobel and Sandra. The Löfgren-Fraser ladies had organized a birthday party for Dan at their home in the Hamptons.

He was celebrating his eightieth birthday. His hair had turned totally white, and he had lost some weight, but he was still fit, both mentally and physically.

———

Ava parked the car and greeted their hosts, "Hi Isobel, Sandra, how are you? What a gorgeous day here in the Hamptons."

"Hi, Ava, Walter. Summer is always stunning on Long Island. That's the reason I've decided to semi-retire here. Hello Dan and Melanie. Hi, Lillian."

Young William rushed toward Lillian; his arms raised. "*Nin hao, nainai.*"

"Come here, little darling," she answered, enfolding him in an enthusiastic hug.

Isobel and Sandra kissed Dan. "Happy birthday, Dan."

"Thank you for organizing the party, Isobel. I like the banner at the front that doesn't mention my age."

"Please come in. Let's go and sit on the veranda."

"How are you keeping, Isobel?"

"Quite good. I walked a couple of miles on the beach with Sandra this morning. It always invigorates me."

Dan looked around. "What an elegant spot you have here, with the vine growing on the pergola, the sandstone paving, and the hardwood garden furniture. You've turned this area into a place of beauty."

"I love gardening these days. It's my pride and joy. I've designed all this and turned the space into a memorial for Sandy. Sandra and I scattered his ashes among the rose beds."

"We all admired Sandy and still miss him a lot. He was such an exceptional man."

They all sat at the table. Isobel and Sandra brought the entrées.

Ava started the conversation. "Isn't it wonderful to be together again. You don't mind if we talk shop, Isobel?"

"Not at all. We'd love to hear the latest. We all follow the developments on climate change, of course, but you're now right on the front line with your job, Ava."

"Sure am. Let me update you. I'm delighted with the achievements over the years, but there are still outstanding issues. What do you want to hear first?"

Walter raised his hand. "Give us the good news first, Ava."

"All right then. Achievements first. In recent years, we've seen significant positive improvements in net zero emissions of greenhouse gases worldwide. The European Union was the first group to reach net zero in 2050, as you know. They have done well to adhere to their policy of carbon neutrality since then. It took the United Kingdom another five years to reach that level. China and the United States have completed this goal only in the last few years.

"By early next year, another 110 countries representing more than 75 percent of the global carbon dioxide emissions and 80 percent of the world economy will have reached carbon neutrality. So, at the UN level, we've managed to build a genuine 'Global Coalition for Carbon Neutrality.' Every country, city, financial institution, and company has adopted plans for net zero emissions. The energy shift has been successful. Renewables power almost all the electricity generation plants operating today. Cars are now mostly powered by electricity."

They all applauded her.

"Well done, Ava," Melanie said, her eyes shining with pride. "What an achievement. You've all contributed to that goal. So can we say coal and oil businesses are part of history now?"

"Not entirely, but overall decarbonization has made a lot of progress. Renewable energy is now the first choice for most economies. On another positive side, the clean energy transition has seen the creation of millions of jobs. Mind you, it's still a struggle for a few parties to the Paris Agreement, even now in 2075. Some of the smaller countries still haven't achieved carbon neutrality yet."

"This is great news, Ava. Our involvement has been worthwhile. Pat on the back, everyone," said Dan.

They all congratulated each other.

"Now, did you say there's a less positive side?" asked Isobel.

"Unfortunately, yes. As you expected, the world has been too slow to react to the emission of greenhouse gases. Most countries have sought remedial action far too late. Sandy and you, Dad, predicted this would happen. The proof is here in front of us today. Despite all our efforts, 2075 is on track to be the warmest year on record. The past decade has been the hottest in modern human history. Ocean heat is at its highest level. Biodiversity has basically collapsed. Sorry, Dad."

"I know. It's terrible. As a biologist, what I have witnessed in my lifetime pains me deeply. Years of mismanagement and neglect have left a trail of destruction. The constant urbanization has been unstoppable. Eighty percent of people now live in cities. Livestock is encroaching further into native animals' habitats and disrupting wild areas. At the latest count, hundreds of species have been declared extinct, including fifty mammals. Entire ecosystems such as wetlands and native forests have disappeared. Deserts are spreading. Most of the fish stocks have vanished from the oceans, which are now heavily contaminated by plastic waste. Today, all the coral reefs are bleached, despite valiant efforts by marine scientists to reseed them. As we predicted, the carbon dioxide released worldwide over the past two centuries will take hundreds of years to be absorbed. Levels have now reached eight hundred parts per million. That's almost three times the pre-industrial level!"

Isobel added, "Methane has soared even higher. Up nearly 1,000 percent since the permafrost started melting."

Ava resumed, "The upward trend of greenhouse gases will continue for centuries, despite our efforts to reduce their emissions to zero. Air and water pollution will take many decades to be remedied, if at all. Our latest United Nations Environment report confirms how close we are to a climate catastrophe. In northern Siberia, we have seen exceptional warming, with overall temperatures more than 5 to 8 degrees Celsius above average."

She looked at Dan. "Dad, do you remember? The Arctic is where you first confirmed the danger that climate change would inflict on the planet. I remember you explained to me how vast quantities of greenhouse gases were going to be released from the permafrost in Siberia. Now, permafrost is melting *everywhere* at an alarming rate. The International Bureau of Meteorology has warned that the discharge of methane is out of control in the Arctic, Greenland, Iceland, Alaska, and Canada. Summer sea ice is at its lowest level everywhere and the re-freezing last season was the slowest on record. On the climate side, extreme weather events are now the new normal."

Dan pulled a small notebook from his pocket. "My latest figures show that depending on the geographical location, we're headed for a temperature rise of 4 to 5 degrees Celsius by the end of the century. We're witnessing extreme weather events in every region, on every continent."

Dan wrote some figures in his notebook. He explained, "It's simple math. Today, we are at 3.5 degrees warming. For every degree increase in worldwide temperatures, the amount of water evaporation increases by 7 percent. Three and a half times seven; the atmosphere holds 25 percent more rain clouds compared to the beginning of the century. A quarter more. This has a proportional effect on the intensity of any storms, cyclones, and hurricanes. Many regions of the planet are in a state of decay. Life is no longer present there. Humans could still hold on as a species for another few centuries, but only if they adopt radical measures. After that? Nobody has any idea how the various parameters will play out. There is no precedent. What do you think, Melanie?"

"We'd better make sure that Explorer 1 makes a safe journey to Eridanus and transmits good news about its suitability for human habitation. How's the construction of the probe progressing, Sandra?" asked Melanie.

"Ahead of schedule, would you believe? The scientists involved are well aware of the risk the planet faces in the future. They understand we're in a race against time to prevent the destruction of our environment. There has been a sense of urgency driving the project. All the components of the first five sections of the spaceship have been assembled and are operational, but the engine has yet to be fitted. Mum, can you tell us where we're at with the propulsion system?" said Sandra.

"Sure. The nuclear fusion engine has always been the challenging part of the construction of Explorer 1. We needed to come up with a way of containing plasma. NASA has now successfully tested a suitable particle acceleration mechanism that does this job. The breakthrough is its lighter weight. The reactor itself weighs under one hundred tons. Its advanced beam-driven field configuration generates plasma in a contained area using Helium-3. The molecules are heated to plasma level and the configuration of the engine doesn't allow them to escape. So, we now have a self-sustaining system which can produce the right amount of energy at the right temperature."

You've been following the mining of the fuel on the moon, Sandra?" asked Isobel.

"Beatrix keeps me posted. The mining crews have now produced all the Helium-3 necessary to fuel the probe. It has been stockpiled in specially designed containers that fit the configuration of the engine. Ready to install. Like cartridges in a gun, so to speak."

"When will Explorer 1 be ready for launch?"

"According to the most recent estimates, between 2080 and 2085. What's holding us up is the stubbornness of the Russian engineers. They want to take control of the construction of Explorer 1. We constantly have issues with them. They're pushing to get their way with the other participants," said Isobel.

"Isn't the project meant to be a collective and international one, Mum?" asked Sandra.

"It is. Unfortunately, the Russians don't see it that way. They tell us that they have the right to make the important technical decisions since they provide most of the shuttles and the technical support."

"I know you're trying your best to get them to share their progress with the other nations."

"I really am. They must be more transparent. We don't want them to install equipment which hasn't been approved by the other nations. We continue to be held back by their bickering and mistrust. Most of the other countries leave the decision-making to their scientists, but not the Russians. Their central government is always interfering. We need to rely on our diplomats to monitor their actions."

Melanie stood up and tapped her glass. "Thank you, Sandra. I think we've covered most of the issues." Melanie beamed at Dan. "Hon, this is your birthday party. Let's enjoy it." Then she looked at their daughter. "Could you bring the cake?"

"Here it is, Dad. Your favorite: honey ale sponge with wild berries. Would you like to say a few words before you cut it?"

"Thank you, darling. Yes, I would."

Dan stood up. "To start with, I'd like to thank Isobel and Sandra for organizing this get-together. On this occasion, we're also celebrating the wonderful friendship between our families lasting more than half a century. We all remember Sandy, of course." Dan lifted his glass. "Cheers, mate."

They all repeated, "Cheers, mate."

"As a biologist, I have devoted my career to trying to understand life on Earth: its origin, its makeup, and its continued struggle to maintain itself. To me, deep down, it's still a mystery as to how this planet became host to intelligent life. Personally, I believe it's a wonderful and unique gift to humanity. One that is both precious and delicate.

As we all know only too well, many people take it for granted and want to enjoy its bounty, regardless of the way their behavior affects the whole planet. They don't realize how vulnerable it is to sudden change. Our group has been trying to protect life in all its forms and the Earth itself. We all understand that we're onboard an exceptional planet in the universe that, through its evolution, has been able to host intelligent people like us. We want to keep that for posterity. Yet, as a species, we are destroying the conditions that make it possible. Sure, we haven't acted deliberately, but we certainly haven't understood or cared about the long-term effects of what we were doing. Hopefully, our efforts to restore the stability of the ecosystems will prevail in the future."

He looked at his friends. His face was full of emotion. "Let's raise our glasses, this time, to the continuation of human life and not necessarily just here on Earth."

They all held their glasses and said together, "To the continuation of human life."

Melanie spoke up again, "Dan has asked me to play the last movement of Beethoven's Ninth Symphony, 'Ode to Joy,' on the piano. It's his favorite piece of music as it symbolizes the hope and fellowship of mankind. A musical celebration of humanity that makes us feel better about human life. Dan will sing the first verse in the English translation of Schiller's original German text, and we'll repeat the text as a chorus. I have prepared a copy of the lyrics for each one of us.

Can you please put a bit extra into the sentence, 'All men will emerge as brothers.'"

She looked at Dan. "Have you still got it, honey?"

"I might be a bit croaky, but the range is still there."

Ava interrupted, "Hey! We need to sing 'Happy Birthday' first, Dad!"

CHAPTER 23
YEAR 2085—CAPE CANAVERAL, FLORIDA

Ava was now the Secretary General of the United Nations. It was no exaggeration to say that this was the most important day of her career. She walked to the podium and smiled at the familiar faces among a gathering of international delegates, politicians, scientists, astronauts, and benefactors.

"Ladies and gentlemen, we have so many people to thank from a staggering array of scientific fields. Today, we recognize their determination in driving project Explorer 1 to its conclusion. What an incredible technological achievement for the people of Earth as a whole! The exploration of space will lead humanity to new frontiers. This is the beginning of our common goal to find alternative homes for mankind.

"Our team of astrophysicists have discovered a suitable planet in the Constellation of Eridanus, ten light years away from our home. They have called this exoplanet THERA. The name contains the same letters as EARTH. It symbolizes our scientific belief that all the basic life-sustaining elements on our planet are present there as well, but in a new environment.

"Our international teams of space engineers have also assembled a vehicle capable of reaching Thera. We have called the probe Explorer 1. It has been assembled over the last fifty years in a joint international effort and is currently orbiting 400 kilometers above the Earth."

She paused, looking at the audience as if addressing each one in turn. "Today, we will witness the launch of the final cargo shuttle. It contains the most advanced scientific equipment available, which will determine whether this planet is suitable for human habitation. This could be the next step for our civilization."

She pointed to a large screen behind her. "I now invite you to watch a short film which has been produced by the engineers of the Roshi Shigora Foundation in Osaka."

A video depicting the construction and assembly of the probe was played in the background.

"Once the probe has arrived at its destination in around two thousand years, it will orbit planet Thera. The various onboard instruments will survey the planet. Several rovers will land on its surface and determine whether the environment is suitable for human habitation. All this information will be beamed back to Earth through a network of relay stations, which will be positioned by the probe on its journey. If the conditions for human habitation on Thera are considered suitable, the next step will be to dispatch another spaceship with human astronauts on board this time."

Ava acknowledged the hearty applause from those present.

"Now, ladies and gentlemen, I'd like to comment about our role as an international organization representing humanity. It is important to understand this space mission is conducted in the spirit of the United Nations charter. We will respect the dignity of any creatures or beings that may live on the planet. We will not appropriate their land as has been done so often on our own planet, when one civilization encounters another one. We intend to protect the natural environment of Thera, its resources, fauna, and flora.

"Should we discover intelligent life on Thera, the moral basis for this expedition will be again our own Universal Declaration of Human Rights. May I remind you of the general principles of our Charter?

"We are all born free and equal in dignity and rights.

"We all have an entitlement to liberty, security, and a decent life.

"As an organization, we have strived to promote the respect of these principles here on Earth. The sad reality is that again and again, these rights have been violated."

She challenged the audience. "At our Security Council, we are constantly trying to solve violent conflicts. Human rights abuses are still committed all over the world. The media show us daily evidence of aggression and exploitation. Is this behavior an intrinsic part of human nature? Are we naturally a violent species? Let me state this clearly: disrespect of basic rights *must* not happen in space. We will ensure our philosophy of freedom and equality prevails."

In a more encouraging tone, she declared, "One positive aspect of this project is that many nations and their leaders have opened their eyes to the terrible danger our own planet is facing. Some of them have decided to take remedial action, put aside their differences, and seek peace amongst their people. We welcome this new constructive attitude. Let's hope it's not too late. Right now, many people are running out of food, water, and clean air."

She concluded, "Ladies and gentlemen, let us all wish this mission an overwhelming success in its search for a potential alternative home for mankind. In the meantime, let us channel all our efforts to ensure the human race will survive on Earth."

The Secretary General received further loud applause from all representatives.

"I thank you, my friends. Now, let's hear a final word from the Director of Mission Control, Sandra Löfgren-Fraser, before the departure of the last shuttle. She will give you the latest technical information."

"Thank you, Madam Secretary. After this last payload is delivered to the probe, the specialist crew on board the shuttle will undertake a final check. Then, Explorer 1 will be towed to an orbit around the moon. The probe will be powered by a Helium-3 fusion engine. While Helium-3 is rare on Earth, it is present in high concentration on the moon. It has been produced there over millions of years by cosmic ray protons hitting the lunar surface without being absorbed by the atmosphere as it would be on Earth. For a few years now, a consortium of Indian and Japanese companies has been mining and super-heating large quantities of lunar rock to produce enough Helium-3 for the interstellar mission.

"This fuel will be loaded aboard the probe over an estimated period of three to six months by a fleet of shuttles already based on the moon itself. Then, Explorer 1 will be towed once more, this time to approximately 1.5 million kilometers from Earth, at what is known as 'the Sun-Earth Lagrange point 2,' a gravitational stable point in space where the nuclear reaction of the engine can safely be sequenced. Then, its long journey to the constellation of Eridanus will begin."

Looking again at the audience and taking her time, she made a light-hearted remark.

"For those who are interested in the direction the probe will be heading, you can look in the night sky for the three bright stars of the shield of Orion. The constellation of Eridanus, known as the 'Sacred River,' is on the right. Ladies and gentlemen, the countdown to the final shuttle blastoff will begin in around forty-five minutes. You will be able to witness its launch live at Cape Canaveral, thirty miles away from the special viewing platform on my right. In the meantime, in the adjacent auditorium, our team of astrophysicists will run a short presentation about Explorer 1 and planet Thera. I thank you for your attention."

The star Epsilon in the constellation of Eridanus is smaller than the Earth's sun and has an overall lower surface temperature. With a mass of around 80 percent of our star, it shines with three quarters of its luminosity. To the human eye, it would appear to be orangey-yellow in color.

The Epsilon solar system itself includes two belts of asteroids, an outward disk of small debris left over from the star formation, and six planets. On the outer edge of the planetary system, two gas giants orbit Epsilon. In the habitable zone, two rocky planets, including Thera, were detected by the James Webb Telescope.

———

Two hundred years earlier, Explorer 1 had approached the Epsilon Eridani system and started to reduce its speed with reverse thrusting. Once the probe had reached the star, a solar sail was deployed to slow its momentum further. An additional and gradual reverse momentum sequence was initiated, lasting for about eighty years. The final retrograde gravity braking began after Explorer 1 entered Eridanus orbit and steadily narrowed.

Then Explorer 1 used the gravity of Thera to further slow down its speed by trimming its initial elliptical orbit around the planet to a near-circular transfer position. The probe was now cruising at a height of 350 to 360 kilometers above Thera, at an orbital speed of 21,600 kilometers per hour and orbital periods of seventy-four minutes. The flight path was suitable for making detailed observations of the planet.

During that time, the spacecraft Explorer 1 remained in safe operational mode. This period was used as an opportunity to gather preliminary data. High resolution cameras took pictures, which provided visual information for comparison with similar environments known on Earth.

A color imagery camera was used to study the planet's dynamic atmosphere. This information was crucial for any future entry of shuttles through their various layers. Several instruments were deployed to make observations of the atmosphere and the geological and chemical makeup of Thera, and to produce imagery of its surface. A climate sounder determined the initial weather. Gamma-ray radiation of the ground was also examined.

The general conditions of the planet were assessed by the onboard artificial intelligence supercomputer, which formulated decisions to determine whether Thera was suitable for a human environment.

After two years of observation and analysis, the primary data was considered favorable for potential human habitation. All this information was transmitted to Earth through a network of relay stations.

CHAPTER 25
YEAR 28—EXPLORER 1, ERIDANUS TIME

"The Ode to Joy" begins to play. The music is pumped throughout Explorer 1.

The dance of life-creating machines has begun. Cooling tank after cooling tank pop up from large stainless-steel consoles with their precious cargo of seedlings. They open, one after another, frosted air rising from their compartments. In each, embryos, which have been stored for two thousand Earth years, are slowly awakened from their slumber. Each represents so much potential for the continuation of the human species. The fusion of the DNA from two gene pools had been activated many years ago; the lives of the future astronauts had been initiated in various laboratories on Earth before the launch of the probe.

The twelve identical machines begin their programmed sequence. The race for the survival of mankind commences. After thawing the genetic material to the appropriate temperature, electronic microscopes scan the embryos. The fertilized eggs are assessed for their cell rate division and preimplantation genetic diagnostic. They have now reached a stage where the individual divisions of the cells are no longer perceptible. All tests are clear.

Then, each embryo is transferred to a separate artificial amniotic pouch.

The bio-monitor bags contain the same key parts of a human womb: a dark cover and interior synthetic sack that encloses the embryos and protects them from the outside world, like the uterus would. In an electrolyte solution that bathes it into the amniotic fluid, an oxygenator circulates blood and exchanges carbon dioxide for oxygen to the fetus. Each small bag includes a cocktail of defensive chemicals, UV filters, DNA repair enzymes, antibodies, and protective molecules.

Then, the rows of the twelve lifelike bellies are placed on the walls of a temperature-controlled incubation room with tubes feeding the oxygen and nutrients into them and disposing of the waste through a circulatory system. Each bio monitor bag has already been electronically tagged with its individual genetic identification.

GENESIS

Day by day, the embryos develop. They are monitored by a bank of miniaturized cameras and life support equipment.

After fourteen days, the body forms are starting to emerge: head and tail, left and right.

First, they consist of two layers of cells from which all the organs and body parts will develop. The yolk sacs provide nutrients until the artificial placenta takes over to supply food and oxygen as well as removing waste. The brain hemispheres and spinal cord form together with the heart, the vascular system, and blood.

Is it a fish, a reptile, or a future astronaut?

The outline of human bodies forms, curved into a C shape. The facial features are taking shape, with dark spots where the eyes will appear and little pits to mark the ears, soon followed by depressions where the nostrils will shape. Small folds are visible below the developing brain, which will grow into tongues, jaws, and necks. Their hearts are beating at about one hundred thumps a minute. The buds that will grow into arms begin to swell, soon followed by those for the legs. Muscle and bone tissues are forming.

The embryos are covered with a thin layer of skin, which has been genetically modified to adapt to a different level of ultraviolet light on the new planet.

Inside, cells that will become intestines are developing, along with the buds of tissue that will become the lungs, liver, and kidneys. The neural tubes continue to close at each end to protect the brain and spinal cord.

After two months, they are about the size of a kidney bean with distinct, slightly webbed fingers. They are starting to move inside the bio monitor bags.

After three months, they have reached the length and weight of pea pods. Their unique fingerprints are now in place.

After a few more weeks, their skeletons are starting to harden from rubbery cartilage to bone.

After five months, their eyebrows and eyelids are in place. Later, their skin will start to become smooth, and they will gain weight.

After seven months, they can open and close their eyes, which have also been genetically modified for the level of light expected on Thera.

After eight months, they now weigh more than two kilos as larger layers of fat are filling them out, making them rounder. Their hair and nails have grown. Their lungs are by now well developed.

After nine months of anticipation, they are now full term, and it is time for the future astronauts to be born in space.

A buzzer rings. The sensors have detected that the babies in two bio monitor bags are ready to be released. The nursoids, who have been on standby, bring the bio monitor bags to a special delivery area in the maternity ward and put them in a washbasin. Extra oxygen is pumped into the room. The nurses open the hatch of each womb, *click, click, click.*

Ten seconds pass, twenty seconds, a cry, a second cry, all the way to three cries. As predicted by the monitoring system, one of the bio monitor bags holds a set of twins. Three newborns are wailing, reacting to the more intense light and the additional gravity experienced outside the watery environment of their bio monitor bags. The noise is loud and, in a way, known since the beginning of humanity.

"Welcome. Welcome. Welcome." The synthetic voices of the three nursoids call out over the cries. The nurses are all identical Japanese robots in light blue uniforms looking very lifelike with an exoskeleton made of synthetic skin.

The three babies have emerged, covered in blood, wet, and shriveled from their long stay in the amniotic solution of the bio monitor bags. Each nursoid picks up a screaming baby and takes it to the nursery station, where each one is cleaned and enveloped in specially designed garments.

The first baby, a boy, has almost white hair and pale skin. He is larger than the other two children.

Next, a set of twins is revealed: a boy and a girl. They have dark skin and a small crop of frizzy hair. They are sturdy-looking.

Each nursoid takes a bottle from the warmer and feeds the babies for the first time. They eat hungrily. It is quiet again now, except for the constant sucking noise of three newborns, enjoying the comfort of their first feed. Each robotic mother looks almost fondly down at their infant.

In the following six hours, a further three children are born. The nurses attend to them. A second girl is delivered. She is fair with blonde, curly hair. Another boy has long, lean limbs, dark eyes, long eyelashes, and a bronze complexion. The sixth child is a smaller boy with delicate features. He has almost no hair and looks very pale. He is already highly strung, full of energy; he is fighting his nursoid.

Soon after, the buzzer rings again. Four more children are delivered to the maternity ward. A light-skinned girl with dark, straight hair and light brown eyes, a dark-skinned boy who has a curly chocolate mop on his head, and two more girls. The smallest one is a lovely girl with thin, straight black hair and little red lips. She has delicate features with almond-shaped eyes. The other girl's skin is like pale honey with sandy hair.

Finally, after a few more hours, the last bio monitor bags are brought in. From them emerge a boy with gingery brown hair, a girl with bright red curly hair and pale skin, and a cute girl with soft brown curls around her chubby, intelligent face.

A total of thirteen human babies have now been born in space aboard Explorer 1.

What a lovely sight. Young human beings, so innocent but unaware of their immense responsibility for the survival of their species. There is so much hope for humanity resting on the future of these children born on a planet in a distant solar system far from Earth.

ACKNOWLEDGMENTS

I'd like to thank the following people:

My wife Ruth for her constant support,
Nadine my daughter who always rescued me when the story hit a snag,
My son Geoffrey who helped me navigate the various computer programs,
My friend Ron for checking the technical facts,
Keith Stevenson, my mentor who taught me how to write a successful novel,
Joanna Niederer, my editor who spent time correcting my manuscript and
Arjan van Woensel for the brilliant design of the cover.

AFTERWORD

Enjoyed the story and the concept?
Please leave some comments at:
climateriskbook@gmail.com